ALSO BY WALTER ABISH

Alphabetical Africa

Duel Site

How German Is It

In the Future Perfect

Minds Meet

99: The New Meaning

Eclipse Fever

ECLIPSE
FEVER

Walter Abish

NONPAREIL
BOOKS

DAVID R. GODINE, *Publisher*

BOSTON

This is a Nonpareil Book first published in 1995 by
DAVID R. GODINE, *Publisher*
Box 9103
Lincoln, Massachusetts 01773

Originally published in hardcover by Alfred A. Knopf in 1993.

Grateful acknowledgment is made to the following for
permission to reprint previously published material:
CPP/Belwin, Inc.: Excerpt from "Stand by Your Man" by
Tammy Wynette and Billy Sherrill, copyright © 1968 Al Gallico
Music, c/o EMI Music Publishing. World print rights
administered by CPP/Belwin, Inc., P.O. Box 4340,
Miami, Fla. 33014. All rights reserved.
Freddy Bienstock Enterprises and *Leiber & Stoller Music
Publishing:* Excerpt from "Happy Together" by Garry Bonner
and Alan Lee Gordon. Copyright © 1966, 1967 by Alley Music
Corp. and Trio Music Co., Inc. All rights reserved.
Used by permission.
Davray Music Limited: Excerpt from "Come to Daddy"
by Ray Davies, copyright © Davray Music Limited.
Reprinted by permission.

Library of Congress Cataloging-in-Publication Data
Abish, Walter.
Eclipse fever / Walter Abish.—Nonpareil Books ed.
p.   cm.—(Nonpareil books; 76)
ISBN 1-56792-036-5
I. Title. II. Series: Nonpareil book; 76.
[PS3551.B5E25   1995]
813'.54—dc20   95-9353
CIP

First printing, 1995
Printed and bound in the United States of America

for Cecile

At the subconscious level nothing is accidental.

—Luis Buñuel, *That Obscure Object of Desire*

I am grateful to the John D. and Katherine T. MacArthur Foundation and the Guggenheim Foundation for their generous support.

Mild

PART ONE

If I or she should chance to be
Involved in this affair,
He trusts to you to set them free,
Exactly as we were.

My notion was that you had been
(Before she had this fit)
An obstacle that came between
Him, and ourselves, and it.

Don't let him know she liked them best,
For this must ever be
A secret, kept from all the rest,
Between yourself and me.

—Lewis Carroll, *Alice in Wonderland*

At One Glance We Can Determine the Years They Will Not Spend Together!

Was it true that the critic had no past to speak of? That the little there was had to be extracted with an agonizing difficulty from the void that marked his early years? More to the point, how relevant was the little he was able to recall? Earlier moments here and there? Critical pleasures? Critical moments? Were they indeed? You mean you have no memory of your childhood? At first Mercedes had been disinclined to believe him. You don't remember your childhood? Nada! Your own room and toys? Nada! Bedtime stories? Nada! Playmates? Nada! Vacations, games in the park? Nada! Fights? Nada! Not even your first love? You must recall something. Nada! One of his earliest memories was cataloguing in the late honorary consul Anadelle D. Partridge's villa a stack of scholarly works, including the codices *Anales de Cuauhtitlán*, *Codex Telleriano-Remensis*, and *Codex Mendoza*, as well as the five-volume *Gesammelte Abhandlungen zur Amerikanischen Sprach und Altertumskunde* and the little-known *A General History of the Things of New Spain*. To this day Alejandro could recall the titles . . . even the appearance of the books. What more? Every detail of the sun-drenched room. The large table on which the books to be catalogued were piled. Francisco, his best friend, who assisted him, sat at one end, he at the other. The huge room was otherwise bare. The house, a two-story villa, modern, functional—the front overlooking the sunken garden located in what once had been the red-brick basement of an industrialist's palatial home that burned to the ground in the forties. By the time he and Francisco had come to work for Anadelle D. Partridge, the villa was empty of its treasures, since most if not all of the honorary consul's precious pre-Columbian collection and possessions, earmarked for what was to become the Partridge Museum, were crated and stored in the basement, awaiting the painfully slow Mexican bureaucracy to sanction their transfer to the museum-to-be, a former monastery to the north of Mexico City, which the state had provided to house them. In return for her collection, a gift to the state, Anadelle Partridge was assured by the then minister of culture that no expense would be spared in the renovation of the eighteenth-century Mexican Baroque building and its conversion into a modern museum with up-to-date exhibition halls and research facilities for visiting scholars. Initially the museum was scheduled to be opened to the public in 1968. This being Mexico, it wasn't anywhere near ready ten years later, when Alejandro and Francisco were hired to catalogue the books intended for the museum library. By then Anadelle Partridge had stopped believing that she'd ever see the end of the renovations. All the same, she kept buying whatever came her way, because these acquisitions gave her great pleasure. She bought from dealers and shady go-betweens and from the plunderers themselves. She bought uncritically. . . . Most of the time she bought without knowing what she was buying. On one occasion Alejandro and Francisco, not fully realizing what her statement "Let's go and study the Mayans in depth" actually entailed, accompanied her to the Mayan ruins in Yucatán. The trip was an outright disaster, since Anadelle proved to be intellectually overbearing, quite unlike any other American woman Alejandro or Francisco had ever encountered, subjecting them daily to hour-long lectures on the Maya kingdoms and the pre-

Columbian rituals and sacrifice, with special emphasis on what can only be described as the gore, of which there was plenty. What else? Memory is ever so selective. Alejandro was twenty-one and short of cash. Cataloguing the books came as a god-send. There was enough work to last the two of them for years. . . . Paradoxically, the otherwise exacting Anadelle D. Partridge didn't rush them. In fact, no one in her household showed much interest in what they were doing at any time or how competent they were to do it. They had the large room on the first floor to work in and a bedroom each upstairs. . . . But after two years Francisco couldn't stand it any longer and quit. When he, too, finally decided to leave, the crates were still stacked in the basement. The museum was opened to the public with great fanfare years later, but he never visited it. He didn't know, much less care, if someone else had finished cataloguing the books. When Anadelle D. Partridge died several years ago, Alejandro received in the mail a black-rimmed notice. Whoever had been in charge of the funeral details decided on the Sagrario Metropolitana, the enormous neoclassical Baroque cathedral on the Plaza de la Constitución, popularly known as the Zócalo, a cathedral that originally was to have been built in Lima but because of a mix-up of plans was constructed in Mexico instead. With all its funerary pomp, it was the ideal setting for someone as renowned as Anadelle D. Partridge, even though she was not a Catholic. But in Mexico, a country that sets great store by the celebration of fiestas and funerals, these matters can be arranged. A major societal event, it was covered on page one by most papers, including the leftist *Proceso* and *Uno más Uno*, all in agreement that since there were no immediate heirs—the one or two "adopted" nephews did not count—Anadelle D. Partridge's considerable estate would be funneled, as intended by her, into the museum, presently under the directorship of Señor

Salas, the money presumably to be spent on the museum's upkeep and the acquisition of art. At the funeral, the aide to the president of Mexico, members of the cabinet, and almost the entire senior staff of the American Embassy made an appearance. Even Francisco, who had come to detest Anadelle Partridge, went to pay his respects. Only Alejandro stayed away. It's nothing personal, he assured Mercedes. I just don't feel like going. Why not? I hardly remember her. I haven't seen her in ages. Don't you think you ought to, in light of your relationship?

In light of what relationship?

Didn't you say that the stipend you received from the Partridge Foundation enabled you to complete your postgraduate studies?

He looked miffed. I don't recall ever receiving any stipend from the Partridge Foundation.

Do you erase everything you find disagreeable in your past?

I don't recall ever accepting any assistance from Partridge. And that's final!

As you please, she said. I won't mention it again.

Critic's Choice

No past to speak of? A black void? Alejandro had insisted on driving Mercedes to the airport, though it entailed his getting up at dawn. In doing so wasn't he fulfilling what he chose to think of as an obligation?—even though on this occasion his compulsive sense of duty was totally misplaced. She was outside the building when he arrived, standing next to the two suitcases and her carry-on bag as if to forestall his entering her studio. When he glanced up, was he hoping to catch a glimpse of someone at her second-floor window? Did he, in fact, detect some movement behind the curtains? An empty bus making its first round of the day stopped to pick up a passenger across the street. The stores were still tightly shut. The few cars on the street had their headlights on. You haven't forgotten anything, have you? he asked as he placed her suitcases in the trunk, conscious of the almost mechanical bobbing motions of his body. He had had less than five hours of sleep and repeatedly had to restrain a desire to yawn. The rumbling sound made by a garbage truck, a sound that invaded his sleep early each morning, was growing in intensity. Any moment now he expected the truck to emerge from around a corner. Despite the forecast for another hot, sultry day, there was yet a slight chill in the air. One never gets a chance to see the city at this hour, he said, deriving a certain perverse satisfaction from his own physical discomfort as they set off. When, as a result of an unintentional detour, he found himself driving past 22 Via Gaspachi, where they had lived for over a year, albeit in a state of war, she had nothing to offer—for all he knew, in her trancelike state, staring into the distance, she may not have noticed it. Moments later, near the intersection of Manuel Macontreras and Antonio Caso, he was startled into a tense upright position, fiercely clutching the steering wheel, fingers paralyzed, eyes riveted on the rapidly receding figure of the helmeted motorcyclist who, astride a red Harley, had come roaring out of an alley, missing him by a hair. Shithead! he muttered, when the motorcyclist to signify contempt raised one hand, the middle finger extended. But his imprecation sounded forced. There was no response from her. She remained composed—face sealed, as he, heart pounding following the near collision, concentrated on his driving. Where exactly is the college where you'll be teaching? She mentioned the town in Massachusetts, giving it its American pronunciation. Though he had never been to the U.S., what Hollywood movie was it that conjured up a picture of the presumably sedate nondenominational women's college, a sheltered environment in a hilly setting, with tree-lined walks and, amidst the low brick buildings, a new glass-faced dorm and an ultramodern-looking library? Young women in a field playing lacrosse with a determination and ferocity that was at odds with the otherwise tranquil genteel panorama, their girlish voices carrying all the way to the heart of the campus.

As soon as you have an address, send it to me.

Her prompt You can reach me care of the Spanish Department sounded like a recording, further accentuating her remoteness.

Who's the head? he inquired, as if there were a likelihood of his knowing the person. She mentioned a Spanish-sounding name. His questions were necessitated not, as she must have surmised, by a compelling need for information so much as by an urge to maintain the sluggish flow of conversation. Throughout, he pointedly refused to mention Jurud—as if Jurud didn't exist! Are you being met at the airport? Did her eyes light up in anticipation when she noncommittally remarked, Someone will be there.

Looking at his watch, he estimated that he had made it to the airport in less than forty minutes. Why are you going now? The summer sessions are not to start for another month?

I want to get to know the place. . . . It's a new experience.

Not persuaded by her explanation, Will you be staying at the college?

Yes. Then suddenly, as if something had snapped inside her, Can't you leave it be?

He noted that she said it, not *me*.

They might have been total strangers!

Reaching the airport, he followed the pictograms at twice the speed limit, while on the alert for the Aeroméxico sign.

There's no rush, is there?

We made great time, he declared, feeling triumphant when he spotted a place to park across from the terminal. Anyone seeing them, side by side, determinedly heading for the Aeroméxico terminal, could only conclude that they must be leaving together.

Given the early hour, there was no line at the ticket counter. He stopped to pick up a newspaper while she purchased *Time* or was it *Newsweek* before they proceeded to the nearest restaurant, their steps enlivened by the fake sprightliness of the background music. There must be another place, he said, when he saw the SELF-SERVICE ONLY sign at the restaurant entrance, but she, not heeding his words, walked to the self-service section, where she proceeded to order scrambled eggs and bacon, then, sliding the tray along the metal counter, helped herself to fruit juice, a roll, melon, and coffee. Her every gesture making plain the need to disassociate herself from him. Their table offered a floor-to-ceiling view of the mist-covered apron taxiway, with a Delta 757 in the foreground. Next to the ground power unit, its cables still connected to the plane, the ground crew, in blue overalls, stood idly by as the passenger loading ramp swung away from the plane's side. One of the men, wearing earphones, gesticulated to the driver of a nearby parked service vehicle. Though the 757 was about to depart, there was in the ground crew's motions a marked apathy. . . . To Alejandro, they appeared to be in a semisomnolent state.

You'll be staying on the campus?

There's no choice, I'm told, she said with a bored expression. She didn't look up as the 757, wing lights blinking, lumbered past, following the bright revolving yellow light of the service vehicle in the general direction of the taxiway. The mist was so dense that in no time the large plane was engulfed. He kept wondering what else Mercedes might be withholding.

You don't have to wait, she reminded him.

Oh, no, he protested, and, by way of a reply, pushed his chair forward, closer to her, unintentionally rocking the table and spilling the coffee in their mugs. I've got all the time in the world!

You? Her sharp negative laugh was intentionally jarring. Seeking a less disputatious subject, he leaned forward, eyeing the bright yellow synthetic-looking scrambled eggs on her plate. Any good?

What? It took her a moment to understand what he was referring to. Want some?

To bridge the silence, he mentioned his continuing effort to locate a book on Jean François Niceron.

She looked at him with a fraction of that former instantaneous attention. Yes?

He tried to jog her memory. Surely you remember? Among all the priceless art in the Palazzo Barberini, those two small seventeenth-century canvases that at first glance seemed out of place?

Yes, she said, seemingly straining to recall their visit to the Barberini in Rome.

I took them for early-twentieth-century paintings.

Yes.

In each of the canvases, the central object, a cylindrical shape, floated in a monochrome field of metal gray. When he whimsically compared it to the exterior view of the spaceship in Kubrick's *2001*, she laughed.

He traced that self-satisfied smirk, her calling card, back to when she was still a student. I don't see what's so funny.

Kubrick of all people to denote the iconography of a seventeenth-century painting . . .

Nothing wrong with that.

Only you'd refer to the movies . . .

People, some with luggage, were wandering in and out of the airport restaurant like so many sleepwalkers whose daily, or was it nightly, routine had been interfered with.

Not about to cave in to her mocking look of amusement, he continued with the description. On the cylinder's surface were painted a sequence of optically distorted portraits.

Like miniatures? she wondered, desisting from any further challenge.

Yes, one was of a bridegroom and one of the bride. . . . His eyes invoked the two faraway paintings, seeing them in a side room of the Barberini that was clearly intended for the *lesser* paintings. Inferring that he intended to go into greater detail, she interrupted. Where are you thinking of going for the book?

The resounding roar of an airborne jet created a faint vibrational hum in the plate-glass windows—briefly Alejandro visualized himself in a window seat of that plane, seeing the mist-shrouded terminal and its facilities hurl past.

In the patient voice of someone addressing a mental defective, she repeated her question: . . . for the book?

As he looked at her bright red lips, carefully, ever so carefully, shaping the words, he was struck by the renunciation they seemed to convey. Delphi books might have it.

Niceron? She mused, Could he have been part of the School of Fontainebleau?

You don't recall seeing the paintings, do you?

You look as if you're working on a critical text, she remarked self-consciously, made uncomfortable by his scrutiny. Despite her reminder—There's no need for you to keep me company—he stayed until they reached the passport control, beyond which he wasn't permitted. Perhaps I'll come and visit, he offered impulsively, choosing not to react to her gratuitous: That won't be necessary. One of these days, he joked, I'll just have to overcome my inhibitions and visit the U.S.

He handed her the present as they parted. She looked at it in surprise, then with what amounted to a confused laugh dropped the little package in her pocket. Well, thanks. I didn't expect any . . . As he waved, he could see himself, a little too stiff, too contrived. . . .

On the drive back, thinking of Mercedes much in the way he might contemplate any difficult text he had undertaken to examine, he was frustrated by the resistance he felt inside himself, an impediment blocking his brain's interpretive capacity—thus preventing him from arriving at anything but the most banal conclusions.

When he asked who, if anyone, would be staying in her studio apartment, Mercedes had hesitated—was she guarding herself against his reproach?—before stating, in a more assertive voice, that a graduate student Jacobus had recommended would be there part of the time.

There was no reason why he should experience that familiar tightening of the throat. Male or female?

Her mouth curved, more pityingly than derisive. Male.

Not one of mine?

Catching his look of dismay, she promptly reassured him. Oh, no! No, no!

What still rankled was her sly, disturbing insinuation masked as an inquiry just before he kissed her: If you were a character in a novel or, given your passion for the movies, in a film, I wonder, who would you turn out to be? What character did she have in mind for him?

Now, heading back to the heart of the city, relieved that her departure had been painless, he reflected on her question, concluding that it wouldn't be Sandro, as played by Gabriele Ferzetti in *L'Avventura*. He also ruled out the love-stricken Don Mateo, as played by Fernando Rey in *That Obscure Object of Desire*, or the writer Paul Javal, played by Michel Piccoli in *Contempt*, or Klaus Löwitsch as the returning husband in *The Marriage of Maria Braun*. . . . Certainly not the narrator, Jean-Louis Trintignant, in *Ma nuit chez Maud*. But what about the cretinous husband in *La Femme infidèle?* The mild-mannered husband who kills his wife's lover? Idiot, idiot, he kept repeating. The epithet an expression of his chagrin, aimed at what he had not explored. The self-denunciation serving, in effect, to immure what he now could relinquish unexamined.

Self-Image

This is *his* story, the twisted account of a man with a face that resembles those massive Toltec stone heads of the pre-Columbian period and a body designed by pre-Columbian gods to scramble up the narrow steep steps of the Pyramid of the Sun. But inside that man can be found an elegant post-Cortés gentleman at ease in the perfect Italian replica of a chrome and leather Mies van der Rohe chair, engrossed in reading Cervantes, evincing no desire to leave this civilized and altogether safe haven.

Alejandro was meant to be a librarian of rare books, Mercedes had once stated—wasn't her mocking voice announcing her newly found independence?—or a custodian, or a caretaker. One of those dedicated conservators of art. When he failed to respond, Mercedes, not content with the effect of her remark, added, I swear, if given one of those marvelous Ferraris or Jaguars of the thirties Alejandro so admires, he'd clean it, oil it regularly, and keep it in perfect working condition in some suitable storage space out of harm's way. Now and then he might even test it, but never, never, no matter how strong the temptation, would he drive it. For that would entail too much of a risk. Was the slightly condescending, musical-sounding laughter intended to soften the impact of her disdain?

Who could she have been addressing? His best friend, Francisco? Or could it have been Raúl? Or possibly Jacobus?

Reviewing Jurud, or How to Avoid the Perils of the Chocolate-Caked Chicken

The actual reason for Mercedes's prompt acceptance of what she claimed was an unexpected invitation to teach at a small New England college—teach what? he'd like to know—was not hard to arrive at. It ineluctably pointed to no one else but Jurud. And it would be Jurud, Alejandro concluded, who'd be waiting for her at Logan Airport, if indeed she was landing at Logan. Instead of proceeding to that doubtlessly Edenic women's college—who did she think she was fooling?—they'd drive, Alejandro was convinced, back to Jurud's place in New York. Still, despite the acuity of his vision, how could he be certain of what might or might not take place once Mercedes reached the U.S.? Given his unerring instinct and intuition, elements without which a critic cannot function, was it that farfetched to picture at her arrival the two of them, she and Jurud, throwing caution to the winds—their great reunion!—embracing, passionately kissing for all to see? All the same, on reaching Jurud's duplex on Central Park West—considering

Mercedes's fierce sexual inhibitions—might she not (was this wishful thinking on Alejandro's part?) resort to some subterfuge and, with that silken laugh he knew so well, allude to her jet lag, the late hour, the onset of a headache, while keeping her palm firmly planted against Jurud's chest and her lips tightly pressed together. Even so, in view of her Mexican background, with all its emphasis on ritual, a writer as insightful as Jurud might interpret her action as only a temporary hurdle, the result of cultural conditioning. Though, in light of her unpredictable mood swings, what assurance did Alejandro have that once in Jurud's bedroom, she wouldn't undress of her own accord? After she had slipped naked between the sheets, would her response to Jurud's passionate embrace be any less cool than before? Alejandro could well imagine Jurud's consternation when his lips encountered the firm resistant line of her lips. Presumably, this resistance would leave Jurud at liberty to roam, free to isolate the nipples with his tongue, free to caress the *firm* breasts and glide his hands over the *smooth* torso, like a collector appraising a newly acquired acquisition, enthralled by her body's *sheer* perfection. Would she finally, inveigled by Jurud's desire, relax her guard, that innate rigidity, that formidable inflexibility? You have such a *funny* view of women, Mercedes used to say. During their lovemaking, Alejandro recalled, her gaze remained obdurately fixed on the ceiling, or was it the sky? Still, without any prompting, without any guidance, she'd compliantly spread her legs to accommodate his desire—but weren't they always parted too evenly, the cool symmetry of her unvarying motion conferring on their fucking a distinct passionless, almost diagrammatic ceremony? All the same, given the unpredictability of the male response, Alejandro was forced to conclude that even her failure to respond sexually, to evince any emotion, to execute anything other than position one cool hand on Jurud's shoulder, might provoke Jurud to previously unknown heights of exaltation.

Still, what proof did he possess that this was true?

Proof? Why, the proof available to anyone capable of reading between the lines of Cervantes, Proust, Flaubert. But of all people, did it have to be Jurud? Of all writers Mercedes might have chosen, did she have to pick Jurud? There was no question that the invitation she had received to teach had come at the suggestion of Jurud. Who else? Examining Jurud's face on the jacket of his most recent novel, *Intimacy*, Alejandro asked himself, What can she possibly see in that face? . . .

Eden

What had Mercedes seen in *him*? Was it in 1983 or 1984 that Alejandro became her lover? By all accounts not her first or second or even third. The others had included a guest lecturer at the Instituto Mexicano de Cinematografía, a fellow graduate student in the Department of Anthropology, and a certain Miguel, who owned a bicycle repair shop in the Polanco district. The guest lecturer, a Romanian, had given her a signed copy of Derrida's *Grammatology*, the grad student had bought her a see-through blouse she never wore, and Miguel had sold her a sixteen-speed French racing bike at cost. As for Francisco? When he had introduced her to Alejandro, was he intent on dumping her? To allay Alejandro's suspicion, Francisco maintained that he and Mercedes had been just friends. Did Alejandro believe him? It's too long ago. Though Alejandro was by far not as outgoing and popular as Francisco, and he certainly wasn't as good-looking, he did, however, already have a reputation as a critic.

Moreover, unlike Francisco, his truthfulness had never been questioned, nor his dependability as a friend. In 1983 or '84, a busy year, he was selected to review the latest book by Fuentes, two by Updike, also a Barth and a Pynchon, and, at the behest of Jacobus, his publisher, he forced himself to write a lengthy, favorable article on Jurud, an American whose work he considered at best antiquated and politically reactionary. To cap his false praise of Jurud's novels, he maintained that they provided irrefutable proof of man's interminable moral striving. To his surprise, no one saw any reason to take issue with his hypocritical appraisal . . . for that matter, no one seemed to realize that Alejandro was mocking the American, whose class-dominated "entertainments" were peopled by a once glamorous WASP ruling class, which continued to cling to values that—in light of America's social polarization and so-called multiculturalism— seemed decidedly dated and more than a little frayed. Reading Jurud, one wondered: did the class he depicted still exist? All the same, these "Arthurian" romances, these advertisements for an upper class whose political power and influence was on the wane, were widely read. Was it that America was loath to give up this genteel, this ennobling fantasy of itself? Or were the books read because Jurud, not a WASP himself, depicted the WASP imperfections with an almost Proustian delight, much as Proust had depicted the shortcomings of the Guermantes, if only in order to elevate them to their proper place in history?

The month his article on Jurud appeared, anyone in proximity to the critic and his girlfriend, Mercedes, as they ascended the Pyramid of the Sun on what proved to be the hottest day that June could have foretold what Alejandro failed to realize, namely that their relationship, for lack of a better word, was not a promising one!

Halfway up the pyramid's steep slope, Alejandro had

stopped to allow Mercedes to catch her breath. Dejected, she sat down, resting her elbows on her knees, hands supporting the weight of her chin, while moodily eyeing the Calle de los Muertos—which traversed the, to her, vast sprawl of unreclaimed history—too unsettled by the intense heat to absorb anything but the scantest details of what was so startlingly revealed. After a swig of the warm, medicinal-tasting water, he offered the plastic canteen to her, incongruously choosing that moment—as she raised it to her lips, throat bared, head tilted back, eyes shut, without appearing to swallow—to broach marriage, saying, We really should get married, or words to that effect, followed by an almost offhand What do you think? which diminished the significance of the proposal, making it sound as if what he contemplated was not the joyous bond of matrimony but something on the order of a weekend among Indians who spoke only Nahuatl or Mazahuatl. He watched her as, silhouetted against the steep steps and the bleached-looking ruins below, she appeared lost in thought, seemingly unaware of the thin trickle of water spilling down one side of her cheek. Finally—reluctantly?—she swallowed, in the process spilling more water down the sleeveless white dress—this immaculate, prim-looking uniform of hers. Well? He looked blindly in her direction, wiping his glasses with a shirttail. What do you think? Her delayed response—Is this a proposal or a suggestion?—wasn't half as playful as she had intended. Was it the heat? Or was his decision not to wait for a more propitious moment the result of his brain's overstimulated response to the spectacle below, or was it something he could trace back to infancy? Ready? he asked, his mechanical smile seeking to nullify the acknowledged awkwardness of his timing. Shielding her eyes against the sun, she looked up, not only to gauge the distance to the top but to take a measure of his ambivalence.

We're more than halfway up, he said encouragingly. She opened her mouth to reply, only to change her mind. Wearing a sundress and sandals more suitable for the reception of a marriage proposal in a tree-shaded garden, she was longing for a cool drink and shade. He may have been about to elaborate on his "untimely" offer, when out of nowhere, stunning them with its horrendous buzz-saw noise, a helicopter swiftly, like an angry giant insect, swooped down on the pyramid and, flying perilously close, created with its downwash a gust of wind so intense it threatened to sweep them off the steps. Alejandro! she shrieked. Hold on! shouted Alejandro, and at the same time, in one of those reflex actions that are impossible to explain, fumbled for his point-and-shoot Konica as the pilot, indifferent to the danger he was causing the ascending and descending tourists, kept circling the pyramid, in ever tighter loops. He'll be gone in a minute! he yelled, wedging himself into the steps to obtain a grip on the camera, trying not to let her shrieks distract him—his face illuminated by a purpose more to his liking—clicking the shutter each time the helicopter showed itself from a new vantage point. She was beside herself—of all dumb things!—while he, once the noise subsided, tried to keep the satisfaction out of his voice as he stated, I may have a couple of good shots, the poorly timed question of marriage deferred for the time being. One moment the helicopter loomed grotesquely overhead, its green undercarriage eclipsing the sun, the next, to her relief, its ear-splitting rotor-blade roar had receded. But before the helicopter withdrew, a blond female passenger, in response to what she may have taken to be a greeting from Mercedes, waved down gaily, while the man at her side, cupping hands to his mouth, yelled something incomprehensible. The words sounded like English to Alejandro. I'll report this, Mercedes said furiously, while he was preoccupied with reloading the camera just in case the helicopter chose to reappear. I've never felt so frightened in my—

Let's proceed, he said firmly.

What if it returns . . . ?

. . . Trust me!

That gust of wind could have—

You won't regret it, he promised. On reaching the top they saw no sign of the helicopter. You see. What? It's gone. Both must have been aware that they had reached not only the apex of this monstrous pyramid but the climactic stage of their seven-month relationship as well. It would have to be now or never. Was it her quizzical look that finally prompted him to ask her to marry him? Her response was instantaneous. Sí. And, once again, Sí. Smile, he said, as he focused the Konica for a closeup of her face. Less than a week later, after the film was developed, they had an opportunity to examine the helicopter with its two passengers—Americans?—peering down at them. The name EDEN on the helicopter's side provided as yet no clue, for at that time, Eden and its president, Preston Hollier, were virtually unknown. Eden? At a time when the air was still reasonably clear and, from the top of the pyramid, that former site of continual barbaric sacrifice, one could obtain an unobstructed view of the tall buildings of downtown Mexico City in the distance, Eden didn't evoke any special response. Eden? Eden what?

The Meeting

The occasion, a benefit concert in the (then) newly constructed $88 million symphony hall, which was closely modeled on the acoustically perfect Berlin Philharmonic Hall at Kemperplatz.

The architect of the replica, a Brazilian who had worked under Hans Scharoun in Berlin, had followed step by step the great German architect's conception, likewise designing the hall from the inside out; hence the exterior, the immediately most visible aspect of the ungainly structure, was shaped by nothing less than the perfect tonal resonance inside—becoming thereby the hall's acoustical skin. Unlike its Mexican twin, the unconventionally shaped golden Berlin Philharmonic Hall, erected on what had been an area devastated by the war, was initially perceived even by its friendliest of critics as aesthetically at odds with Berlin's formerly rich architectural history, whereas the Brazilian architect's oddly shaped creation for Mexico City was immediately accepted as an anomaly only the Aztecs or their unknown precursors might have created in a moment of aberrational bloodletting inspiration. In no time, with true Mexican disregard for historical veracity, even the German original, Scharoun's inspired creation in Berlin, completed in 1963, came to be viewed by Mexican architectural historians as a structure that must have been intended for Mexico. The Mexico City symphony hall was so popular that tickets were sold out for the entire season two weeks before they officially went on sale. When Jacobus, the publisher, unable to attend the premiere performance—the Israeli Philharmonic Orchestra was playing Mahler's second— offered Alejandro a pair of tickets—tenth row, house left—he jumped at the opportunity. During the intermission, as he and Mercedes were standing in one of the several long lines at the refreshment counter, she pointed out Preston Hollier, his wife, Rita, his sidekick, Terrence, and the Brazilian architect, the men in formal attire and Rita striking in a backless black satin dress, the four sipping champagne as they leaned against the red-velvet-covered railing of the upper level, closely watched by what Alejandro took to be their bodyguard. Do you want to meet him?

Mercedes asked, taking pleasure in his surprise. I can introduce you, she maintained, with an almost coquettish toss of her head.

He grimly assessed her smile of satisfaction.

Well, do you? If anything, her smile identified a separateness he all along pretended wasn't there. They had been married for four years and thought they knew every incriminating detail of each other's lives, without appearing to acknowledge the extent of their disunity.

Why not? Reluctantly preparing himself for the encounter with Preston as they pushed their way through the throng of middle-class Mexicans gaily sipping domestic champagne and headed toward the floating stairs that led to the upper level—or was it stratum?—where the four, like royalty, were beneficently radiating approval on those below. But by the time they reached the upper level there was no trace of them, other than their now empty champagne flutes on one of the stand-up tables, next to an empty bottle of Dom Ruinart rosé. You never once mentioned him, he said when Mercedes cheerfully went on about how she had met Preston in Jacobus's office. I'm sure I did. You don't remember, do you? Slipping her hand under his arm, the conciliatory gesture a subtle sexual promise, coupled with the suddenly confiding tone of her voice: I've been told that Preston is now Jacobus's chief backer.

He never mentioned that to me.

That's because you never ask the right questions.

The bell sounded, and people began to drift back to the concert hall. Do you ever run into him? Alejandro asked, once they were back in their seats. Mercedes, not looking up from the program she was reading, frowned: No. Just before the houselights dimmed, Alejandro located the four in one of the boxes—which, like every other component in that structurally unconventional interior, seemed suspended in midair—taken aback to find Rita, leaning forward between Terrence and a bored-looking Preston, training her opera glasses directly on him. Turning to Mercedes, he began, almost jocularly, I don't know if all the things I've heard about Preston Hollier's wife are true, but— quite unprepared for Mercedes's instantaneous metamorphosis. The moment a woman is halfway independent, she stated angrily—not letting him complete his sentence— everyone is ready to make the most god-awful insinuations. An elderly woman in front of them turned in her seat, her eyes two daggers. As if it were impossible for a woman to achieve anything without having to jump into bed with a man, Mercedes went on, ignoring the irate woman.

Who's talking independence? he said disparagingly. I'm told the lady in question screws around—period!

No doubt with good reason, Mercedes replied evenly.

And what might that be?

Pretending not to hear, she applauded enthusiastically as Leonard Bernstein made his appearance on stage.

Well, no one is free to do whatever they want, he began, only to be shushed by a woman in the row behind. Unable to contain himself, he sneaked another look, catching Rita, the white, fine-boned face irradiated by a smile that could only be interpreted as licentious, listening to what the young Mexican in tuxedo (was he a visitor to their box?) in the row behind her, his face intimately close to her ear, was saying. As Bernstein raised his baton, an expectant hush fell over the acoustically perfect hall, and the rapt Mexican faces, not all that different from their music-loving German counterparts, revealed a boundless expectation. Lenny wouldn't let them down. Mahler might, but not Lenny.

After the concert, when they providentially ran into Preston, Alejandro concluded that they must have been destined to meet. As a Mexican, he had learned to recognize and accept fate. Now he wasn't going to let his critical faculties obtrude. Solemnly he shook hands as Mercedes introduced him to Preston Hollier, who in turn introduced him and Mercedes to his wife, to Terrence, and to the self-important Brazilian, all on their way backstage to congratulate Bernstein on his masterful performance. Aren't you coming? Rita asked Alejandro—from the sound of her voice, he might have been an old acquaintance. I think it's that way, said Terrence, distractedly looking in the direction of a small group of people passing through an inconspicuous door that was not marked with an Exit sign. They seem to have changed things about, the architect admitted. I could have sworn the door leading backstage is over there. . . . And he pointed in the opposite direction.

Come on—join us? said Rita impulsively, and then, in the manner of someone accustomed to having her way, folded the two of them into the group with an all-enclosing gesture, even as Mercedes looked doubtfully over to Alejandro, anticipating his refusal.

After surveying the rapidly emptying hall, Preston, their square-jawed battlefield commander, having determined the best strategy for his forces, gave the order to advance: Let's go. Avanti!—both Alejandro's and Mercedes's participation, or was it their allegiance, already taken for granted.

I've not met Leonard Bernstein, Alejandro felt the need to explain, to ensure that there be absolutely no misunderstanding.

He's a darling, said Rita automatically, her eyes focused on some detail a light-year's distance away as they set off down a maze of corridors until, more by luck than by design, they reached the long queue of Lenny's fans snaking up the gunmetal stairs. Unlike himself, Alejandro noted, a number of the men were impeccable in tuxedos, the women in the shiny ivory silken evening gowns they seem to wear on occasions of this sort, although a number of others, possibly music students, wore jeans—but all were united by the passion and desire to press the hand of the Maestro. Preston said, Come on, ignoring the fans, who, correctly acknowledging the admixture of authority and determination on his face, let them pass. Moments later, as Alejandro watched a perspiring Bernstein in a light blue terry-cloth robe, a white towel slung around his neck, hug Preston, kiss Rita, and fold the architect in his sweaty embrace, which for a split second lifted the short man completely off the floor, he wanted nothing so much as to slip away unseen. When his turn came, he stepped forward, shaking Bernstein's iron hand, politely murmuring something to the effect that he had been overwhelmed by the Mahler, not failing to notice that Bernstein had already shifted his attention to the next in line. We've been asked to join them for dinner, Mercedes said in a low voice. Was he accepting fate, or was it destiny? Why not? he replied as they made their way out of the now empty symphony hall. Before joining the others, already seated in a black limousine, Terrence gave Alejandro hasty directions to the restaurant. Rita waved: See you later!

Sure you want to go?

Absolutely, he said, surprised by Mercedes's question.

Preston and his party, consisting of Rita, Terrence, the Brazilian architect, and two American friends Alejandro had not seen before, all in the best of spirits, were still waiting for Bernstein and his retinue when Alejandro and Mercedes arrived. Sit there, Preston said, pointing him to a seat across from Terrence, while beckoning with a welcoming finger to Mercedes—amidst laughter, saying, She sits here, placing her next to himself. Red or white wine? the waiter asked. Notwithstanding the attention Preston was paying Mercedes, Alejandro felt he was among friends. Terrence, across from Alejandro, diffidently inquired if he had liked the Mahler. I'm fond of his songs, especially *Kindertotenlieder*. Then, unable to resist—was he testing taboos?—he remarked, In Mahler's time, the Germans, I believe, tended to ridicule his music, referring to it as Jewish wailing. Really? said Terrence in a frosty voice of disapproval. Later, following Bernstein's arrival, Terrence, like some well-rehearsed salesman, at what must have been a cue from Preston, launched into a detailed history of Eden's latest projects. Looking at Mercedes, Alejandro could plainly see she was enjoying herself, laughing effortlessly at all of Bernstein's and Preston's ribald jokes. When Terrence, having exhausted the topic of Eden, inquired if he'd be free for lunch the next week, he promptly said, Yes—wishing to be agreeable—that'll be fine. Though he could see no reason why they should ever see each other again. How about Tuesday? Terrence asked. Fine. Whereupon, to Alejandro's puzzlement, Terrence tried to catch Preston's eye, but the latter, as much for the benefit of Mercedes as anything else, was engaged in a raucous exchange with Bernstein and the Brazilian architect on the merits of the Sydney Opera House and paid no attention until Terrence was forced to raise his arm: their ensuing exchange, as far as Alejandro could determine, consisted of only two words. Lunch? mouthed Terrence, to which Preston responded with a vigorous affirmative nod. Tuesday? mouthed Terrence, and received another affirmative signal. Alejandro now perceived Terrence's suggested "lunch" in an altogether different light—seeing himself as the object of some as yet undefined stratagem. Wishing to leave, he tried to catch Mercedes's eye, but she was deep in conversation with Rita. You're not leaving, are you? It's getting late, he told Terrence, and I have an early class. Mercedes, still in animated conversation with Rita, did not see him stand up. Realizing how little time he had, Terrence came straight to the point: We're hoping you might help us. Our intention is to garner the support of intellectuals such as yourself for a project that Eden Enterprise is to undertake with the approval of the Ministry of the Interior. What's the project? He sank back into his seat, dumbfounded, when Terrence explained that Eden Enterprise was installing an elevator in the Pyramid of the Sun. What—the height of the pyramid? Absolutely. Run a shaft to the apex. I see. But he didn't. To what end? To make it and all of Mexico's remarkable antiquities more accessible . . . Alejandro gravely nodded, as if this preposterous idea were the most reasonable venture in the world. In what way can I be of help? Preston will explain it all, Terrence promised. Candidly, I suspect both Terrence and Preston are ready for the loony bin, Alejandro complacently told Mercedes as they were driving home. I'd stay away, she advised. They want me to publicly approve of their plan. Say you're busy. I may do that, he decided. But he didn't. The next week, following their lunch, he and Preston drove to Teotihuacán to inspect the site of the commission—just the two of them, with Preston Hollier using his considerable power of persuasion to win Alejandro's approval. What did Preston hope to accomplish? Was he under the impression that a favorable article by Alejandro might soften or, better yet, blunt the anticipated criticism and attacks from the left? As for Alejandro: I didn't expect to like Preston, he admitted to Mercedes. But there's much more to him than one would expect.

I'm not surprised, she said. I knew you'd take to him.

That's unfair.

I bet you couldn't resist telling him how we spotted his helicopter the day we climbed the pyramid. Well, did you?

I may have. . . . So what?

What else did you say?

Nothing, he replied, although the look on his face failed to confirm this. Nothing whatever. What do you take me for?

The Magnitude of My Love
Is Beyond Measure

Almost to the day of her departure, to indicate to their friends that no rupture had taken place, and in part, no doubt, to appease Alejandro's rancor, Mercedes continued to spend at least a night every week in their apartment. Sometimes she even condescended to share his bed. However, if she undressed in his presence, wasn't it to indicate her utmost indifference, if not her control of the situation? The one time he came close to touching her, she stopped the exploratory impulse guiding his extended arm with one sharp word: Don't! Now that she was gone, he was able not only to measure her absence with greater critical clarity but, given his wide reading of American literature—everything from Melville's *The Confidence Man* to the current Pynchon—to establish and familiarize himself with the terrain in the U.S. where she might be staying: seeing Mercedes as clear as day. As clear as one of those slick Englishy Polo advertisements in *Vanity Fair*. *What did he see?* That Jurud's bedroom windows were flung wide open? That the blinds were raised? As if there was no need for concealment. No need to fear Mercedes's distant unsuspecting Mexican husband? It wasn't a strain on his imagination to get an overhead view of the location, as he looked for Jurud and Mercedes, holding hands on the nearby park's broad stretch of green, called Sheep Meadow, or strolling under the stately elms (or were they beeches?) that shaded the broad avenue lined with weathered statuary of statesmen, both a short walk from Jurud's duplex on Central Park West. As for the mementos of Jurud's former existence, weren't they secreted away from prying eyes? Presently all that was to be seen were the new acquisitions. And the family? There wasn't a trace of them. Could it be a Jewish family? Given the city? The odds were two to one in favor. Given the location? Just asking. It wasn't difficult to ascertain the topography of this discreet illicit love affair. With windows overlooking the small garden at the back, the daughter's sunny room contained the traces of a contented childhood—or did it? Young women resist interpretation. In addition to an accumulation of once treasured dolls and stuffed toy animals she cannot bring herself to discard were piles of CDs by Motley Crue, Led Zeppelin, Metallica, B-52's, Guns n' Roses, and Mudhoney, and an assortment of catalogues from Tweeds, Smythe, J. Crew, and Victoria's Secret to satisfy the needs she was only now beginning to discern. By now she had even outgrown the wallpaper. Who had given her the tarot cards? For the past four years she had been fulfilling the role not only of custodian but also of seer. A controlling force? The one who determined so much of what went on in the house? She accompanied Jurud, the congenial American dad, to Carnegie Hall, to MoMA openings, and everywhere he went closely scrutinized the single women who, despite her vigilance, managed to get themselves invited to dinner afterward. And *now?* Right now! This minute? Just past breakfast? While Mercedes, facing the former wife's three-way mirror, with the aid of skin toners, eye shadows, and fragrant lotions bearing foreign-sounding names refashioned the finer details of her Spanish face, a face that could be traced to Velázquez, Jurud—the predictable American Dad? the lovable American Dad?—swiveled in his chair to face a belligerent daughter, sternly demanding to know: Bonny, why are you being so rude to our guest?

Whom does she resemble? Her mother? Her father?

The larger setting? A preponderance of Hondas, and throngs of compliant visitors who, dreading the worst, brandish their blameless foreignness as if it were a document of safe passage, while New Yorkers outdo each other in their skeptical assessment of the city: It's gone to the dogs. Central Park West, as Alejandro envisioned it: essentially a carefully scripted paradisiacal Woody Allen location in which Mercedes, strikingly beautiful, exotically foreign, wouldn't be out of place. She was, let's admit it, Mexican in the most positive sense. A walking advertisement for the beaches, the resorts, such as Acapulco and Puerto Vallarta, the mariachi music, the fiestas. Light-skinned, possessing an irresistible smile. By now her even white teeth, Alejandro was convinced, would have left their precise imprint on Jurud's shoulder. Even her delightful accent and almost imperceptible mispronunciations were an asset. In their initial exchange of letters, she and Jurud had deliberated over the preferable use of a word: the word for "intimacy." Could it be anything but *intimidad?* And Jurud's boundless need to know: What is "entertainment" in Spanish?

What is "cruelty"?

What is "The magnitude of my love is beyond measure"?

What tranquillity! We are pals, Jurud asserted, his arm around Bonny's waist, while Bonny looked up, not for a second persuaded by his maneuver. Yes, Dad. For the benefit of their guest, Mercedes, the two boisterously played in the small garden with Chico, the retriever. *What else?* Well, there was also Tim, recently back from a six-month stay in Sde Boker, a singularly bleak kibbutz in the Negev, tall for his age, bookish, suffering from a slight case of acne in addition to bearing the incurable trait of a loner, the teenage outcast, whose travail no amount of communal living could ever hope to alleviate. Tim's availability, always, at a moment's notice, stood strongly in his favor. Bonny's fondness may have extended to permitting Tim's fingers occasionally—well, not more than once or twice—under her tight panty crotch to gently probe the outer reaches of that mysterious region of pubic hair within which lay the pink opening, a soft fleshy upheaval protected by the censuring word *Don't!* the instant the intruder's fingers overstepped the limits. If not for Tim's readerly insight, how would she have known that in one guise or another she appeared in each one of her father's novels? You mean you hadn't noticed? How could you miss it? Nevertheless Tim, despite his "loners"'s perspicacity, was not a factor in the familial equation. He didn't even come close, though in the small garden, in full sight of her father's study, she playfully straddled Tim, taking pleasure in her feeling of abandon, wildly calling out his name, Tim, Tim, Tim. Her voice imitating, as best it could, the voice of an older woman in the throes of rapture: Ahhhh . . .

What else did Alejandro see?

He, the expert, the man who preferred to read between the lines, missed nothing. . . .

When Mercedes undressed for Jurud, she deliberately kept on her gold earrings and the heavy gold necklace: the gold serving to accentuate the wide cheekbones, the smooth, pale skin, the sensuous lips, the perfect curvature of her breasts. Have you ever tried this, she asked, with legs parted, eyes narrowed, as Jurud looked up at her expectantly, in a flash seeing over four hundred years compressed in her unexpected independent motion. No . . . He struggled in the grip of a powerful pumping motion, pinned, it seemed, to the pinnacle of a tall pyramid in the center of an impenetrable jungle. Never. Ahhhh . . .

How could a foreigner—for instance, one of those lean six-foot-tall good-natured Americans—provided with an unenviable panoramic close-up of Mexican history, this pre-Columbian bloodletting, on the one hand not recoil in horror, for what in his entire TV viewing experience would have prepared him for the brutality with which the pre-Columbians dispatched their victims, the priests slicing open the victim's chest with a mosaic-encrusted flint knife and, after ripping out the living, bleeding, beating heart, holding it aloft to replenish (would you believe it?) the sun's power; and, on the other hand, not feel overawed by the remarkable stoicism, a characteristic Mexican virtue to this day, with which these horrifying deeds were endured?

A Day in the Life of a Critic

Having driven Mercedes to the airport, Alejandro on his return to the city made a beeline for Librería Delphi, the mammoth bookstore in the vicinity of the Plaza San Ángel, where a clerk in the art section, after checking the shelves and his reference books for anything on Jean François Niceron, the seventeenth-century mannerist painter, found a brief entry in the *Nouvelle bibliographie genéral.* He was born in Paris, said the clerk reading from the encyclopedia. At nineteen he joined the Friars Minor. He studied mathematics. Spent time in Rome. A life of duty—he died at thirty-three. He got to know Descartes and two years before his death in 1646 presented him with his book, *La Perspective curieuse.* There's also mention of a translation he did of a work by Antoine-Marie Cospi: *L'Interpretation de chifres,* from the Italian.

Any mention of his paintings?

No, the clerk said, and suggested that he might have more success in the rare-book section, on the sixth floor. Informed that the elevator was temporarily out of order, Alejandro, having set his mind to acquiring a book on Niceron, climbed the five flights despite his fatigue, noting when he stopped on the fourth floor to catch his breath that the Ballerini Gallery had an exhibit of eighteenth-century Fantastic Architecture. By the time he reached the sixth floor, he was not only out of breath; he also had a blinding headache. Looking down the corridor, he could make out the roof of the university library in the corridor windows at the far end, and then, approaching the rare-book division, glimpsed in the windows a silvery jet against the overcast sky. You should never have married a critic, was one of the last things he had said to Mercedes. She, by now far less constrained, responded instantly, You should not have married, period. He had felt too depleted to challenge her gratuitous remark. Walking to the end of the corridor, he struggled to push open one of the windows. It didn't budge, but to his dismay he had managed to trigger an alarm somewhere in the depths of the building, its shrill sound coming up the shaft of the nearby freight elevator. Hastily he retraced his steps and was about to enter the rare-book division, when the frosted-glass door was flung open and a wiry, disheveled-looking young man, a briefcase clutched to his breast, literally skipped out, his elongated olive-skinned features pinched into a look of near ecstasy, like some apparition out of one of El Greco's canvases. As he turned to watch the phantomlike figure sprint toward the stairs, he was knocked down by the man's pursuer, who, bellowing Alto ladrón! as he came charging out of the rare-book room, collapsed on top of Alejandro with the deep grunt of a sumo wrestler. Alejandro managed a groan. He felt he was dying. But when the man, now sprawled on top of him, scrambled to his feet, he paused only long enough to ask, You OK?, and then, not waiting for a response—a response

Alejandro was anyhow too stunned to give—resumed his chase. Alejandro continued to lie prone on the floor, his cheek resting on the cool marble, even after the pain from the sharp, immobilizing blow had eased somewhat. What was it about the cool marble floor that, however briefly, made him recall the school corridor? Standing in front of the principal's office, waiting to be censured. In this memory glitch, in this suddenly reclaimed picture of the past, he stood ramrod straight next to the door, flanked by a watercooler to his left and, to his right, a glass trophy case—though none of the trophies bore his name, of that he was convinced—as the tall, forbidding principal, a balding man in his late forties, strode past, entering his office without stopping to inquire why Alejandro was there, thus prolonging his agony. At last, when Alejandro picked himself up, he not only had a throbbing headache but also an aching back. Holding his side, he stiffly proceeded to the frosted-glass door, which was ajar. The books on the floor and the overturned green metal filing cabinet, were the first things that caught his eye when he entered. Seeing the only employee, a wiry young man with shoulder-length hair and rimless glasses, on the telephone, in a high state of agitation trying to prevail on an operator—I keep telling you it's the sixth floor . . . get me the police!—Alejandro decided to leave. I'll come back later, he announced, as the man, not acknowledging his presence, frantically dialed again. Passing the nonfunctional elevator, Alejandro made for the stairs. Despite his pounding headache, on reaching the fourth floor he headed for the Fantastic Architecture exhibition, determined that at least his morning wouldn't be a total waste. When he spotted his friend Francisco, together with Preston Hollier's wife, exiting from the gallery next to the Ballerini, was it paranoia that convinced him that if not for his forced rhapsodic greeting—*Qué mila-*

gro!—they'd have passed him by, pretending not to see him? Rita was laughing at something Francisco was saying in an exaggerated wispy voice. It sounded as if Francisco was mimicking one of the gallery personnel. Alejandro caught only the words It's worth every . . . Hearing his *Qué milagro!* Francisco spun around, greeting him with a spontaneous smile. Alejandro . . . what brings you here? At the same time gesticulating to indicate that they couldn't stop, apologetically mouthing, as they kept going, We're late . . . while Rita, to Alejandro's dismay, gave no hint of recognition, her eyes blank, as if willing herself not to acknowledge Alejandro's presence. I'll call you, Francisco promised cheerfully. Alejandro was so discomfited by the encounter—the way Rita had gazed with obvious adoration at Francisco as they emerged from the gallery made it plain, even to a less observant eye than his, that they were having an affair—that on entering the Ballerini Gallery he at first failed to appreciate the artfulness of the eighteenth-century architectural designs by Boullée, Ledoux, and Lequeu, including the "Projet d'un Musæum au centre du quel est un Temple á la Renommée" and, by Ledoux, the "Temple of Memory," as well as the "House of Communal Life." In the second room, Alejandro saw a man in front of the glass-encased model of Scharoun's symphony hall which was standing next to its Mexican replica. The acoustics are not to be believed, Alejandro began, mechanically, like a wound-up toy, less out of a need to communicate his enthusiasm for the Berlin symphony hall than a desire to efface the troubling encounter with Francisco as well as the mishap on the sixth floor. Undeterred by the man's lack of response, he focused his attention on the architectural model. Its chief drawback, he declared, is that every sound, every cough, every whisper, is audible in the acoustically perfect interior. Still failing to recognize the man—

after all, why should he, having only caught a glimpse of him?—he asked, Have you ever been inside it? The hesitant, almost timorous No ought to have alerted him. In the tenth row, said Alejandro—warming to his subject, the headache now a thing of the past—one experiences an odd doubling effect, for in addition to the perfect resonance of the instruments, there's an almost imperceptible fuzziness . . .

The mistrust visible on the man's agitated face, Are you playing with me? he asked.

Am I? Alejandro was taken aback. Should I be? This grotesquerie was more suited to fiction. Staring closely at the man: Didn't I see you . . . ? Alejandro's bemused condescension yielded to an admixture of grudging respect on his recognizing the man. You're the . . . He couldn't bring himself to finish the sentence. The man reacted defensively, as if anticipating a fight, setting his briefcase on the floor, buttoning his faded, narrow-lapel cotton jacket, warily eyeing Alejandro, who, watching the man's uncoordinated motions, felt a surge of pity. Because of you, Alejandro said in a nonaccusatory voice, I was knocked to the ground.

The man took a hesitant step sideways preparatory to flight, only to remember his briefcase—picking it up, he muttered something about: the withheld components of our pre-Columbian cultural heritage . . .

Seeing the gallery assistant in the doorway, eyeing them distrustfully, Alejandro decided to leave, disconcerted by the other man's inexplicable brazen goodbye—Adiós, amigo.

The filing cabinet was upright, and the books picked up from the floor when he returned to the rare-book department. The man who had collided with him was busy behind the counter, quite deliberately, it seemed to Alejandro, withholding recognition. Accusingly, Alejandro identified himself as the one who had been knocked to the ground. I was chasing a book thief, the bookseller explained—as if that was sufficient cause. Then, after a moment's delay, the bookseller mumbled an apology in the disgruntled manner of someone entirely unaccustomed to such social niceties. Was he trying to provoke the bookseller, when— feigning concern—he asked Did you catch him? The man shook his head. What did he steal? Grudgingly, as if to indicate that this wasn't a topic to be discussed, the bookseller revealed that the book thief had tried to make off with a codex. Then, leaning confidingly over the counter, he declared himself at a loss to explain how the man could have known the size and color of the container in which the codex was boxed. How did he do it? While I was being distracted by a call from what must have been an accomplice, he tried to switch the boxed codex with a box the same size and color, which he had brought with him in his briefcase. Alejandro made a commiserating *Muhhh* sound. We didn't suspect a thing, the man continued, looking sideways at his assistant, who nodded in agreement but then, perhaps flustered by the gaze of the two men, smirked inappropriately. To think that he almost got away with it, reflected Alejandro. He had handed me his card. Said he was acting as a consultant on behalf of an institution interested in purchasing the codex, stated the bookseller. Still, you spotted the attempted switch. He just wasn't fast enough for me!—his triumphant look turning to surprise the moment Alejandro asked to see the codex. Abso- lutely not, the bookseller said reprovingly, sounding as if Alejandro's request was, given the circumstances, somehow in bad taste. It's extremely rare. I'm a scholar, persisted Alejandro, his hand reaching for his wallet. If you'd like to see my credentials ... No, no. Obdurately shaking his head, the bookseller returned to his desk, only to rise again when Alejandro complained that in falling he had wrenched his back. Exasperated, the bookseller gave in, OK, OK, he said, as he stalked into the back room to fetch the codex. Returning, his face all puffed up, he placed the codex on the counter, watching vigilantly as Alejandro extracted it from its heavyweight gray archival portfolio box. To Alejandro's astonishment, the codex, entitled *The Origin of the World*, was one he recalled having catalogued for Anadelle Partridge. The front page even bore in his own hand the penciled Dewey decimal system classification number. Leafing through the codex, which he assumed must have been stolen from the Partridge collection, unless Salas, the curator, had sold it or exchanged it for something else, he could not resist asking its price. The bookseller, already piqued by his initial request to examine the codex, looked as if Alejandro was stretching the bounds of human courtesy. With a deep sigh, he stated the price.

Really? Alejandro was impressed. That much? Do you expect to get it?

Yes, said the bookseller, removing the codex from the table, eager for him to leave. I have every confidence that we will.

Thank you, said Alejandro, feeling elated.

Well, you know where to find us, the man replied peevishly.

Like an April Morning in Summer

Had Bonny read her father's books? She certainly made a valiant attempt to. Each time, she'd begin, more than ever determined to maintain her high opinion of him, and then, fast losing her place, involuntarily start to skip . . . the eyes showing an alarming independence, shifting downward or across to another paragraph—her uneven reading, as she was carried along by the little eddies and rivulets of the text, augmented by the picture she carried in her mind of her father the novelist, like a conscientious historian, adding luster to his favorite societal group, the present-day WASPs, who, though by no means idle or rich, had lost the ruthless acquisitiveness of their forefathers. Now, by comparison with the "new moneyed class," they seemed depleted of energy, spending more than half their lives simply waiting to inherit. All the same, the WASPs provided inimitable fictional characters. Like the Polo ads, they offered a dream. . . . Tina Barney's bounteous color photo of these engaging WASPs relaxed around the dining room table in their Connecticut or was it Rhode Island country home, perusing *The New York Times* just before or was it after Sunday brunch, summed it up so well. It was absolutely enticing: the appealing family one wished to be part of. But what was it about Jurud's novels that addressed itself to women readers? Was it that Jurud, an outsider, a non-WASP, had the temerity to introduce into that indefectible WASP existence an element of *Verneinung* and repression? In fact, all too often, a female character—was it to demonstrate her distinctiveness?—would pick herself up and disappear. Walk off the pages, as if to test the reader's credulity—never to reappear in the book. What is he doing to those women, one reviewer, clearly irritated with their perplexing disappearances, demanded to know. Bonny preferred to believe that her father was simply fulfilling an authorial task by giving and sustaining life—or, in this case, artfully withdrawing a character he had invented out of whole cloth.

Whom does she resemble? Mother or father?

She wasn't taken in by her father's so-called candor, as he leaned far back in his chair, legs on the desk, with that amiable, ask-me-anything grin on his face, and tried to reassure her about his relationship with Mercedes. Listen, Buddy, I couldn't refuse my Mexican publisher's invitation, could I now? Why not? He looked earnestly at her, fumbling for the right words. Too much is at stake. His hands futilely sculpting an offering in the air to comfort her. If not for the Spanish translation, I wouldn't dream of going to Mexico without you. He fidgeted nervously in his chair, adjusting the angle of its back, as if overnight the contours of his body had changed. Mercedes will be there, she pointed out. I'm not privy to her plans, he replied stiffly. As if Mercedes were a stranger and not someone presently in his bedroom, in his bathroom . . . He tried to steer clear of Bonny's silent reproach. Buddy, she's my translator, my go-between. This is business! But Bonny knew every detail of what had taken place. Wasn't he still carrying Mercedes's imprint on his skin, in his uncombed hair? In his bathroom, nothing could clear the air of the sweet smell of Mercedes's exotic perfume. Soon the troubling scent made its way downstairs. Bonny found traces of it on the pillows on the couch and in the inner recesses of the closet. It pervaded everything. Unaccountably, Jurud's voice had thickened—he now spoke as if his tongue was swollen. Could Mercedes have bitten it? It's hay fever, he declared. At this time of year? I'll take some antihistamine. But the flush on his face refused to recede. Don't come near me, Bonny shrieked, stepping back in alarm when her father tried to put his arm around her. Even his shirt and jacket reeked of Mercedes's perfume. Flustered, he explained that it was for ten days only. Buddy, believe me, it's the last thing in the world I want to do. It's not as if it were a vacation. They'll have me running from morning to night. Sure, with Mercedes, she thought. Buddy, I love you. You're my muse. . . . No longer! . . . When we go, you and I, he promised recklessly, we'll drive down to Yucatán and together explore the ruins of Chichén Itzá, the center of the once flourishing Mayan-Toltec civilization, and to El Tajín's tantalizing Pyramid of the Niches, near Veracruz . . .

And Now?

Even though Mercedes, at her most charming, attempted to win her over by taking her shopping, by advising her, woman to woman, on what to wear, on what cosmetics to use—a skill Bonny had not yet truly mastered—she felt increasingly threatened by the Mexican intruder . . . She had no option, she felt, but to leave! After withdrawing from her savings account one thousand dollars, most of it a gift from her grandma intended for the coming year's trip to Europe, and redeeming three U.S. Savings Bonds, a gift from an aunt, and using her dad's credit cards to obtain an additional three thousand dollars from cash machines, Bonny left the house, convinced that she was setting out in much the same way her father proceeded with his text: *in a state of not knowing!* He was not, she cautioned him in her first letter from L.A., to misjudge this adventure, this voyage—what else to call it?—as retribution: it was intended as a gift. After all, he had trained her to be his eyes, his ears. . . .

I'll apprise you of everything that happens, she warned. Everything! But could she be mistaken? Could she be just another confused teenage runaway and not his literary or was it historical conduit? All the same, in her letters she'd omit nothing—nothing! No matter how painful! Nothing! Nothing, she screamed, as she began her first, detailed, accusatory letter.

Bonny

The bus trip, one way to Valhalla from L.A., where she had spent her first week away from home, came to $26.25. The ticket clerk held the hundred-dollar bill up to the light, a quick, experienced scan, before handing over her change. Near the bus terminal Bonny had bought a cheap scarf, black, earplugs, a yellow waterproof Sony Walkman for $54.95, Spearmint gum, and four tapes, by The Downtrodden and The Geezers and, her favorite, The Kinks. She caught the bus as it was about to depart from the platform. The driver's sunglasses were as dark and impenetrable as her own. She picked a seat near the back. Alone, chewing gum, she listened to "Make Waves" and "Come to Daddy," as the tinted panorama presented a life outside that was not inherently at odds with The Kinks.

Sunday afternoon is something special,
Just like another world,
Jogging in the park is my excuse to look at all the little girls.
You see I'm not a flasher in the rainbow,
I'm not a dirty old man,
I'm not going to snatch you from your mother.
I'm an art lover! Come to Daddy.

How does a young woman all of seventeen—well, almost—dressed in a cantaloupe-colored tank top, stone-washed denim jeans, and a pair of Tony Lama western boots, consider the world? With preciseness and a clear-eyed longing? With wariness and innocence? With suspicion and defiance? Dispassionately? In her case, from birth—well, almost—came the need to provide GJ with the insight he lacked. There was only one road to Valhalla, the one that leads to Point Tuna. The cars passing the entrance to Valhalla did so at speed. Was it the speed of thought, the speed with which GJ put his thoughts to paper, the speed with which he entered the captivating world of his novels? Only days later was she able to distinguish the local drivers from those on their way to the Point. To the south, there was a nondescript shopping center; a mile beyond that, the ramshackle airport, with five or six planes on the tarmac in addition to the dozen or so derelict, cannibalized C-14s. Bonny spent an hour in the main building, hypnotically watching the single-engine prop planes land, while the air controller, a heavyset woman who also presided over the candy and the coffeemaker, issued instructions into a huge old-fashioned mike in a clipped, mechanical voice. As Bonny unwrapped a peanut rice cake, marked Kosher, the black attendant, old enough to be her grandfather, leaning on his broom, shyly remarked that fresh doughnuts were available in the morning. Best you come early. She asked for the nearest mail drop. Mindful of the air controller, fearing her disapproval, he lowered his voice: Just drop your letter in that wire tray over on that nice lady's desk—then he beat a hasty retreat.

And now?

In her letters to Jurud she omitted nothing! Nothing! For the letters were intended to cause pain . . . acute pain. Was it a cleansing pain?

Between the airport and Valhalla there were several cinder-block restaurants, including a usually empty Italian, with red-checked tablecloths and candles and giant travel posters, and its competitor, the Mexican, down the road a little, displaying sombreros, tooled western saddles, assorted riding gear, fake timber, and glazed pottery for sale, with colored balloons as a halfhearted attempt to inject gaiety. Steward and World's drugstore had a soda fountain with red bucket swivel seats, and in The Happy Few, one of a string of bars, there was a pool table and two pinball machines. To the north, nothing but utility poles for what seemed a long, long while. To the south on Route 102 one could find a few motels, one drabber than the next. The missing black plastic letters on the illuminated yellow signs cast doubt through their absence on the offering of such delights as VI RATING BEDS, XXX MOV, and XTR-WIDE SCRE, as well as TEAK DINNER with BAKED POT and SAL BAR for $8.95. The so-called public beach, advertised in the illustrated booklet available to tourists wherever they stopped, and so engagingly depicted on the billboard at the entrance to the Iguana Motel, was a narrow uninviting pebbly strip. The Valhalla Spa was in a league of its own: a tranquil setting, a sanctuary secure from intrusion, its beach accommodatingly wide, with soft white sand. Nothing in the area came close to it. There was no sign at the entrance to attract the passing traffic and no mention of it in the local paper. The guests came from afar. Most had been there before. Year after year they returned for the deep-sea fishing, the calm, the seclusion. Pete Rawlings, the owner, was curious to know why Bonny hadn't called to inquire if they were hiring. Despite her evasive answers, there must have been something about Bonny that he found acceptable, for she was hired on the spot even though there were hardly any guests and she had no credentials or references to speak of. She lied not convincingly about her experience and age. I'm twenty, she declared, looking Rawlings straight in the eye. We accept people on trust, Rawlings's wife, Joan, a tall, sprightly woman with a forthright manner, said as she showed Bonny the small maroon-painted room that was to be hers. Facing the parking lot, it had no view of the beach or ocean. Everything, from the single bed to the Conran drop-leaf table and folding chairs, not only looked, it even smelled brand-new. The kitchenette cabinet contained an unopened pound bag of brown rice, two packages of Muller's spaghetti, tomato paste, cans of split-pea soup, Folger's coffee, and in the tiny refrigerator there was a container of milk, frozen Tropicana orange juice, two sticks of

Hotel Bar butter, unsalted, and a dozen brown eggs. The framed pastels of boats at sea above the white commode were flanked by tall flowering rushes and cattails in a copper-colored vase and a nine-inch Zenith color TV. *The Believer's Diary* had been left on the GE alarm clock radio next to the bed. *Trust Christ to enter your heart,* the Reverend Del Banko exhorted the reader on the first page. *Have faith!* There was no mention of guilt. Nor was the Christian God ever irate. . . . If anything, there was the promise of a spiritual redemption. Another Eden? And doubtless as reassurance to the diarist, every reference to the Old or New Testament gave the reading time—never more than three minutes. The Rawlingses had thoughtfully provided a ballpoint pen. Other reading matter consisted of the *Homeowner's Eternal Sanctity,* a couple of *Christian Maturity* magazines dated 1966 and '67, an issue of *Health First,* and a *National Geographic* from 1912, containing a large fold-out map of Kiangsi Province. On the Xerox of the roughly drawn map that pinpointed the Valhalla resort in relation to the Kmart, the post office, Ffloyd's Pharmacy, Gable Pizza, The Pancake House, Dock's Plumbing Supplies, Flo's Diner, Jerry's Body Shop, C & D Cleaners, and Central Savings & Loan, there were half a dozen bars, including Aces, a topless one, but the US2 was the only one to have been awarded four hand-drawn asterisks by someone who, Bonny surmised, might have been, despite the newness of the room, the room's former occupant. The days passed quickly. The work wasn't demanding. She and Marina, a nimble olive-skinned woman of indeterminate age who was never seen without the commanding presence of the large gold cross suspended over the deep cleft of her ample bosom, were responsible as a team for twenty units—half of which were unoccupied. The week passed uneventfully. She felt swept by a powerful desire to please the Rawlingses, wanting their approval. Each evening she made an entry in the diary, dutifully following the guidelines by referring to Jesus the redeemer and the rewards of prayer. Though her entries were guarded, she didn't fail to mention her father and her boyfriend Tim by name. As she lay in bed, listening to The Kinks, she tried to visualize her father's reaction to her sudden, unannounced departure—was he angry, concerned, baffled?

After a week she felt as if she had spent her entire life in the sheltered environment of Valhalla, deriving an unqualified contentment, as she was pleased to mention in her letters, from the daily ritual of changing the bed linens, vacuuming, cleaning bathrooms and kitchenettes, while—as GJ's observer and muse—keenly assessing the pleasantly carefree visitors, who, this being their vacation, arrived with children and wives or girlfriends. They came in boisterous groups for a week of relaxation, surfing, snorkeling, deep-water fishing. Little escaped her as she almost voraciously examined the women's possessions, their dresses, their underwear, their knickknacks, as if to determine their precise indebtedness or obligation to the swaggering men, of whom a disproportionate number seemed to be in construction. Even the perfume the women wore was deemed significant. But what was she to infer from a preference for New Balance, or Nike, or Adidas? Marina marveled: The things you notice. I mean . . . who has the time? We'll never see them again! Not that those scrutinized by her remained unobservant. But as Jurud's daughter, she was conditioned to being stared at. She almost expected it. Not by men only— however, the women's gazes, less explicitly sexual, struck her as unnervingly penetrating. Finely attuned to the conduct of their own gender, women were far less likely to be hoodwinked by a sixteen-year-old, even though she might pass for a year or two older. With one glance they could intuit what the men were likely to overlook, namely Bonny's determined, even deadly resolve. Unlike the others, Bonny kept her door locked, though anyone the least determined could easily have gained entrance. She tried to be inconspicuous about it; still, Marina noticed. We don't lock our doors, she said in rebuke. It's second nature where I grew up, explained Bonny. Well, you can relax, Marina said. We just don't have muggers around here. Besides, what's to hide? To Bonny's surprise, Rawlings, in what she took to be an overture, without ado handed her a 120-minute videocassette of his sermons, though he must have known that at present she had no means of viewing it. Somewhere, she speculated, on that cassette, entitled "The Christian Return to the Eternal Eden," was a truth waiting to be transmitted to Jurud, who'd eventually work it into one of his novels. In her imagination she could see and hear Rawlings imploring his audience, "Hear the truth!" in a voice not dissimilar to the half-dozen late-night AM-dial evangelists battling Satan's evil empire until the break of day.

Just don't you fall for him, Marina cautioned.

Bonny's response: an incredulous Whaaat? followed by the spurning: You must be kidding, he's ancient—to which Marina's rejoinder mouth tightening in disapproval, As long as you remember! sounded like not a censure but a warning.

Bonny was beside herself. Old enough to be my . . . Besides, I'm waiting for Tim.

At night, passing outside Marina's room, she overheard a long sustained moaning and wondered who the man might be. The orgasmic moaning, as she thoughtfully listened (Ah, this too was for Jurud!), grew more intense and then peaked with a quaver. Armed with a handful of quarters, she used the public telephone in the shopping center just in case anyone were to trace her call, speaking to her best friend, Crystal, as well as, of course, to Tim. Don't worry, Tim said, but she didn't fail to detect the note of uncertainty in his high-pitched voice. We'll head for Mexico. There's a solar eclipse in Yucatán on the eleventh. An eclipse? It was the first she had heard of it. A total eclipse. The most spectacular in memory, he explained, going on at far too great length, so that she felt less and less reassured. Then why aren't you here already? He had so many excuses—I'm leaving as soon as I—that she stopped listening. Car after car slowed to a crawl alongside her as she walked back on 102, not turning her head to meet the sex-crazed stares of the leather-jacketed drivers, deaf to their hoarse entreaties: Honey, please, let me take you home! Beseeching her: We'll have a great time, I promise! Followed by their imprecations: Bitch, you know what you want? Here, baby—feel between my legs! Fed up, she gave the finger to the eighteen-year-old who, under the misguided belief that any moment now she'd succumb, had been trailing her for half a mile in his souped-up '78 Mustang.

Daily, she'd double-check to see that her cash remained wedged securely in the ice bucket under the beige wool blanket and spare pillow on the top shelf of the closet.

Do you like it here? Joan Rawlings inquired, showing maternal concern. We like our staff to be happy. I'm happy as a lark, Bonny said promptly. That's good. In the evening she was able to observe from up close as couples, fueled by slabs of semirare steaks, half-pound portions of lean hamburgers, or the catch of the day, along with fries and countless Buds, Miller's Light, or Kronenbourgs, indicated a strong romantic albeit robust longing. Watching a busty, freckle-faced woman squirm with pleasure in the embrace of a big-chested man in cowboy boots, she readily understood that the words EASY RIDER on the woman's T-shirt were an allusion not to her equestrian skill but to something far more sexually inviting.

Placidly chewing gum, Bonny sat back in the deck chair, a dog-eared copy of *Intimacy* on her lap, all innocence, listening to "Come to Daddy." She couldn't help but be struck by the absence of any sign of furtiveness as couple after couple retreated to their rooms and respective king-size beds for the express purpose of—what else?—wanton, bestial, insensate, lustful love. After eleven there was no one left on the beach as she headed back to her quarters, seeing Joan Rawlings on the jetty gazing pensively out to sea, with only the Irish setter for company, while the nearby row of identical white power boats, ropes neatly coiled, everything spick-and-span, gently bobbed up and down in their mooring. In the parking lot, Marina, at the wheel of a brand-new red Toyota still sporting a sales sticker on the rear side window, offered her a lift. I'm driving to Kmart for some birdseed for my canary. Come along, and I'll buy you a Coke. No, thanks. Was she testing Marina when she mentioned seeing Joan on the jetty by herself and then, with a childlike E.T. smile bound to infuriate Marina, wondered where Rawlings might be holed up at this hour? Turning the ignition key, Marina snapped, Won't be long now before you'll be in a position to know, though some of her words were drowned out by the noise of the engine.

By the time she met Emilio she'd seen *The Return of the Jedi* and *Friday the 13th*, and gone through at least four trashy paperbacks, and twice ingloriously spent the night, or part of it anyhow, with Rawlings. The first time, after knocking on her door, Rawlings, a bundle of religious tracts in one hand and, in the event she didn't drink Coors, a six pack in the other, had stood expectantly in her doorway, while she, flustered by his presence, in her most adult manner, excused herself: I was just about to wash my hair. Don't let me stop you, he said, striding past her into the room with the proprietary air of someone coming to inspect the premises. Nonplussed, she didn't move—this microsecond indecision her undoing. Why the delay? Had she realized that she was incapable of generating the necessary indignation to make him leave? She chose the least confrontational option, leaving the hollow-core door of her room wide open. But Rawlings, having made himself comfortable on the Sealy Posturepedic bed, didn't seem to care that anyone passing outside might see them. For that matter, even after the door was shut, anyone passing by would have had no difficulty identifying Rawlings's ministerial voice, as he inquired loudly: Do you, Bonny, believe in everlasting life? Are you able to recognize happiness? Do you seek salvation? I don't think I . . . Do you believe that perfection is attainable? I really must go to sleep, she said finally. What's your perception of divine inspiration? I haven't given it much thought. He treated her response as evasive. Are you a Christian in body and soul? Answer! Gosh, of course, if you . . . By then she was experiencing a decided time warp. Here was something even her capacious, ever accommodating brain was unable to comprehend. Who dimmed the light? Seeing in the strategically located full-length mirror—a customary motel feature, as entrenched and splendidly American as the ice machine and the vibrating bed—a pair of strongly veined hands, which may well have resembled in more ways than one those painted by Michelangelo for one of his elongated figures on the Vatican ceiling, clasping her by the waist, and then, for the mirror does not deceive, she observed how one hand, cannily poised, took the initiative to boldly pull up the ribbed J. Crew tank top and liberate her startling in their white beauty, small, youthful breast. Nothing escaped her. Nothing. Her overactive mind raced through her father's fiction—was it in search of a similar heart-pounding experience? Why else would she boldly, but seemingly out of context, remark, I'm the source of my father's creative imagination? What source? Rawlings couldn't have been less interested. Men are afraid of the emotions women invest in love, Bonny asserted bravely. They think they're making love, and are experiencing intimacy. But in truth, they come to regard love and intimacy as yet another form of warfare. Did you know, for someone your age you're kinda gabby, Rawlings acknowledged matter-of-factly. Finally—was it to appease his irritation?—she stepped out of her skirt. Seeing this act of capitulation as an irrevocable step in the right direction—it now remained only a matter of time before the decisive moment of, ahhhh, penetration—his face conveyed the shine and conviction of a ship about to be launched, just prior to sliding into the deep water that would, from then on, forever be its home. This is me, she thought, and then, little realizing how unsettling her remark was, complained, D'you realize you're making love to a text?

He paused, flushed from the exertion, and querulously demanded, What text? Gazing at her with pinhole eyes. What the heck are you?

A book waiting to be written by . . . , she started to say.

A statement dismissed as irrelevant. There's only one book, he replied, resuming his slow in-and-out motions.

I'm his text, she thought, tranquilly. Seeing the words typed on twenty-pound Minerva bond her father bought by the ream.

Hours later, gently nudging him awake, knowingly whispering his name: Rawlings, wake up.

What? The eyes opened, and as the unfocused mind struggled to diagram the darkened interior, his muscular, sleepbound body was prepared, if need be, to leap into action.

Time to go, she heard herself chant, her cheerful American cheerleader's voice sounding years older, as if the sexual experience had infused her with an insight, a knowledge that put her on a par with the braless waitresses in The Pancake House. Joan's waiting. Uncertain if, by saying his wife's name, she hadn't trespassed irredeemably. Believing his wife's name, not their sexual act, to be the taboo. If anything, waking him had the reverse effect. As he placed his arm on her warm belly, the fingers promptly rushed a rich patina of information to the still dormant brain.

When he playfully inquired, Do you know why I hired you? she patiently waited for his explanation.

Because of the unconvincing way you lied.

She protested, I did not.

Like someone pleading for counsel . . .

What? Bewildered: What do you mean? How?

That's it, he exclaimed, That's the look!

Puzzled, twisting her neck to gaze at her reflection, but in the dim interior light her face and upright figure in the mirror could have been those of any slim, adventurous young woman of seventeen, no, sixteen.

What look? she demanded, now annoyed.

The look of someone struggling to acknowledge that God is keeping an account of all history.

Frustrated, she pounded the mattress with her fist. I wish you'd make yourself clear. . . . Finally, exhausted, she let her head fall against the broad chest.

He breathed in the youthful scent of her hair. He was contented. Holding her close. Don't misinterpret what I say. Don't rebel.

But how do I look?

Willful.

In the dim light of the TV, its sound turned low, everything was in its appointed place. The digital clock radio indicated 2:32 as the muscular torso of the middle-aged man continued unabated his nocturnal activity, to the rhythmic squeak of the bed.

There's nothing I can do about it, she reflected, not missing the opportunity to imprint this event, both painful and enlightening, on her ever receptive brain. In the mirror she could vaguely determine, as he rested his hands on her haunches, his intense internal struggle for self-control. She could also see that the blinds were tilted in a way to permit someone standing outside to peer into the room.

How is he seeing me? she wondered.

After their second time in bed, an occasion that threatened to become routine, she went out of her way to avoid him, spending the entire evening by herself in US2, a bar frequented by pilots and mechanics and the local rejects who liked to hang out at the airstrip. When she spilled her stein of beer on the already beer-impregnated dark-stained wood counter, the Mexican dishwasher with the—to her mind—Aztec face rushed from the kitchen to wipe up the spill. Watching *Wheel of Fortune* on the wide-screen TV, she could see the Mexican within the kitchen repeatedly turn to look at her while rinsing plates. I'm his TV, she thought contentedly. Spurred by the intensity of his gaze, she returned his look, staring back until finally, in confusion, it was he who withdrew. An hour later, when Emilio—straight black hair, dark-brown skin, wearing a biker's black leather jacket—came up behind her as she was watching the late-night TV news and, in a Mexican-accented voice, blithely asserted that the announcer, just then describing a drug bust in Camargo, failed to have the slightest comprehension of what was going on in Mexico, she swiveled a quarter turn on the barstool and, smiling accommodatingly, listened to his explication as if he were an extension of the TV. How long have you been working here? she finally asked. I don't work here, he said. What makes you think . . . ? Then, as his eyes shifted to the now empty kitchen—concluding that she was confusing him with the Mexican help—he said reproachfully, You mistook me for that Indian in there, didn't you? Oh, no, she said, I simply took you to be the . . . As she was thinking of an appropriate word, he concluded the sentence: Dishwasher. Manager, she corrected him. After that she couldn't refuse when he bought her a beer. She hesitated briefly when Emilio offered her a ride in his 1972 VW Squareback. I didn't know they're still making these. Well, not in Germany, that's for sure. They don't. He drove straight to Valhalla without stopping or slowing down, not daring to look at her now that she was next to him, while talking nonstop about the effects of the '85 quake in Mexico. Where were you when it took place? It took him a moment to reply—Mexico City. He accompanied her to her door. To her relief, he didn't press her to let him in. What do you do? With the ingratiating smile of an experienced salesman, he pulled out several three-by-five colored photos of pre-Columbian pottery. They're beautiful, she said. I dug them up, he continued. Really? Disbelief in her eyes. Are they for sale? Sure, he said, not able to read the face of a sixteen-year-old. I sell them to collectors in California, Arizona, and New Mexico. Isn't it dangerous? What? Bringing them across the border? He grinned. Not if you know the ropes. Rawlings was nowhere in evidence the entire next day. Marina, more than usually remote, asked, Well, where's that Tim of yours?

The occasional appearance of a squad car and the sight of the local police didn't alarm her. When she called Crystal, euphorically describing the Valhalla beach, the octagonal house, as well as the people staying at the motel, she wasn't prepared for the anguished note in her friend's voice: Bo, how could you? What? What did I do? You left him high and dry. My dad had more pressing things on his mind. You're being spiteful, Crystal insisted evenly. Got to go, Bonny said in response, and hung up. Most couples renting powerboats stayed out as long as they could, the ones with a nice sized catch on their return—posing jubilantly next to the huge fish. What? Anything large. Swordfish, shark, barracuda, or tuna would do nicely. Anything that would put up a decent fight, while Rawlings obligingly took a couple of shots with the Polaroid. I'm having fun, Bonny assured her dad in a postcard, going so far as to reveal that not far from where she was staying there was an airport with a bunch of C-14s dating back to the war. Did you ever see a C-14? Can you tell it from a C-16?

What did she know? At seventeen, no, sixteen, she hadn't even heard of less read José Vasconcelos's book on the cosmic race or Fuentes or Rulfo or Paz or Arreola or Vicente Riva Palacio or, for that matter, the incomparable B. Traven. She had no clue as to the Mexican character. The only Mexican she had encountered so far was Emilio. With respect to his profession, she reasoned: Some people realize their potential by pumping gas, others manage self-service laundries or drive eighteen-wheelers. Some, like her dad, spent their days and nights worrying sentences to death while pecking away at their ancient manual typewriters. So if Emilio chose to smuggle pre-Columbian art into the U.S., what was to stop him? At their next meeting she tried to describe to Emilio how, at home, she and her father would discuss history as if it were the most farfetched fiction and fiction as if it were an outrageous form of history. That makes perfect sense, Emilio readily agreed.

There's little to distinguish one from the other. Miffed by his ready assent, she maintained that notwithstanding her father's point of view, one tends to get a more accurate view of a society's concerns and tribulations by reading fiction. I love Mexican comics, he agreed. She looked at him suspiciously but caught no hint of mockery.

What else? She could without much difficulty locate herself on the map of California. She could trace the route she and Tim intended to take to reach their destination in Mexico. She could also, at one glance, determine what approach, direct or circuitous, a man, any man staring longingly at her breasts and legs would take simply from his general demeanor, the way he stood, the way he walked. She had attempted to explain her actions to Crystal. But how to explain what remained largely inexplicable? How to justify her sudden recklessness? I really didn't plan it this way.

Crystal, unconvinced: All the best.

One call out of the way, Bonny reassured herself afterward.

Every day around 6:00 p.m., when the wheezing, sputtering, antiquated prop plane from L.A. came in for a landing, she'd wonder if Tim would be on it. Tim failed to call, but he'd come. Tim wouldn't let her down. In the end, was it Emilio's tape, "Accidents Do Not Happen in a Perfect World," that persuaded her to give up on Tim and travel to Mexico with Emilio instead? Instinct, intuition, or seizing an opportunity? Who can tell? Emilio seemed far more agreeable, more competent, more responsible, and more versatile than Tim. On the downside, his Mexican passivity conveyed an absolute incorrigible fatalism. Did you know there's soon to be a total eclipse in Yucatán? We have the best, he agreed politely. They left after she had picked up her paycheck at the end of the week. She didn't inform anyone she was leaving. They're accustomed to that, Emilio assured her. In fact, they expect it.

Nightly, as she worked on a letter to GJ, she felt her anger waning—it made the task she had set herself a more arduous one. Did you know, she wrote, that to protect themselves against the dangerous effects of the solar rays during an eclipse, the Mexicans wear red? Red is said to repel the rays. . . . In a P.S., she referred to her traveling companion, Emilia, a young Mexican Indian woman: She and I are driving to Mexico via Phoenix. Love, Bonny.

Villa

For once, a hint of blue in the sky when they left the D.F. Rita regarded it as an omen of good luck. But Preston, as if to negate her optimism, her cheerfulness, decided against taking the scenic—at any rate, the more pleasant—route because it would add another forty or more minutes to the trip. Just ignore him, Rita told Terrence, who with the look of a martyr sat upright in the back seat. He's accusing me of pushing this house down his throat. I've done nothing of the sort, Preston complained, raising the volume of the music to drown out her voice. Here, she said, handing Terrence the manila folder. Have a look and tell me if it isn't worth the trip. . . . Glancing at the assorted material, which included several photos, a blueprint, and the prospectus the real estate broker had sent Preston at the behest of their mutual acquaintance, Salas, the curator at the Partridge Museum, Terrence agreed, much to Preston's annoyance, Looks good! No reason why it shouldn't be a sound investment.

It's a setup, Preston muttered. The real estate broker and Salas. As usual Rita is falling for it.

Is that a below-ground garden? Terrence asked, as he looked more closely at one of the photos.

A sunken garden.

For Christ's sake, it's in what once was a basement. Can you imagine anyone in their right mind . . . ?

Rita, trying to sound conciliatory: It contains a swimming pool as well.

What do you know about this guy Salas?

Preston is seeking an excuse to turn back, said Rita.

It's a fool's chase.

You'll be the first to find out, she replied equably. The next instant she shrieked, Stop! for on their left she had glimpsed a small nondescript frame building, really a shack with the magic word RESTAURANTE in large red letters.

No way. I don't want to eat there, said Preston, eyes unwaveringly focused on the empty road, foot resting firmly on the gas, until she repeated her request, if anything, a little louder. I said stop! Reluctantly slowing to a crawl, he attempted to dissuade her. We'll be in Megalen in less than an hour—

I don't care.

I wouldn't eat in there if you—

I'm ravenous!

I know there's a Kentucky Fried Chicken somewhere near Tulancingo—

You must be joking.

He looked to Terrence for much-needed reinforcement, but Terrence, lost in thought, was hypnotically staring at the barren, treeless landscape. What do you say, Terrence?

But Terrence refused to be pulled into the dispute.

Turn back, she instructed, in a steely voice.

We'll never get to Megalen at this rate, Preston complained

as he made a U-turn. Look at it! he warned as they neared the cantina, which was set back from the road in a grove of trees. I smell bad food! He was still trying to discourage her even as he parked alongside a battered VW van.

Well, what are we waiting for? she asked.

Jumping out, Preston slammed the car door and rushed ahead, but on reaching the entrance he stopped to peer inside, pretending not to see the welcoming smile of the owner.

It's dark, complained Preston.

Terrence, the peacemaker, proposed that they sit outside. There are tables in the garden.

It's cooler in here, Rita maintained, forging ahead, her advance watched by the still smiling owner, who, perhaps encouraged by her facial expression, had readied a chair for her at a table for four.

I say we go on, said Preston.

Disregarding his anger, she sat down, accepting from the owner a mimeographed menu that listed dishes in a garbled English.

Is that identical to the menu on the blackboard? she asked of no one in particular.

We'll sit here, Preston decided, seating himself at a table in the vicinity of a window, even though it was set for eight.

They might not wish us to sit here, Rita remonstrated, as she stood up to join them.

He's happy we're here, Preston replied firmly, then, addressing Terrence, What are we drinking?

Tequila, señor? suggested the owner, standing to one side.

Beer, said Terrence. Have you got Carta Blanca?

I prefer diet Coke, said Rita.

I'll have the Negra Modelo.

Will you share a chili con queso? Rita asked.

I don't share, said Preston, ordering sopa seca and shrimp with red rice. Rita was the one to bring up the Partridge Museum. The chief curator was extremely forthcoming.

You mean Salas? said Preston.

Is he Alejandro's pal? Terrence inquired.

Of course, Rita said. Alejandro put us in touch with him.

They're all in cahoots, Preston grumbled.

Why do you say that?

He looked at Terrence, who laughed as if on cue.

Alejandro maintained that he and Mercedes were climbing the pyramid the day we flew over it, Rita remarked.

I'm sick of Mexican hyperbole.

Having to read between the lines of what they say, Terrence agreed.

What's wrong with that? Rita said, just to be contrary.

Tell her, said Preston. Explain to her how those inconclusive conversations we keep having with our Mexican bankers can drive one up the wall. She laughed as Preston glumly inspected the shrimp on his plate, then, with exaggerated relish, bit into the flauta she had ordered. Mmmhh . . . This is fantastic. . . . Would you care for one? Offering her plate first to Preston, who declined, then to Terrence, who gingerly took one with his fingers.

Well?

He cautiously tasted it. Very good, he assured Rita, pretending to like it.

The trouble is that you've been eating in far too many four-star restaurants, she taunted.

Not true, said Terrence. Preston and I—

Don't let her pull your leg.

If that's how you feel about it. I think I'll order some refritos.

Don't blame us if you come down with one of those unmentionable diseases from the lard drippings.

Poor Preston, he's just in a bad mood today, said Rita complacently. Being dragged against his will to look at a villa. Being forced to eat in a dive like this.

What can we do to ease his pain? Terrence joked.

This will, said Preston with a broad grin, as he signaled to the owner that Terrence would be paying.

He's steadily getting worse, complained Rita as they walked to their car.

I liked the dessert, said Terrence.

The churros?

No. I had sopaipillas.

Preston made a point of looking at his watch.

Are we that late? Rita asked.

It's two-thirty, said Preston, blaming her.

The broker doesn't expect us to be on time, said Terrence.

I wish we could get on a more scenic road, said Rita.

Is there anything else you would like, my pet?

She had no intention of letting him upset her. I'll tell you later. Terrence looked at her, signaling his approval—and his secret love.

The dark-haired, "Rubenesque" Señora Maggi was waiting for them in her office, one of six new stores, two of which were boutiques—the row of stores, more effectively than anything else, proclaiming the town's recent prosperity. I hope you didn't lose your way? Señora Maggi's question served simultaneously as a greeting and a statement that she was a busy woman and not one of those dilatory Mexicans who, as most North Americans would have you believe, exist in a blissful state of timelessness.

We're keeping Mexican time, Rita couldn't resist saying, not failing to recognize the telltale signs of petulance on the fair-skinned, unblemished face—a face that the large colorful Indian necklace and the gold loop earrings effectively enhanced. This is nice, said Preston, settling himself in Señora Maggi's capacious chair and nearsightedly peering at the large color photos on the wall of villas for sale, while fanning himself with a file he had picked up from her desk. Gripping the large shiny black purse under her arm as if it were an automatic weapon, Señora Maggi, not wishing to allow them time to settle down, remarked that her car was outside. It's only a twenty-minute drive, she explained. Unconcerned, Preston continued his scrutiny of the photos. Now that's what I call a great-looking house. No, no, said Señora Maggi as she gently urged Rita in the direction of the door. Hold on, Preston said, I'd like to— No, no, she repeated, oblivious to his irritation. He scowled. I just wanted to— When we come back, she promised, consulting the tiny face of the watch in the gold pendant that dangled from the collar of her dress—the kind of loose silky print favored by ladies who desire to camouflage or, at any rate, diminish their ample proportions. His face radiating anger: If you don't mind, I'd like to— We must go now, she insisted. I have people waiting for us. Now, Preston, don't get hot under the collar, Rita warned. When we get back, Señora Maggi promised, you can study the photos to your heart's content. Waving to Rita to proceed, We'll take my car. It's so much easier that way. Compliantly they piled into her ancient Ford station wagon. Magisterial, isn't she? whispered Terrence. We have quite a few Americans in the area, Señora Maggi explained as she drove past the tall walls and massive gateway of a villa on the outskirts of the town. That one was just sold. Nice people. But far too many pets. Wrinkling her snub nose. A guard dog in its place is all right, but they overdo it. They have six, would you believe it? Twice more along the way she slowed down to show them houses purchased by Americans, each time providing a capsule history: That's Forster, former CIA. He was in Nicaragua. I was told in strictest confidence that he served there as your Bush's personal link. Not that he'll ever admit it. His wife has taken a Mexican cooking course. She gives great garden parties. Turning to Preston, in the seat next to her: Everyone will tell you it's a good time to buy. He grunted, then closed his eyes, to convey his total lack of interest in anything further she might have to offer. We're almost there, she promised, noisily shifting gears as she made a sharp turn into a narrow bumpy country lane. Tree branches scraped the sides and roof of the car. It's made for people who like their privacy. Then, with that little ladylike laugh she seemed to have cultivated: If you don't know the way, you'll never find it.

At first sight, the building, shaded by tall trees, was plain, almost boxlike. Facing a sunken garden located in the former basement of an estate that had burned to the ground in the forties, the house looked surreal, something Magritte might have chosen to paint. It was larger than the photos had led them to assume. It doesn't look particularly Mexican, does it? commented Preston. It's quintessentially modern, said Señora Maggi, in a voice of reproof. A strong architectural statement! The architect studied with Corbu. Preston looked puzzled. Corbu? Corbusier, Rita explained. Modern Palladial, said Terrence. Yes, the broker said exuberantly, as she parked on the gravel drive. Yes. Just look at the symmetry! Magnificent, isn't it? Have a look at that, said Rita as she got out of the car, gazing at the statuary in the sunken garden. That's Pan; Hermes is over there somewhere near the fruit trees, said Señora Maggi, pointing vaguely to the far right of the garden, as Preston snorted in derision. They're remnants of the former estate, said the Señora. The front door was unlocked. Briskly leading the way, Señora Maggi stopped in the large hall. There should be someone around. Paulo, she called out. Paulo? María? Exasperated: Where can they be? How many rooms are there? asked Preston as he gazed at the stark interior in dismay. Oh, dear, I think it's eight bedrooms, if you include the servants' quarters; then, laughing: But don't hold me to it.

If you have to ask . . . , quipped Rita.

Señora Maggi, chuckling to show her appreciation of Rita's wit, beckoned them to follow her. As they traipsed into the wood-paneled music room, she pointed to the Art Deco windows. Aren't they marvelous? You don't see many of those, Terrence said, referring to the dark, high-gloss mahogany Bösendorfer baby grand. Yes, Señora Maggi agreed. It dates back to the beginning. Rita, pointing to the shelves of LPs and the stereo: Did those belong to Mrs. Partridge? To tell the truth, we can no longer determine what precisely belonged to her and what belonged to various members of her circle. Did they all live here? She was exceedingly *fond* of young people, replied Señora Maggi. She laughed as if at a private joke they couldn't possibly understand. I see, said Rita, looking out the window at the sunken garden: Why ever did she choose to build here? I mean, on the site of the former estate . . . Anadelle Partridge was a most resourceful and inventive woman. She immediately saw the possibilities of converting the basement into a lush garden. Fond of drama—I mean, the theater—she staged plays in the sunken garden. Believe me, this was a lively house. Did you ever attend any of the performances? Terrence inquired. Me? No. She giggled. No, never! Was the owner of the former estate an American as well? Rita asked. Oh, no. Jewish; from Kiev. A structural engineer. He built railroads and bridges. They used Chinese laborers. Rita was amazed. Here too? Señora Maggi raised an eyebrow. Did you have Chinese laborers also? Maybe on finishing your railroads they came to work here. Isn't it amazing, said Rita. Divining Preston's predilection for history, Señora Maggi said to him, Given its present context, doesn't it, by comparison with any of the other buildings, convey the grandeur and sweep of Mexican history? Preston nodded in agreement. That it does. Suddenly drained of all energy, he looked around for someplace to sit down. The former estate was grandiose, she reminisced. Richter had close to a hundred stonemasons imported from Italy to work on it—they lived in shacks on the now divided property. I'm told it was a replica of a European estate. It may interest you to know that quite a few of the Italians have stayed on and prospered. Richter also stocked the grounds with pheasant and, in the greenhouse, raised all kinds of exotic fruit. His son inherited the mansion and promptly sold it, to a man named Jenkins.

Jenkins, mused Preston, as he sat down on a bentwood chair, only to rise quickly when the cane seat began to give way. I've heard that name before. . . . Not now, said Rita, turning to Terrence, with a comic look of disbelief waving her hands—Do something to stop him, will you?—when Preston asked how Anadelle Partridge had died. She was getting on—at least eighty and in poor health. If we could postpone the history for a moment, said Rita. *Where* are the bathrooms? This way, Señora Maggi said, quickly leading the way, remarking that the consul had the bathroom fixtures imported from France. Whatever became of Jenkins? Preston inquired, pretending not to see Rita's look of mounting frustration. He was about to sell the estate when it burned to the ground. Was he selling it to the consul? Oh, no. The Señora was amused. No connection. As they walked from room to room, Terrence, as befitted a "friend" of the family, remained noncommittal, while Rita, for Preston's benefit, found numerous occasions to show her delight at the spaciousness of the rooms, the parquet floors, the chandeliers, the tall ceilings, the thick walls, the dumbwaiter. There have been a number of articles on this house in the architectural journals, Señora Maggi stated with befitting solemnity. Anything we might have seen? When we get back, the Señora promised, I'll dig up what I have. Can't you just see what a great party one could give in here? Rita said to Terrence. It needs work, Señora Maggi admitted, but it's not an insurmountable task. Our local craftsmen are experienced. I'm sure of that, Preston said as he stepped into the next room. I can recommend several excellent painters, she said, not appearing upset by his ironic tone. Also, my husband might be helpful. He owns a foundry and does ironwork. The roof . . . She waved a manicured hand. A minor detail. Some windows may have to be replaced. The south wall might need to be reinforced. Gazing from the balcony at the huge terrace overlooking the underground garden below, Señora Maggi pointed to the tall shrubs blocking their view. Once you get those out of the way . . . A good gardener can work miracles, said Rita. Precisely, said the Señora. What's more, the former gardener, Rodríguez, is available for a pittance. As for the swimming pool, I'm told it needs the barest attention. Since it's in the sunken garden, one can swim in the nude. Of course, Rita said, it comes down to the price. The Señora, with a radiant smile, declared that the executors for the estate had authorized the Mercano Bank to accept what *it* considered a "fair" price. Do we need it? Preston inquired, as much for Rita's ears as for Señora Maggi's benefit. It's practically a giveaway, stated Rita as they entered the huge, old-fashioned kitchen. The Señora kept her eyes on Rita, knowing it was Rita who would decide. Think of the meals they must have prepared, said Rita. Preston swung open the oven door. My, my, have a look at this antique. There is no family to speak of, Señora Maggi explained. After her retirement, the consul settled here, though she retained her town house in Mexico City. Maybe we should see it as well, gibed Preston. To unravel Anadelle Partridge's many affairs has taken considerable time: For that reason the town house has as yet not been put on the market, Señora Maggi said reprovingly. The nephew who tried to prevent the sale turned out not to be a nephew after all. Not everything is settled yet, but the estate has been empowered to sell this house— I thought you said it was the bank. The bank is better equipped to handle the sale of this property. Rita stayed at the window, looking out at the unkempt sunken garden, at the lush tropical plants. I love it. Preston scowled: Have you considered the amount of work it'll require? Don't you agree it's the most beautifully designed— Yes, yes, he said testily, but who'll see to the repairs? I don't expect you to, she replied.

Asked by Terrence if Salas, now curator at the Partridge Museum, had ever stayed in the villa, Señora Maggi tactfully stated, For a time he was her secretary. Whether he spent any time here, I cannot say. In response to Terrence's question Was the consul already planning to leave her collection of art to the state? the Señora replied, All I know is that by the time Salas worked for the consul, the plans for the museum were well under way. I wonder how Salas came to head the museum? Preston mused aloud, as he tested the large, unwieldy louvered wood shutters, opening and closing them. I'm told Señor Salas had a way of influencing people's decisions, said Señora Maggi, with the look of someone whose source was unimpeachable. Delicately she added, He is, you know, a most astute organizer. If one is to survive in Mexico, one had better be, Rita agreed. The Señora laughed shrilly, a disconcerting shriek that reminded Rita of the brightly plumed birds at the pond near their home. Preston, controlling his impatience: What years precisely are we talking about? The sixties, the seventies. Another wave of the Señora's plumpish hand, on which glittered a massive diamond ring. I'm told even the President had come to visit. The American or the Mexican? Rita wanted to know. Both, both, the Señora said gaily, as Rita, standing at the open window, peeling dead wood from a windowsill, closed her eyes. Terrence felt his heart go out to her. A year before her death, Señora Maggi continued unabated, a number of Señora Partridge's investments had gone sour. Preston had the impression that Señora Maggi was enjoying herself. The late consul was accustomed to adversity—one could say she thrived on controversy; she took risks. But she was getting old. She was being cheated by former colleagues.

You know, nothing in this house really works, Preston noted. Not the doors, not the shutters. They need oiling, said Señora Maggi. Placing the ball bearing he had brought for this very purpose on the floor, he watched it slowly roll in the direction of the adjacent room. Did you see that? Smiling, he challenged Señora Maggi like a teacher awaiting an answer, but he was not unduly surprised when none was forthcoming. Rita stared at him, lips compressed, nostrils flaring: You've made up your mind, haven't you?

If you'd rather I didn't look at the house, just say so.

Being your circuitous self?

I couldn't possibly hope to compete with you in that department, was his reply.

As she looked around the vast living room, the thought suddenly occurred to Rita that the aging Anadelle Partridge might have been a perfect victim for someone like Salas. In the end, the sale hinged entirely on Rita's ability to overcome Preston's reluctance to acquire what he said was a needless extravagance. This house will never again be on the market, Rita asserted.

Preston sighed. Aren't you losing your sense of proportion?

We can't pass up this opportunity, she replied.

Fixing Terrence with his unblinking stare, Preston asked, What's your thought?

I've not seen anything quite like it.

It's a white elephant, isn't it?

Outside my limited experience, Terrence said, trying to maintain his position of neutrality.

See, Preston declared. That's Terrence's polite way of saying that we're out of our minds.

No he's not. . . .

If I had the means, Terrence impulsively began, I'd probably— then, realizing the potential danger of what he was about to say, stopped in midsentence.

Yes—what? Rita asked.

Precisely, interrupted Preston, effectively silencing Terrence. It's extravagant and ludicrous.

I'm glad you've got Terrence, said Rita.

It'll change your lives, promised Señora Maggi.

We already have a large house, thank you, said Preston.

Not in the country we don't, Rita corrected him.

Where do we eat? Terrence asked when they were getting into the station wagon for the return trip. This time, at a signal from

Rita, he sat next to the statuesque Señora. Goodbye, house, said Rita.

Once Rita sets her mind on something, Preston loudly complained, she never lets go.

Have you lived here long? Terrence inquired, engaging Señora Maggi in a conversation to give Rita the opportunity she needed to exhort Preston to purchase the villa. The Señora obliged by talking nonstop of her twenty years in the area. Terrence could hear Preston's muffled objections—all overridden by Rita. As she stepped out of the car, Rita winked to Terrence to indicate success. Preston has decided to go ahead, she stated triumphantly.

If you're prepared to sign the papers, I don't see why you shouldn't be able to take possession by next week, Señora Maggi stated in an offhand voice when Preston informed her of their decision—really, Rita's. Rita's smile spoke volumes. When Preston referred to the mower/tractor and other power tools in the garage, most of dubious value, the Señora agreed straightaway to include them. Jotting a reminder in her notebook. Carefully pouring a measure of what Rita took to be Cointreau into very ancient-looking dusty green liquor glasses set in a row in front of them, Señora Maggi raised her glass in a salute. With set smiles, they faced each other.

With respect to the carpets? Rita inquired. Oh, the bank is most understanding. They're leaving everything. Rita's eyes widened. You mean the piano, the stereo? The Señora, archly eyeing Preston: You know how financial institutions operate— they just want to close their books. On their drive back to the city, Preston had nothing to say. Disgruntled, eyes on the road ahead, he drove as fast as the rutted roads permitted. Terrence, seated in the back, free to admire Rita's bare shoulders and shapely neck whenever she leaned to the side or forward, wondered what at that moment could be going through her mind.

That evening, long after Rita had gone to bed, Preston joked about Rita's latest infatuation, the villa, and observed in mock dismay: One needs to keep them happy. It's difficult, believe me, not ever knowing what they *really* want. Terrence was quick to agree. He felt gratified that he wasn't the only one totally in the dark regarding women's multifarious motives and desires. The next day, emboldened by Preston's remarks the night before, he ventured to Rita that women remained an absolute mystery to him. Her extemporary reply, They're a mystery that's easily penetrated, hit him like a bolt of lightning. He couldn't believe his ears. She said it with an amused look of resignation—as if it were a fact so well established it hardly bore repeating. There was no mistaking the point she was making. With one simple sentence, *Women are a mystery that's easily penetrated,* she had brushed aside years and years of obfuscation on his part. With one sentence she confronted him with news he was ill prepared to receive. Poor Terrence, she said, patting his arm. Life's not been all that easy, has it? A mystery that's easily penetrated, he thought. You're a wonderful person, she said. Someday you'll make *someone* very happy.

Getaway

CLASS-A MOTOR HOME! 67K miles, V-8 eng., new tires. Refrig., gas range. Excel. cond. Slps 4. Body like new. Garage kept, one owner. Lowest Price Anywhere! it said on the three-by-five card pinned to the bulletin board in the local Kmart. When Emilio asked for directions to State Street, the store manager's lewd smile seemed to imply something sexually aberrant in their intentions. Still, his directions were accurate. The large lake the store manager had mentioned was not hard to locate, but State Street presented a problem, for the streets, mostly narrow unpaved lanes, were missing street signs. It was a forlorn world. What was to be seen—a cluster of tall, emaciated trees, their bark peeling, next to ramshackle frame buildings—looked as if it had just barely survived a hurricane. Now aimlessly turning left, then right, Emilio refused to admit that they were lost. They might have been in darkest Africa. At least stop to ask for directions? When he did come to a halt, trying to decipher the paint-encrusted number above the doorway of what she took to be an uninhabited shack, an elderly black man materialized, asking, Watyolookinfo? She yelled out, State Street, before Emilio could drive off.

I aks wat yo lookin fo and yo give me a street? Wilkins, she called out in that young, confident, unbiased, Dalton-Schooled white voice. We're looking for a Mr. Wilkins.

Into pit bulls, are you? No. We're looking for— But as soon as he took a step in their direction, Emilio floored the gas pedal. Damn fool, the man shouted in exasperation. Goddamn. You headin the wrong way. Still, there were other signs of life. A desiccated goat tethered to a tree stump was nibbling at the few surviving blades of grass, while a bunch of emaciated dogs, ribs showing, noses to the ground, were running in concentric circles in a seemingly futile quest for something edible. How are we ever to find State Street? It was Emilio who spotted the squat cement-block structure—the only substantial building in the area. The corroded gas pumps in front had not seen service in years, despite the misleading sign: CHEVRON—SERVICE WITH A SMILE. Above the entrance, the sign in red, its first two letters missing, announced RAGE. Pulling up behind a metallic-blue '86 Isuzu Trooper with roof rack, running boards, tinted windows, and oversize wheels, they found themselves surrounded by four pit bulls in prime condition, growling menacingly. Why don't we just forget about the car . . . , she said, when the garage door opened and Wilkins emerged, in a shiny dark suit. Bonny took him for a minister or at least a funeral director—though from up close the trousers were too short by an inch or two, and protruding from beneath the jacket sleeves were frayed shirt cuffs and a couple of inches of bony wrist. Not heeding the dogs, now frantically leaping at the tightly sealed car windows, he approached them. What are you folks doing here? Emilio lowered the side window a crack to explain that they were looking for a Mr. Wilkins.

What would you want with him?

We'd love to have a look at that motor home he advertised at the Kmart, Bonny said sweetly.

I've never heard of a Wilkins. I know everyone in these parts, and there ain't no Wilkins here.

It might have been another name, Bonny was quick to agree.

Well, I don't know you from a hole in the wall. You might be from the IRS, Wilkins concluded, coming here to entrap folks. Responding to her look of astonishment: It's happened. People come by, innocent like, asking for Wilkins or some such person. Before you know it, they're going through the house. . . . Perplexed, shaking his head. Why on earth do you want to look up someone who don't even exist?

Could we just look at it?

At what?

The car?

It so happens I have a motor home, Wilkins admitted. It so happens I am willing to part with it. With a grimace, as if resigning himself to the inevitable, he motioned Emilio to drive into the yard, while cautioning him, Son, try not to hit anything. The aroused pit bulls kept running wildly back and forth, as Emilio carefully weaved past several scrawny brown chickens, in a state of high agitation, and piles of fenders, carburetors, tires, and a row of what to Bonny looked like brand-new car seats with adjustable headrests.

It's a piece of junk, Bonny concluded when she saw the bookmobile next to the dune buggy and the rusting hulls of four cars. Wilkins was prepared to let the RV go for three thousand dollars—far below its market value. The dogs kept their distance, guarding the driveway. Appearances are deceptive, Wilkins said in a soft voice. You better than anyone else ought to know that, he told Emilio.

What about that? Bonny pointed to the fading sign, LUBA-VITCHER PRAYER LINE BOOKMOBILE, on the side of the car.

A can of spray paint will take care of it.

Who are they? Emilio asked.

The bottom line is that these bookmobiles were built to last, Wilkins assured Bonny. Check it out. The dogs had stopped growling, but their pointed ears indicated a wariness, a never subsiding alertness. Take it for a spin, he suggested to Emilio. Drive it around the block. Emilio hesitated. It's got a new engine, Wilkins said impassively. Go on, she said. Care for some tea? Wilkins asked. She followed him into the house, with the dogs close behind—unprepared for the singular display of a Star of David on the kitchen wall above a framed map of what appeared to be ancient Israel, showing the route of the Exodus and the conquest of Canaan. Red Zinger? he asked. I love Red Zinger, she said, only now seeing the black velvet cloth on which were stitched in gold the Hebrew words *Shabbath Sha-lom*. You're not Jewish, are you? He drew himself up, scowling. You mean I do not conform to your stereotype? No, no, she protested. As you see, I'm not an Ashkenazi, of Polish descent.

Or even a Sephardi from Spain. Or one of those forlorn Yemenite Jews rescued from Aden in what was called "Operation Magic Carpet." No, no, that's not what I meant. . . . He would have none of it, reprovingly raising a palm, its light skin color in startling contrast to the dark pigmentation of his face, sternly saying, I know what you meant. I'm a descendant of the Habirus. You've not heard of the Habirus? Where did you go to school? We're the ancient Israelites. But then I expect you haven't read Malamat's *Campaigns of Amenhotep II and Thutmose IV in Canaan.* He pointed to the map. Now that piece of land has become the property of the Sephardim from Spain and the Ashkenazim from Europe. The Habirus, mentioned in the ancient Mari and Nuzi documents and repeatedly referred to in the letters of Amenophis IV, all now in the El-Armana archives, are presently dismissed because we're nothing but a historical embarrassment for the Israeli government. You see, we invalidate their ideological account of ancient Israel. But even they cannot disprove the link between the Habirus and the ancient Hebrews. Both were outcasts. The Habirus carted stones to the great pylon of Rameses. They and the *Ebed ibri,* the Hebrew slaves, joined forces . . . if they weren't one to begin with. Black, black, black.

Black? she asked.

Well, dark-skinned. Irate, scowling, banging his fist on the kitchen table. They do everything to diminish our countless exploits—how Moses took an African wife . . . that we and the Nubians fought the client kings of Egypt in Canaan. Finger pointing to the map. They even disregard that we occupied Canaan, preparing the ground for Joshua. They expelled us. She saw his eyes tear. Why else would we leave? Return to Africa. Again, a long finger stabbing the map. That's how Menelik, the son of Solomon and the Queen of Sheba, came to be our king in

Ethiopia. Now see how everyone treats us. His finger angrily stabbing the white wall to the left of the map, Here, in the sub-Sahara, it all took place. Here the Nubian princes of Egypt established Egypt's twenty-fifth dynasty. Why, I asks you, are the archaeologists so reluctant to publish the El-Armana archives, which would provide evidence that in 3000 B.C.E. the Cushites, the Nubians, were the backbone of the Egyptian society. Black, black, black. And why, I asks you, are the scholars so hesitant to decipher the thousands of tablets in Ebla? Are they afraid they'll be forced to admit that the rabble under Moses were as black as my own face? How's the tea? I like it. Of course, you're an Ashkenazi Jewess, he said, appraising her. He was beaming. Your eyes give you away. My eyes? That look of anxiety, he explained. It's written all over you. What is? Privilege! White privilege. Then, with hands outstretched in her direction, as if receiving signals her body was emitting: You're a little fearful. But ah, so observant . . . You miss nothing. Right? Say I'm right. Everything you experience is to be conveyed to another. Right? You're the go-between. Who is relying on your information? Not that Mexican hustler . . . A boyfriend somewhere? No? It must be your father . . . Does he believe in the man upstairs? Well, does he? Sure, she replied. But why are you rejecting him? Why hurt him? Tell me I'm right. Then, slapping his leg: You're a runaway, that's why. How old are you anyway? Fourteen? Am I right? New York—right? Liberal Jew—right? Say I'm right. Bet you're not a virgin. Ptula, in Hebrew, right? At fourteen—hell, at twelve—no, by ten—the girls . . . Watch your pocketbook, he advised. I've met Mexicans like your boyfriend. He's not my boyfriend. He certainly ain't sleeping with you—right? Watch it—first thing, they need five thousand dollars for silicone shots. Laughing as with his hands he formed two huge breasts. Why don't you just mind your business, she snapped, losing her patience. As soon as they heard the car outside, the dogs were at the door, clamoring to be let out. Down, yelled Wilkins. Down, boys. Well? She asked Emilio when he entered the kitchen. How does it run? Better than you might expect, he said. An hour later, after Wilkins agreed to throw in a microwave and a new refrigerator, she paid twenty-four hundred dollars in crisp new hundred-dollar bills of her own money for the blue and yellow twenty-seven-foot motor home, which still had steel shelving along one wall with a row of books stamped *Property of Lubavitcher Prayer Line Bookmobile*. You're not going to regret it, Wilkins assured them as they drove off, she in Emilio's VW, following the smoke-belching bookmobile. Shalom, shalom. The next day, they unloaded Emilio's VW for three hundred dollars, spray painted the exterior of the bookmobile an azure blue, and set off in the direction of Barstow, with Emilio showing a marked preference for secondary roads, though once they reached San Francisco he became less jittery. At his suggestion she bought herself a leather halter with fringes in Tulare. You look terrific, Emilio assured her when she modeled it for him in their RV. She waited expectantly as he ran his eyes up and down her body. It goes well with the flaming boots. Annoyed, she said, Not flaming boots—it's flame stitch. That's what I said. Feeling frustrated, she asked, Don't you even like to kiss? To her dismay, Emilio shrieked with laughter. Only a mature sixteen-year-old, or was it fifteen, she withdrew into the protective shell of her age . . .

The Longest Possible Detour

It wasn't what she had expected Death Valley to be like. The mountain range to the south, the salt flats shimmering in the sun, and from where they were parked on the rubble-strewn plateau, rows upon rows of RVs: Winnebagos, Allegros, Pace Arrows, Dolphins, in every conceivable shape and form—mini motor homes to thirty-four-foot-long Bounders as far as the eye could see. The sleek forty-foot Starcraft with aerodynamic fiberglass exterior design and dish antenna, the Gulfstream 2000 with shower/tub and whirlpool and backup video systems, the forty-foot Ultrastar bus motor home that was towing a twenty-three-foot stretch Lincoln limo, were located on the high ground, an exclusive enclave nearer to the grocery and gasoline station. . . . She and Emilio were parked near the Indian village, at least that's how it was marked on the map, though it wasn't a village by a long shot but a fenced-in group of neglected-looking motor home rejects. None of the RVers Bonny asked seemed to know what tribe the Indians belonged to. Maybe Hopi, guessed the mechanic in the garage. They were poor, dirt poor—that much she could see. What mattered was that no one paid the least attention to her or to Emilio, despite his Mexican Indian appearance. Now she sat at the foot of the bed Emilio had installed, trying to concentrate on what the couple in the RV parked alongside theirs were quarreling about, while saying Yes and Sure to Emilio, who had suddenly voiced a strong desire to visit his friend Cash in Flagstaff. It's only a small detour, he explained. Sure, she said, carefully wiping the pointed toes of her lizardskin boots, no problem, still listening intently as the man in the other RV, a 1982 Roadtrek van camper with a convertible dinette and twin beds, accused his companion, a slim woman in cutoffs and a cotton halter, who round the clock played country and western—*There's been hot spells and cold spells ever since we met, I've seen your small fires, your big fires, I won't give up yet*—of making eyes at the driver of the black and silver thirty-six-foot 1990 Limited by Fleetwood. Indignantly she denied it. It's in your head, she said. What's in my head is the knowledge that the moment I turn my back you're ready to leap into the sack with anyone who owns a thirty-six-footer with a large color TV and VCR. You'll like Cash, Emilio assured Bonny. Does he have a pool? Of course he has a pool. Aren't you going to call him first? I have a standing invitation. What if he won't be in? He'll be there, said Emilio confidently. But they were in no rush to leave, staying long enough for Bonny to overhear the enraged man in the adjacent camper threaten to shoot the woman and then himself. What with? scoffed the woman. Your BB gun? Don't you worry—when I'll need to lay my hands on a gun, I'll find one. After debating with herself whether to call the state troopers, Bonny decided against it, happy to have her judgment confirmed when, some twelve hours later, she heard the joyous, explosive sounds of the couple's reconciliation, to the accompaniment of *I was your first, I'll be your last, no matter whom you have in between.* Later that day she and Emilio set off for Flagstaff. To her disappointment, it wasn't all that different from the other towns. One could take it in at a glance. Everything was, so to speak, on the surface. What you see is what you get! Though that wasn't necessarily true about Pablo and Pedro, who to Emilio's alarm greeted them at Cash's house. Well, look who's here, Pablo said. She had no inkling of who they might be and, from Emilio's disconsolate response, couldn't figure out what they were doing there. She knew that Emilio had met Cash and his mother in Guaymas or Chichén Itzá (the story had a way of changing), but he had made no reference to a Pedro or a Pablo. True, by focusing on Cash, the wealthy American and his mother, wasn't Emilio emphasizing the respectable side of his multilayered history? Initially, Emilio explained, he had served as Cash's guide . . . producing several letters and half a dozen photographs of Cash to overcome any lingering doubt on her part. Later he became Cash's interpreter and preferred dealer of pre-Columbian artifacts. There was a partner or two somewhere in Emilio's still nebulous artifacts business, but the partners, on the few occasions they were mentioned, remained nameless. Emilio explained that in the jungles he employed a crew—disparagingly referring to them as his gravediggers. Once he told her that being a go-between was not without its hazards—yesterday's allies soon became tomorrow's enemies. Which ought to have prepared her for Pablo and Pedro. Do we let them in? joked Pablo. He was wearing his friendliness like a silly mask he was, at any moment, about to discard, as he playfully blocked their entry. There was no one on the street to witness their arrival. The only sign of life was the flickering light of a TV in an upstairs window across the street. Hi, Pablo. Where's Cash? I can't wait to see him. To her ears Emilio sounded stilted. We'll let *her* in, Pedro decided. But I don't care for the dude's attitude. Her trepidation was somewhat assuaged by the brightly lit interior—as if it were inconceivable to her that anything could be amiss in so congenial a setting. She laughed with relief when Pablo, as if reading her mind, said in mock resignation, OK, I guess we'll have to let him in as well. Then, spotting their vehicle, he cried out, What's that funny thing on wheels?

It's a converted bookmobile, she volunteered.

Cash didn't warn us you were coming, said Pedro, keeping his eyes riveted on her.

I told him we were coming, Emilio said, sounding more confident, as he preceded her into the house.

Sure you did. Pedro's high-pitched laugh, an exaggerated, spiteful laugh, was echoed by his friend.

Friendly, aren't they, said Emilio, his voice, the barometer of her confidence, sounding less and less assured.

When they sat down at the huge bare refectory table beneath the slow-revolving ceiling fan, she looked around, seeking in the pre-Columbian pottery on the mantelpiece, the Navaho rugs on the floor, for some evidence at least of Cash's presence.

Pablo slapped Emilio affably on the back. You're staying overnight, right? The hard slap, a benign sign of friendship, was intended to convey, in case Emilio had forgotten, the true status of their present alliance.

Overcoming his inhibition, Emilio again inquired, Where's Cash?

Do we tell him? Pablo's quizzical voice made it sound to her like the beginning of a comedy routine.

What's happened?

Poor Cash, Pedro said in a mock-falsetto voice.

Emilio's guarded Uh-huh disclosed only polite interest.

How long have you been on the road? Pedro's question was directed at her.

We've driven nonstop from Vegas, she explained, with the apologetic look of someone as yet unacquainted with the house rules.

You should have called first, Pablo said in reproof. Pedro, thoughtfully rubbing the stubble on his chin, offered to fix her an omelet. A Mexican omelet.

Her face lit up, as if the offer could be taken for a declaration of friendship. Her immediate affirmative reply conveyed a willingness to disregard all previous signs of dissension.

Pablo was amused. Do you like Mexican food?

Breathlessly, she said, I love tacos and enchiladas and tamales and chilies and refried beans.

Emilio tried again. Where'd Cash go? his voice, low and what is considered in that part of the world as respectful—just one friend inquiring about another.

When Pablo informed Emilio that Cash's mother had died, Bonny was left with the feeling that neither of the two men expected him to give this statement much credence.

As she listened she tried to derive comfort from her awareness that the map securely inside her head ultimately would lead her to her Mexican destination.

What a shame, Pablo commiserated for Bonny's benefit. Cash's mother was so fond of Jesús . . . there's something about him that ladies find attractive. Isn't that true? he asked Emilio.

She was nice. Was Emilio accepting their account?

Did you refer to Emilio as Jesús? Bonny asked, as she was intended to.

He's got more names than I have buttons on my shirt, Pablo said contemptuously.

Pay no attention to them, said Emilio.

Our Jesús is one great kidder, said Pedro.

Bonny followed Pablo into the kitchen, standing as if in a trance while he, affecting a look of anticipation, lifted the lid of a pot simmering on the stove. Stew. Inhaling. Ahhhh. When Pedro entered, Pablo said teasingly, I didn't know you had something on the stove.

It's a stew.

To her relief, Pedro's voice had lost its menacing edge.

He's a good cook, Pablo assured her. Even if, unlike our Jesús here, he only has one name.

Emilio darted a look at Pablo. What about the funeral?

Pablo smiled expansively. Cash made the arrangements.

It was so sudden, said Pedro.

Heart, explained Pablo, dolefully pointing to his own.

They were toying with Emilio.

Placing his arm on Emilio's shoulder, Pedro asked, What did you bring him this time? Again that cruel, teasing voice. A little artifact . . . pre-Columbian pottery?

Addressing her, Pablo said, Jesús is very modest. He was the best of the *vaqueros* in Yaxchilán. He could smell out burial sites from a distance of five kilometers.

Cut the crap, said Emilio.

Pedro guffawed.

Jesús was their nose, continued Pablo, eyes twinkling. Am I right? She couldn't understand why Emilio simply did not take what he had come for and leave. When the phone rang, neither man made a move to answer it. It rang and rang. Apprehending her mistrust, Pablo said, It's not Cash.

Pedro snorted. He's got other things on his mind.

Inside Cash's bedroom, surrounded by his belongings, she felt no nearer to Cash. He's at the funeral, said Emilio. Was he trying to reassure her? In one corner stood an exercise bicycle. The large bed was unmade. It looked slept in. On the shelves were dozens of pre-Columbian figurines. There were more on the cabinet.

I'm afraid, she said.

We'll be leaving in the morning, he said, nervously opening and shutting several drawers, checking their contents—hearing someone running barefoot up the stairs, he pulled a picture album off a bookshelf crowded with cookbooks, hastily flipping it open as he fell back on the bed next to her. There you are, said Pedro, arms akimbo, eyeing them indulgently from the threshold as Emilio, not looking up, kept leafing through the album, intent on his search for a particular snapshot he wanted her to see.

Show her the ones of Cash and his mom at the Casa del Balam Hotel? said Pedro, explaining: Jesús always stayed with them.

Just a hotel, Emilio stated offhandedly.

Only the best for Jesús! She could see that Pedro was enjoying himself. Jesús even planned their itinerary, he said. Usually he'd have to bone up first. Right, Jesús? He used to buy all the tickets. Right? Plan their evenings. Pick the restaurants. Right?

Emilio settled back, hands behind his head.

She turned a page of the album. That's Cash and me at one of the sites I uncovered, said Emilio.

She marveled, You really detected them?

Mostly they're covered by the jungle, said Pedro helpfully. Jesús has the right instinct. . . .

When the front doorbell rang, she saw Pedro tense imperceptibly.

What happened? Emilio softly asked, his voice pleading for reassurance. What happened?

What can I tell you? said Pedro wearily.

Tell me the truth.

His mother . . . he began, then hearing the sound of the door being shut, Pedro walked to the landing and called down, Everything OK? She heard Pablo laughingly reply that a woman had dropped off a large philodendron.

Cash has so many friends, Pedro remarked in wonderment. Then, glancing slyly at the impassive Emilio, Maybe our Jesús can explain what they all see in Cash.

We're tired, said Emilio.

Sure thing, said Pedro. To her relief he left at once. He even closed the door.

Where do Pablo and Pedro sleep? She asked in a barely audible voice. She had never been so afraid in her entire life.

On this floor.

Can you lock the terrace door?

Don't worry. I'm a light sleeper.

What happened to Cash? she whispered. When he failed to reply, she said, If it's so bad, let's get out of here. This minute!

Next morning Pablo surprised Emilio inside Cash's office, in the act of examining the ledger in which Cash recorded his so-called transactions. Looking for something? Just checking my account, Emilio retorted calmly, forcing himself to smile.

Does everything meet with your satisfaction?

I was going to offer him a pot . . . , said Emilio, closing the ledger and returning it to its place in the desk drawer.

Leave it here; we'll show it to him.

It can wait.

He'll be back soon, Pablo reassured him. Come back . . .

Yeah. I just came to pick up something I left with him.

What's that?

A package. With his hands, Emilio measured its size.

You sure? Pablo's voice trailed off.

She walked into the kitchen in time to see Pedro expertly debone a red snapper.

You do it so well, she marveled.

I used to cook in a fish restaurant in Salamanca.

By now she didn't quite know what to believe. Is that in Mexico?

Whatever he's looking for, it's not in our room, Pedro muttered as he cut up the remains of a large green pepper he had taken from the vegetable bin in the fridge. Throwing the pieces helter-skelter into the sizzling, oversize frying pan.

Need some help?

He raised his eyes, Where did you pick up that faggot?

She walked to the window next to the spice shelf and looked down into the garden, addressing no one in particular: What a great pool.

Don't even think of staying, warned Pedro.

Was it the sound of yet another door upstairs that impelled him to drop what he was doing and dash out of the kitchen, bounding up the stairs, two at a time, shrilly screaming, I said no one is to— She heard Pablo trying to calm him down. It's OK . . . He's just . . . Let him . . . He's just taking what's his. He's just going for . . . No one's . . . Then a scream, followed by imprecations in Spanish.

No you don't, yelled Emilio.

From the foot of the stairs she could see Pedro, holding a knife at waist level, seething with anger as he advanced on Emilio, who, a brightly colored polychrome effigy figure tucked under one arm, kept retreating while looking desperately about for something with which to defend himself.

Hand it back, Pedro shouted.

Don't be a fool, Pablo cautioned. Put the knife down. Looking relieved when Pedro with an expression of disgust flipped it backward. The knife, which had tightly wound black electrician's tape in place of a handle, glinted as it spun in an arc high over the banister, before falling straight down and with a soft thunk piercing the bright red diamond-patterned Navaho rug and the varnished wood floor beneath.

Something's burning, she yelled, in panic racing to the kitchen. Pedro, cursing Emilio, came tearing down the stairs, taking two at a time. The red snapper! he yelled.

Pablo winked at her when they sat down to breakfast. Scowling at Emilio, Pedro placed the pot on a ceramic plate in the center of the table. Look how angry you've made him, Pablo teased Emilio, who continued to calmly chew his food.

Great fish stew. But her compliment had no noticeable effect on Pedro.

You mustn't take what happened seriously, said Pablo. Pedro was only kidding, isn't that right?

Pedro grimaced as he took a large mouthful of food.

Has he shown you the Anasazi pottery? Pablo asked, beginning to sound more and more like a solicitous host.

She looked in the direction of a row of Indian pottery on the wall unit. Are those the ones?

That's recent stuff, Emilio exclaimed.

Jesús and I are— Pablo began, and after what seemed an internal struggle, completed the sentence —partners. He taught me everything I know. Before they left, as if to confuse her further, Pablo urged her to make use of the pool. Go on, take a dip. It'll make you feel better.

I feel fine.

Go on, Emilio encouraged her. I'll pack.

I don't feel like it.

Sure you do. All three looked at her.

I don't have a bathing suit, she said finally.

That's OK, said Emilio. We always swim in the buff, don't we?

Yes, the two chorused.

Too lethargic to swim, she just floated on her back. When she came out of the pool, she sensed Cash's presence. Could it have been his initials on the large towel she wrapped around herself that activated her awareness? On her way to the shower upstairs, she saw Emilio with Pablo and Pedro in Cash's den, studying a map. We're going to let them have the bookmobile, he informed her. We'll take good care of it, Pablo assured her gravely. They've got to move some of their belongings, Emilio explained lamely. We'll meet in Mexico. What are we supposed to be driving? The Olds. What Olds? It's an '84 Cutlass Supreme. Whose car is it? It's Cash's. . . . He always lets me have it. I paid for our car, she protested, the tears rushing to her eyes. It's *my* car. . . . Only heeding when he pleaded, You do want us to get on with our trip, Bonny. If you do, please . . . please. Please, Pablo echoed, this time not sardonically, until she gave in not because she was persuaded but because finally the full measure of Emilio's fear began to sink in.

Unsettled on seeing the two suitcases with Cash's initials on the blue velour back seat, she demanded, What are those? Just things Cash let me have the last time I saw him, Emilio said, avoiding her accusing stare.

Looking out the car window as Emilio turned the key in the ignition, seeing no one at either door or window, she was filled with foreboding. Is he dead? she asked.

Remind me to tank up at the next station, said Emilio.

Something terrible has taken place in that house! I know it . . .

To possess that degree of intuition, you need to have Indian blood.

What intuition?

To see what happened in there . . .

Something did happen, didn't it?

Sidestepping her question, he tried to describe the dread the Aztecs experienced just before the arrival of the Spaniards. They anticipated Cortés. They could look into the future.

I'm referring to the past few days . . . here!

As they pulled away from the house, he said, Montezuma consulted the soothsayers. He wanted their dreams. When they displeased him, he had them killed. People went into a panic—they stopped having dreams. They . . .

Her tears took him by surprise. I'm sorry. I can't seem to help it, she said.

Be reasonable. If they harmed Cash, they wouldn't still be hanging around, would they now? They'd be far away.

Now tears were streaming down her face. She was unable to stop. It was as if something inside was compelling her to cry her heart out . . .

I wish you'd control yourself, he said, concentrating on his driving—his face stony, unapproachable.

When they reached the Mirabel Motel just outside of Phoenix, Bonny's tear-streaked face caused the desk clerk, a motherly woman in her forties, to ask if anything was the matter. A friend of ours had an accident, Emilio explained. In their room, in an effort to distract her, he showed her pages from the codex.

It's part of a codex, and worth a small fortune.

She thought he was boasting and laughed in disbelief, no longer knowing what to accept as truth.

It was written by the Indians after the arrival of Cortés. It describes their history.

She pointed to a gruesome drawing of dozens of skulls impaled on racks. Is that history?

By now she was able to read his face. She could see conceit, smugness, and incertitude. How did you come by it?

Well, for your information, ownership in Mexico is a frame of mind.

. . .

After Emilio had turned off the lights, she lay on her bed, staring at the full moon that hung in the center of the wide-open window. Is your name Emilio or Jesús?

Pedro's full of shit.

I prefer Emilio, she said. Then, taking a calculated risk: I bet you've never slept with a woman. If true, was it her intention to remedy this fact?

Enraged, he dragged her out of the bed and slammed her against the wall, thrusting his perspiring face into hers. You slut! I could easily break your neck. When he released her, contemptuously saying, What are you anyway, fourteen, fifteen? she felt so weak that she sank to her knees, lowering her head to the floor, incoherently babbling and weeping.

What did she know?

Despite her total lack of awareness about the existence of the vulvas engraved on the walls of the caves in southern France—those first crude depictions of female sexuality, the possible precursors of all art, dating back to the Aurignacian period, approximately 30,000 B.C.—Bonny understood, at least subliminally, that the crude depiction of female as well as male genitalia on the walls of the toilets—those other indications of male yearning—were signs that referred explicitly to her: she, however young, was already made the object of desire.

Blurred Vision?

Because of the traffic, the three of them, here to celebrate the contractual agreement for the pyramid project, were over an hour late. Which may have been the reason why Preston failed to heed the warning from the Mexican in the business suit, who, when they entered the building, realized that they were Americans and warned them in English that the elevator instead of ascending had plunged to the basement. It dropped like a brick, he said. He was still badly jolted. To Preston, who had more pressing things on his mind, it sounded like *jilted*. Don't you think we ought to wait for the local, no matter how long it takes? said Rita. But Preston, on receiving assurance from a beaming uniformed attendant that there was absolutely nothing the matter with the express elevator, stepped into it, followed, albeit reluctantly, by Terrence and Rita. Four more passengers crowded in as the by now exasperated Preston kept pressing the CLOSE DOOR button. When it finally began its ascent, Preston counted a total of fourteen in the elevator. No hitch until the thirty-fifth floor, where, to Preston's relief, six passengers stepped off. The elevator continued its ascent but less smoothly, every few seconds emitting a shudder of protest. Two more stepped out on the forty-third and two on the forty-ninth floor. On the fifty-first, the doors opened on a large man wearing a straw hat, an unlit cigar in his hand. Abajo? he asked, even though it must have been evident to him from the green light above the door that they were ascending. No, arriba, said Terrence. But the man, annoyed at having had to wait so long, stormed past Terrence, disregarding or not wishing to understand Preston's plea that he wait for the elevator to descend. It was now proceeding in fits and starts. On reaching the PH level, to their relief, the doors parted with a satisfying whoosh of air, but the moment Rita stepped off, it began to sink before anyone could follow. Preston retained a glimpse of Juan, the banker, coming forward to greet them and the look of outright dismay on Rita's face as she half turned, seeing the elevator—its doors still wide open—with Preston in it, beginning its plunge. It's grotesque, thought Preston, seeing in front of his eyes the headline: Eden's President in Freak Accident. Or was it only later, as he was describing the mishap to Juan, that he began to flesh out the particulars, embellishing the details of their precipitous descent, which could not have lasted more than a few scary minutes. In truth, there hadn't been time for any thought. As the floors whizzed past, Preston had flicked on the alarm, only to switch it off when all it accomplished was to trigger a deafening bell inside the elevator. He was conscious of an absence of fear or panic as he indiscriminately punched the floor buttons on the panel, illogically hoping—though he should have known better—that by some fluke, the random combination of floors might emit an electronic impulse that would slow their fall. During the descent, which to him seemed to take forever, they had, with not a word spoken, positioned themselves against the waist-high railing of the metallic Art Nouveau interior. It was as if language had become redundant. When they finally came to a jarring halt, Preston felt convinced that they were dangling by a thread in that bottomless shaft. Where the hell are we? Terrence had hoarsely yelled at the alarmed face of the Mexican handyman who peered at them through the small oval window of the outer elevator door. Preston heard the man say, Sótano. We're in the fucking basement, Terrence translated, with a look of relief.

When they finally reached the penthouse, this time using the service elevator, Juan clasped Preston in a tight abrazo, then lightly clapped him on the shoulder. Amigo, you gave us a little scare. This statement was followed by a drawn-out Mexican laugh, capped by a jubilant whoop. We still have need of you, remember? A number of guests watching from the nearby table applauded. So do I, said Rita, kissing Preston on the cheek. To Juan's delight, she then rubbed off the offending traces of her bright red lipstick with her lace handkerchief. More applause as the thick-jowled senator, wearing a double-breasted suit with a tiny gold eagle in his buttonhole, stepped forward. I am greatly honored, Your Excellency, said Preston with a little bow that, if anything, conveyed not deference but an inappropriate and quite unintentional mockery. Beckoning to Terrence to step forward, Preston introduced him: This is my colleague. His right hand, Juan commented unnecessarily. I'm his Sancho Panza, Terrence said. His ingratiating bow was lower, as if he intended to make up for Preston's negligence. Face-to-face with the senator, the near brush with death all but forgotten, Preston exuded confidence. He apologized for causing a delay. I thought the bearer cable had snapped, he admitted. Not omitting to mention that the misfunctioning elevator was not designed or installed by Eden Enterprise. Emphatically stating, Our elevators do not break down. Their table bore a sign that said Reservado. Juan Ariello ceremoniously bid the senator to take the seat at the head of the table and, with pride, stated to Preston that while the food might not be equal to that at La Chantelle, on a clear day the vista from the restaurant was something to behold. Unlike Juan, the investment banker, the senator seemed immune to Rita's charms, she, in her most revealing silk dress, receiving only his perfunctory attention. Act nice, Preston reminded her in a whisper. But try as she did, the senator remained impassive, uncommunicative . . . Clearly his stonelike face, taking its shape from one of those enormous heads of a Toltec god, was waiting for something more rewarding.

From the fifty-seventh floor of the Melancine Building, the outlines of the Pyramid of the Sun could be discerned in the orange haze despite the photochemical smog.

It's good to be here, said Preston, surrounded by one's amigos. He might have been addressing his compliant executives. Voice exuding confidence, If there's one thing I've learned after my recent travails, it is the value of friends!

Down the hatch, said Juan chummily. He had gone to Louisiana Tech and affected all sorts of quaint terms that now, twenty years later, were outdated.

The senator obligingly raised his glass—though nothing on his massive face indicated any inclination to participate.

We're looking forward to seeing Your Excellency this coming Sunday, said Terrence.

The unblinking eyes of the senator might have been scrutinizing an entry in a business ledger.

As you know, Eden Enterprise is underwriting the performance by the Teatro de la República and the Orpheus Singers, Rita chimed in.

For the general public, in Chapultepec Park, said Preston.

Free of charge, added Rita.

More drinks were consumed. More talk, more relaxed laughter, nothing to prepare Terrence, when he inquired, Has Your Excellency had an opportunity to examine the plans for Eden Housing on RF 85?, for the senator's reply: It's on my desk. The gruff rejoinder triggered an instant alarm in Terrence's head. Well, that puts my anxiety to rest, he chuckled.

If you have as much stuff piling up on your desk as I do, Preston chimed in—struggling to sound lighthearted—it's hardly surprising, ha ha ha.

It doesn't clarify Eden Enterprise's branching out into housing construction, stated Senator Augusto Galindez, his eyes shifting from Terrence to Preston.

We not only have the requisite approval from the ministry, Preston declared. He was breathing heavily. We have it from the minister himself.

They have it in writing, Juan assured the senator, with just the barest suggestion of anxiety in his limpid dark eyes.

Terrence, in an attempt to head off a possible clash, lifted his champagne glass: A toast to a beautiful couple—may they continue to enjoy the beauties and the good spirit of Mexico.

We're glad that despite the recent spate of unpleasantness in the news with respect to Eden Enterprise, Preston is not withdrawing from the pyramid project, Juan said to the senator, as if to cue a forgetful actor.

I pay no attention to the vultures, Preston replied, fully expecting a sympathetic response from the senator.

We wouldn't dream of leaving, Rita assured Juan.

The senator remained sealed in his fortification.

Was this really Mexico City, soon to be the world's largest city, the capital of the twenty-first century? No, that was premature. Give them time. If you've never been here before, how on earth could you tell? By the chaos, the turbulence, the mind-numbing noise? By that unmistakable vast sprawl? The highways packed with midday traffic? The dense haze? Traffic snarls at every major crossing?

All the years I've known Preston, he never ceases to amaze me, Terrence said. It's people like him who've given Mexico the much-needed shot in the arm.

He has helped to revitalize it, Juan agreed.

Preston, with an expression of acute pain, stared at the city in the picture window. It was enveloped in a pink haze that seemed to glow. It's a challenge, he said. Juan correctly understood him to mean a personal, manly challenge.

The senator's vigilance should have warned Terrence that he was simply biding his time. When Terrence pointed out that their brightly lit red neon EDEN ENTERPRISE in the distance was more conspicuous than either the SONY or the TOSHIBA sign, he may have provided the senator with both an opportunity and a provocation.

I'm not an expert in housing, Senator Augusto Galindez said in a deeply accented English, his jaw jutting out combatively, as he chose to confront not Preston but the less formidable Juan, the banker, who earlier, in a brash aside to Preston, had recklessly maintained that he had the senator in his pocket. I may not have mastered the art of promotion and packaging so essential for any American undertaking, but I understand the principles of investment.

Get on with it, Dago, thought Preston, clenching his teeth as well as his grip on the wineglass, which under the pressure of his hand threatened to explode, as he balefully stared at the senator, who continued: Yet I regret to say that I am at a loss to understand this enterprise.

It's housing for American retirees, Terrence said, trying to placate the senator. An alternative to Arizona. They come for the weather, the pleasant surroundings, the—

Slyly tapping his nose, as if sniffing a deception, the senator asked, Why build in the proximity of the Pyramid of the Sun?

It'll be the main attraction. Preston leaned forward, to ensure that he was making himself understood. To enable Mexico to develop to its full capacity, the project will of necessity have to be connected to a U.S. infrastructure.

I should caution you, said the senator mildly, though the eyes bulged: We do not care to serve as a convenient outlet for you. We have experienced our share of American generosity.

Far from it, said Preston. It's an exchange between equals.

It's a pipe dream!

Two hundred million U.S. dollars can hardly be considered a pipe dream, murmured Terrence.

Our weather is hardly suited for American retirees, and once the novelty of the pyramids has worn off—

Preston was quick to respond: Eden Enterprises sees a need to diversify. This is a market with great potential.

If Juan's bank agrees to make this loan to you personally, or to some entity independent of Eden, the senator contended, I'd endorse it.

Our program is quakeproof, said Preston with a forced laugh.

Not if you leapfrog . . .

If anything were to go awry, the Melancine Bank will be holding the real estate.

Holding what, said the senator derisively. The pyramids?

I fail to see the reason for the senator's disagreement, Terrence complained, whereupon what Preston had most feared, namely a rupture, almost occurred as the senator, glaring at Terrence, half rose in his seat.

No, no, you mustn't, Juan cried, hands beseechingly in the air, palms outward, imploring the senator to give him a minute. I can clear up this . . . misunderstanding.

Aren't we here to celebrate? Rita asked, looking at one then another of the men with a suggestive smile.

The senator sat back, painstakingly wiping his mouth with the oversize starched linen napkin. Señor Hollier, he said finally, will have to acknowledge the risk *we* face.

Seeking to disassociate himself from the present heated exchange, Terrence put on his glasses and ran his eyes down the menu, as if the choice he was about to make outweighed anything presently being discussed. I had the sautéed scallops with creamed spinach and bacon last time, he told Rita. They weren't half bad.

In light of the present inquiry into Eden's vast real estate acquisitions, noted the senator, all future bank loans would doubtless require additional collateral.

Terrence, unable to restrain himself any longer, burst out, As you well know, we've been targeted by people who are openly hostile to Eden Enterprise. They consider us inter-lopers. . . .

I can't endorse any future bank loans, said the senator, dabbing at the froth at the corners of his mouth with the folded napkin, until there's sufficient proof of—

If it comes to that, there's always my collection, Preston murmured, half in jest.

But pre-Columbian artifacts cannot be taken out of this country, Juan stated, much to Preston's dismay. Looking apologetically at Preston, Juan went on to declare, That dimin-ishes their value as collateral. Whose side are you on? Preston's aggrieved look seemed to say, as he pointed out that Eden Enterprises was a joint U.S.-Mexican venture.

You control fifty-one percent, stated the senator.

We proceed only with the express approval of our Mexican partners.

Juan flashed a broad smile of impartiality: Precisely.

A waiter approached with fresh rolls. Another solemnly poured the wine. From their somber expressions, they might have been there to offer their condolences.

I suggest the red snapper, murmured Juan to Rita, as she attentively studied the menu. She had spent over an hour on the makeup. One hour on her face. After accepting his suggestion with a smile, she looked provocatively at the senator: Have you ever dialed the 800 number for Eden support services? It's the most innovative service available in Mexico. . . .

The senator didn't even care to understand what she was saying. For all he knew, she might have been discussing the merits of Dial 900 Best Phone Sex. Helping himself to one of the crisp white rolls, he savagely tore it in half, before addressing Preston. Señor Hollier, the problem can easily be resolved if you were to consider restitution for the displaced pepenadores families who made their living off the garbage dumps you've acquired. It was tantamount to a declaration of war. Alarmed by the turn of events, Juan, echoing Rita's words, pleaded, Aren't we here to celebrate? Come, he cajoled, holding up his empty glass in a toast.

Another in what was an endless row of waiters stood patiently while Preston quickly scanned the menu, settling on Norwegian salmon. Rita picked the sautéed snails in garlic butter. Juan, after some indecision, selected the leek and onion tart. The senator, without glancing at the lavish menu, ordered pâté de maison.

What did we accomplish? Terrence inquired when an hour later they left the building, stepping into the heat of the afternoon.

A three-month respite, said Preston, mopping his face with an oversize initialed handkerchief.

What's the senator up to? asked Rita.

Resigned, Preston said, We'll just offer him another two percent.

Is that what it's about? Piqued, she looked at Preston. All along I thought it was for real.

And where are we off to? Preston asked. His eyes belied the voice's disinterest.

Smiling, as if it were a familiar joke between them: A little shopping, she said, holding out her tanned hand, on which gleamed a pre-Columbian gold bracelet. My reward for being nice to guys like the senator.

I've been admiring it, said Terrence, his eyes traveling up

the smooth skin of her forearm, well beyond the gold bracelet.

Olmec, Preston declared.

Beautiful, Terrence agreed reverently, eyes lingering on the golden color of her skin, now that he'd been given license to do so.

And whereabouts are we headed? Preston asked again, with an ironic tilt of his head.

Plaza de la Ciudadela.

He looked to Terrence, not concealing his misgivings. What's there?

One or two shops, Terrence conceded with an embarrassed shrug. Preston nodded, then by his abrupt question to Terrence—What are you up to?—dismissed Rita from his presence.

Terrence, long accustomed to Preston's quick changes of mood, mockingly, as much for her benefit as Preston's, clicked his heels: *Su servidor!*

Preston, not displeased: Drink?

Para servirle!

After we drop Rita.

I'll hop in a cab, she said in a voice as finely chiseled as her face.

First you, Preston insisted. We have the car.

She shook her head. No, no. I want a cab.

Terrence, correctly interpreting her wish, looked up and down the street. Spotting a cabstand at the far corner, he set off at a trot in that direction. In the minute it took Terrence to return with a cab in tow, Rita and Preston didn't exchange a word. Hasta la vista, she said, as Terrence opened the cab door for her. Plaza de la Ciudadela, she told the driver. Both of them waved, then Preston, with Terrence at his side, jauntily headed for the bar in the nearby Barbizon Hotel. Preston was snapping his fingers and, so to speak, thumbing his nose at danger. Before entering the bar, Preston suggested a pit stop. Inside the john, like a pre-Columbian statuette, a Mexican attendant stood waiting with a supply of towels as, side by side, they somberly faced the immaculate glistening white of the urinal as if it were the site of an oracle.

Everything OK?

Preston wasn't listening.

You OK?

When Preston said, Why don't we pick up a couple of those amiable-looking young ladies that are always killing time in the bar . . . ? He seemed to be testing not Terrence but himself. Pass a pleasant few hours in this establishment . . .

Terrence, zipping his fly, thoughtfully assessed Preston. It's been a long day.

Just kidding, said Preston. Peering at Terrence in the mirror, Preston smoothed his graying hair: I guess I'll settle for a drink. Then, confidingly, placing a leaden hand on Terrence's shoulder, while the latter was drying his hands on one of the spotless white towels handed him by the attendant: Frankly, I'm so bushed, I doubt I'd get it up.

Sure you would.

You think so?

If it's the last thing you'll ever do, Terrence said, giving Preston the assurance he craved.

Gratified, Preston strode into the dimly lit bar, warmly greeting the Mexican barman—Hi there, John—as if he remembered him from a prior occasion.

All it took was the barman's solicitous inquiry—Gentlemen, how can I serve you?—for Preston to feel unreasonably pleased. It was good to be alive. He looked around, blissfully contented. Everything was in its right place. Bars are essentially a microcosm of our existence, he explained to Terrence. Here each move we make conveys a particular need. By the time he was on his third Scotch, he was in favor of sending the senator a case of Napoleon brandy, to show that he bore no grudge. There are things, he said confidingly, about which it is best not to talk . . . even to one's best friend.

Are you referring to the senator?

Preston frowned. I was speaking about Rita . . . I'm not oblivious to her impulsive behavior, her high-strung actions, her lack of emotional stability . . .

I've been reading Cervantes, said Terrence. If you wish to probe human inconsistency—if you ever hope to grasp the fantasy world of the Spanish mind—I recommend you . . .

Thrown off by Terrence's interjection, Preston frowned. I've never managed . . . Honestly . . . As for the Spanish mind, I don't give a shit what . . .

You've been reading him in translation.

I think you're full of bull, said Preston. Taking hold of Terrence's arm, he asked cajolingly, How about another?

Oh, no.

Preston looked at their reflection in one of the many mirrors: Some people would maintain that our elevator project is a quixotic act. . . .

The bartender, who had retreated to the other end of the bar, was assiduously polishing glasses that did not need to be polished. Terrence extracted his wallet. I say we head back.

With glazed eyes, Preston stared at the barman. I admire competence. A bartender in control is as worthy of one's appreciation as the most skilled bullfighter. In fact, given a choice, I'd rather observe a bartender any day. Take our man. See how he has withdrawn . . . That's discretion.

That's common sense, replied Terrence, placing money on

the bar. Preston didn't resist when Terrence took him by the arm. I admire consistency, said Preston as they walked along the dimly lit, carpeted corridor to the hotel entrance. I admire stoicism.

Stoicism?

Yes. In the face of adversity.

No you don't.

You're probably right, he agreed with a laugh, as they reached the lobby. Then, wistfully, I wouldn't mind taking a room and just going to sleep.

No you don't, said Terrence, taking his arm again to steer him in the direction of the street.

What do you see, when you look around you?

A microcosm, said Terrence obligingly. The perfection of life. Preston, having decided that Terrence wasn't ridiculing him, agreed: Well put. He stopped to stare at the high ceiling, from which a giant crystal chandelier was suspended. When you come down to it, it's aesthetics that provide the only relief from this unrelenting need we have to succeed.

You've succeeded.

Tell me, Preston asked as he drunkenly headed for the revolving door, What do you want to be when you grow up?

To be as convinced of my destiny as you are of yours, Terrence said, to Preston's appreciative laughter. After you, said Preston with a mock bow, letting Terrence exit first.

Siesta?

If the Savoy was frequented by prostitutes and other lowlife, they weren't in evidence that Wednesday afternoon. Where are we? Rita asked, trying mentally to identify the area they were in on that special map of boutiques, galleries, and jewelers in the Distrito Federal she kept securely locked in her head. The entire neighborhood, a district she never visited, struck her as offensively squalid. However, no one they encountered looked remotely threatening—the few men standing about were too enervated for anything but the bottle. The area had nothing to offer her. There was nothing to see—not so much as a mailman's shadow or a truck pulling up in front of a store to make a delivery. On the second floor of the six-story hotel, a dusty relic from another era, each window was flanked by a ram's head of stone. How very odd. Francisco—was he trying to entertain her?— mentioned that until well after the revolution it was one of the city's most fashionable hotels. Given the context of their visit, the items in the pawnshop window visible from their second-floor window across the street—really the usual assortment of unusable TV sets and Emerson clock radios, manual typewriters, saxophones that had lost their gleam, jazz guitars and percussion instruments, in addition to the half-moon spread of worn Omegas and Schaffhausen watches within a semicircle of now less than reliable Contaflexes, Rolleiflexes, and Leicas predating World War II, not to overlook the lethal array of knives that even to the most gullible eye could have only one purpose— carried an unmistakable sexual imprint. Each pawned object, retaining some physical attribute of its former owner(s), or so she fancied, indicated a sexual quandary, or was it preference? She saw the hotel in the full sun of the early afternoon. Later, much later, musing aloud: I wonder what it's like here at night? I wonder . . . They were there for a most intimate purpose—sexual pleasure! He looked at her as yet uncharted older body, as she, deriving pleasure from the unfamiliar hotel room interior, the illicit bordellolike use of the room, even the universality, the almost cliché of their respective roles, without any urging slipped out of her clothes in a state of high sexual readiness and, long accustomed to male scrutiny, male desire, stretched her body accommodatingly, like a skillful actress awaiting her cue . . . laughing as he pulled her to the bed, all slippery eagerness to mount her, this first coupling, a kind of sweaty initiation, ending shortly with Rita's sharp cries of delight, while he, more subdued, with an admixture of ardor and effort, turned instant lightning rod to the intense discharge.

The noise of the afternoon traffic from as far away as Zócalo, the heart of the city, the site of the National Pawnshop, the Suprema Corte de Justicia, the Palacio Nacional, and the now partially exposed Aztec Templo Mayor, was muted, a distant sound as they dug into guacamole con calabacitas, campechana, and flan especial, which she, under his careful tutelage, had selected from the hotel's room service menu, then rested on damp sheets in the sweltering heat, cooling off under the overhead fan, the wooden shutters tightly shut against all intrusion, their conversation unhurried, unconstrained, at times even loving. . . .

But how did you . . . ?

He, still chewing, his hand holding a spoon, arrested in midair: I didn't know how you might react, but seeing you, I felt a sense . . .

You're teasing.

On my honor.

She laughed as he swallowed a mouthful of flan.

He came close to blushing. You're making fun of me.

Oh, no. As she leaned forward, he cupped a drooping breast.

She smiled. Let me finish the flan. . . .

Now and then, as a further stimulus, they caught an enticing glimpse of each other in the discolored mirror. I've scratched you, she said solicitously, seeing the marks of her bracelet on his upper back. Leaning over him, on impulse she licked the scratch, tasting blood, as he eyed the bracelet: Pre-Columbian?

Preston has his sources, she said, not without a certain pride.

Really? Eyes narrowed, he inspected it more closely. The bracelet conveying, more than anything, a sense of Preston's acquisitive power.

The floor outside creaked as someone passed their door. Nonthreatening sounds. Once, there was an altercation below. As a bottle shattered beneath their window, she sat up, startled, hand to her breast, the other seeking his hand, her protector, feeling their safe environment invaded. But from the sound of it, the fight never transcended the intense verbal clash, the acute Mexican insults, *chinga tu madre, hijo de puta, hijo de la chingada,* fighting words that had their origin in the violent Spanish and pre-Columbian past. After a final *vete a la chingada,* the adversaries were gone, and there was quiet.

She asked, How do you spend your day?

Adept, a skillful lover, he strained the unlimited Mexican supply of his sincerity, responding, I think of you.

Though gratified, she revealed a lover's skepticism, teasingly. Surely not the entire day?

Why not? Alert, he looked ready to prove it.

What do you do when you wake up?

He persisted, adamantly: I think of you.

When he inserted the rigid upward-curving expansion of his concupiscence into that cunningly designed aperture at the juncture of her ever so white legs, so that the extent of their coupling positions was limited only by their imagination— when he repeatedly, moistly, with her active participation, as the mind clocked the rapid acceleration of the pleasurable to and fro, thrust himself forward, *into* her, *into* that often, on school toilet partitions, graphically replicated, iconically loaded opening, that tantalizing orifice beneath the vaginal hair named coño, the hand-drawn slit—sometimes clumsily embellished by little curlicues to designate the hair—as the fitting signal of that singular otherness schoolboys are quick to respond to, didn't Francisco, simultaneously, also enter that to him still elusive, paradisiacal American world in which she, a former cheerleader, had once been nurtured? Didn't she, as well, provide him with unlimited access to her convictions, to her identity, not excluding her sense of individual worth, which back in the U.S.A. well may have included (who could say?) the Buick and Pontiac in the suburban driveway—her unmistakable cordiality and open-faced candor serving to mirror a laid-back way of life that was shared by the most disparate elements, from the black gasoline station attendant (well, not quite) to the coiffed blonde in the real estate office with colored snapshots of available houses under four hundred thou in the window. But how could he possibly appreciate the cherished values that unite Americans, rich and poor, black, Hispanic, and white alike? How could he, given his innate ambivalence, his forceful Latin passion, appreciate the American virtues that conditioned her?

I wouldn't be surprised if over here things start jumping around midnight. You bet, he replied. Let's do it, she said impulsively. Come here one night. Please. Francisco agreed only in order to preclude the possibility.

For all they knew, a more choice room was available, but this one on the second floor, with its high ceiling, light green wallpaper, tall shuttered windows, and redundant curtains of ancient, musty, discolored heavy brocade, their pattern no longer discernible, suited them. A room in a Spanish bordello?

On the far side, above the old-fashioned washbasin on the wall, was a circular fluorescent lamp that cast an unpleasant greenish light. The massive TV on the brown imitation-wood bureau had a large exterior omnidirectional aerial, which she remembered being in use in the 1950s; the attached black metal receptacle for coins also served as a timer. Wishing to follow the football match between Oaxaca and Mazatlán, he inserted five thousand pesos, after politely asking, You don't mind, do you? To his chagrin, only the sound came on. Nothing ever works here, he said half apologetically, half proudly, as he settled himself next to her on the bed, listening to the fast-paced announcer's account of the game so far, everything except what he needed to know, namely the score. She studied his Mexican features: the sensuous lips, the dark eyes that stubbornly were focused on the blank TV screen as if willing the hidden images beneath to come to life. Useless, he said. The bed creaked. Seeing her naked body in the large mirror on the wardrobe door, blurred by the rust-colored stains, he was reminded of the ample-bodied females in Bellocq's renowned photographs of the New Orleans brothels. She examined her figure critically. Worrying over every sag, every line? Trying to see herself as he saw her? She didn't look a year over thirty-five. Thirty-seven at the most . . . No, she could pass for thirty-two. When she said thirty-two, Francisco didn't even blink.

At the front desk, the receptionist, a taciturn man in a mismatched stained brown shirt, green tie, and navy blue jacket, had handed Francisco the key to 23D and nonchalantly watched this tall, appealing blond gringa with the fabulous legs preceding the Mexican up the stairs. No one else so much as glanced in their direction. 23D, the only interior they saw. The first room they were shown. Later she'd make use of the telephone booth in the lobby, while Francisco tactfully moved out of hearing range. Hotels like the Savoy, in all its squalor, abound in the major world cities. To Francisco, knowing the area as well as he did, it was a familiar landmark. His family used to live in the area, moving away only when the neighborhood deteriorated. Rita was amused to learn that in the 1800s his family, conservatives, even right-wingers, had supported Maximilian. How come? On my father's side they are direct descendants of the Spaniards, he explained, only to correct himself: Well, partially Spanish. They were drawn to the pomp of Maximilian.

He had chosen the Savoy not for its history but, as he explained, because they stood a chance of being recognized in any of the better-class hotels. It's not worth the risk, is it?

How do you want to make love? she asked gravely, as if it were a menu from which he could choose. In this instant, was she not inviting a foreign sensibility, in her opinion a foreign inventiveness, arguably steeped in Mexico's savage past, to seek pleasure in her body? History as an instrument of pleasure?

The bathroom contained an ancient discolored tub with claw feet, a torn shower curtain on a rod enclosing the shower, a bidet, and a toilet incongruously set on a raised tile platform. The washbasin was located in the room. He observed her graceful and to him still foreign (American?) motions as she, thoughtfully, gazing at herself in the mirror, sponged her breasts at the washbasin. She didn't seem to object to the discomforts, the suspicious yellowish stains on the linen, the flattened pillows that contained something repulsively dense or the stale odor of over fifty years of neglect.

The clock on the bureau didn't keep correct time. He placed his wristwatch on a chair.

Who introduced you to Preston? she asked.

Alejandro. He told me that Preston was looking for some-one to write a favorable article on the elevator project.

It's absurd, isn't it?

He pursed his lips, politely considering her statement. No. Not really.

You can speak candidly, she said.

Preston, he replied, speaking as if Preston were some distant figure and not her husband, has provided us with a kind of fantasy of the future we can accept.

He doesn't have a clue about the Mexican psyche.

He shrugged. Who does?

Do you trust Salas?

He frowned. Salas? He's not a bad guy. I know what you think. There's something disreputable—

Slippery.

OK. Slippery. But he's dependable.

She laughed, As a crook?

No. No way. He's been living by his wits. As Anadelle Partridge's secretary, he managed to—

Put aside a little nest egg for himself.

He was trained as an art historian . . . so his curatorial skill is strictly . . .

Did he and Anadelle have . . .

Of course . . . But she wouldn't have made Salas curator unless he had the elementary knowledge to—

She cut him short. What about Alejandro?

We've known each other for ages.

A ridiculous man—so opinionated.

He's a prominent critic.

I'm not at all surprised his wife left him.

We're friends. Years ago we traveled together in Yucatán. We both catalogued the Partridge library. Then, seeing what she was thinking: No, he didn't have an affair with Anadelle. . . . She was ancient when we came to work for her.

She wasn't through with Alejandro. He strikes me as someone incapable of expressing any emotional truth.

He married Mercedes not because he loved her but because she was perfect. Someone to idealize . . . to constantly observe . . . to listen to . . . It wasn't so much what she said, but how she said it. He married her for that and for her family and for her history . . .

Love?

Of course. That too. I'm sure he loves her. Above all, I suspect, Alejandro wanted to become part of her family. They rejected him. Still, in one way or another by marrying her he was marrying into her family . . . Into that Spanish arrogance . . . that supreme self-confidence . . . that enviable bias. Not only was she perfect, but—

What about Mercedes?

He had to think for a moment before replying, I guess, I'm partly to blame. I introduced her to Alejandro. . . .

I know, she said impatiently, but what's she like?

Her parents are socially prominent. Spanish. Her father is in the foreign ministry . . . a powerful man. She married Alejandro despite their disapproval.

You still haven't told me what she's like.

Given her background, she's not what you might expect— she's supremely independent. Intelligent. Carved like an intricate ivory figurine, delicate and . . . He hesitated, then settled on the word *strong*.

Tough?

Not tough! he demurred.

You're fond of her.

She's OK.

Did you ever sleep with her?

He felt that Rita wanted to penetrate his unyielding mind. To invade it. She was insatiable. Impatient, he mounted her again, making love as though attacking a fortified position, assaulting an enemy, giving no quarter. While she held her legs in a raised position, to grant him total fulfillment, total access— then afterward, unable to contain herself, she fiercely declared: God, I'm crazy about you. While he, immobile, disengaged from all thought, isolated, in a puddle of sweat, said nothing to either encourage or discourage her.

What does he want? He prefers not to think ahead. Not even four hours ahead. At intervals they ate and drank. He chewed loudly, his brain dulled so that nothing, not even taste, registered.

Though he had no way of knowing what she was thinking, he was able to categorize her thoughts, her musings, as part of the American perfection, that unattainable, antiseptic perfection. You make me feel so Mexican, he admitted. To his dismay, she had a retentive memory. Total recall. Nothing escaped her. She remembered everything he had said. She was the one who alerted him that it was time to leave—though all along he had been glancing at his watch. He watched her telephone Preston from the lobby. As they left the hotel, he experienced an inexplicable feeling of relief.

I'll mention to Preston that I ran into you today, in case we were seen together.

Is that wise?

Trust me.

There's No Telling, Is There?

The tiny red dots on the white wall to the right of at least six of the sprightly paintings indicated, if they could be accepted at face value, a moderately successful exhibition. Aren't they just wonderful? voiced the young blond woman with a sunny smile from behind the desk. They certainly are, said Bonny. The young woman's smile was contagious. Are you from the West Coast? Bonny wanted to know. The one to my left is my favorite, the secretary said, pointing to a woman reclining in a bathtub, her head resting on the curved white ledge, her eyes half shut, her face self-absorbed.

Pop art?

No. It's an appropriation. The painter had Thiebaud in mind when she painted it.

Oh, it's a she?

Earnestly, as if so much depended on Bonny's understanding this, It's a genuine comment—a sign of appreciation.

I see, said Bonny, unconvinced.

Would you like to see the catalogue? Hastening to add, It's free. Bonny accepted it, then, prompted by Emilio's irate look, We've come to see Mr. Pech.

Is he expecting you?

Emilio, the small box under his arm, nodded vigorously. Yes.

Your name, please.

Emilio, Emilio Monte.

Pech, tall, lanky, in stone-washed jeans and western boots, the blond hair looking a little faded, stepped out of his office with a welcoming smile. Ushering them into his office, where Bonny, looking to make an impression, gazed rapturously at the sculpture on the glass tabletop. Beautiful, she said. Archipenko, Pech stated. Beautiful, she repeated reverently, while focusing her gaze on a frayed Indian blanket. Early Navaho. And that? That's an Artschwager. They're getting harder to get hold of, he remarked. She absorbed the many details—everything from his tooled belt with the shiny silver buckle to the high-tech bookcases, the Formica desk, the Mies chairs, the Italian swivel lamp. There were Indian pottery and pre-Columbian figurines on the white Formica shelves. He pointed to a Futurist painting. That's on consignment. That's not . . . Yes, it is, Pech replied.

She shook her head in disbelief.

He concurred. When I first arrived, years ago, you couldn't give them away. Now everything's changed in Phoenix. We have visiting string quartets performing Stravinsky and, as you can see—with a nod in the direction of his gallery—the requisite taste. You want an Agnes Martin, a Bruce Nauman, a Neil Jenney, a Beuys, or a Malevich—you name it, we've got it. If we don't, we'll have it for you by the next delivery. Our collectors are no longer restricted to the prairies and the southwest landscape and heroic bronzes of rider and horse. I think we can safely pass the test with whatever you have brought me, don't you? He beamed at them. That's why we're here, Emilio said, eager to get past the preliminaries, explaining that Pech's name had been given to him by someone in Mexico. Right move, Pech agreed, his laugh resembling the strangling sound made by a dog with food caught in its windpipe. Let's have a look at what you've got in that box.

For crying out loud, he said when Emilio extracted the fourteen-inch-high red clay squat pre-Columbian figure of a man with one hand gripping an erect penis. Look what we have here. She realized it was also a pot, with a funnel at the back of the head, while the disproportionately large penis served as its spout. Where did you get it? Pech marveled, holding it up to the light. I've got my sources, said Emilio stolidly. Bet you do. Liz, my secretary, will get a chuckle out of this one. Is it Aztec? she wanted to know. He couldn't resist showing off. If I'm not mistaken, it's a seated shaman. Colima, I'd guess. Protoclassic. That's approximately 100 B.C. to 250 A.D. Is that good? Pech smiled at her encouragingly. It's definitely not without value. Do you mind if I test it? Emilio looked annoyed but gave his assent. She looked to Emilio when Pech took the figurine into the bathroom. It's OK, he said. He's just checking to see if it'll discolor in water. What are you asking for it? Pech wanted to know when he reentered the room, the pot in his hand.

Three thousand.

Pech, pretending to be surprised, carefully placed the pot on the table slightly beyond Emilio's reach and pulled a fat, much-thumbed book off the white Formica bookcase filled with art catalogues and books. Our bible, he joked. Flipping through it, he read a description that fit the seated shaman. Fifteen hundred, he said solemnly. Here, look for yourself, handing the reference book to Emilio. That's not the same pot. Just as a frame of reference, said Pech. Besides, your bible is dated 1985, said Emilio, seeing the date on the cover. It's the last issue, Pech explained. It's the most authoritative source. I can offer you seventeen fifty—no, in a spirit of generosity, I'll make it two thousand.

At auction it would fetch seventy-five hundred.

This isn't Sotheby's. I'm not saying it's not worth it. But my collectors won't shell out more than twenty-five hundred. They're skinflints.

When Emilio stretched out his arm to retrieve the pot, intending to put it back in the box, Pech mentioned his overhead. Do you have any idea what the rent on this place is today? I have a two-year lease. Then, God knows. What the hell . . . and he went to $2,250. After more to and fro, they settled on $2,500. Cash only, said Emilio, when Pech pulled out his checkbook. This is made out to the local bank. They're down the street. You can— Sorry, no. Without a change of expression, Pech pulled open his desk drawer. Extracting a wad of hundred-dollar bills he kept next to a pistol, he counted out $2,500. Would you be needing a receipt? he asked jokingly, while stroking the pot with his forefinger.

Instead of leaving, Emilio settled himself in the chair, explaining that he had something that might interest Pech. It needed discretion. I'm the heart of discretion, Pech assured him. It wasn't his, Emilio explained. Do you have it with you? Yes and no. At any rate, it should fetch more than the pots, he said, standing up.

Let's have a look at it.

The fax machine started up as Emilio, without a word to her, left the room. More illicit business, Pech joked. Looking through the partially raised blinds, she could see Emilio walk to the Olds in front of the gallery. The car was broiling in the midday sun when Emilio carefully extracted the codex from its place of concealment. Package in hand, he returned—the young woman coming forward to lend a helping hand with the door. What professional packaging, Pech marveled as he surveyed the bubble-wrapped carton. With three deft cuts of his mat knife, he slit open the side of the carton, quipping: So this is the treasure?

That's for you to decide, Emilio said with innate Mexican courtesy.

Having extracted the bubble-wrapped codex, Pech gingerly placed it on his desk. The bubble wrap was hot and sticky to the touch. A hot piece of art, Pech quipped, then, seeing Emilio's angry reaction, quickly said, Just joking.

Emilio explained that he was selling the codex for a friend, only to have Pech interject, We can always arrive at a plausible reason for your ownership, as he cautiously opened the accordion-folded pages made of beaten bark paper that was surfaced with a thin layer of plaster. Where's the rest? I assume there's more to this.

Yes, there are a total of sixty-two pages.

In similar condition?

Emilio lined up for Pech's approval a dozen Polaroid shots, each depicting four or five of the missing codex pages. After glancing at them, Pech directed a small but intense light on the codex. As he proceeded to examine each page with the aid of a magnifying glass, he explained—his voice having shifted in tone in order to stress his know-how—that most if not all codices were documented. It can't have materialized out of nowhere. Consulting a reference book, he began to read out the list of known codices. The Codex Mendoza is preserved at the Bodleian Library, Oxford. The Vaticanus as well as the Borgia are at the Vatican, the Dresden is in Dresden, the Codex Borbonicus is in the Assemblée National in Paris. . . . There aren't all that many. The famous Florentine Codex is at the University of Utah. . . . Then there are the four Maya Codices. . . .

She stared at Pech. What are you driving at?

This particular codex corresponds in more ways than one to the Codex Laud, Pech said. I wonder if it isn't a more recent copy. . . . She looked blankly at Pech. What are you saying?

He looked at her, arching one eyebrow. Clearly we're in a quandary.

Emilio stared at the bookcase to his right, as if the titles on the metal shelves were of greater interest than anything Pech might have to say.

How do we establish the authenticity and value of anything, Pech continued rhetorically. We rely on evidence, records of previous transactions, the correspondence of painters, subsequent letters to and from collectors, the correspondence and bills of sale and receipts of the painters.

Are you interested or not? Emilio demanded.

It'll have to be sold to a dealer or collector who doesn't ask any questions.

Something about the conditions of this exchange did not appeal to Emilio. What's it worth? he demanded.

Pech swiveled in his chair to face the white metal bookcase. Codex, he murmured to himself, as he ran his eyes up and down the shelves in search of an elusive reference book. I can offer you . . . Eyes now tightly shut, head thrown back, he calculated. Fifteen thousand for the entire codex. Opening his eyes in order to appraise their faces: Fifteen thousand, he repeated.

Emilio, impassive. Eighty.

Pech burst into laughter, then wiped the spittle from his mouth. Look at it. See how brittle it is. This—pointing to it disparagingly—by itself isn't worth much. Fifteen for the total.

Emilio, rising from the chair, said to Bonny, I don't think he understands.

We can advance you—say—three thousand, if you leave this with us.

Emilio, indignantly turning to face the congenial Pech: Who's *we*?

Pech, unperturbed by his outburst, smoothly complimented him. For a Mexican, you have an excellent command of English. What part of Mexico—

Are we talking business or what?

This will be safe in my gallery, Pech assured Emilio. We have a vault in the basement. Though the gallery may not look it, this building was once a bank. If you'd care to inspect—

You're trying to—

Emilio, please—

We take good care of the art in our charge. This fragment cries for care. If it's bounced around a few hundred more miles, there won't be much surface left.

Emilio, rewrapping the codex in the sticky bubble wrap, insisted, It's worth more.

I'll take it off your hands . . . plus the remaining sections. Yes.

Seventeen thousand for the total, but first I'd like an expert to take a look at it. Why not wait? Two days—what's the harm? I'll put you up. Seeing Emilio's stony disapproval. That was a ballpark figure. It could be more. I'll tell you what: twenty thousand for the total, and I'll advance you five thousand, cash.

Emilio, softly: I'll be in touch. . . .

Pech, eyes more alert, mouth tightening, hand stretched out on the desk, touching the photos. Be reasonable, he appealed to Emilio.

It could be worth a small fortune, Emilio blurted out.

During my thirty years in the business, I've had people, their faces full of expectation, come by with their Titians, Holbeins, and Rubenses. If you like—playing his last card— I'll have Horning, at the Phoenix Museum, look at it. He's a top-notch scholar. Then, in the face of their recalcitrance: What more do you want?

Emilio, openly hostile: I consider forty thousand a fair sum.

Who'll take it off your hands? Pech asked wearily. You're barking up the wrong tree. Do you really expect to walk into a gallery or auction house—or a museum—and sell it without any embarrassing questions?

I'm in no rush, said Emilio, standing up.

You're talking lots of money, conceded Pech. In this part of the world, people are prepared to kill for one tenth that amount. I wouldn't rate your survival as very high.

OK, Emilio said wearily. Thirty-five thousand. Take it or leave it. He held out the package to Pech, who accepted it.

OK, said Pech, unlocking another desk drawer. It so happens that some money came in today, he joked, as he counted out the money in hundreds. Handing Emilio five thousand dollars, along with his card. That's my private number. It's unlisted. Call me when you're ready to deliver the rest.

Thirty thousand.

If, as you say, there are sixty-two pages. Pech extended his hand in agreement. Yes.

They shook hands. I'll have them for you in a week, promised Emilio.

Give me a couple of hours' notice and I'll have the cash for you, said Pech as he walked them past the smiling secretary— who said, Goodbye, now—to the street, where he watched as they got into their car. Drive safely!

We will, said Bonny. A nice man, she decided.

Crossing the Great Void

Their border crossing at Nogales was uneventful. To her relief, the border police didn't show any interest in them or the ancient yellow Olds. Instead, grinning insanely, they looked at her tanned legs. At her blond hair. They were, she felt, feasting their eyes on her. Do we offer them a Coors? she asked Emilio, who, trying to appear respectable, wore a faded seersucker suit and a broad jazzy tie that evoked the sixties. Asked what he had been doing in the U.S., he solemnly stated that he had been working as a typesetter. One of the border customs officials said something to his colleague, who laughed. Emilio, his dark face flushed, handed him a five-dollar bill. It was done casually, in the open. The man waved them on.

What did he say?

Chinga tu madre.

What does that mean?

It's the equivalent of fuck you. These mestizos hate our guts.

Where to now? she asked as he gunned the accelerator. To the heart, he replied, grinning.

Teotihuacán was deserted when they arrived. They had the central axis, the broad Street of the Dead, to themselves. Emilio explained that the Aztecs felt that if they did not feed the god the blood he needed, the sun would cease to burn.

Then this is Aztec?

No. Pre-Aztec. By the time the Aztecs arrived, these people were long gone.

Did they practice human sacrifice?

Most likely.

And eat their victims?

He looked uncomfortable. The Aztecs did. Not the entire body . . . mostly the arms and legs. It was a ritual.

And the heart?

Yes. It was a delicacy. They referred to it as the eagle-cactus fruit. Then, changing the subject, Over there's the Pyramid of the Moon. Cash's mother, who must have been seventy at the time we were here, insisted on climbing to the top.

Your best friends, she mocked.

Go on, he said. Make fun of me. Spit on my grave.

. . .

Sufficiently alert to Emilio's sensitivity to criticism, she didn't speak up when he had bought himself a Rolex in a Phoenix pawnshop, maintaining that it would fetch twice the amount in Mexico. But when he suggested that they sell the Olds before it fell apart, she felt she had had about enough. Where's the car I paid for? she demanded. Where's my car?

He was indignant. Don't you trust me?

Answer! she screamed.

They'll meet us in Mexico City. It'll be waiting for us in Mexico City.

Frustrated beyond belief, she yelled, Why should I believe you? Give me one good reason. One!

Because without me you're nowhere, he said, stalking away, leaving her by herself in front of the Pyramid of the Sun.

Now What Do We See?

This is a surprise, Preston had said when Bonny called him from La Piramide, a restaurant near the Teotihuacán Museum and gift shops. Of course he remembered her. To her finely attuned ears, he sounded more wary than surprised. You're just leaving Teotihuacán? On your way to Yucatán to see the eclipse? Calmly he took what she said in stride, then, sounding resigned, said, I guess you'd better come around. She put Emilio on the phone to receive Preston's detailed directions to the house, which turned out to be a villa protected by a tall wall overflowing with bougainvillea. It was everything she could have hoped for.

In the circular foyer, a floor-to-ceiling metal scaffolding obscured the partially restored mural, which, as far as she could determine, presented the past Aztec city intertwined with the present, by an elaborate method of layering, so that two cities could occupy the same space . . . a confusing if agreeable mix. The colors, a faded blue, purple, red, and magenta.

I didn't think you'd ever show up, Preston said.

She hadn't expected him to be so old. We had to find our way. . . . Yes, it's hard to find one's way in Mexico City, then courteously, to Emilio, Though, I'm sure in your case it presents no problem at all. . . . What a beautiful house, said Emilio. Looking at the mural in the large circular lobby, he asked, Who's the artist?

A colleague of Orozco. It was commissioned by the former owner.

Amazing.

It will be if the man restoring it ever decides to finish, Preston said, as he contemplated the half-restored mural.

You can always find another restorer, suggested Emilio, sitting down on one of two Barcelona chairs, which were covered with a plastic drop cloth.

Preston, still gazing at the mural, bemusedly observed, Like everything in Mexico, I expect it'll get done one of these days.

The eclipse won't be for another fourteen days, Bonny explained.

You'll find Yucatán an exciting place. But are you sure it's Yucatán?

That's what I was told.

I was under the impression that the best view of the eclipse would be from Baja California.

I was told it's Yucatán!

That's it, then! He wasn't about to dispute her assertion.

Could we rest up? she asked hesitantly. We've come a long ways.

Sure.

I meant here.

We have a spare apartment above the garage. I've told the chauffeur that you'll be staying there. It's fully equipped.

Just for a week, she assured him.

We'll put you to work, said Preston to Emilio, half in jest.

Sure, Emilio agreed.

Well, said Preston, eyeing him a little dubiously, we can always use another watchman. A lot has changed in the past few years. People are more suspicious. Worried about their safety.

Emilio picked up a walkie-talkie in Nogales, Bonny offered.

That'll come in handy, said Preston.

And now?

Settling in? Preston inquired in a friendly voice when he found Rita reading in the tub.

Eyes wary, she asked, Something troubling you?

Having a little read?

She rested the book she was reading on the tub's ledge, her other hand in the water, covering her breasts. I feel like a little privacy, if you don't mind.

Making any headway? he asked, referring to the novel.

Why don't you run along, she suggested. Join your guests.

He looked undecided, as if questioning his own emotional response, or lack of. I had to invite her. . . .

After what Jurud wrote about you?

And now? What is she doing? Still in the tub? At ease amidst the pearly whiteness of the tiled walls, ceiling, and floor? Everything, from where she was immersed in the large white tub, turned into an agreeable, timeless, mistlike lull; void of past or present, it stretched beyond the glistening interior walls of her vivid

imagination. Serene? All calm, she stayed tuned to those gratifying signals from afar, experiencing this tranquil condition, as one
might an out-of-body experience. Serene? She rested her head on
the white rounded ledge of the tub, gazing contemplatively at the
water's dancing reflections on the ceiling, allowing the passing
seconds and minutes to peel away layer after layer of short-term
memory, exposing a bleached cinematic view of Francisco in the
Savoy Hotel room, pulling her onto the bed, the next second,
with her assistance, inserting himself *into* her, then fast forward,
to the moment of ultimate pleasure.

Preston had left the bathroom door ajar, enabling her, from
the sound of their voices, to follow their slow progress from
painting to painting, statuette to statuette, from room to room.
Now and then, in response, she permitted a sound to leave the
bathroom, as if in acknowledgment of their presence. How
much is it worth? she heard Bonny inquire shyly. Rita could
distinguish Emilio's voice. Emilio's admiring *It's a fine piece*
made her conclude that they were looking at the life-size jade
mosaic mask of Lord Pacal from the funerary crypt, Temple of
Inscriptions, Palenque.

Ten years ago, Preston declared, I made a killing. Ten years
ago I was on top of the world. Ten years ago . . . But why am
I telling you this? He stared at them intently.

Ten years ago I was living by my wits, began Emilio. Then
I met— Stopping abruptly when Bonny kicked his shin.

Ten years ago, Bonny said pensively, my life changed when
my mother left Dad for someone else. Now they have three
children, two from the man's former marriage. . . .

Yes, I know, Preston said, not unsympathetically.

Did you ever meet my mother?

Yes, he said reluctantly. She was very beautiful. You resemble her, you know.

Did my father tell you anything about their breakup?

No. By then we weren't on good terms.

I thought you were close friends.

Not anymore. You might say we had a falling-out.

GJ never told me. Whenever he mentions you, he calls you his dear friend. Had I known . . .

Don't give it a thought. It's ages ago.

Dad never once mentioned any disagreement.

I've put it out of my mind.

I'm so embarrassed.

No reason you should be.

Ten years ago, Emilio began again, only to stop abruptly on seeing the warning look on her face. What's the use of going over the past?

Ten years ago, said Preston, on my way to Madrid, I found myself seated in the plane next to the former Mexican minister of information. . . .

From the bathroom, Rita could make out Preston's fake hearty laugh. She had no wish to see Bonny or her Mexican friend. The milky bathroom window was open wide enough for her, when the three of them stepped out on the balcony, to catch every word. There was no avoiding it. As she listened, it seemed that both men, the one fifty, the other half his age or less, like sudden adversaries, were speaking for her benefit—as if what they were saying was intended for her ears only. She was their true recipient. Within reach, next to the large potted fern, lay the book she had put down on hearing their voices. Not wishing to encounter Emilio, she remained in the tub. Soon Preston began dropping names, not because he had any desire to impress Emilio, but because for some reason Preston regarded every male he met as a challenge, someone to appraise, someone to mollify and ultimately subdue. They reminded her of strangers who, on finding themselves thrown together in a train or hotel, trade stories of their lives. Preston couldn't resist telling Emilio how once, at some risk, he had smuggled some valuable artifacts out of Mexico. I grant you, Preston appealed to Emilio, they are available in the U.S. One can get everything over there. But, there's little challenge in buying it in New York.

What would have happened if they had caught you red-handed? Bonny asked.

Preston, offhand: I don't know. I guess they'd confiscate the lot. They might even fine me.

Toss you in the can?

They once tried, though for other reasons.

Stepping out of the tub, Rita dried herself in front of the full-length mirror. Over an hour had passed. In that period Preston had referred to her several times, as if inviting Bonny and Emilio to inquire about her whereabouts. Thoughtfully, pursuing the truth, she looked at the fine blue veins coursing down the inside of her white arm. Dispassionately checking her body—impartially observing, as only a woman can, her future and her recent past in the firm flesh of her belly, breasts, buttocks. Each receiving a quick approval: Still OK. Still OK. Still OK.

Even though Bonny and Emilio declined another drink, neither showed any inclination to leave. Exasperated, she put on her robe, slamming the door as she left the bathroom. Hearing the door, Preston stood up, a tall courtly figure, giving them the signal to leave.

Still, I didn't think they'd put us up in the garage, Bonny admitted, with an indignant twist of her chin. After all, he used to be an old friend of Dad's. . . . Fight or no fight, she maintained illogically, he stayed with us countless times. Sure, it was ages ago. All the same . . . they must have lots of guest rooms. This is fine, said Emilio, stretching out on the bed, the remote control in his hand as he flipped TV channels.

And now? What are they doing? Sitting on folding chairs, plugging into the cable network, receiving the latest weather report from CNN? Reading books they had lifted from the San Diego public library, or following the climactic comic strip adventures of Hermelinda Linda?

I know nothing about you, Bonny said, with a look of exasperation. I don't even know what part of Mexico you come from.

My life began after I ran away at fourteen.

How old are you?

I only count the years I have left, he said.

How many, she joked. Go on . . .

Less than the fingers on my left hand . . . In my occupation, anything over twenty is pure gain.

Still, that did not explain Emilio's panic the following day. Was it something he had seen? Some message he had received? A phone call he had made? She was asleep when he left, taking his suitcases—really, Cash's. She found the warning he had received in the form of a Polaroid shot of a knife with a thickly wound tape handle and the words NO HAY ESCAPE, There's no escape, in the trash. Wasn't she the thorough investigator? She took the photo to be the message. But how had he received it? In the scribbled note to her, using a page from her notebook, Emilio had written that he'd be back. It was a short note.

Where Is She Now?

You're well rid of him, Preston comforted Bonny. She burst into tears.

Why don't you call your dad and arrange—

No, she wailed. I came here in order to surprise him when he arrives in Mexico. . . .

All the same. He'll want to—

I've had it all planned. He's going to be here in a few days.

What about the eclipse, then?

That's later . . . I want him to take me there.

Did Emilio take your money?

Well, not exactly . . . I paid for a car that he loaned a couple of his pals. . . . Not this Olds. It belongs to someone in Phoenix. Emilio left me a note—he had to settle an urgent—

Yes, I'm sure. Just move your things into one of the guest rooms, and forget—

You won't call Dad, will you?

I know Rita shares my feelings—we ought to inform your father.

No. She was adamant.

Well, then, he said with a look of resignation. You better stay with us until your dad arrives. He *is* coming, isn't he? She assured him that he was.

Moderate

PART TWO

I am less upset by the affair now that I think I perceive how unlikely it is to come to any decisive crisis, imminent as that sometimes seems to be; one is easily disposed, especially when one is young, to exaggerate the speed with which decisive moments arrive; whenever my small critic, grown faint at the very sight of me, sank sideways into a chair, holding on to the back of it with one hand and plucking at her bodice strings with the other, while tears of rage and despair rolled down her cheeks, I used to think that now the moment had come and I was just on the point of being summoned to answer for myself. Yet there was no decisive moment, no summons, women faint easily, the world has no time to notice all their doings.

—Franz Kafka

A Critical Concept of Dread

What in heaven's name made him undertake to interview Jurud? What's more, agree to host a dinner in Jurud's honor? A dinner bound to be a grotesque event! Was it that by his acceptance he was ensuring that Raúl or Francisco would not take his place? Or could he have been concerned that his refusal would be misconstrued?

The Critic Thinks

Then there was the painting of the old critic Mercedes had inherited. At first they hung it in the living room, until Mercedes, finally at liberty to disagree, gave voice to that petulance residing deep inside her, claiming, It's oppressive!

He's nonthreatening, Alejandro declared, referring to the critic. A benign presence.

Just look at that cluttered nineteenth-century interior. Those piles of papers accumulating on every surface of his crimson-walled study—aren't they a measure of his decrepitude?

Has living with a critic made you so unbending?

And all that art on display—are the paintings we see in the painting the gifts of grateful artists thanking him for past reviews?

It's his life. Grant him that!

But she wasn't in the mood. Admit that this painting is made to encapsulate his glorious career.

I see no reason to quarrel with its elegiac tone, Alejandro stated mildly. At his age, most distinctions become blurred and meaningless.

It announces to the world, Me, me, me!

I see resignation—

Each object in that portrait bears the imprint of deliberate prevarication.

It's a splendidly conceptualized tragic work.

Then hang it in your study! Go on . . . hang it in your study! Who knows what wealth of information you might extract from it.

The Critic's Mother

His mother, an inveterate analyst and interpreter of human character, hadn't concealed her foreboding as soon as she met Mercedes. At one glance, she detected the adversary and rival, although Mercedes hardly said a word. The problem, his mother concluded, was clear-cut: In her opinion, Mercedes was too striking in appearance, too self-reliant, too self-absorbed, too independent, and far too rich for him. You'll be at a decided disadvantage—she comes from old money. Her "blanco" family will disparage your values, your manners, and your mestizo background. They'll make jokes behind your back. And you, you'll become ashamed of us. You'll pretend we do not exist. You'll think of reasons to stay away and not to invite us to any family celebrations. You and I will never again go to the bullfights. Never share that aesthetic ritual. Wasn't it his mother's prerogative to warn him? Not only will you sever your ties to us, you'll exert all your devotion on her. But in doing so, you'll change. You'll give up your own self. You'll become another, disdaining your heritage. We're passionately fond of the same things, he said. Things? What things? Irritated by the vagueness of his response. He rattled off a list, an endless list: *Don Giovanni,* Manet's *The Funeral,* Spohr's Octet, Saint-Saëns's Piano Trio in F Major, opus 18, *Le Mépris* by Godard, Buñuel's *That Obscure Object of Desire,* etc., etc., as she, in her matter-of-fact manner, concluded that he'd never know what Mercedes was up to. She'll conceal everything from you—above all, her emotions. He repeated that he loved Mercedes. Poor Alejandro, she said, you disguise your naïveté so well. Your sophistication is exclusively derived from the movies. You'll never provide Mercedes with what she really craves. He looked at her squarely: What's that? Try to understand, she's been conditioned to excellence, to perfection! He could tell his mother was dissembling even as she triumphantly gave him proof: Never as much as a hair out of place. One is made to feel that she has stepped off the pages of a fashion magazine. She's impeccable. Every graceful motion, every gesture, every word, has been rehearsed. She exists to be admired. Everyone is or becomes part of her audience. His mother's voice conveyed the sadness of someone able to divine the future. She was right. After their marriage, Alejandro saw her less and less frequently. Months would go by—no, as much as a year—without their seeing each other.

Sometimes, unexpectedly, on the street, in a crowded café or a theater lobby, or at a bullfight, Alejandro would still hear his mother's distinct voice, clear as a bell, a distant reminder, even now that she's long dead.

The Critic Sees

When did it happen? Months and months ago, on their return from an evening in the swanky Bar Inglés with Preston, his wife, and some of their American friends. How did it occur? Mercedes, unaccustomed to more than three glasses of champagne, had coyly asked, What is it that you love about me?

Was he surprised by her question? If so, he didn't show it. I love every fiber of your elusive, ever perplexing, ever astonishing self.

What else?

I'm captivated by that kernel of doubt in your eyes, that pensive, hesitant, thoughtful expression on your face . . .

Yes?

I cannot get enough of your face. That penetrating, questioning stare . . .

Go on.

Gladly. The way you impatiently push back your long black hair . . . the soft petals of your lips, parted as if in expectation. What are you concealing? I ask myself.

What else?

The alert, anticipatory way you probe and worry every event before it reaches fruition. The way you methodically shape whatever task you've set yourself.

Go on.

The way you assertively frame what you see . . . identify and label it.

What else?

The way you pout, the way you reveal your impatience, your irritation . . . I even love the manifestations of your anger.

My anger?

Yes. Your questions go to the heart of the matter. But you speak as if you feel that no one is listening.

What about the rest of me?

Why couldn't he bring himself to respond more easily to that question as he looked at her naked in front of him. Naked! Stark naked! Her small pointed breasts, erect nipples, taut belly, perfectly shaped thighs and buttocks, the smooth skin, cool to the touch. . . . She stood relaxed, one hand flat on her hip, looking him straight in the eye.

Perfect, he said, in appreciation, his eyes hesitantly shifting from the breasts downward, finally becoming aware of an inhibition, something that tangibly, like a barrier, prevented him from stepping forward. Dry-mouthed, he stared at her pubic mound. . . . She laughed at his inhibition, taking strength from her nakedness. He, still dressed, seemed at a decided disadvantage. He was to remember her derisive laugh. Perfect? Perfect what?

The Critic Examines a Painting

The old critic in the painting that now hung in his study was the source for endless rumination. One hand holding the gray and white cat pressed against his jacket, the old critic was lost in thought. The loose brown tweed suit, the greenish V-necked sweater, the white shirt and the wilted bow tie, not just garments but like a supporting framework holding him in place. Not a picture of ease. The gaze beneath bushy eyebrows, occluded, inward. The pinkish gleam of the cheeks, high forehead, bulbous nose conveying a sprightliness belied by his age. Mercedes, when she first received the painting, guessed him to be eighty. Arms akimbo, eyeing the canvas, she taunted Alejandro, declaring,

He's your age, all of eighty. It had taken Mercedes the years of living with Alejandro to refine that particular laugh. She had shaped it as one shapes a weapon. The pink on the critic's face matched the pinkish cast on the oversize sheets of paper piled on the L-shaped desk in the painting's foreground. The crimson tapestry of the critic's study was crowded with paintings, several of which, hanging on an opposite wall, could be seen reflected in the large gilded mirror over the mantelpiece. As in life, the mirror made the interior seem larger. Every other available surface in the painting including the three chairs against the far wall and the mantelpiece was cluttered with heaps of manuscripts and bric-a-brac. At the center of this fantastic maelstrom, really in a pocket of calm, totally detached, sat the old critic and his purring cat, its eyes green slits of vigilance. Wasn't the old critic adrift in his Parisian past, more dead than alive? One had to respect his determination. . . . Sitting for one more portrait, one more testimonial, wasn't he showing an indomitable will and stamina?

I still love Mercedes, Alejandro admitted to the old critic. I dream of her. . . . I still make love to her in my dreams. Passionate love. But the old critic, clutching his pussycat for comfort, was beyond caring, beyond doubt, beyond desire, *beyond* . . .

The Critic Waits

Without consulting him, Mercedes had accepted an offer to translate one of Jurud's earlier novels. She maintained it was for the money. It'll come in handy. Alejandro was incensed: Not Jurud! It's my opportunity, she said. Then, voicing resentment, Besides, I hardly exist other than as your "beautiful" companion, your showcase wife. What was it about her statement—I'll enjoy conveying the complexities of Jurud to our culture, a culture so emotionally inimical to America—he could possibly fail to understand? Not wishing to exacerbate this ill feeling, this mutual rancor, Mercedes packed a few essentials and re-treated to her one-room apartment in the San Angel. Her translation sold uncommonly well for Mexico, a country in which over seventy-five million so-called readers confined themselves to the more immediate enjoyment of *fotonovelas,* as the comics are called. Something the Ministry of Education was proud to record as evidence of its triumph in the ongoing battle against illiteracy. Her translation briefly made the best-seller list. Mercedes appeared on TV as if born to that medium. Truthfully, it hardly mattered what she said. To Alejandro, however, it seemed as if she was directing an unmistakable challenge at him—something that couldn't have escaped the notice of his more alert graduate students. He understood her to say, by translating Jurud: So much for your critical predilec-tions, your literary juggling and positioning.

By the time she agreed to do the translation of Jurud's latest novel, *Intimacy,* at the urging of Jacobus, they were seeing each other once a week, at most. Since she liked to work at all hours, Alejandro explained to his friends—more his than hers—she found it more convenient to stay in her studio. What else did he say? As little as possible. Before *Intimacy* appeared in Spanish translation, Jacobus informed him that it had been sold to fifteen foreign publishers, including Jacobus's company, within the first six hours of the Frankfurt Book Fair. A further indication of Jurud's immediate success were the stacks of the American edition available in the multilingual bookstores in San Angel. We're so pleased with Mercedes's decision to translate *Intimacy,* Jacobus remarked. Her uncanny grasp of Jurud's intentions as well as the smoothness and verbal richness of her translation accentuates the boldness of his work. What boldness? He felt tempted to inform Jacobus that what most readers were responding to was not boldness, since, as far as Alejandro was concerned, they couldn't distinguish boldness from a cat caught by its tail in a sliding door. As for Jurud's attempt to denigrate authority even as he gave lip service to it—didn't it mark him as a subversive? What was it about Jews that made them rock the boat? Were these people never satisfied until they destroyed all harmony? Take Proust, for example. Misreading Alejandro's morose expression, Jacobus apologized for working Mercedes so hard. What's the use? thought Alejandro in disgust. Why even try to explain, if he's going to be so dense about it?

Does the Critic Dwell on What He Doesn't Know?

Driving along 2 de Octubre, Alejandro caught sight of Mercedes, determinedly striding past the crowded stores, looking straight ahead, walking like someone late for an appointment. What was she doing back in Mexico? Despite the heavy traffic, he slowed down, craning his neck to catch another glimpse of her. For a split second he thought he had spotted her gripping her tan briefcase—his gift to her. He was convinced it was she, but by the time he was able to find a place to park and dash across the street, no mean task at midday, she had disappeared. She could have been going anywhere. Undecided, he strode over to Pepe's, a restaurant he used to frequent at the time they met, not recognizing a single face among the relaxed-looking crowd eating lunch on the long, narrow restaurant balcony. No one so much as glanced in his direction. What could he hope to accomplish by running into her? In that first impulsive rush he had failed to consider the complications that might arise. What if she was meeting a lover? Overcoming his irresolution, he strode past the maître d', ostensibly heading for the stairs leading to the toilets and telephones downstairs. Skirting the marble pillar, he looked into the rear dining area, spotting among a sea of diners what he took to be Mercedes, her back to him, immersed in a conversation with Jacobus. He lingered in the doorway, only half convinced that it was Mercedes and not some other chic, slender, dark-haired woman—torn between the compelling need to advance and an equally strong wish to withdraw, until the moment that Jacobus glanced in his direction and he, freed of the magnetic bind, fled, trying as best he could to reassert a minimum of self-control over this embarrassing "escape," not certain as he strode past the maître d' if the latter's question, Were you waiting for a table, señor?, was addressed to him or not. Once outside, glimpsing the banner of the Desafío bookstore down the street, he headed toward it. In the midst of the row of recently restored stores, in what only a few years ago had been a tumbledown area, the Marxist bookstore, drab and uninviting as ever, stood out as an eyesore. He was still outside, gazing at the militant titles in the bookstore window, trying to put his thoughts in order, when from somewhere across the street behind him a high-pitched alarm erupted. Passersby froze, and a man came tearing out of the antiques store next door, face distorted by an anticipatory fear—still there was nothing whatever to see. False alarm, the man at the cash register said when Alejandro entered. The message in red on the man's black T-shirt—DEFIANCE FROM THE VERY BEGINNING!—had a Freudian rather than a militant ring to it. Alejandro tried to focus on the reason for his own ill will. Was it the makeshift rustic interior, the cheaply made bookcases, the scarred, badly stained yellowish wood floor, the untidy boxes piled next to old green metal desks, the improvisational look? Or the underlying assumption that these titles, arranged by regions and areas of conflict, represented not only an authoritative analysis but also the essential cure.

Outside, the fire alarm fell silent just before the first fire engine, its siren going full blast, pulled up with a great hiss of brakes. Is this their latest issue? Alejandro inquired, seeing from the date that the issue of *Disolución*, a magazine he used to edit in the seventies, was more than six months old. From where he was standing, he was able to see a number of firemen, shouldering oxygen tanks and other bulky equipment, rushing into the large apartment building across the street. It's their latest issue, the cashier assured him. When Alejandro joined the small crowd on the sidewalk outside, a man was pointing to a telltale wisp of smoke rising from the roof—over there! As he looked up, two cool palms lightly covered his eyes, and a woman's husky voice close to his ear whispered, Guess who? The voice was familiar. I knew it was you, he said, when he turned to face the as always keenly observant and now patently amused Patricia. You still aren't able to lie convincingly, she said. She hadn't changed, except, perhaps, for her clothes, which now seemed more stylish and expensive. As he kissed her cheek, her perfume, like some mysterious Proustian secretion, reminded him of the occasion, shortly before their rupture, when she stopped wearing her perfume, from one day to the next—was it to serve as an admonition or a signal? The extravagantly rich, malleable fragrance was deliberately withheld, its absence marked by the piercing, distressingly raw, harsh, naked odor of her *self*, for what reason other than to challenge him? Now, seeing the magazine under his arm, Patricia raised an eyebrow: Not playing the militant again?

Killing time, he explained.

She mischievously glanced at the bookstore window. I didn't think this would still be your kind of store.

What about you?

Gesturing to indicate the street: I've just come from one of the dealers.

Is that what you're doing now?

Her matter-of-fact rejoinder, One has to live, seemed to receive its mandate from that same dispassionate source of self-appraisal that, each and every time she was turned down for some part in a movie, had prompted her to state, Just another rejection. Let's face it, they don't like me. Nothing I can do. Showing no lingering anger, just acceptance.

How about a drink?

OK. She suggested Pepe's, then, seeing his grimace, took him by the arm: I have just the place. Passing the row of antiquarian stores, she waved to one of the elderly European-looking dealers, who promptly came forward from behind an enormous assortment of massive black ebony and elephant tusk furniture, a veritable colonialist's nightmare, to inform her with a beaming countenance that he had put aside a small ladies' vanity chest, seventeenth century, Spanish! Oval mirror.

Her face shone full of optimism. I'll come by.

I often come here; it's tranquil, never crowded, she explained as they entered the outdoor café.

This used to be the Tibor if I'm not mistaken. No, no. The Tibor is on Río Nasaz. This was Molino's. He was convinced she was wrong. Then, seeing the small, ornately carved stone fountain in the center, felt less certain about it. Could the Tibor have been elsewhere? The tall acacia trees, harboring dozens of twittering birds, looked new. Intertwined with their chatter, like a musical accompaniment, was the sound of glass breaking, but only after they had sat down at a table not far from the tall building looming over the garden did he realize that they had in fact circled the burning building. More shattering glass. She pointed to several firemen high up on the roof, the thick dark smoke pouring out of one of the upper stories. One of the firemen, poised against the sky, perilously close to the edge, looked down at them, as if lost in thought. Still more glass breaking. Do you want to move? he asked, but not making a move to do so. Balancing himself hazardously on the steep incline of the roof, a fireman wielding a long-handled ax began chopping a hole, only to jump back as flames, the first they'd seen, leapt out of one of the windows. Two couples hastily evacuated their nearby tables as the jets of water were aimed at the flaming windows and a mistlike spray descended on their section.

Unconcerned by the fire raging above them, the waitress wiped the metal tabletop with a quick practiced circular motion, before setting down their drinks. At a table in the far corner, he spotted one of his former grad students, Alva, with a dark athletic-looking man in suit and tie—and, unsuccessfully, tried to catch her eye.

Patricia, following the direction of his gaze: Someone you know?

One of my students.

Sexy, she said, staring at the young woman with that intense appraisal only a woman can bring to bear on another. Nothing, he felt, was omitted in that feminine scrutiny. Do you ever? Moving her forefinger in and out of the circle she had formed with the thumb and forefinger of the other hand. The explicit gesture substantiating, as if he might otherwise have forgotten, the preeminence of her sexual forthrightness.

You haven't changed.

Choosing to misunderstand his comment, she countered, self-disparagingly, I'm older.

And more beautiful! To his ears his insincerity was jarring, the words, more suited to a film starring Adolphe Menjou, bordered on the ludicrous.

Makeup, she said.

At my urging, my father used to run every one of your movies.

I don't trust you, she said seriously.

Why ever not?

You're too unpredictable.

How so? But he knew he was treading on dangerous ground.

Have you forgotten? In her eyes he could easily replay his departure—his rejection of her.

When he failed to respond, she said, I see your articles everywhere. It didn't escape his notice that she hadn't said, I read your articles.

The waitress passing near their table shot a glance in their direction, but he decided against ordering more wine.

On the main street, not far from where he had parked, they ran into Salas. Always with the most attractive women, Salas exclaimed. Always . . . They embraced. The customary Mexican abrazo. Where does he pick them up? Salas asked, exaggeratedly rolling his eyes but not failing in one of those rapid eye movements to absorb the shortness of Patricia's skirt and her still beautiful legs.

Salas is chief curator at the Partridge Museum, Alejandro said, as he introduced him, a little dismayed by the eagerness of Patricia's response. I'm available, her stance seemed to suggest. Salas, not to be outdone, though far less subtly, promptly recalled all the films in which she had appeared, professing disappointment when she said, Those days are over. *Finito!*

Come and visit us, Salas urged, extracting a business card from an expensive-looking black wallet. If you're fond of pre-Columbian art, we have several gems. Then, not wishing to exclude Alejandro, he handed him his card as well. What's the use? Alejandro said. Each time I want to visit, I'm told it's closed for repairs. Call me first, said Salas. He could tell from the way Patricia was eyeing Salas that she was taken with him. Something Salas would be quick to comprehend. Alejandro couldn't think of two people he had more reason to keep apart.

Can I drop you? he asked after Salas left them to cross the street, heading for the restaurant.

Don't bother. I'll get a taxi . . .

Not at this hour. As they walked to his car he glanced fleetingly at the restaurant.

Patricia, still animated by the meeting: Isn't the Partridge Museum a private collection?

A minor collection, he said disparagingly as they reached his car. Hardly warrants the designation museum.

Didn't you once tell me that you catalogued a collection of rare books for an American woman—wasn't she the one who started the museum?

What an incredible memory you have, he marveled.

I can't forget anything, she said, as if that was a liability.

Yes. I was twenty-one. Somehow Francisco and I, without any prior experience, attempted to catalogue this amazing collection of scholarly books that Anadelle Partridge had amassed—don't ask me how. . . .

You described her house . . . with the curious below-ground garden.

He professed amazement. Did I?

It reminded you of that palacio in Pasolini's *Salo*.

Really? How odd. I don't remember.

In your opinion, it was the perfect setting for violence.

Nothing ever happened while I was there.

You were so impressed.

By what?

Her wealth . . . and the carefree lives of her friends.

I don't recall!

You felt attracted to their outright decadence.

I have no recollection whatever. . . .

Incidentally, was Salas one of her lovers?

I wouldn't know. Trying to disassociate himself from Salas. He came via the dealers who were combing Yucatán for pieces for her collection.

She laughed. Whatever happened to Francisco?

I see him all the time. The other day, when I ran into him, he was coming out of an art gallery accompanied by a striking blond gringa—

Married, I bet!

What makes you say that?

She was, wasn't she?

He doesn't want to become entangled . . . no danger of that with a married woman, I guess.

There's always the likelihood that the husband will catch up with him.

If there's one thing Francisco can do, it's talk himself out of any predicament.

Blond, you say?

Yes.

Young?

That depends entirely on what you—

Ah, that age . . . a *mature* lady!

A woman of a certain age.

Ripe, lush . . .

Precisely.

She has money.

Her husband certainly does.

Ripe, lush, blond, and money, she mused. Do I know her?

It's a small world, he conceded.

Settling into the passenger's seat, she changed the subject. New car?

It's a year old.

She touched the dashboard, feigning admiration. What is it?

A Honda.

An Accord?

No, no . . . a cheaper model.

When he stopped in front of her building, on Avenida Miguella, he had no plan to visit. But there happened to be a spot for his car. He chose to read it as a favorable sign.

Nothing in her tiny apartment had changed. When she opened the windows, the noise from the street below was deafening. Over her bed was the same large movie poster of a film in which she had starred. He kept sniffing for the presence of another. A row of *fem* magazines and cinema periodicals leapt to his eye. So, of course, did the mirrored tile wall.

Wasn't there something beside that mirror?

As a matter of fact, yes. A settee. I got rid of it.

Had she been able to decipher his mind, she might have encountered her undressed self on the floor, head twisted, both audience and participant, eyeing their combined sexual theatrics in the mirror. Was that why he had come? To spy, to elicit information? Did that entitle him to ask, Who's your present lover?

No one. Seeing his skeptical look: I swear. When she handed him a bottle of wine to uncork, she did so with an amused, playful expression that was intended to convey a sexual memory.

There must be someone, he insisted, looking around the room as if for confirmation.

There isn't.

I don't believe in celibacy.

Is this why you came up? To interrogate me?

Only to catch up on old times.

It's more than five years, she said. Going to her desk, she extracted a playbill from the top drawer. That was the last time we went out. . . .

What's this . . . He frowned, not remembering the play.

You and your friend Jacobus took me to see it.

Do you still see Jacobus?

Do you feel the need to keep track of my love life?

It's a perfectly harmless question. I introduced you. Remember?

How can I forget. You were so solicitous in providing Jacobus with your reject.

Are you being deliberately brutal with me?

Jacobus suggested that I write an autobiography.

Why don't you? It would be sensational.

Because he doesn't mean it.

How can you tell. If he—

How can I tell? She laughed. You're all so transparent. However, to give credit where credit is due, Jacobus didn't ask questions. I don't know if he's lacking in curiosity or if it's the result of old-fashioned tact.

My curiosity is simply a means of remaining attached to you.

Is that what you believe? At the beginning I took your curiosity to be the result of an inordinate possessiveness, even jealousy. I felt gratified until I realized that you were simply coming here to obtain material.

Never! He looked earnestly at her. Repeating, Never, emphatically.

Admit you were titillated. My so-called adventures appealed to you.

Seeing her light a cigarette and hungrily inhale, he remembered how, on that first occasion, before making love, before undressing even, she had to have a cigarette while he sat in a chair, waiting. Standing at the window, barely listening to what she was saying. There's more traffic than ever, he stated.

Why did Mercedes leave?

She's teaching at a women's college in the U.S.

Ignoring his explanation: You have an arrangement?

She sprawled on the sofa in what was, at least cinematically, a sexually provocative pose, a little dated perhaps, for it reminded him of Delphine Seyrig in *Last Year in Marienbad*, the legs seductively exposed, her face almost masklike under the sexual constraint. Yet something continued to hold him back. He turned to the street, resting his hands on the windowsill: Mercedes returns in August. Then, quickly reacting to her teasing—Well, what else would you care to know?—willed himself to sit beside her. What was the name of that intoxicating perfume? She laughed as he lightly ran one hand up her leg. A skittish laugh. A compliant laugh. Kissing her lips, he was taken aback by the taste of wine . . . an acrid taste. No matter how hard he tried to keep up the banter, he must have communicated his waning interest, for she stood up, her face hardened to meet what she saw as his rejection. After pouring herself another glass of wine, she stepped into the bathroom and turned on the shower. I really have to go, he declared a little too forcefully. When she appeared in the bathroom door, she had unbuttoned the wine-colored linen shirt. The intent was by no means sexual but to indicate her dismissal of his presence. It was like a replay of a former occasion. You do that, she said quietly, somberly considering him.

There was a message from Jacobus on the machine when he got home. Has the editor of *Excelsior* been in touch with you? Jacobus wanted to know. He's interested in having you do an interview with Jurud. I mentioned that you're working on a full-length article, the publication of which is to coincide with Jurud's visit. By the way, was that you at Pepe's today? Then, in a voice more querulous than baffled, What the hell has come over you? One minute I saw you standing in the doorway, the next minute you darted away.

When he reached Jacobus, the latter sounded genuinely upset. Why didn't you come over?

That wasn't Mercedes you were having lunch with, was it?

So that's it, said Jacobus. You took the woman at my table to be Mercedes. Well, my friend, as usual you're way off the mark.

Liar, thought Alejandro, allowing himself the luxury of suspecting a conspiracy . . . What did it mean? Was Jacobus deriving a certain schadenfreude at Mercedes's affair with Jurud?

The Critic Smiles

The still life of modern existence! The heavy chrome and glass coffee table sat squarely on the rare Chinese rug. Why was he displaying a broad, accommodating smile? Was it simply in order not to scowl? Señora Galindez across from him was partially obscured by the lilies in the tall vase. The Señora called it a working breakfast, but no food was served. The tall cut-glass vase with the two dozen or more lilies was set with a decorator's eye next to the three oversize artbooks. The one on Manet contained a reproduction of *The Execution of Maximilian*. The two books beneath were on Spanish castles and European Baroque gardens. A Pekingese that he at first mistook for a stuffed animal watched him unblinkingly from an upholstered chair. He was offered coffee and biscuits. Unless you prefer something stronger? the Señora inquired archly. She looked at him, seeing, he felt, not a critic or a scholar, but an attendant. So far he had counted four servants, not including Señora Galindez's social secretary, a young woman in a black silk blouse and pearls, who, in a wispy, girlish voice, informed him that the invitations had arrived that morning from the printer. He could see that both women expected him to be pleased. The Pekingese did not stir. It just sat there, following the proceedings. All the tables are taken, said the Señora, with a surprised laugh. It's quite gratifying. The Señora, the secretary stated, has decided against an outdoor reception. He helped himself to a handful of biscuits, a move that did not escape the vigilant eye of Señora Galindez. We've also decided, said the Señora, that it would be far wiser not to have the press attend the dinner.

No need for their presence, he agreed.

Except, of course, for the photographers.

All he had to do was acquiesce, Yes.

You said two would be ample, the secretary stated, making a notation in her leather-covered notebook.

We'll want the photos . . . and so will our guests.

Smiling, he leaned forward to cautiously pick up the fragile gold and white coffee cup.

I look forward to the event, though I must say Jurud is hardly my favorite writer. . . . She glanced at her secretary for support. But if it has been decided that it shall be Jurud, so be it . . .

It'll be a stimulating evening, her secretary reassured her.
Will Jurud read from *Intimacy?*

It's the one being promoted by Jacobus.

I've tried to read him. I simply don't know what all this fuss
is about. As soon as I open one of his novels, I feel an
instantaneous resistance to his characters. . . . All he looks for
is the gangrene. She appealed to him, her face searching for a
discerning acknowledgment.

He nodded sympathetically. It's a question of sensibility. . . .

Jurud is remorseless, the secretary said with the furrowed
brow and fixed conviction of a former grad student who had
studied the Greats.

I was never so startled as when someone in our discussion
group mentioned how years ago Preston Hollier—*our* Preston!—had been a patron of Jurud . . . Imagine! Hand toying
with a string of pearls that were, if anything, more lustrous and
larger in size than the secretary's, the Señora gazed at Alejandro. Apparently Preston was even helpful in finding him his
first publisher . . . only to be slapped in the face for his efforts.

Slapped? Alejandro looked puzzled.

Figuratively. People get what they deserve. Help the needy
and— She stopped herself midsentence, as if to bridle her
emotional outpouring. Her cheeks were flushed as she remarked, It's common knowledge that Jurud in one of his earlier
novels slandered Preston and his wife.

I've heard some talk, Alejandro said vaguely, not disagree-
ing.

I wonder if Jurud is the right author for this occasion. . . .

Intimacy is doing very well, Alejandro assured her.

Have you read the book?

I read everything Mercedes translates.

No, no. I meant the one in which Preston was maligned—he portrayed as rapacious and totally unprincipled, while Rita chases after younger men. . . . But you'd know!

He sighed. This conversation wasn't what he had bargained for. It's by no means clear that the couple in the novel are Preston Hollier and his wife.

No? Showing her disappointment.

There are resemblances.

A servant came to remove the coffee cups and what was left of the biscuits before he could help himself to more.

The Pekingese noiselessly descended from the eighteenth-century carved and lacquered armchair, to follow her out of the room.

There was a gleam in the Señora's eyes when she said, You know the Holliers well, don't you?

Oh, no, he said, a little too hastily. We've met a number of times. . . .

You'll be glad to hear Mrs. Rita Hollier is on our entertainment committee.

He waited for more.

I don't see why men find her so attractive.

She's knowledgeable in matters of art, he said in Rita's defense, as he was meant to. She has impeccable taste.

You mean, she has a fondness for revealing dresses, said Señora Galindez, exchanging a knowing look with her secretary. Then, addressing him: I wonder if there ever was anything between—she paused for maximal effect—her and Jurud.

It was something he hadn't contemplated. Jurud? He stuttered, I-I d-don't have the s-slightest idea—

I was under the impression that in the United States, affairs are as commonplace as the daily workout, she stated with impish delight. Or is what I've been told incorrect? What with Preston so engrossed in his business affairs . . . It makes one think.

He smiled, the stutter now under control: Affairs are the essential ingredient of soaps and Hollywood movies.

You disagree, then? Showing her extreme annoyance when he remarked that North America did not have the advantage of the siesta. Their day is simply not designed to include a leisurely sexual encounter. As a result, most are short-lived. They hardly warrant the term *affair*. . . . They are quickies!

Quickies? That sounds like a cereal being advertised on TV, said the secretary. Eat your quickies.

Is there a Spanish translation? The Señora asked in an icy voice.

Intimidad will be out in a week or so, Jacobus tells me.

No. I meant a translation of the other . . . the one in which the Holliers are depicted?

I don't believe so.

A pity . . . At first glance, the world Jurud describes is an appealing one, the characters are attractive, even seductive. . . . But let's face it, Jurud is not satisfied until he drains his characters of their best qualities, leaving them without any . . . She paused to search for the word.

Redeeming qualities?

Precisely. The moment his eye settles on some virtue, something one can be proud of, he demolishes it.

The smile, almost a permanent embellishment on his face, as he sat facing her barely concealed what? His contempt? His boredom? His insecurity?

It seems doubtful, doesn't it, that those so-called WASPs Jurud describes could be the people who steered the U.S. to its greatness?

His smile was less constrained as he stared at the portrait of a woman he took to be the Señora's mother. There was a distinct similarity. . . . He saw bottles on the sideboard, but he couldn't bring himself to ask for a drink.

There's a cynicism pervading his novel, suggested the secretary. A rejection of life-sustaining values . . .

The Señora, still furious—was it for his allusion to the siesta?—remarked coldly, This obsessive self-scrutiny is foreign to me.

It comes down to a question of taste, said Alejandro lamely.

I keep thinking it's my fault, said Señora Galindez. I've even picked up one of his earlier books. . . . Would you believe it, I've even tried to read him in English. I'm told he's a Jew. Is that true?

As far as I can tell, Jurud doesn't concern himself with Jews. The circles he describes wouldn't welcome Jews into their midst. . . . I'm sure there's bound to be the odd one, who belongs to the club . . . a Morgenthau or Brandeis or Frankfurter.

No matter, said the secretary swiftly, at last finding an opportunity to communicate her continuing literary interest. After all, Kafka doesn't have a single Jewish character in his work, and can there be a more Jewish writer than Kafka?

I wasn't aware, murmured Alejandro, that there aren't any. Not a single Jew? I must look into this.

Not that it's all that significant, she shyly admitted, seeking approbation.

It's something to consider.

If I'm not mistaken, you've reviewed Jurud?

Years ago. But I've just let myself be talked into writing a full-scale article on him. He shrugged deprecatingly. I don't know why. . . .

Then he's not your cup of tea either?

The rumbling sound he made did not commit him to either a *yes* or a *no.*

Your wife should be able to help you with the article, said the Señora cattily.

He felt his face redden. We stay out of each other's work.

I find Jurud somehow too inquisitive, the secretary opined.

Please, I've had enough. We in Mexico have been more than kind to all of Jurud's compatriots now living in the lap of luxury in the Polanco district, the Señora said with the mild contempt she reserved for her social inferiors. You've been there lately. . . . Well, there's no bias in Mexico. Unlike North Americans, we aren't racists. . . . There were Jews, or New Christians as the converts were called, here from the very beginning. They arrived with Cortés. Father Sahagún was a New Christian. The Garza and Sada families that control a vast business empire are of Sephardic Jewish origin. No one objects. They are Mexicans— However, if the Jewish people choose *otherness* as their territory, then they ought to restrict themselves to its confines. No shilly-shallying, back and forth . . . no little deceptions. It's high time *these* people be made to understand that they either become full-fledged members of our society or stay strangers within their distinct separateness.

What about the recurrent theme of the disappearing woman in Jurud's fiction? asked the secretary, who was impatient to challenge him on his own ground—eager to demonstrate her perspicacity. Could it be that the WASP female is on the lookout for a sexually bolder partner?

I'm sure this is of great interest to you both, the Señora said chidingly before he was able to respond. But aren't we here to discuss the upcoming dinner?

Now it was the secretary's turn. He saw her cheeks redden as she endeavored to find an escape in her notes.

Is there anything we have omitted? the senator's wife asked Alejandro.

No. You've thought of everything, he said, and indeed, she and her secretary, doubtlessly with some assistance, had spent long hours planning every detail, from the menu, the flower arrangement, the wines, the music, to his introductory speech and Jurud's response. Alejandro listened to the secretary read the list of those attending.

As you can see, we've had to omit—the secretary hesitated—some of the names you suggested, but for this dinner we needed to provide a degree of excitement. We've added several actors and actresses—naming four movie celebrities.

As well as our friend Carlos Rozar, said the Señora, naming an industrialist who was known to be a supporter of her husband.

As he was leaving, Alejandro—the inquisitive visitor who, given the way things are, might never again set foot in this splendid old mansion in the Lomas Chapultepec neighborhood—seeing that the door to the large wood-paneled reception room off the hallway was ajar, seized the opportunity and knowingly intruded, curious to see what paintings it might contain. There was no one to stop him, no one to prevent him from examining the paintings on the near wall. The only one he was able to identify was a Courbet of a shadowy cave entrance, *The Source of the Loue,* which on close scrutiny bore a marked resemblance to a pudenda. The immense room's lavish furniture, which was in keeping with the rest of the ostentatious interior, included an eighteenth-century mahogany settee, a tall armoire with wood and bone inlay, a black lacquer Chinese screen, and two hideous ebony and ivory tusk armchairs. There was also a profusion of flowers. Not lilies, but freshly cut orchids, in an inverted pear-shaped vase with a narrow neck and serpentine handles. Though the two men, both in shirtsleeves, playing billiards in an alcove at the far end could not have been unaware of his presence in the doorway, neither so much as looked up from the billiard table. He stayed long enough to see the older man, grim-faced as he bent over the table to aim his cue, effect a perfect shot . . . hearing the satisfying double click as the ball hit one, then the second ball at the intended angle, followed by the congratulatory, Good shot, Senator, from the earnest-looking younger man, who might have been his aide.

I hope your wife will be happy with our arrangements, the Señora had mischievously said as they parted. Her comment struck him as quite gratuitous.

I'm sorry; she won't be able to attend. At present she's teaching in a small college in the U.S.

I admire independent women, said Señora Galindez. Don't you? He wasn't certain if this remark was intended for him or the secretary. She, at any rate, thanked him as she handed him the envelope containing the list of guests. I don't know how we would have managed without you.

Su servidor, he said, bowing—though he had not intended to.

Art Source

Bonny didn't care how they intended to spend the day. Eyes closed, she sat in the back, drowsily listening to Rita's self-assured voice. It was a relief not to be responsible for herself. It was a relief to leave the planning to others—quite satisfying to speak only when spoken to. What a relief to be

young . . . How young? A child. At the moment, all of twelve
or thirteen . . . A precocious adolescent flooded by the intensity
of a sudden acute psychological awareness of adults. For the
present, intent on finding their way to the Anadelle Partridge
Museum, the adults paid no attention to her. In spite of that,
Bonny felt she was in the secure embrace of a family—even
though she couldn't understand their cryptic exchanges or
figure out what they were after. Twice Preston took a wrong
turn and had to turn back. Rita, who was holding the map,
became more and more irritable. These damn Mexican road
maps, she complained. They're definitely not out to attract
visitors, that's for sure, said Terrence, when they finally came
across a faded road sign marked MUSEO, the arrow pointing in
the direction of a side street. No one was in sight when they
parked in front of the colossal old building. This is quite insane,
Rita asserted as they got out. Bonny giggled nervously. Circling the large compound, they knocked to no avail on several
doors until Preston located what appeared to be the entrance.
A gleaming plaque read *Museo Partridge* and, beneath it, the
word *Filantropía*. To their dismay, the guard there was unre-
sponsive. Invitación, Preston said loudly. El licenciado Salas
invitación! Señor Salas not here. Go away. Distrito Federal,
said the guard brusquely. Finally, seeing that they were not
going to budge, the guard picked up an antiquated phone and,
after dialing, spoke rapidly into the receiver. Then, turning to
Preston, he said, Cerrado—the word accompanied by an em-
phatic gesture of dismissal with his free hand. No cerrado,
Preston repeated adamantly. Absolutamente no! Sí, sí, the
guard said heatedly. Vuelva en septiembre. Preston, outraged:
No! Ahora, do you hear! Then, seized by inspiration, produced
the word *Inmediatamente!* This time, after the guard had
relayed Preston's forceful demand, a young man in shirt and tie

appeared. Sorry, folks. We're closed, he announced in a cheerful voice. The museum is being renovated. You'll have to come back next year. I am Preston Hollier. We're here at el señor Salas's invitation, Preston explained curtly. I am to use the museum facilities. El licenciado Salas's secretary in Mexico City made the call in my presence. One minute. The young man, whose pale face and heavy-lidded eyes reminded Bonny of the theology student she had sat next to on her Greyhound bus ride from New York to California, picked up the phone and, after a brief exchange, waved his hand, Por favor, to indicate they could enter. The guard, losing all interest in their presence, sat down. To Preston's inquiry, Dónde está la entrada a la galería de arte? he made a lazy sweeping motion with his arm, a motion that included the entire courtyard and what lay beyond. Derecho. Gracias. De nada, said the guard. Facing them as they stepped into the vast courtyard was a cluster of life-size busts, their condition so lamentable and their placement so arbitrary that Rita concluded they were being discarded. From where they stood they could see that crisscrossing the entire courtyard were deep trenches, with untidy heaps of funerary sculpture and gravestones next to the mounds of freshly dug up reddish earth. On the far side, two bare-chested men were digging energetically, but not with the caution required for an excavation. Why all these trenches? Bonny wondered. Half a dozen sprinklers directed an intermittent circular trail of water on the straggly uneven patches of yellowed grass. In the full glare of the midday sun, everything looked parched, worn to the bone, hopelessly neglected. Even the shady arcades did not appear inviting. What had she expected? On the wall to her right, a bewildering display of stone heads and torso fragments, hands, feet, chests. In the first hall, a twelve-foot frieze lay on the stone floor, while the bare walls were covered by ceiling-high metal and wood scaffolding. One wall was partially repainted. Dented buckets of paint and brushes had been left in one corner, as if discarded by the painters. Following the trail-like drips of beige paint on the floor, they finally reached another courtyard, in a similar state of disrepair.

Several transparent green plastic hoses were directing water to the fountain at the center, which, in addition to debris, contained goldfish. The fish were darting in and out between jagged pieces of concrete that looked as if they had been forcibly wrested from the ground.

To crown this state of disrepair, a tall dead tree, incongruously held in place with metal supports, sprouted a live branch with leaves at its apex, like some grotesque aberration of nature. Reaching the main staircase, they climbed the marble steps to the second floor, where Preston was greeted by Vinicio, the chief restorer. I have orders from Señor Salas to make everything available to you, he said in faultless English. Please, follow me. Proceeding at a fast pace down the vaulted corridor.

Does he understand why we're here? Rita asked Terrence in a low voice as they tried to keep up.

Take my word for it, Preston assured her.

It's so implausible, Rita murmured.

All the same, Terrence maintained, it is a museum.

So far, Rita observed, there's nothing I'd like to own.

Folks, this way, please, said the restorer, holding open a door. As they stepped into the office, the assistant director, sitting at his desk, jumped to his feet, greeting them with Mexican exuberance. Apologizing for not having been apprised of their arrival, he lied disarmingly: I was expecting you next week. Over drinks they could not refuse, despite the questionable ice cubes in the glasses, he went on to explain that he had just been on the phone to Señor Salas and it was agreed that the restorer was to take them on an *extensive* tour.

Alarmed at what an *extensive* tour might entail, Rita protested, There's really no need—we've just seen the place.

It's a beautiful museum, said Preston, who correctly assumed that the restorer intended to take them to the artifacts they had come to see. I'm most impressed! As his foot nudged Rita's, signaling her to be patient, his broad smile imparted the boundlessness of his amicable disposition.

Wait till you see the restorations completed, was the director's smug response.

Slow to catch Preston's signal, Terrence spoke up, annoyed by what he took to be a further indication of Mexican procrastination. Aren't we speaking at cross-purposes? After coming all this distance— He was about to mention their long-standing interest in pre-Columbian art, when Preston, in what was made to appear as a friendly pat, forcefully jabbed a thumb into Terrence's rib cage. Ahhhh . . . Terrence gasped, eyes widening in surprise. Ahhhh . . . Flushing a deep red, he coughed to mask his distress.

You all right? Preston asked with a look of concern.

Terrence recoiled when he saw that Preston was about to clap him on the back. I'm f-fine, he stuttered. Pretending not to notice their idiosyncratic behavior, the chief restorer gave the signal for them to leave, holding open the heavy wood door, and, with innate Mexican courtesy, making a little bow to each as they passed through.

Goodbye, my friends, said the assistant director, sounding like a recorded voice for a beginners' English lesson.

If this turns into a wild-goose chase, I swear, I'm going to scream, said Rita.

Dearest, shut up, Preston said through his gritted teeth. We're all anxious to see art!

Is there a ladies' room? Bonny asked.

Not now, said Rita.

It was on their tour of the studio where pre-Columbian artifacts were being restored that the restorer handed Preston the list, a creased carbon copy containing over one hundred artworks, each listing accompanied by a brief description and, in parentheses, a coded identifying number. Preston, not comprehending, asked, What are these?

That's what's presently available, the restorer informed him casually.

Rita, unable to contain her excitement, asked, Aren't there any photos?

If you wish, just give me the number of the ones you'd like to see.

How are they priced?

Patience, patience, urged Preston.

That one! Without even consulting Preston, Rita pointed to one of a dozen black-and-white eight-by-ten enlargements she had been handed.

Absolutely, Preston said when he saw it, for once in agreement. It's magnificent. It was a crouching goddess giving birth. The price was within reason.

Are there any discounts?

Sorry, what do you mean? asked the restorer.

Galleries in the U.S. customarily offer a discount to their customers, said Rita, to Preston's distress. You know, to serious collectors like us.

Discount? said the restorer, not trusting his ears.

Forget it, said Preston, glaring at Rita. My wife must have been thinking of the sales tax.

Ah, sales tax. He looked relieved. There's no tax.

Yes, I understand.

You don't accept American Express, do you?

No. I'm sorry, madam. We're unable to accept credit cards or traveler's checks.

When, on receipt of their check, Preston was asked to sign a form, he balked, peering suspiciously at the tiny print in Spanish. What does it say?

The restorer tried to reassure him: Pro forma, simply for our files.

What does it say?

Terrence painstakingly deciphered a word here and there. Something to the effect that for your contribution to the museum . . . and this word looks like *borrowing,* or *on loan.*

Pro forma, the restorer insisted.

Pro forma, hell, Preston said irately. According to this form, what we acquire is considered a loan.

No, no, it's not a loan, the restorer politely insisted.

Exasperated, Preston looked to Terrence. What do we do now?

It's your baby, said Terrence noncommittally.

I want it, Rita insisted. Whatever, I want it. Sign it.

We'll have our lawyer look at it, Preston promised, folding the form and pocketing it. By tomorrow I'll have it in the mail to you.

No. The restorer adamantly refused. You must sign for it.

Rita, losing patience, reached inside Preston's breast pocket for his pen. Let me—

You can't, protested Preston. Wait. You'll be liable—

Bull, she said. Demanding the form from Preston, she scrawled her signature.

The museum official did not raise any objection.

Beneath her signature she printed her maiden name, then, under Address, she entered their former New York address.

Fine. Grimly, the restorer nodded. It's just for the files, he said, wiping his brow.

Peeking into an adjacent room, Bonny glimpsed a young man in a white lab coat in front of an easel—he was wearing a protective mask, and the light strapped to his forehead cast a strong beam on what to her looked like a painting she had previously seen in reproductions. Urgently she beckoned to Preston, only to have their guide and escort, Vinicio, with a look of alarm, walk hastily to the door and shut it in her face. That's private, he warned sternly.

Trying to establish goodwill with the restorer, Rita reprimanded her. Haven't they taught you not to poke your head into other rooms?

I wasn't, she said, tears coming to her eyes. I was just—

That's all right, said Preston. She's tired.

Speak for yourself, said Rita.

When the restorer and an assistant brought the wrapped goddess to their car, Rita insisted on having the sculpture on the front seat, beside her. I'm so pleased with it, she declared, her hand resting on it as they headed back to the city. Who'd have thought that Alejandro would—

Preston, exultantly: It's a treasure trove! Then, peremptorily to Terrence: First thing next week I want you to go back and get photos of whatever else is available and pay Salas a visit. Thank him properly.

I'll do that. All the same—

Properly, you know. Show our appreciation.

We also have to thank Alejandro, Rita reminded Preston. He's the one who put us in touch with Salas.

He'll get his cut from Salas.

It would be a nice ges—

Not only does he not expect it; he'll regard it as an insult, Preston insisted.

I didn't say cash, Rita protested. I meant it to be a token of our appreciation.

Trying to be conciliatory, Terrence agreed. It can't hurt.

Well, I bow to your combined greater wisdom, said Preston in a huff—gazing straight ahead at the outskirts of Mexico City.

The Critic Sees?

Somewhere on the building's exterior was a small bronze plaque to confirm the café's literary significance and history. By the time Fuentes, Paz, and their friends came here in the sixties, the place had been sold to a Panamanian, who enlarged it to its present size. Visitors included Alejo Carpentier, Julio Cortázar, Manuel Puig, and Juan García Ponce. There was as yet no art gallery on the second floor and no TV program. It was a relaxed, rustic sort of establishment. Now, as a result of Raúl's bimonthly TV program, it had come to be regarded as nothing less than another Mexican edifice, another literary pyramid.

But what's all this to do with history? Now the only history of significance transpires on the TV.

Why do we keep coming here? Alejandro asked rhetorically—was he seeking to ensnare his companion? But Francisco, enjoying an afternoon seeing friends, had no intention of examining his feelings with regard to this old meeting place of theirs.

To Alejandro's dismay, the moment Raúl stopped at their table, his eyes sparkling behind the gold-rimmed glasses, openly seeking an invitation, Francisco promptly invited him to join them. Gladly. Sinking into the chair next to Alejandro. Beaming contentedly. What are you drinking? Not seeming to mind when Alejandro didn't answer. What a beautiful day. Alejandro, inwardly raging at being seated next to Raúl, glared at the waiter, whose self-conscious smirk when he came to take Raúl's order was to Alejandro an acknowledgment of Raúl's sudden rise to prominence—nothing less, nothing more. In the tree-shaded courtyard below, several people were openly looking their way. Because of Raúl?

Just another sultry afternoon?

It's his smugness that I resent, thought Alejandro as Raúl jubilantly described his new three-room apartment on El Guero nearby and how with some finagling he had managed to acquire the next-door apartment as well and now was having the dividing walls torn down.

Did you need a building permit?

Raúl rubbed his thumb and forefinger together. I took care of that.

Alejandro sipped his wine, thoughtfully measuring his antipathy for Raúl. But why? Raúl, who remained sublimely unaware of his dislike, had never harmed him. Recognizing someone, Raúl stood up and waved to a slim young woman in black turtleneck and tight black leather trousers, standing at the bar with friends. Gaily she waved back. Raúl beckoned almost too eagerly—an eagerness that Alejandro was quick to interpret as the latter's inherent need to please. Was it Raúl's keen eagerness that he so detested? My assistant, Alva, Raúl explained as he pulled up another chair. At first Alejandro failed to recognize her heavily made up face. A face that could easily have doubled for that of any of the young inexpressive women who made a career modeling the mass-produced dresses on the fliers and catalogues of the less expensive department stores, such as Sears or El Puerto de Liverpool. Blankly staring when she greeted him by name, the filing system of his brain somehow awry as it strained to identify her, but if anything, he was led astray by the black leather trousers and the tooled western boots. Only on hearing her disarming remark, I'm glad that Raúl has finally snared you for his program, was he able to identify her. It was none other than his former student, whom he had seen only days before in the outdoor café. Was he right to remember her as being taciturn and withdrawn? The one who in class never opened her mouth? The one who promised to have a paper ready for the next class and never presented anything? Now, in their presence, she seemed transfigured— uninhibited, flaunting her sexuality. I kept urging Raúl to have you, she began.

Alva! I didn't need you to urge me to invite Alejandro, Raúl protested. It was my intention all along. . . .

Francisco, accusingly, as if for Alejandro to appear on Raúl's program was somehow inconceivable to him: You never told me. . . .

Alejandro has agreed to interview Jurud, said Raúl, with the aplomb of someone who had every reason to expect only approval for his decisions.

An excellent choice, said Francisco, though he failed to show a corresponding enthusiasm.

Raúl winked at Francisco. Bringing the oddest fellows together is my business.

You're going to let him get away with that? asked Francisco.

Alejandro shrugged. I have no intention of making a fool of myself on TV.

When is this event to take place?

You'll be informed, said the imperturbable Raúl, oblivious to Francisco's ironic tone.

When? Francisco persisted. When?

You don't want to be there, said Alejandro. Take my word for it.

Two weeks next Thursday.

I've just finished Jurud's last book, Alva stated, as if this deserved praise from him.

He looked at her fleetingly. And?

Your wife's translation is outstanding, she said ingratiatingly. As for the novel, doesn't it capture what in Jurud is intended to pass for candor? Some readers erroneously equate it with fearlessness. They think he is outspoken. To Alejandro, it sounded as if his former student was repeating some of his off-the-cuff remarks to the class. And skillfully weaving, Alva continued, an extravagant tale that one could compare to . . . Here she paused, as if she had suddenly lost her place, looking to Raúl for guidance. But he was of no help. So recklessly she named the first author who came to her mind, Isaac Bashevis Singer. When to her dismay Francisco burst into laughter, she substituted Erico Veríssimo, a writer of popular novels in Mexico. Alejandro stonily continued to stare at the half-empty bottle of tequila.

There you are, said Francisco, taking pity on her. She's making my point. Singer, Veríssimo. Aren't they all skilled manipulators of the reader?

Jurud accommodates himself to the reader, said Alejandro. The slickness stands him in good stead.

I tend to see an obsessive quality there. That's how they are. . . .

They? Raúl asked, ready to pounce on Francisco.

Francisco, embarrassed: I was just kidding. . . .

You don't have to like him, Raúl protested virtuously. I happen to.

Well, why does anyone care to read Jurud? Francisco said dryly.

He disarms the reader, responded Alejandro with quiet dignity. He entertains.

Their biases.

I don't take him that seriously, admitted Alejandro.

Is that why you never once referred to him in your course? Alva said in a sultry, sexy voice he found curiously appealing.

I did. More than once, Alejandro protested.

Francisco yawned and pointedly looked at his watch.

Raúl, face flushed, showed signs of wishing to leave, just as a young waiter Alejandro had not seen before brought their drinks.

You must be new here, said Raúl.

Yes, señor.

He looks promising, Raúl commented as Alejandro took the opportunity to order another bottle.

I can no longer drink white wine, Francisco maintained, staring disdainfully at the people in the courtyard below. I get the most awful headaches.

It's the additives, said Raúl.

Alva kept looking at Alejandro.

But why go on? Just another wasted afternoon? Humid, overcast sky. Raúl reacted with suspicion to Alejandro's deliberately provocative remark that they were saddled with a turbulent and irrational history.

Why should history be anything but? Raúl interjected.

A history, Alejandro continued, so intensely bloody, so insanely chaotic, so driven by dementia and rapacity and passion and greed, that it puts all our fiction to shame.

It's a fool's occupation. Raúl waved his hands, behaving as if he were on camera. In a state of fluctuating doubt one nourishes illusion. True, there's always the encouraging success of Fuentes, Paz—

Francisco objected. The serious Mexican writer has little freedom left to select . . . to invent . . . if he wishes to remain true to our society.

To Raúl's astonishment, Alejandro furiously opposed Francisco's contention that the Mexican writers weren't free to employ Mayan ball courts, Aztec ruins, Baroque churches, the Toltec pyramids, in their novels without casting over the entire text an appallingly solemn air of gloom, putrescence, and mass extinction.

Alva hugged herself, as if to contain her delight at being present—her elongated pale face suffused by an almost sexual intensity. She couldn't be more than twenty-one or two, Alejandro decided. With a possessive gesture—was it to demonstrate an intimate attachment?—Raúl placed his arm around the back of her chair, his fingers grazing Alva's bare shoulder.

Francisco's further assertion—In Mexico we aren't free to produce a paragraph that's devoid of our constricted Mexican symbolic content—may have been intended as a challenge to Alejandro. When he failed to respond, Francisco continued, Saddled with this "Mexican" formula, our writerly stratagems are of little avail.

Fuentes, for example, is free to locate his novels wherever he chooses, Alejandro finally said.

Wherever he chooses? Francisco expressed amazement. Our ceaseless contemplation of conquests, colonization, revolution, mass executions, betrayals, sieges, and the omnipresence of death, this loathsome celebration of death, dictates what we write, and foremost what we think.

Bullshit, Alejandro said. Utter, total bullshit.

How not to envy that innate optimism of the writers to our north . . . ? Was Raúl trying to spur them on to further combat?

Alejandro objected, Hardly the same. . . .

Your known dislike of Jurud because he is a best-selling author marks you as an elitist, said Francisco.

Alejandro, indignantly: My dislike? How do you come to that conclusion? Isn't it enough that I grant him a technical virtuosity as he concocts his well-crafted, seamless entertainments?

Unconvinced, Francisco leaned back, lighting a cigar. All the same, Jurud's virtuosity is the measure of an all-too-accessible world unfettered by the interlocking jungles, pyramids, peasants, and torments of our spirits.

We cannot escape being Mexican! Raúl said flatly.

Francisco, choosing his words carefully: In spite of the inequities, the destitution, the demographic explosion, the poverty, some, a few, pleasures remain. . . .

Once, this place was one of them, Alejandro murmured.

Raúl, having poured what was left of the Don Pedro Reserva Especial into Alva's glass, signaled the waiter. The check? No, another . . . Despite the warning signal of an oncoming headache, Alejandro did not stop the waiter from filling his glass. What was it about Raúl that made him welcome the pain? He fumbled in his pocket for aspirin.

When the check was presented, Raúl made a grab for it. Mine, he said triumphantly. Alejandro felt too depleted to even make a show of trying to take the check away from him.

. . .

I'm working on a novel, Alva said as they parted.

Good luck.

Despite the disapproval in his voice, she ventured, I wonder if I might . . .

What? He looked at her sharply.

Your comments would mean so much to me. I mean . . .

You want me to read it? He eyed her with exasperation.

He's not going to read it, Francisco laughingly warned her. It's a waste of a good Xerox.

If I may, she persevered. Please, please!

Oh, go ahead, he said against all better judgment.

Her voice husky with emotion: Thank you, thank you ever so much. Can I bring it by?

Put it in the mail. Raúl will give you my address.

Less than pleased, Raúl asked, How's Mercedes? as they shook hands.

Oh, to escape this morbidity! To leave Mexico's explanations behind forever!

Intrusion

When Francisco rang from around the corner—with the not altogether plausible request that Rita would love to see the painting of the critic—wasn't an immediate *no* called for?

We won't stay long, Francisco promised. We just want to—

Alejandro, incredulously: Now?

Please, said Francisco, uncharacteristically sounding in need of help. Looking out the window, he saw them emerging from under the striped green awning of the Café Rivoli, where they must have made their call, Rita firmly—no, possessively—holding Francisco's arm. When he had suggested that they make it an hour later, Francisco had pressed him to let them come by immediately. Now would be convenient, please!

Alejandro waited on the marble landing in front of the metal and glass elevator shaft, greeting Rita in English—Hi, good to see you—as soon as she stepped out. My buddy, said Francisco, embracing him in a bear hug. As they entered the apartment, Alejandro caught Rita glancing at Francisco as if for guidance, or could it be reassurance? What could they possibly want? Stopping in the entrance to the large living room, she said in a contrived voice, What an absolutely fabulous place, as if thereby paying her due.

Did he show his resentment at this intrusion? This interruption?

As soon as I described the painting of the old critic, Francisco said apologetically, Rita wanted to see it.

She met Alejandro's gaze with a calm smile. Sanguine? Feeling complacent about her beauty. If you don't mind? Just a peek. Preceding them into his study. Is that it? Rapturously gazing at the canvas from the doorway. Magnificent, she said. It's been shown, hasn't it?

We let the Museum de Art Moderno have it for an exhibition, not realizing what it would entail, said Alejandro. It was damaged in transit. . . .

Staring intently at the painting, she gave an involuntary shudder.

Satisfied with her response, Francisco urged her to look closely at the paintings within the painting, especially the one to the left, shown hanging above the chair piled high with papers.

It's a Modigliani, he said.

Amazing, she marveled.

Few painters have so effectively created an intimate space, said Alejandro.

The desk is the size of yours, she observed.

And just as untidy, Francisco stated.

When the "critic" hung in the living room, most people took him to be a relative of Mercedes, said Alejandro, taking pride in the fact that the "European" critic was assumed to be an ancestor of his wife.

I find it entirely appropriate that you would have a painting of a seemingly incapacitated critic in your study, Francisco remarked incautiously—and then, disconcerted by the malice his statement revealed, tried to laugh it away—I meant to say, the painting is desirable as a framing device. A matter of reference. N'est-ce pas?

He's immersed in his past, Alejandro insisted. A past, after all, that he may have helped create . . .

One shouldn't forget, argued Francisco, that the critic, and what he may have stood for, is being brought to life by a far more persuasive critic—the painter himself.

But Alejandro, not about to be drawn into a dispute with Francisco, deflected the implied assault. By the time this was painted, he said, the critic had, in effect, ceased to function as a critic.

She looked astonished. Because of his age?

I equate criticism with energy. It's an assertion. A form of domination, whether we admit it or not.

I would have thought that at his age a critic would achieve his greatest work and arrive at self-illumination.

Francisco, bemused: Total awareness?

He's just less disputatious, less judgmental, said Alejandro.

You love him, she concluded impulsively.

Look at him—he's feeble, asserted Francisco. Why not

admit it—we find him agreeable because he's no longer intellectually contentious.

He listens to me, said Alejandro with a fatuous smile.

Does he respond? Francisco asked.

Alejandro didn't bother to reply.

Francisco pulled him aside before he and Rita left,
apologetically requesting a favor. If the subject of our visit is
ever brought up, would you agree to say that you had invited
Rita to look at the painting? Seeing Alejandro's perplexed
expression: Just in case Preston should inquire . . .

Is that why you came?

Francisco, checking his watch: Will you?

OK.

Say two, two-thirty p.m.

What?

Time of our arrival, Francisco explained. Make it three.

Alejandro couldn't resist: And when did you leave?

Francisco saw the humor of the remark. Smiling broadly:
Why, now. Whatever time . . .

Alejandro glanced at his watch. I have five-thirty.

Fine. Thanking him profusely, he joined Rita, waiting in
front of the elevator.

Thank you for having us over, she called out.

The Critic Is Outraged

Raúl wanted his "honest" opinion the minute he entered the
apartment. I just had the carpenter construct the cabinets.

Nicely done.

Raúl pointed with pride to the bookcases. The shelves are
adjustable. That's oak finish. He also scraped the floors.

Nice!

And those are hand-painted tiles.

Looks good.

He's only twenty. If you ever need a carpenter . . .

Nice print, said Alejandro, eyeing the framed print on the exposed brick wall.

It's by Tamayo. I was flabbergasted when he gave it to me. I had admired it in his studio. And after he appeared on my TV show, he sent it over. A housewarming gift. Mind you, I had never suggested . . .

Alejandro picked up a heavy candlestick that was placed next to its gleaming silver mate on the table.

Spanish, said Raúl, with an air of satisfaction. I picked them up in the Mercado de Antigüedades.

Alejandro looked at him somberly. Was there something you wanted to tell me?

Instantly Raúl's pride of ownership, his glow of satisfaction was extinguished. It can wait.

As you please.

Raúl took a deep breath. This was not how he had planned to proceed. It's just this: After listening to some of your comments about Jurud the last time we met . . . well, are you sure you—

What comments? I recall it was Francisco who cast doubt—

I was left with the impression that you hadn't read Jurud's latest book closely. I now realize that a best-seller is not your kind of—

What makes you say that?

I mean, you aren't fond of him. . . .

Come on, I've read him. . . .

I wouldn't want you to feel coerced into—

I wouldn't dream of accepting anything that—

No, no, no, protested Raúl. I'm not suggesting. Just that a few people I know seem to concur. . . . They too have the impression that in your heart of hearts you consider him antiquated. Predictable. Someone who fails to present a challenge. He paused, looking upset. Let me get you a drink. Brandy, cognac, French wine— He could have gone on had Alejandro not cut him short.

Wine.

Any preference? I have—

Red.

His back to Alejandro, Raúl uncorked a bottle of Spanish red wine and then, having wiped the inside rim of the bottle with a napkin, proceeded as if in slow motion to pour. They seem to believe that Jurud is antithetical to everything you believe in, he stated in a low voice.

Name them, barked Alejandro, his feeling of indignation if anything fueled by Raúl's hesitancy.

Taken aback by the acrimony in his voice, Raúl protested, I can't reveal their names.

You have no compunctions about going behind my back.

I? Turning with his glass of wine. Behind your back? Here I am—he dramatically waved his free hand—opening myself to you. The posters with your name on it announcing Jurud's visit have been printed.

Why are you questioning my motive? Alejandro asked.

When Jacobus spoke of your admiration for Jurud, I saw no reason to doubt him. Especially since Mercedes is translating Jurud's novels. Raúl laughed a little hysterically. Now I discover . . .

You think I'd agree to appear on TV to make a fool of Jurud?

You might humiliate him.

I am simply functioning as an interviewer.

Well, Mercedes . . . Miserably he left the sentence unfinished.

What about her?

I was told you resented her translating Jurud. That you were the last person on earth to—

If you feel that way, I'll step down—

I invited you—

And I accepted, Alejandro interjected. Where's the problem?

The rumors. These horrid implications that you at heart despise Jurud and everything he stands for.

Because he's a Jew?

No, no, please. Don't further muddy the waters. I don't even want to get into that.

Because of the way he depicts a society that only someone with his background—

Please, don't patronize me.

The seamlessness of his—

You dislike his work. Mouth tightening. I have no quarrel with that. I just don't want it to take place on my program. I didn't invite Jurud to this interview in order to have him ridiculed.

Why should I stoop to—

Because, fool that I am, I have provided you with a God-sent opportunity. With two million viewers, you can put him through the wringer.

If that were the case, I wouldn't have accepted, Alejandro said. Amigo, trust me.

Raúl took a step forward, with a beseeching look on his face, his hand gesturing an earnest appeal. I want to, my friend.

Don't you see, if I were to ridicule him I'd end up attacking my wife, his translator?

Of course.

Well, then, agree that your assumptions are absurd.

Raúl, if anything, looked even more miserable. Not with your wife as his ally . . . He'd have to grin and bear it.

This is intolerable.

You might wish to engage in a messy brawl. It would be the end of my—

Who said that? Alejandro was incensed. Bolting out of the chair, angrily gesticulating. Who? Tell me. Who? Give me a name.

Raúl retreated, his face now ashen.

This is a deliberate attempt to eliminate me from the TV event.

Absolutely not, said Raúl—Will you allow me to make one suggestion? One? Then we'll erase this event from our memory.

Scenting more trouble, Alejandro raised his head. Yes?

Would you consider sharing the interview . . . ?

Never, said Alejandro emphatically.

Hear me out, Raúl pleaded. You and a colleague of your choice—for instance, Francisco—jointly interview Jurud. The two of you, old friends, would make it a more congenial—

You're insulting me.

There's no question of splitting your fee, I promise you . . .

Seeing his grim face, Raúl made a sweeping gesture with his hand to indicate that the troubling event had been brushed aside—then, as a sign of appeasement, he asked, What do you prefer, Ciceros or Les Caves? I've made reservations in both.

Either one. Looking at his glass of wine, Alejandro said,

This is good wine. Then, looking around, reappraising the apartment—you're doing well.

Their altercation all but forgotten, Raúl beamed at the mention of the apartment. Since moving in, I feel I've been given a new lease on life.

It's quite a find, said Alejandro, walking to the far end of the room and peering into the next.

Our reservations are for one, Raúl reminded him.

I'm starving.

Incidentally, Alva told me how much she enjoyed taking your course, Raúl said as they descended the stairs.

Known her long?

Raúl appeared eager to provide him with information.

I know her father. He's appeared on my program.

What does he do?

He's an official of the PRI.

Useful.

Well, that's not why . . .

I envy you.

Raúl, as he stood holding open the front door, turned a bright red. She thinks the world of you as a critic, he said.

On their way to the restaurant, Raúl ducked into a small photo store—You don't mind, do you?—to pick up some pictures he had left to be developed. From where he was standing on the street, Alejandro could see Raúl glancing at a few as he stood waiting in line at the cashier, then, before leaving the store, pocketing the package with a look of inordinate satisfaction.

At least a dozen people were waiting to be seated in the restaurant when they arrived. Raúl stepped up to the maître d' and, after giving his name, watched as the man, with the aid of a pince-nez, inspected the ledgerlike reservation book on the table in front of him. What was that name again? Only to declare, when Raúl repeated it, I have no such name. Alejandro saw the well-dressed woman next to him exchange a knowing look with her companion. More people were arriving. A woman selling tuberoses slipped past the maître d', who, suddenly all smiles, unctuously informed a couple that their table was ready. As he passed the maître d', the man slipped him a bill, which the maître d', with a conjurer's skill, made disappear up his jacket sleeve.

I made the reservation yesterday, Raúl insisted.

Impossible. Like a teacher disappointed by an incorrect answer, the maître d' showed his disapproval. If the gentlemen would care to wait an hour, perhaps . . .

Why don't we just lunch elsewhere? Alejandro proposed.

I'll mention this on my program, vowed Raúl as they exited, their departure followed dispassionately by the people still waiting for their tables.

At Alejandro's suggestion, they settled for the small restaurant around the corner. It was crowded with office workers on their lunch break. They both ordered the special, only to have the waiter inform them that they were out of enchiladas. Raúl was disconsolate. We could go to La Calesa de Londres, he said.

This place is fine, Alejandro said, while watching Raúl toy with the tape that sealed the bright yellow package of photos, peeling it off, then replacing it. . . . For God's sake, he said finally. Go ahead and look at them.

Well, just a quick glance. Opening the envelope, he removed the color snapshots, scanning them avidly, then after some deliberation, he selected one, hesitatingly offering it to him. Here's a shot of Vegas . . .

Beautiful, Alejandro agreed. When were you there?

Just recently. It was on the spur of the moment. I needed to get away. . . . Shuffling the photos, he extracted another. Here's one with your former student.

You took her along?

Becoming bolder, Raúl handed him one of Alva in a robe, parted in front to reveal a hint of her breasts and her bare legs.

If you've never been to Death Valley, Raúl said earnestly, you owe it to yourself to go. . . .

I've never been to the United States.

I keep forgetting. He laughed nervously. You have this aversion.

No. I avoid it out of fear that it will not approximate the United States of my imagination.

Raúl remembered a trip they had taken to Nogales.

They turned us back at the U.S. border, Alejandro reminded him.

Is that it? You've not forgiven them for that rejection?

I'm sure I'm still on their blacklist for my past political indiscretions.

You? Raúl laughed, as if he couldn't conceive of Alejandro as a Marxist. All you need is a letter from your father-in-law to clear up the matter.

He probably could do it with a phone call, Alejandro agreed.

Do you recall the gringa? The two of us driving around in the pitch dark trying to find her apartment? We were completely lost.

Alejandro pretended not to remember, as if fearing what this recollection might lead to.

Raúl sighed as he deliberated over his next choice. Death Valley, he said finally, handing him a photo. The hotel was built into the side of a mountain. Those palms are sixty meters tall.

Alejandro looked at it, disappointed to see only a hotel.

That's the oasis. . . . That brook is fed by a natural spring.

On seeing that the group of four at a nearby table who had been seated after them were already being served, Alejandro was put out. What the hell is keeping our waiter? Raising his hand . . . to no avail.

Raúl, immersed in the photos, didn't look up. You and I were the absolute incarnation of innocence. Getting soused and then sleeping it off in her apartment.

What are you talking about?

That failed trip of ours.

Grudgingly almost, Alejandro remembered. It's a long time ago.

I keep asking myself, what was she doing in Nogales? Why would an American woman rent an apartment in Nogales?

All I remember is having a dreadful hangover, said Alejandro. He was taken aback when Raúl, in an aggrieved voice, blurted out, Alejandro! Admit you did sleep with her.

He couldn't believe his ears.

We had an unstated agreement—

Unstated agreement? Flabbergasted by Raúl's allegation and the magnitude of Raúl's perturbation Alejandro raised his voice. Here's some floozy we picked up . . . We stayed up late, talking into the night. I don't recall much of anything else.

They broke off when the waiter finally brought their soup.

I remember listening to the two of you at breakfast. . . . You were making a fool of me. . . .

Raúl! Where's your sense of proportion?

Raúl shuffled the photos like a deck of cards. Sorry. I don't know what came over me.

Before they parted, an hour later, Raúl mustered his courage. As to the interview. If—

Alejandro waited. Yes?

Oh, never mind.

The Three-Legged Dog

They were showing *La Femme infidèle* by Chabrol at 4:10 and 8:20 and Godard's *Contempt* at 6:15 and 10:30, both with Spanish subtitles. Since Alejandro's last visit, the lobby had received a new coat of the dark red paint his father seemed to love with a passion. The red-haired, freckle-faced young usherette didn't recognize him. Little had changed. The same worn red carpet. The same posters. The same uninviting red-upholstered seats.

I knew you'd show up for this double bill, his father said with genuine exuberance when Alejandro opened the door a crack and peered into the tiny cluttered space his father called his office. Alejandro, come in! To do so he had to step over a large bundle of freshly printed programs. Max, lying under the desk, feebly thumped his tail. Alejandro bent down to pat him as Max let out a muted strangled sound of dog devotion.

I like the red paint in the lobby and the recessed lighting.

His father fished for the list of forthcoming films among the pile of papers spread on his desk. Here—he held it up—have a look. Antonioni, Buñuel, Fassbinder . . .

When he inquired after his brother, his father said that it was Diego's day off.

His father, who had once harbored a desire to establish a

chain of art-movie houses, inquired, as he did each time Alejandro came by, if he owned a VCR, looking pained but not surprised when he said yes.

Do you rent videos? It was a sore point, Alejandro realized.

I don't have the time. . . .

Is *La Femme infidèle* available on tape?

No, he lied.

You could have helped us, his father said sadly. With your imagination.

Imagination is a drawback. Then, regretting his flippant response, in a gentler voice: You need business acumen.

You look worn out. Is everything all right?

What about you? Alejandro countered. When did you last take a vacation?

His father, pretending not to hear his question, mentioned Patricia. Remember her? She came by when we were showing *Ich Liebe Dich, Ich Töte Dich.* Is she still in the movies?

No. She's in the antique business. I ran into her a couple of days ago.

His father, eyes sparkling, lips curving into a smile of remembrance. She had a distinct flair!

He was always taken aback when he saw his father evince the slightest sexual interest. She wasn't getting anywhere . . . all those small parts.

No; once she had a main role, his father corrected him. It was a little-known Mexican movie. Dreamily his father looked at the poster of Buñuel's *That Obscure Object of Desire* on the wall over his desk, as if seeking from it a confirmation. She undressed in it, and her lover, a mercenary soldier, caressed her breasts.

On the screen? he asked in disbelief.

Absolutely.

Nude?

Partially, his father said defensively. Do you think I'm making it up?

You sure you're not confusing her with another actress? For instance, *La Furia de un Dios*, with the Spanish actress Assumpta Serna?

Well, the next time you see her, ask her.

I will.

You were sweet on her? Eyeing him thoughtfully, as if to determine how he and Alejandro's mother could have produced someone so devoid of affection, of familial loyalty, of emotions, of all the virtues Mexicans swear by.

She needs someone more stimulating, more flamboyant— she needs constant excitement.

Why are you selling yourself short?

I'm merely describing Patricia's—

Is she married?

She'll never marry.

How's Mercedes? As usual, his father had difficulty in saying her name.

Fine. What else could he say?

Their eyes met. Out of politeness to Alejandro, his father's skepticism was quickly veiled. It took an effort for him to ask, You sure you two are still together?

What an odd question. Why shouldn't we . . . ?

I never see her. The laugh concealed embarrassment. Does she exist—except, of course, in your overactive imagination?

After buying a bar of chocolate, for which the concessionaire refused to take money, Alejandro took a seat in the empty house to watch the ending of the film by Chabrol, that remarkable master of endings. Was it farfetched to believe that Chabrol began *La Femme infidèle* with the ending in mind?

After all, in every scene he could see the director reaching out to that indeterminate ending. An ending that would, he sensed, fill Chabrol with satisfaction. Even pleasure. The film's intimacy was highlighted by the fact that the actress Stéphane Audran, starring in the movie, was then still married to Chabrol. That stocky, amiable actor Michel Bouquet, playing the serious, dedicated lawyer, could easily be Mexican by the way he failed to reveal his emotions, Alejandro decided. By that studied reserve. That inwardness! That stoicism! By that inability to give of himself. Thereby, or so Chabrol might have one believe, setting in motion an irreversible sequence of fateful events that would undermine the orderly continuum, the enviable stability, that the lawyer, his strikingly beautiful but somehow detached and calm wife, and his young son seem to share—a stability that was established the moment the film began, focusing as it did on the contented lawyer and husband, his well-to-do law practice, and his Edenic house in its tranquil suburban setting. Acquiring proof of his wife's infidelity, he pursues the matter not as a vengeful husband but as a competent, inquiring, if constrained lawyer in order to better understand his wife's aberrant behavior. For her inexplicable behavior threatens not only a quintessential stability but the public good. Given the essentially peaceful, law-abiding nature of the husband, the element of surprise at seeing him, the inexperienced avenger, deliver, to his own amazement, a sudden blow to the back of the lover's head, clumsily killing him, cannot be sufficiently appreciated. Unplanned? Seeing the spreading pool of blood on the floor, while watching the perspiring husband mop up, and then, having wrapped the body of the lover, a larger man than himself, in plastic, going about disposing of it, the viewer cannot hold out any hope for a good ending. Good endings virtually have been ruled out by Chabrol. Seeing Chabrol, one might conclude that there were no good endings, period. The killing and the clumsy disposal of the body conveyed Chabrol's farcical intent to undermine any empathy for the inept husband, who contains his tremulous emotions with the stoic smile one so often can see on the face of a boy rejected as a player by his teammates. What was it about certain movies . . . ? The post-Cortés gentleman inside Alejandro moved restlessly. Alejandro had kept his mind concealed from him even though he shared his principles, his detached literary taste, and his morbid attachment to duty.

Alejandro accompanied his father home, Max at their side doing his utmost to keep up with them by a combination of walking and hopping. Each time they stopped, Max, teetering slightly on his three legs, stopped to gaze up at them mournfully.

Yesterday Diego brought Enrique along. As always, he asks after you. . . .

Enrique?

Diego's son. Your nephew.

How old is he?

Fourteen.

I have no memory, nothing, Alejandro complained.

His father leaned forward to pat Max. . . . Ready, Max?

My past remains a blank, said Alejandro bitterly. I feel as if I never experienced childhood.

His father now the one becoming impatient with the conversation: I'm worried about Max. I have to take him to the vet. . . .

Well, the strain of hopping about on three legs . . . , said Alejandro. They waited as Max sniffed the base of a streetlamp, then squirted it with a thin stream of urine. These are bad times for Mexican cinema, said his father. Our middle-class viewers are fixated on Hollywood films. He grimaced. But I'm not discouraged. Something always comes along. The six-story building looked grimier than he remembered. Was this where he had spent his childhood?

Alejandro was reassured to see that the names on the doors they passed were the same. The same doctor practicing on the ground floor. Does he still treat prostitutes? I wouldn't know, said his father. There was the tailor and his family on the second. Max's loud panting accompanied them as they climbed the stairs. Don't you think it's high time you moved to a more comfortable place? This is our home, his father said, unconsciously using the plural pronoun. The apartment was smaller than he remembered. Will you settle for soup? Why don't you let me invite you to a restaurant? Alejandro said. There's that local place you once took me to. It's too late. Besides, I'm too tired. While his father was feeding Max, he tried to locate Buñuel's autobiography, which the cinematographer had inscribed to his father. Everything's helter-skelter on your shelves, he said, finally giving up in exasperation. There are several boxes of books in the closet. If you want to go through them . . . Another day. Don't worry, it's there, his father assured him. Diego doesn't read. How *is* Diego? Surprised when his father casually mentioned that in his will he was leaving the movie house to Diego. It's Diego's only livelihood, he explained. Unlike you . . .

Diego doesn't give a damn about good movies, said Alejandro.

You don't need it, do you?

No. You're right.

I'm leaving you my books, my paintings, the letters from Buñuel . . . mementos . . .

Why mention it?
His father was surprised. Because I never see you?
What are you showing tomorrow?
Zero for Conduct.
I'll come if I can.
Will you visit my grave?
Don't make life so difficult.
What kind of a son are you?

Severe

PART THREE

In the unleashed eye of noon
these and other terrible things are written, yet it seems
at the time as mild as soughing of wavelets in a reservoir.
Only the belated certainty comes to matter much,
I suppose, and, when it does, comes to seem as immutable as roses.

—John Ashbery, "Flow Chart"

La Condition Humaine

They *still* meet at the Maximilian, as if nothing of substance had changed. As if the old caring waiters in their dotage were *still* solicitously hovering over them. As if the air were crisp and clear, the sky that long-forgotten azure blue and the peaks of Popocatepetl and Ixtaccihuatl, the snow-covered volcanoes in the distance, *still* visible from the roof of any five-story building in Mexico City. They get together out of habit, as if their camaraderie had not yet worn thin. As if they were *still* able to derive pleasure from each other's successes. As if they *still* confided in each other—instead of grudgingly listening with one ear as they spoke of everything under the sun except what mattered. As if they *still* luxuriated in that singular fragrance of their past, confident that their one driving purpose, a single-minded ambition that could be traced as far back as Cervantes, would indubitably enrich all of Mexico, revitalizing the now discredited "institutionalized" revolution and their moribund society.

Food for Thought

In the Distrito Federal alone, the capital of Mexico, soon to be the largest city in the world, there were, at last count, more than thirty thousand restaurants, for every taste, for every pocketbook: a limitless selection—from the Middle Eastern, Adonis, to the Japanese, Daruma; from the English fare at King's Road to the superior French cuisine at Fouquet's or Normandie. For fresh-made pasta it was La Lanterna; for steaks, La Tablita, the Argentinean steak house; for hamburgers, fries, strawberry cheesecake, and milk shakes there was always Delmonico's; and for "nouvelle" Mex, Bar Isadora in the Polanco district was a good bet. . . . So that an overly finicky visitor, such as Jurud, need never sample anything remotely resembling asado de puerco en leche or patas de puerco en escabeche, or tostados grandes or chimichangas; never be compelled to taste such dubious local delicacies as chicken covered with layers of chocolate, or pre-Hispanic exotica such as iguana in pumpkin sauce, prairie dog, or armadillo meatballs in nut sauce.

What did the Aztecs eat? Nutritious meals of corn, sweet potatoes, tortillas, beans, and fruit. They also relished the fungus called huitlacoche, which spreads over diseased kernels of corn and is used in soups and stews. According to historical sources, in Montezuma's court xocoatl, chocolate, was drunk in vast quantities. Chili peppers and vanilla beans were added to enhance the taste. For dysentery, the ground bones of their ancestors were recommended in the chocolate. As for meat . . . that remained an open question. A debatable issue. The ruling class enjoyed turkey, duck, deer, rabbit, wild game, fish, and dogs—a hairless, chubby breed that didn't bark and had no sense of smell. As for the special fragrant stew called tlacatloalli, according to Father Sahagún, still the most authoritative source, the Mayans put "squash blossoms" in the meat, which was served on a stew of dried maize—while the victim's heart, the "precious eagle-cactus fruit," only to be savored by a privileged few, was prepared on a brazier. As for the skulls of the victims, they were strung, like so many beads, on poles and put on display.

What was Alejandro? A descendent of the Toltecs or the Aztecs, or simply part of the Spanish soup created with the able assistance of Cortés's Indian adviser, guide, interpreter, mistress, La Malinche? His response was equivocal: Even though no two people can ever completely agree on any given event in history, history need not derive its impetus only from ruthlessness, rapacity, distortions, and lies. That Cortés with five hundred men and sixteen horses toppled an empire truly verged on the chimerical. Assuredly the timing of his arrival was a contributing factor. Moreover, Cortés had the support of Montezuma's enemies. Still, five hundred against untold thousands? Then with impunity, having enslaved or decimated the Indian population, the Spaniards, with a total disregard for the history of their captives, proceeded almost unwittingly with the evolution of a mestizo nation, implanting in the native Indian women, along with their sperm, their vision of the world. Implanting, along with their spermatozoa, their genetic history, their features, their pale olive skin, their arrogant lies, their greed, their myth-driven quest for the Amazon, their obstinacy, their self-centeredness, and their distrust of woman. Is it any wonder that with regard to history and literature Alejandro remained ambivalent as to his affiliation? Should he side with a Spain that colonized Mexico but also yielded a Cervantes, or with the pre-Columbian empire? At best a difficult choice.

His favorite dishes? His mother used to prepare calabaza guisada con puerco, and hongos guisados con chile estilo querétaro, and nopales al vapor estilo otumba, and the famed mole poblano, chicken in chile and chocolate sauce.

Mercedes, however, couldn't cook to save her life. Her preferences included chocolate. The best chocolate available.

From France, Belgium, Switzerland. Godiva? Wilbur's? Droste? Valrhona? Laederach? But whatever the case, never in chicken mole.

Further Food for Thought

There was no trace of its foreign-sounding name on the unassuming exterior of the restaurant where they were to meet Señor Salas and his assistant, Vali di Vanini. Terrence, after casting an experienced eye over the somber interior, indicated the table of his choice to the headwaiter. Francisco sat facing Señor Salas. Terrence's pleasantry, a comment about the Polanco district, in which they found themselves, was greeted with a knowing smile by Vali di Vanini. If they keep adding more high-rise condos, chic boutiques, and office buildings, stated Salas in Spanish, it'll soon lose all its charm. As Francisco translated for Terrence, Vali remarked, It's our little prosperous Jewish enclave. . . . I don't begrudge them that, said Salas. You should see their country club, said Vali. Does one have to be Jewish to belong? It helps, said Francisco, to the appreciative laughter of Salas. Terrence chose the antipasto del mare, he ordered carciofi con finocchio in pinzimonio. It promised to be a leisurely lunch. In broken Spanish, Terrence consulted with Señor Salas before deciding on a white wine. Señor Salas drank sparingly. He ordered prosciutto e melone. From the almost intimate manner in which Vali di Vanini asked Francisco if there was any truth to the rumor that Mercedes had left Alejandro, Terrence concluded that the two must know each other well.

I wasn't aware that they were ever truly together, Salas asserted.

If your conjecture is based on the fact that she has a place of her own in the Zona Rosa, remarked Francisco out of loyalty to Mercedes, that's her studio, where she does her translations.

Vali gazed at Francisco mischievously. Unlike you, I consider our critic totally inscrutable.

I've always found him rather inoffensive, said Terrence.

I dare say, she said.

I ran into him last week, said Salas. He was with Patricia Estrada. Remember her? Her last film, *Midnight Reckoning*, was a disaster.

They've known each other for years. . . .

There you are. . . . Anyhow, he looked vexed at meeting me.

Doesn't this indicate something's in the air? said Vali.

Seeing that Terrence was having difficulty following the Spanish, Francisco appealed to Vali: Speak a little slower, will you . . . ? I'm so sorry, she said to Terrence. Señor Salas prefers to speak in Spanish. His English is far from fluent.

Terrence grimaced. I understand, but you see—

Señor Salas has less than half a dozen words in English, Francisco interjected, deliberately exaggerating.

I'll have to depend on you to translate, said Terrence. Addressing Salas, speaking slowly: I'm so sorry. I just don't have the time to study Spanish. Tapping his forehead: What's more, I don't have a head for languages.

We'll manage, Vali assured him.

What were you saying?

Just that Mercedes seems to have left Alejandro.

Isn't she teaching somewhere in the U.S.?

Oh, has she given up translating? asked Vali.

Not that I'm aware, said Francisco.

Señor Salas nodded, sympathetically. Sí, sí. Then let slip the word *cabrón*.

What's cabrón? asked Terrence.

Vali, looking embarrassed, said, Oh, dear.

Cuckold, Francisco stated baldly.

Just a joke, said Vali.

Terrence forced a laugh, deftly changing the subject. I expect you heard that Preston, Rita, and I visited the Partridge Museum . . .

I hope you found it a rewarding visit? Vali said with a practiced knowing smile that he found enchanting.

An enriching experience, was Terrence's straight-faced response. I consider the museum to be on par with Dumbarton Oaks in Washington, D.C.

Acknowledging the extravagant compliment, Señor Salas raised his glass. Terrence, glad he had decided to wear his linen suit, responded in kind, then, speaking for Preston, assured Vali of the latter's gratitude for their kind assistance.

We're counting on Francisco to accept the assignment, Vali said to Terrence, as if he and not Francisco were the one to make the decision. The assignment, a book on the museum's prime benefactor, the American consul Anadelle D. Partridge, was made to sound uncomplicated, entailing, at most, several brief visits to the museum. Now turning her attention to Francisco, she promised their full cooperation. Señor Salas will personally see to it that you have access to the museum's files.

If anything, a book on Anadelle Partridge will make the collection more widely known, Terrence asserted.

Francisco, who understood him to say that Preston Hollier was behind the project, looked at Vali inquiringly. I'm not sure that I have all the details . . .

We'll just have to persuade him, said Terrence.

We're counting on *you* to convince him, said Vali.

No, you're the one to do it, Terrence prompted, gazing at her expectantly, eager for the words to come forth—which, at his urging, they did, alluringly, to convey, if not the exact ring of truth, then the pleasant sound of poetry. There it was. They had combined forces, she and Terrence, in order to convince Francisco to accept their offer. Vali indicated that the museum board was in full agreement with their choice. You're the man for us, she said to Francisco. It's as simple as that. Terrence nodded his agreement, then beckoned to the waiter, ordering another bottle of Bordeaux with the composure of someone who expects to pick up the tab—while Señor Salas, in his customary low, measured voice, said in Spanish, Now, having Preston's generous offer of assistance, it's imperative that we begin right away!

Get the show on the road, Vali quipped for Terrence's benefit. Isn't that how you say it?

You bet, said Terrence, looking pleased.

And Vali, like a bird responding to the call of its mate, twittered cheerfully, The material for the book can be augmented by selected diary entries, letters, and notes by the late Anadelle Partridge. In short, everything that concerned the founding of the institute . . .

As you know, she told Francisco, who until now knew nothing of the kind, the publication is to be underwritten by both the museum and Señor Preston Hollier.

Eden Enterprises, Terrence gently corrected her. He was captivated by her voice, the elegance of her gestures, and that magnificent "blanco" face of the Spanish aristocracy. From what sixteenth-century portrait had she emerged?

I've never undertaken such a project before, said Francisco.

She, persuasively: You'll have complete access to the archives. Moreover . . . She paused, querying Francisco. You've had the advantage of having worked for Anadelle Partridge.

Alejandro and I were in our early twenties when we attempted to catalogue her extensive library.

Didn't you once accompany her to the ruins in Yucatán, asked Terrence.

We certainly did.

There you are! she said triumphantly, ignoring his ironic tone. Who better than you?

I hardly knew—

I wonder if the Department of Antiquities would be willing to make available any material they might have, Terrence said, cutting him short.

Not the Department of Antiquities, protested Vali. They've done everything in their power to vilify her. Sheer spite. Professional jealousy. Don't you worry, we'll provide Francisco with all the material he needs.

This book requires considerable research . . .

Rest assured, she said in English, we'll answer any questions you may have . . .

How much of the book is to be devoted to the private as opposed to the public persona?

Skirt the political, Salas advised in Spanish. As for the private—pressing the fingertips of both hands together in a gesture of sincere piety—that must be treated with circumspection!

Yes, Vali was quick to agree. Avoid the political. Anadelle Partridge had the support of President López Portillo. But that's not something to flaunt. As for the private person . . . There's no need, is there, to invade the privacy of the bedroom?

Francisco caught the barest hint of a smile on Señor Salas's smooth round pale face.

You'll find it a rewarding assignment, Vali said encouragingly.

I was told they have a new chef here, Terrence declared. From Del Lago.

Has Señor Terrence eaten here before? Salas inquired in Spanish.

Sí, sí, said Terrence with a broad smile.

To Terrence's chagrin, Francisco equivocated. Could we discuss this again, say in four months. Explaining to Vali, By then I'd be in a better position to reach a decision.

Terrence frowned. I wouldn't hastily reject any offer these good people—

I'm merely stating that I need time to consider—

I hope Francisco doesn't envision obstacles where, in fact, none exist! said Terrence in a voice that was at once colder and more caustic than he might have intended.

Please keep in mind the consul was held in high respect, Señor Salas was quick to add. He then went on to say: Thus far, it has been the left, especially the Marxist-dominated judiciary, that has exercised its inordinate power to prevent the success of the museum!—his remarks effortlessly translated by Vali.

What do you want this book to accomplish? asked Francisco.

It's to serve as a companion to the as yet unpublished museum catalogue. It's to provide a succinct history of Anadelle D. Partridge and the subsequent expansion of the museum under the able directorship of Señor Salas.

That's it?

I won't conceal from you our intention of seeking assistance from American philanthropic institutions such as the Rockefeller, the Ford, and the Getty. Their support would enable us to proceed with our archaeological exploration of Mayan sites.

I wasn't aware that the museum had any such plans in mind.

The paucity of excavations are due to a lack of funds. We know the sites and would prefer to have our own, not predominantly foreign, archaeologists study the many as yet unexplored Mayan sites and areas, such as El Tajín, before they're reduced to rubble by looters, vandals, and the elements. . . . Señora di Vanini extracted two booklets from her briefcase. This is for you, handing one to Francisco; the other she gave to Terrence.

Why, it's in English! exclaimed Terrence. Then, taken aback by the title, *Human Decapitation in the Codex Laud:* A little on the gruesome side, isn't it?

I assure you, it's a scholarly work, said Vali.

I don't doubt it. But is it good publicity?

We desperately need to attract outside attention. This particular booklet, soon to be available in French and Swedish, will serve that purpose.

You realize the book you wish to commission might well provoke adverse reaction from both the left and right, warned Francisco. Consider the equation: a former American consul, a female to boot, a valuable collection of pre-Columbian art, a museum. Not to mention rumors of impropriety—

Señora Partridge donated her entire collection to Mexico, interjected di Vanini.

Anadelle Partridge's opponents carry a lot of clout in the media.

However, nothing Francisco said could shake Vali's conviction that he was the man for this project. No, no, it must be you! she insisted. Terrence ordered osso buco. Francisco chose the rognoncini trifolati. Señor Salas, without glancing at the menu, ordered triglie. When she ordered petto di pollo, she looked to Señor Salas, seeking his approval.

Given my cursory knowledge of museums, I think you'd be better off with a competent art historian.

You've got nothing to fear on that account, Vali said. Then for Terrence's benefit she translated Señor Salas's wishes, really an appeal to Francisco, as Salas, a dignified rotund figure in his tailored dark pin-striped suit, pulled out his checkbook. Francisco, behaving as though this matter were of no direct concern to him, politely watched Señor Salas write out a check, using a large fountain pen. After signing the check with a little flourish, Salas handed it to Vali. As in everything, she, his able assistant, was the conduit. The retainer, she explained, waiting for Francisco to accept it from her.

Francisco's bewilderment was genuine. I don't follow.

Don't pass it up, urged Terrence.

Whose money is this?

It's the advance.

Francisco, seeing the amount on the check, raised his eyebrows.

If after six months you are dissatisfied with the arrangement, you may withdraw, di Vanini announced.

And keep the retainer, Terrence added, as he, with a tiny involuntary sigh, extracted a folded check from his billfold. And this is from Eden Enterprises. You see, you can't lose! After presenting it to Francisco, he turned in his seat and tried to catch the waiter's eye. Vino, he mouthed, pointing at their empty bottle.

Mesmerized, Francisco stared at the two checks. What role does Eden Enterprises play in all this?

We're most eager to be of assistance, said Terrence, trying to sound sincere.

I would need to have something to that effect in writing.

Absolutely, Vali replied. With the stipulations that we retain editorial control and that the book be ready for publication by the time the museum renovations are completed.

And that is to be when?

Ahhhh, we still have some time to go.

Years?

Yes, she laughingly conceded.

Francisco guessed, Two, three, four?

Possibly.

My customary fee, said Francisco, solemnly scrawling the amount on a piece of paper, which he then slid along the white tablecloth to Señora Vali di Vanini. Or fifty percent of royalties, whichever is greater.

She looked to Salas, who, scarcely glancing at the paper, sorrowfully blinked in agreement.

Good enough, drawled Terrence when she handed him the piece of paper on which Francisco had scribbled the amount.

Then we have a deal, Vali said in that marvelous contralto voice.

Terrence ordered melanzane. Vali and Francisco chose the insalata di stagione. Señor Salas, murmuring something to Vali in Spanish, stood up. He was inches shorter than she. Señor Salas apologizes, Vali said, glancing at her elegant gold wristwatch. We have an appointment. Please forgive us. As soon as you have the contract, may I ask you to fax it to the museum. They shook hands.

Terrence and Francisco watched them leave, with Salas preceding her out of the restaurant.

The food is not as good as it used to be, brooded Terrence, his hooded eyes contemplatively following their departure. I should have ordered the mullet sautéed in olive oil.

Francisco was put out. How do you explain their abrupt departure?

What?

Leaving like that before the meal has ended. It's simply not done.

I am going to test the zuppa inglese. What about you?

Looks like they stuck you with the bill.

Terrence, unperturbed: All in a day's lunch.

Francisco ordered macedonia di frutta. When Terrence requested the check, he was ceremoniously informed by the Italian waiter that everything had been taken care off.

Rumors

Once again he had broken out in a rash, and his skin was itching all over. By now rumors were as abundant as the beggar children with hands outstretched near the Zócalo. Faces Alejandro had never seen before solemnly focused their entire attention on him. What had he done to deserve this unwelcome scrutiny? Was it some telltale sign on his medio moreno Mexican face that signaled the deplorable state of his affairs. *Could it be that visible?* Idle gossip. She's left him! he overheard a woman shopper casually mention to a friend in the Bazar del Centro, where he was buying an alarm clock to replace the one he had given Mercedes. *Was the remark aimed at him?* Tattletale. I wouldn't be surprised if she doesn't return, her friend gleefully replied. But who pays any attention to what people in the street may say? He was exploding with anger. The pleasure it gave people to discuss a breakup! With what glee they'd say, She threw him over! Abandoned him! Out of sight, rumors multiplied like the pestilence, contaminating everything in their path. By now Mercedes's whereabouts in the U.S. were common knowledge. *She's with Jurud!* Of course, where else? *She's with Jurud!* Allusions to her absence were everywhere. Slander, defamation . . . Was there really any point in concealing that Mercedes had left him? Suddenly, for no particular reason, he'd read into the most innocuous occurrences—a woman's bare arm reaching out to close a window, a woman's taciturn face in a passing bus, the sight of an empty parked car, its motor running, a man glancing up at a window—a meaning not unrelated to his present quandary. The *abandoned* husband? In a country where the transmission of this deadly pestilence had been perfected to an art, poisonous rumors spawn paranoia and ill will. She's gone. She? Who? What precisely was she to him? His *love?* Didn't she also denote his preferential station as critic, his dignity, his manhood! Each day another blemish. Feverishly he scratched until he drew blood on his forearm. The cuckold adapts himself to the vilest misrepresentation, until each morning he can hear the intolerable song of the birds madly chirping away in the dying trees: *She's left him! She's* . . . The rumors gnaw at every impediment, clearing a path, insidiously tunneling their way from one home to the next, attacking every barrier. *She's with Jurud!* Nothing can be done to obstruct their pernicious advance. *She's in the U.S. with Jurud.* In Mexico, where betrayal is so well understood, every man has grown up with the dread as well as the anticipation of it. . . . Because La Malinche, who slept with Cortés and bore him a child, betrayed every one of her countrymen, modern Mexico began with an act of treachery. The mestizo race is simply the consequence of this apostasy. One might say that these all-too-credible rumors of perfidy call to mind history's irreversibility. Now how was he to react to the rumors that despite the announcements, the well-laid plans, the TV interviews, the festive dinner, the panel discussion, Jurud wasn't coming to Mexico? Was he, Alejandro, being a little too rational, a little too restrained, or, perhaps, even too fearful to let anyone glimpse the actual dimensions of his bitterness? In the face of these insinuations, would the unassuming lawyer in *La Femme infidèle* be any more capable of controlling his disquiet? As for the rumors . . . Don't they proliferate in order to animate the fiestas and the parades? To enliven the church gatherings? It is even said that due to the rich availability of rumors, there's little interest in the novel. Truly, what need do they have of fiction, since women's turpitude is readily acknowledged . . . even women sadly come to recognize themselves as mirror images of La Malinche, that evil feminine spirit who, fluent in Maya and Nahuatl, the language of the Aztecs, pointed Cortés to victory over her people, her society, her gods. Here, she indicated, that's how you'll defeat *us!* Without La Malinche, Cortés would not have succeeded. Never! Not in a thousand years. Is it any wonder that Mexicans, cursed with a total recall of past inequities, cannot shed their distrust—seeing in each woman the potential betrayer, the potential La Malinche. With their self-esteem at stake, Mexicans, knowing as they do the weakness and the emotional instability of women, can exclude none of them, even their wives, sisters, daughters, from the suspicion that, left to their own devices, they'd promptly succumb to the first man's sexual overture.

By now Alejandro had taken appropriate countermeasures—grim-faced, armed with a deadly resolve, he daily swept the cafés he visited, the houses of his friends, even the public parks and the museums, for the presence of rumors. By now he was willing to deal with them. To confront the slander. To have it out, once and for all.

Critical Limitations

By the time Raúl arrived, an hour late, Alejandro and Francisco were well into the large bottle of tequila an enthusiastic soccer fan at a nearby table had sent over with his compliments. They're over there, Alejandro heard the waiter inform Raúl, who, like them, for the coming game wore the loose-fitting red shorts and yellow tunic, with the letter *M* for Maxi emblazoned in red on his back. I just had a call from Jacobus, Raúl said breathlessly, as he sat down. He wanted to know if I had any inkling of Jurud's whereabouts. . . .

He's in a panic, calling everyone, Francisco declared with an uncalled-for expression of delight.

Raúl, looking to Alejandro, as if expecting him to know: Well? Where is he?

How should I know? For the time of year, it was an unusually cool day—a day that would remain firmly fixed in his memory.

I needed to put myself in the proper frame of mind for tonight's game, Francisco declared, so I took the morning off.

What did you do?

Just walked about aimlessly, ending up in the museum, where I spent a couple of hours with some of my favorites.

Raúl, evincing incredulity at the coincidence: Just what I had in mind.

You don't say? This morning?

I left my house at eleven.

So did I.

Then I changed my mind.

Pity. We could have met.

Francisco poured liberally from the half-full bottle. It was a domestic brand he wasn't fond of.

Bring us some of the fried shrimps and baby cactus, Alejandro told a passing waiter.

But when the small dishes were served, after one mouthful he pushed his plate aside.

What's the matter? Raúl asked.

Mine are not tasty.

They're a little off, Francisco agreed, putting down his fork with a grimace of distaste.

Mine taste just fine, Raúl maintained, continuing to eat with apparent gusto.

I'll inform the waiter, said Francisco.

Why bother, said Alejandro. It's time we left.

Again it was Raúl who, as always, insisted on paying—who struggled with Francisco over the check. Oh, let him have it, said Alejandro, losing his patience. As they were leaving, he remarked that for the next three days his father was showing Buñuel's *That Obscure Object of Desire*.

An infuriating movie, exclaimed Francisco, with an expression that matched his reaction to the shrimp.

Why so? Is it because Buñuel loves to denigrate respectability?

He toys with his characters in a most disagreeable manner—

Disagreeable or not, Raúl said heatedly as he halted outside the bar—for this was an emotional issue—the humiliating spectacle of the older man's passion for the younger woman in *That Obscure Object of Desire* resonates with a painful truth. . . .

Francisco winked at Alejandro as he stated, Two actresses playing the identical role to confuse the audience is not my idea of exploring any truth.

Truth is truth, no matter what, Raúl maintained stubbornly, ignoring Francisco's condescending tone. Once we lose our grip on the truth——

Not unmindful of Raúl's evident reverence for the Spanish filmmaker, Alejandro quoted Buñuel as having asserted that most of the film's audience wouldn't notice that two young actresses who didn't even resemble each other were alternately performing the identical role.

Isn't that precisely what you'd expect him to say, Francisco burst out, to Alejandro's surprise. The prig!

Not if you accept the interchangeability of our love objects, Alejandro remarked.

For that matter, said Raúl, undeterred by Francisco's derisive hoots, truth has little or no bearing on desire. Our emotions are not swayed by truth.

What drivel, commented Francisco. I'm surprised that you take seriously what at heart is sheer improvisation. Most likely, when one of Buñuel's actresses failed to show, he used another in her stead. Movie directors have no principles. They improvise, they adapt . . . and the audience, fools that they are, try to read a meaning into this extemporaneous divertissement.

Nothing could be more reasonable than Buñuel's depiction of the frustrated, aging lover, Alejandro countered. In the grip of desire, the poor man's longing impairs his reasoning.

For me, Buñuel's film defines the privileges of an old-fashioned "gentleman" who idealizes women. . . . I can't tell for sure if the fool is trying to regain his lost youth or his lost class.

The love object is a fantasy, argued Raúl. In case you didn't notice, the aging protagonist is simply an updated version of Don Quixote accompanied by his Sancho Panza.

That only goes to show that Buñuel, whose films refer to the past, was himself hopelessly mired in that past, said Francisco.

Unwilling to acknowledge Francisco's animosity, Alejandro said, Buñuel was terrified.

Francisco stared at Alejandro, as if he couldn't believe his eyes. Of what?

Of their rampant sexuality. Why else would he set out to misrepresent their seductive power? Why else would he resort to all these cinematic stratagems?

Frankly, I never expected such a vacuous comment from you, said Francisco. Thank God you're not a movie critic.

Raúl bared his teeth, anticipating an altercation.

The two actresses alternately playing the same character are consistent with Buñuel's upstaging of the viewer, Francisco continued. It comes down to a kind of infantile showing off: See what I can do. . . . See how clever I am. . . .

Nonsense, said Alejandro. The two actresses playing the same role were cynically designed to reify the force of the feminine. . . . But you should know by now!

I don't waste my time in stuffy movie houses being diddled by a supercilious Spanish hypocrite, Francisco said, with a self-satisfied look. If you allow yourself to be taken in by cinematic chicanery . . .

I admit I do not possess your expertise with women, Alejandro began, taken by surprise when Francisco punched him forcefully in the arm. What the hell! Clenching his fist to retaliate.

Stop it, shouted Raúl, laughing as he grabbed Alejandro by the arm. You're behaving like schoolboys.

He's been goading me all along, said Francisco furiously.

You're off your head.

Coming from you, that's a laugh.

Raúl intervened: Now, look here. But Francisco, looking aggrieved—I've had my fill—strode ahead, leaving them behind.

Still nursing his arm, Alejandro complained, Has he gone berserk?

He'll get over it.

What's got into him?

He's pissed.

Why?

How should I know?

I feel sick. I'm leaving.

Not till after the game you're not.

Now!

You're our goalie.

I'm tired to death of being goalie.

Hey, Francisco, Raúl yelled. Wait for us. But pretending not to hear, Francisco strode ahead, if anything he increased his pace.

Let the fool go, said Alejandro, feeling slighted. His former animosity to Raúl temporarily forgotten, he persuaded the latter to join him for a drink at Max's. Side by side at the crowded bar, he sought Raúl's advice: What's got into Francisco?

I wouldn't read too much into it.

I don't know what's come over him. Ever since he accepted the commission to write a book on Anadelle Partridge . . .

He's being well paid, Raúl pointed out.

All the same, there are limits.

You disapprove?

I wouldn't touch the assignment for all the money in the world.

He's not in your position!

Why do you say that? Alejandro asked querulously. Given the noise level in the now crowded bar, he soon found it a strain to listen to Raúl's convoluted rationalization. What did you say? Speak up. Then, exasperated by Raúl's meandering account and the increasing din, he turned to leave. I need some air, he said, slapping money on the counter. No, no, protested Raúl, let me. . . . Alejandro pushed his way to the door, only to be waylaid by Humberto, a colleague from his department. Gripping his arm to make sure that he did not escape, Humberto, who was much taller, thrust him toward the statuesque blonde at his side. Meet Dr. Alejandro Mucho, Humberto said deridingly, our reigning critic and goalkeeper. Accepting her cue from this maladroit introduction, she greeted Alejandro with a playful: How are you, Professor? Suppressing his annoyance, Alejandro chatted with them about the forthcoming game, aware that Humberto, in a deliberately provocative gesture, was stroking her buttock with the palm of his right hand. She pretended not to notice, but her voice, becoming more and more high-pitched, gave her away. See you later, said Alejandro. Once outside the bar, he joined the mostly good-natured throng heading for the nearby parking lot, happy not to speak to anyone. There were far more people than anticipated on the makeshift football field. The hastily constructed goals had no nets, but they seemed sturdy enough. In the growing dark, Alejandro spotted Jacobus in earnest conversation with a reporter from *El Heraldo*. Jacobus, with whom he had lunched at Fonda del Refugio that day, seemed to take pains to avoid looking in his direction. Alva, on the other hand, standing out in her black leather trousers, arm in arm with the man he had seen her with once before, was more forthcoming, shrilly calling out, Good luck, Alejandro!

Salas, less well intentioned, came over to inquire, Aren't we getting a little old for games?

Alejandro, not a bit upset, quipped, Is forty mid-life?
Do you intend to reach it?

What's it like? he countered.

Salas grinned idiotically. Anything can yet take place.

I take it, it still has promise?

In Mexico, the ending is inscribed on our skulls and in our hearts the moment we are born.

Returning to his goal, Alejandro strapped on his chin guard, then, with eyes closed, took a deep breath, expelled it, took another deep breath . . . with each breath expelling his rancor, his misgivings, his antipathies. Thinking: It's good to be alive, good to be alive. . . .

Tensing, he watched the center forward take aim before kicking a low, accurate shot at the goal. To his relief, he caught it easily, exuberantly tossing it back to the players waiting for a practice shot. Crouching in front of the goal, Alejandro readied himself for the next. . . . It was high, drifting to the left. Leaping, he saved it with his fists. With each practice shot he was gaining confidence.

The game itself remained a blur. Some prankster had broken a set of lights at Alejandro's end. Half an hour into the game, the other lights went on the blink. The players continued as best they could in the glare of truck headlights. The bystanders, in some places standing two deep, were howling with laughter at the antics of the players, who kept fumbling the ball in the semidarkness. Now and then—was it to enliven the scene?—someone chucked an empty bottle into the parking lot. Screaming, the viewers ducked as it shattered. Minutes before halftime, Alejandro saw the Fortunas' center forward receive the ball and kick it in the direction of the goal, a split second before the headlights were inexplicably extinguished. Divining the ball's direction, Alejandro dove for it in the near-total darkness, exhilarated as he felt the rewarding thump of the ball against his chest. Ball tightly clasped in his arms, he fell to the ground, only to receive a kick in his back, then another. The less vicious kicks that followed seemed to come from another source but, like the first two, were intended—of this he was convinced—not to dislodge the football but to cause injury. As he blacked out, he could hear the sound of his half-stifled scream reaching him as if from a great distance. He was still clutching the ball when the referee came running with his flashlight. . . . Someone brought a first aid kit. Helped to his feet, he managed to stagger toward a limousine parked conveniently near the goal and throw up, seeing particles of a leisurely consumed lunch with Jacobus at the Fonda del Refugio spattered all over the license plate. He then collapsed and had to be driven to the emergency room. He didn't get home until well after 2:00 a.m.

In bed, he tossed and turned, unable to sleep. He was just dropping off when the elevator door slammed shut. Barefoot, he walked to the window in time to see a woman leave the building. Her high heels made a sharp, urgent feminine sound as she crossed the street. Though she didn't resemble Mercedes, something about her walk reminded him of her. Leaning out the window, he watched until she was out of sight. When he checked his watch it was twenty to four. He still hadn't slept a wink.

Rude Awakening

Next morning he was wakened by the telephone. Father's dead, his brother announced. It took him a moment to grasp the essence of what had been said. Dead? Groaning slightly, he tried to raise himself into an upright position. Every part of his body still ached. Did you say . . . ? Listen! Diego shouted. Father's dead! No matter what, Diego couldn't shake his rudeness, not even when he called to convey the news of their father's death, so that Alejandro was compelled to deal with the sudden impact of his father's death and his younger brother's characteristically blunt and discourteous voice as well. Alejandro couldn't recollect the last time he and Diego had exchanged more than a few words. Was it at their mother's funeral? Rudeness was the shelter behind which his brother seemed to live a more or less contented life with his wife and children. Alejandro often wondered how Diego was able to hold on to any of his friends. . . . I don't find him rude, his father had said. Diego's simply impatient. Once you overlook his irascibility, he can be extremely considerate. However, each time they met, after less than a minute in Diego's presence Alejandro felt a strong impulse to punch that smug expression of complacency. Needless to say, a good-looking face, a handsome face Diego had inherited from their mother's side of the family. You used to squabble endlessly, his father acknowledged. You were always at each other's throats. As far as Alejandro was concerned, Diego didn't even have to say anything—just that insufferable look of aloofness sufficed to set his teeth on edge. Women mostly mistook Diego's rudeness for self-confidence. Infuriated, Alejandro wanted to announce to the world, Diego's got no money, he's got nothing. Nada! He's dependent on my father's handouts. But then women are notoriously inept when it comes to assessing handsome men.

It was an easy death, Diego said. With a tiny inappropriate chortling sound, he mentioned that their father had died while watching a movie.

Oh? Instantly alert. What film?

Diego snorted. He was watching *That Obscure Object of Desire.*

Had his father chosen to show that film as a farewell gesture?

An overrated movie, his brother said disapprovingly. All that Christian balderdash, with its absurd emphasis on the virgin . . .

He could not remember the last time he and Diego had agreed on anything. Yet Mercedes had not found him disagreeable. He seems nice enough, she had said after speaking with Diego, who had shown up for their wedding, only to leave early, not attending the dinner. I don't find him rude at all. Now, with his head throbbing, Alejandro tried to think of what needed to be done.

We'll have to make the arrangements.

They're made.

He was outraged. You didn't consult me.

I must have tried at least a hundred times to reach you.

Was anyone present when he died?

No. Angela was closing the premises.

Angela?

She's a new girl I hired. The last reel of the film was still running. Father had slumped over in his chair. From all evidence, he must have died peacefully. His face was serene.

Then what?

Angela called me. As you can imagine, she was in a state.

And you did what?

I rushed over. . . . There was nothing I could do. I called his doctor. He came over straightaway and, after I had pressed him, reluctantly made out a death certificate. . . . I then called the undertaker he recommended.

And all this time you didn't try to reach me?

Remember, Diego said, not raising his voice, I did have a lot of things on my mind.

Where are you calling from?

At the moment we're at Dad's apartment, just straightening things. . . .

I'm coming over.

I'm just locking up.

I'm coming over! Did it sound like a threat?

I won't be here. . . .

I have a key.

Diego was incensed. How did you get it? As if he had no right to the key. Dad never mentioned that you had a key. Then, petulantly surrendering to the inevitable: Well, if you insist . . . But before hanging up, he couldn't resist a final admonition. Just try not to disturb anything, will you? Father has left a will, I believe. . . . A deliberate slap in the face! You son of a bitch, Alejandro said into the dead phone. You fucking bastard!

Flawed Connection

Mercedes returned his call soon after receiving the message he had left with the secretary of the Spanish Department—she promised to fly back at once for the funeral. There's no need, really. Everyone knows you're in the U.S. How will it look if I'm not there? she said. The next day, she called once again to give him the time of her arrival. But then, to his dismay, she failed to arrive at the given time. Exasperated, Alejandro made inquiries and was told that there was another Delta flight, this one from Kennedy Airport, landing an hour and a half later. He reasoned that she might have missed her flight. While having a drink in one of the small bars in the terminal, he spotted an old girlfriend, Alicia Menzel, who was waiting for her boyfriend, a journalist, returning from an overseas assignment. Knowing Alejandro to be an acquaintance of Preston's, she mentioned that the evening news on Channel 13, where she worked, would focus on Preston and his shady Eden Enterprise. What's so shady about it? Any American entity named Eden Enterprise that is investing heavily in real estate must be, she concluded. They had a drink together. Her leg grazed his like a question mark as she explained that her divorce had just been finalized. I hardly know anyone who's still married, she declared with a look of satisfaction. I guess you and Mercedes have always been an exception. As she laughed, he could see that she was missing an upper tooth. It left an unsightly gap. He mentioned his father's death, not expecting her to break into tears. Such a considerate man, she said. I wasn't aware that you knew him. You introduced me. You used to take me to see the movies . . . or have you forgotten? Reluctantly Alejandro gave her the details for the funeral. I'll be there tomorrow, she promised. Before leaving, she kissed him on the lips, an ardent moist kiss. Take care of yourself! As soon as she was out of sight, he scrubbed his lips with a handkerchief to remove the unpleasant wet reminder. When the next plane landed without Mercedes, he checked to see if there were any messages on his answering machine. He then tried to reach the college in Massachusetts, but the secretary in the Spanish Department was gone for the day. He was trying to come to some decision on what to do next, when he was hailed by Irena. It's me, Irena, she said when he failed to recognize her. She had just returned from a book tour in Canada. In Canada? I didn't know they were interested in Mexican writers. They're interested in Mexican feminists, she explained. At least the people who invited me to lecture were. . . . When he mentioned the reason for his being at the airport, she embraced him warmly. I was fond of your father, she said. It was the second time that afternoon that he found himself being ardently kissed on the lips. I'm so sorry, she said. Deciding not to wait any longer for Mercedes, Alejandro offered Irena a lift to the city. She was overjoyed. What good fortune, letting him carry her suitcase to the car. I don't believe in accidents, do you? she said, her look of inquiry changing into an unsettling stare. When she repeated, I don't believe in accidents—as if thereby revealing a momentous inner truth—he tried to mollify her, saying, Sure, sure, though by no means certain if by "accident" she meant chance or misadventure. While driving, he noted a tiny scar on the inside of her wrist. It was a self-inflicted scar produced by a sharp knife or a razor, he decided, unsuccessfully trying to determine if there was a matching scar on the inside of her other wrist.

What are you working on?

She pursed her lips, then, looking past him, revealed that it was a book on desire—that is to say, women's desires.

Trying to lighten the mood, he joked, Why do women keep them so well concealed?

Her laughter had a hysterical edge to it, he decided. To his relief, she ignored his question, asking instead, What'll happen to the Riva Palacio now that your father is dead?

Diego, my brother, will run it, he said morosely.

It won't be the same. Empathically, she touched his sleeve. By now he regretted having offered her a lift.

As they reached the city center, she looked out the window, shaking her head. I should have stayed in Canada. I felt so free up there. Then, once again fixing him with that unnerving stare of hers: If only men would learn to lie more convincingly.

Is that what you really want?

As long as they tell a woman what she wishes to hear, yes.

He was debating whether or not to inform her about the funeral if she asked, but she didn't.

Next morning he called the college in Massachusetts and left a message for Mercedes. Within an hour she returned his call. He could barely control himself. Why the hell didn't you show up yesterday? You told me it wasn't necessary, she protested. That I needn't come . . . that people would understand. I did, and your response was to say that you were coming. You then called to give me the time of your arrival. Or have you forgotten?

As soon as you made it clear that my presence wasn't essential, I canceled—

Are you mad? Are you completely insane?

If that's your attitude, then we have nothing left to say.

Wait a minute. I'd like to clear up this misunderstanding. There's nothing further to—

He hung up. She called back, shrieking, Don't you ever hang up on me again, before banging down the receiver.

Flowers

What are those? Rita asked the florist, pointing at a bunch of pale blue flowers.

African marigold.

And those?

The florist lifted his gaze from the giant bouquet he was assembling. With a trace of irritation, he said, Brazilian bleeding heart, a fumariaceous flower.

And those?
Love-lies-bleeding, an amaranthine flower.
No, to their left.
Delphinium.
Undecided, she looked at the vast array of flowers in the enormous glassed-in refrigerated unit, trying to find the right color, the right message for this particular occasion.
I'll take those. What are they?
Brazilian hotspurs.

Charlie, their chauffeur, admired the flowers Rita was carrying when she returned to the car. Beautiful.
She, pleased: Aren't they.

Funeral

Diego, for once subdued, the rudeness held in check, sat beside Alejandro in the front row gazing mournfully at the coffin of their father. The tiny neighborhood church was packed with an overflow congregation that included filmmakers, film critics, members of the influential Cineteca Nacional and IMCINE, the Mexican Cinema Institute. Was it in order to demonstrate a more than passing knowledge of the cinema that the elderly priest, in the middle of his sermon, rhetorically raised the question: Was our dear departed friend, in choosing *That Obscure Object of Desire* as his going-away movie, trying to tell us something? Launching himself into the emotional caldron of the movie, written and directed by none other than Luis Buñuel, a devoted if often iconoclastic friend of the Church, he stated: This film is to be regarded as a baptism . . . an unexpected initiation for Don Mateo, a worldly, cultivated man—an aesthete, a connoisseur of life who, blessed with worldly resources, has been able to skirt the inconveniences if not the terrors of existence, until his fateful encounter with Conchita, whose actual name is Concepción, as we discover belatedly when she and her mother, Encarnación, at the instigation of Don Mateo, are being expelled from France as undesirable aliens. A man in his late fifties, Don Mateo, who admits that he never had a relationship with a woman he did not love passionately, is being put to a severe test . . . a test for which he, a reasonable man at heart, finds himself ill equipped. "You only want what I refuse you," Concepción maintains. "That's not all of me." Concepción is willing to live with him, but, to his dismay, she rejects his idea of sexual union. Why? Because I am a virgin. The more she resists, the more his infatuation clouds his judgment. It is as if Buñuel, in his final film, has gone out of his way to proclaim that the inability to attain fulfillment is the key to our humanity. Two dissimilar actresses playing the role of Concepción deny Don Mateo the attainment, the fulfillment of his desire. As her name implies, Concepción is the act of becoming, the capacity, function, or process of forming ideas. Her refusal becomes the stimulus . . . until, goaded beyond a rich man's endurance, he acts forcefully. But, Concepción, like the source of belief, remains outside the reach of reason. The benignly smiling elderly Mexican priest resisted reaching a conclusion. Instead he spoke of Alejandro and Diego's father's extreme dedication, his prescience, his magnanimity, his altruism, compassion, and popularity. He concluded by stating that the Church, notwithstanding its reputation as a stern upholder of morality, was not unsympathetic to the aims of the young Mexican filmmakers. Entreating the filmmakers and critics among the mourners not to dismiss the Church: We are here to serve you. Arms outspread, he said, We welcome diversity. Following the sermon, a board member of IMCINE, as a mark of the institute's appreciation for the services their father had rendered to the Mexican cinema, presented a posthumous award to a grief-stricken Diego.

I can't get over the dumbness of it, Patricia said as they were filing out of the church. Francisco was under the impression that she was referring to the minister's interpretation of Buñuel's movie. Oh, that? I wasn't paying attention. All that intellectual drivel . . . No, I mean handing Diego the award. How inappropriately timed . . . Besides, shouldn't Alejandro have been the recipient?

Francisco found himself with Rita and Terrence in the back of the air-conditioned Lincoln stretch limo, which in addition to a bar and a telephone contained a CD player and a TV with VCR. Looking jaunty in his dark suit, with a yellow tie to set off the blue shirt, Terrence commented, Not a bad turnout . . . Even the senator's aide showed up.

How long do we wait? Rita asked Francisco, as if he was apprised of the scheduling.

Shouldn't be too long.

I didn't see Mercedes.

She didn't return in time.

Who's with Alejandro?

His family, in addition to Jacobus.

Why Jacobus?

Alejandro asked Jacobus to ride with him in the lead car, said Rita, stretching her feet, snuggling up against Terrence. He can't get along with Diego. He needed an ally.

Whatever has happened to Jurud? Terrence asked Francisco.

Francisco, morosely: Your guess is as good as mine.

Will he show?

Rita laughed. Have you ever known a writer to turn down a free trip?

Jurud has a room reserved for him at the Astoria, Terrence said.

Why do the publishers always pick the most antiseptic hotels?

Looking out the car window, Francisco kept seeking, in the motions of the young Mexican in jeans who was steering a power mower back and forth across the wide expanse of lawn, relief from the oppressiveness of the funeral.

I sure could use one of Preston's daiquiris, Rita admitted. Where *is* Preston?

He had a meeting he couldn't cancel, said Rita. . . . Yesterday Alejandro waited over three hours for Mercedes to arrive . . . and she didn't. Rita's laugh sent a shiver down Francisco's back.

The imperturbable-looking chauffeur kept reading an *El Financiero* someone must have left behind in the car. Francisco noticed that the red and yellow button on his lapel bore the map of Cuba.

Terrence, badly in need of diversion, leaned forward to inquire, in his broken Spanish, Have you got any hot tips? But the driver, an old hand at dealing with foreigners, pretended not to hear.

After further delays, the line of stretch limos began to move forward at a snail's pace.

When the time comes, I'm for cremation minus stretch limos, Rita baldly announced.

I know for a fact that these cremation societies retain every ounce of gold they find in the teeth, said Terrence. They sell it to dentists at half price. . . .

You're being ghoulish, Rita complained.

Terrence chuckled. I'm not, but this country is.

Is that right, Francisco? Rita asked.

Yes. We are obsessed by death. A fascination, a—

No, what Terrence said about the teeth. That they remove the gold . . .

Oh, I wouldn't know.

Promise?

Now what do we see? Was it the finely tapered finger of fate? Calm, detached, Francisco's brain was prepared to overlook everything that was injurious to the function of the self.

The tall palms still fronted the old apartment building on the south side of Río Churubusco Avenue. Now and then the phone rang; intermittently the doorbell. Signals that might, as far as Francisco was concerned, have been triggered from outer space. Now contemplating the icons of his surroundings, the row of pre-Columbian figurines Rita had given him, seeking what remained stable, though his eyes could not help but return to the weblike crack that continued its inexorable advance up the apartment wall. Now on the phone, renewing life, as he listened to Rita's resonant, even, precise, untroubled voice— the fine, persuasive extension of a cultivated mind that was able to see light-years into the future.

But you'll come with me, she concluded.

Preston isn't going to be happy about it, Francisco stated flatly. He was simply presenting his case. It was not intended as an argument. I get the distinct impression that he suspects. . . .

Nonsense. You have an overactive imagination.

I think—

Trust me!

Francisco trusted her timing, her impulses, her selections, and especially her impeccable taste. Taste was her trademark. How could her exquisite taste not win over those visitors who happened to wander into her and Preston's bedroom and come face-to-face with the goddess Tlazoltéotl, twenty centimeters high, from postclassical Mexico, in gleaming aplite speckled with garnets, on a white Formica shelf, crouching in the act of childbirth, her teeth bared in a frightful grimace, as the baby the goddess was bringing forth emerged from between her legs with a gargoylelike frown, its hands thrust forward, as it poised itself to dive into the world?

Yet to Francisco's mind, there were fleeting moments—such as the time when she pressed him to accept her gift of the silk pajamas he'd never wear—when her heartfelt good taste seemed a trifle overstated.

Jurud's Reception

As soon as they passed through the cast-iron gate of the massive turn-of-the-century building, a man in formal attire and black tie, whom Francisco at first took to be the embassy butler, ceremoniously welcomed them. From afar, several guests glanced expectantly in their direction, but the man marched them to the guestbook, in the opposite direction. Glimpsing Francisco's look of incomprehension, Rita whispered, He's the ambassador. Would you be so kind, the ambassador said, paternally presiding over them as they signed. The task completed to the ambassador's satisfaction, they were approached by a uniformed maid bearing a tray of Mexican delicacies. Francisco observed a tall, elegant woman in an off-the-shoulder dress detach herself from a small group of guests, all looking distinctly forlorn as they stood near the bar at the far end of the cheerless wood-paneled reception room, and unhurriedly make her way toward them, only to change her mind midway and head for the sideboard instead. . . . The ambassador's wife, Rita whispered in his ear at the first opportunity, while the ambassador pretended not to hear. After a quick look at the food on the sideboard, the woman picked up a tidbit, which she popped into her mouth. Even with her mouth full she lost none of her incomparable self-assurance. Though other people kept arriving, the ambassador remained steadfastly at their side, amiably talking about the weather, a recent trip he had taken to Paris, and raising orchids, until Francisco, feeling himself conversationally depleted, wondered peevishly why the ambassador didn't have anything better to do. It was a relief when they were joined by the two Mexican diplomats Maximino Cardona and Moreno Velasco, both in the city between overseas assignments. The two, having met Rita and her husband at some prior function, greeted her enthusiastically. However, seeing Francisco at her side, they tactfully refrained from asking after Preston. We're celebrating, said Moreno. I've just turned fifty, his friend volunteered, then executed a little Spanish dance of exuberance that elicited from Rita an amused look of incomprehension. In Mexico the fiftieth birthday is serious business, Francisco explained. Don't listen to him, he's far too young to even hazard a guess, Moreno joked.

Sitting in front of a giant blowup of the jacket cover of *Intimidad*, the mariachi band in their silver-studded black uniforms, until now concealed behind the curtained-off section, began to play with wild abandon as the black curtain was swept aside. The ambassador's wife, who had joined the little group that included Francisco and her husband, covered her ears in mock dismay. Where is our guest of honor? Moreno loudly demanded to know, twisting his neck, as if expecting to spot Jurud in the crowd. He still hasn't come, Francisco explained. The ambassador smoothly changed the subject, mentioning that Ring Lardner had once stayed at the embassy. Marvelous writer, said Maximino, while his friend Moreno took this opportunity to laud American writers. They're so unlike us. They're so transparent.

The ambassador's wife wondered, Transparent?

Well, without textual guile.

Moreno agreed, However, there's a concreteness to their world, a welcome lack of abstract thinking. Things exist to be identified. There's still the belief that negativity, which we prize, is to be challenged and overcome. . . . But he looked puzzled by his friend's reservations. Aren't the Americans overly determined to read either success or failure into every one of their pursuits?

On the contrary, their drive, their intensity, their lack of inhibition, is not reduced by historical or metaphysical speculation. . . . The imagination is not endangered, as it is in Mexico, if you follow my meaning. Everything in the U.S. is set in that eternal present. That carefree Now.

Surely not carefree? protested Rita.

Besides, one learns so much about their latest contraptions. It's like reading a Sears catalogue. Even the landscape is compartmentalized and numbered.

Are you going to let them get away with it? the ambassador's wife asked her husband.

He smiled. I welcome an opportunity to listen to critics of their caliber.

Well, I, for one, mistrust the superfluous details, said Max-imino. American fiction doesn't just provide the breakup, or the purchase of a house, or the destruction of a car. . . . The reader is supplied with the minutiae, the incidental details of these circumstances. I ask you, do we need this willed verisimilitude?

That's what's so exciting, said the ambassador's wife.

I'm troubled by anything that is so devoid of the mysteri-ous, declared Maximino. In America, one look and everything is clarified. This instant supermarket discernment can be fatigu-ing. The contents are listed on everything.

Have you read Jurud? Rita asked politely.

Of course. I'm to sit near him at the forthcoming gala dinner. . . . He's not going to catch me napping. I know the ins and outs of his WASP pecking order.

Poor Jacobus, he's fit to be tied, the ambassador's wife cheerily remarked.

He'll come. He has to . . . after my taking all this trouble to read his book in English and getting to know the behavioral idiosyncrasies of the upper middle class, said Moreno.

I'm sure Jacobus has all kinds of contingency plans, said the ambassador.

We once met him, Maximino announced.

Really? What's he like? the ambassador's wife wanted to know.

Smooth, urbane . . .

He's unobtrusive, Moreno concurred. A tallish sort of man . . . With his hand he tried to estimate Jurud's height. Very reserved . . . almost withdrawn.

Personally, I thought he was angry-looking, said Maximino.

Angry?

Well, he glowered at me.

Come now.

He certainly didn't radiate friendship.

Candidly, I doubt that we'd recognize him if he were here. He was indistinguishable from the others—don't you agree?

You mean, for all we know, he might be in this room, listening to us. . . .

I assure you he's not here, said the ambassador, in a voice of disapproval. I for one—

He never completed his sentence, for to Rita's relief, his wife gaily interjected, Darling, did you know that Mr. and Mrs. Hollier have purchased the former consul Anadelle Partridge's country house?

Villa, murmured Francisco.

Ah, the late honorary consul . . . a formidable lady, said the ambassador, trying to show interest.

Did you ever meet her? Rita inquired.

Never had the pleasure.

She had lots of influential friends, I'm told, remarked Rita, looking to the ambassador's wife for corroboration. Isn't that true?

Given her looks, she seemed to have done remarkably well, the ambassador's wife confirmed—capping her irreverent remark with the rhetorical question: Didn't she have a thing with El Señor, the former minister of the interior, or was it tourism?

Though the ambassador showed little outward reaction to his wife's undiplomatic assertion, his silence served as a rebuke.

Francisco is to write a book about our Anadelle, Rita said archly. . . . For the Partridge Museum, that is. If she hoped for some further grandiloquent response from the ambassador's wife, she was disappointed, for sensing her husband's disapproval, the latter limited her response to: How timely.

A daunting project, stated the ambassador.

Francisco, behaving more and more like an incompliant

youngster who was present against his wish, nodded with an unbecoming petulant grimace: You might think so.

Seemingly unperturbed by this rank incivility, the ambassador managed a genial: Good for you . . . his voice appearing to issue forth from a distant set of stereo speakers.

In fact, I may soon have to visit Washington to get more material on her, Francisco announced. The remark took Rita by surprise. The ambassador could see she was upset as she faced Francisco. Is that really necessary? Francisco, whose new Italian-cut suit was a little too broad in the shoulders and a little tight in the waist, squirmed as she dismissed his explanation. Finally, not able to contain himself any longer, he burst out, I don't see why I have to justify my research. To prevent an all-out altercation between Rita and her lover, the ambassador loudly stated to his wife, We really must take a day and visit the Partridge Museum. It's an exceptional collection, I've been told.

Darling, have you forgotten? You're on the board, she said with a tiny laugh, then impishly exclaimed, Men! as if men couldn't possibly keep these functions that are so essential to any sort of social interaction straight in their head.

That may be so, said the ambassador, but I've never attended any of their board meetings.

You're listed on the letterhead—that's what counts.

Rita, still glaring at Francisco, offered that she and Preston had been roped in to assist the museum. And that after just visiting it once. Then, adopting the tone of the rich who all too often are saddled with these honorary obligations, she said, in a voice of resignation, I suppose it's a worthwhile cause.

Trying to appease Rita, Francisco explained to the ambassador that he needed background material on the late consul. She was married to an influential Washington lawyer. . . .

I remember him, said the ambassador. I was in Washington at the time.

Didn't he die in a . . . ?

Something quite absurd. It was a freak accident. . . .

Surely you were too young, said Rita. This happened ages ago.

I grew up in Washington, the ambassador explained. My father served in the State Department under Acheson.

You and our Fuentes, remarked Francisco a little illogically, gazing at the ambassador as if he belonged to some distinctly odd species in the zoo.

I believe his father was the Mexican ambassador to the U.S., the ambassador stated stiffly, as if to distinguish his American boyhood from that of Fuentes, who, after all, was a foreigner.

How I envy Fuentes growing up in a country that wasn't his own, said Rita unexpectedly.

Francisco, more annoyed than perplexed by what he took to be social prattle: What makes you say that?

The idea of foreignness . . . Don't you agree? The thrill of being free of the constrictive familiar . . .

In Mexico we are never free of the familiar, Francisco maintained, studying her reaction, intent on finding fault whatever her response. Unless physically prevented from doing so, we familiarize everything.

Why do you sound so downright sad about it? the ambassador's wife asked with a little artificial laugh.

Any sign of Jurud? inquired Raúl as he joined the group.

Have you just arrived? asked Rita.

Yes. Where is he, my guest-to-be on the program?

That's the question, said Moreno.

Raúl, looking from one to the other: He hasn't shown?

The ambassador, rocking gently on his heels, said that he wasn't going to let thoughts of Jurud's absence spoil the party.

And How Is the Weather?

What lies ahead? The satellite was one of those low-orbiting, short-endurance satellites that read the everyday patterns to determine the magnitude of the fluctuating drug traffic, the ever-shifting illegal border crossings, or, depending on its origin, any recent shifts of priority in the aerospace industry. As it streaked over southern California toward Mexico, its high-resolution, highly detailed photographs included a view of the Pemex station that lay on the route ahead. There was nothing singular about the station other than that it might, to hazard a guess, serve as an occasional rendezvous for drug runners and other nefarious travelers to the north. As for the individual now sitting on a tire, watching the cars speed by, his back to the '82 Mitsubishi pickup on which there was a Yamaha motorbike . . . All over Mexico, nondescript people just like him could be seen sitting for hours, for days, it seemed, patiently waiting for something—for what was never made clear. In any event, there was nothing unusual or especially noteworthy about the young man now puffing on a cigarette, or, for that matter, the attendant pumping gas, or the driver of the old Studebaker drinking a Coke, or the pile of discarded tires, the oil slicks, the ancient tow truck, the malfunctioning tire pressure gauge, the cigarette dispenser, or the general derelict atmosphere. The young man, now reading someone's discarded newspaper, was still waiting as if time had stopped. As for the basic needs of the tourist? Maps? Forget it. Repairs? Only in the direst of emergencies. As for the rest? The desolate scenery? Predictable brush, cacti, and wildlife in this land of Sangre de Baco and tequila and Corona beer. What have we here? Endless vistas of mesquite trees and as many as sixteen hundred species of cactus that bloom for perhaps a single day. Nothing memorable, nothing noteworthy for miles and miles other than skunks and raccoons, tarantulas, beetles, grasshoppers, desert chipmunks, miniature ground squirrels in their burrows under the bushes, and mice. And here and there, half buried, the traces of past incursions . . . Now and then someone on foot or on a mule will cross the emptiness. From where to where? Does it really matter? It certainly wasn't the Mexico the tourists had come to visit—that's for sure. The fiestas, the processions, the fireworks, the Spanish Baroque churches and cemeteries, the passion plays, not to mention the Aztec and Mayan ruins, the picturesque inlets and harbors on the new tourist coast, with its broadly smiling Mexican faces and its inviting American-Express-and-Visa-recommended fish restaurants and four-star hotels—these were elsewhere. On the same highly detailed photograph taken from approximately two hundred kilometers above the Pemex station, the satellite showed heading south the advancing line of cars—a Honda Accord, a Ford Impala, a twenty-six-foot Gulfstream Conquest class C RV, and a speedy Nissan Maxima, an old Silver Mercedes, a BMW two-door sedan, two VWs—a Beetle and red Sirocco—and a nondescript delivery van, in groups of threes and fours and fives spaced less than a mile apart. By the time the '84 yellow Cutlass Supreme, now trailing the first group by a quarter of a mile and traveling at approximately ninety kph, would reach or pass the Pemex station, the satellite would be in a perfect position to take an accurate reading of the thirty-square-mile stretch of El Tajín's unexcavated pre-Columbian civilization, at the center of which stood exposed the mysterious Pyramid of the Niches, with its 365 now empty niches.

Driving with the window wide open because the a/c was on the blink, Bonny tried to take her mind off the troublesome knocking sound that seemed to be coming from the engine. Searching for an English-speaking station, she came across a station playing the Beatles' "I'm a Loser." The car had had 87,870 miles on it when she left Mexico City, and she wanted to see the meter read 88,000, but by the time she remembered it was 88,003.

She was going too fast. Seeing the large lizard darting across the road, she swerved, then, looking in the rearview mirror, saw it squashed on the road between the tire marks. Still fiddling with the dial, she tried a religious program and then settled on what sounded like an English lesson. *Life,* said the speaker in well-modulated English, then followed the word by a rapid string of Spanish words. *Slipping away,* he continued in English with barely a hint of an accent. After repeating *Life slipping away,* he spoke at length in Spanish. She tried another station as the first of the four cars including the twenty-six-foot recreational vehicle with Alabama plates whizzed past, then, in despair, returned to the English lesson.

After describing the pleasures of shopping in Perisur, the largest shopping mall in Mexico, just thirty minutes' drive from the Zócalo in the Distrito Federal, the language instructor entered into an exchange with a woman in the all-too-familiar role of solicitous saleslady. And how much are the shirts? he asked. I like the red one. I prefer the striped button-down ones. What size are you? A pleasant, lighthearted exchange, it relieved her anxiety: That feeling of acute distress at her father's failure to show up.

At the gas station Bonny told the attendant, *Lleno, por favor,* then, needing to use the toilet, *Dónde está el baño?* The key hung from a hook in the office next to a calendar showing a smiling nude Mexican woman with legs parted enticingly. Bonny walked to the back, discovering that everything, from a puddle of oil just outside the door, to the strong odor of Lysol intermingled with the sour stench of urine, to the crudely drawn female figure impaled on a giant prick on the wall of the windowless toilet, was overwhelmingly familiar. There was a cracked sink but no water. There was a sliver of soap but no paper towels. After returning the key to the hook, Bonny looked to see what the candy machine in the office had to offer. After purchasing a candy bar, she fed several coins into the Coke machine, only to end up with a fizzy Mexican drink. Looking at the road, she could see the heat shimmer on the tarred surface. With the attendant in the soiled overalls closely watching from the office, the young Mexican made his move, his face emitting a hopeful look, as he timed his approach just as she was getting into the car. In a fair imitation of an American, he said, Waddayaknow! When she looked up, he said, I bet you're from North Hollywood. All the prettiest girls come from there. . . . Seeing that she didn't outright reject his overture, he went on to ask if she was driving south. She hesitated, then, looking straight ahead, turned the key in the ignition. Please! he pleaded. Hastily explaining that his bike was damaged, pointing to the new-looking motorbike that was resting on top of the Mitsubishi pickup. I need to get money to pay for the repair. It sounded plausible. OK, she said, against her better judgment. Hop in. In the mirror she could see the unshaven attendant, arms folded, watching with evident disapproval as the young Mexican casually swung his knapsack onto the back seat and then slid into the seat beside her. Bonny asked him where he was going. South, he said.

Ten miles later, when she had a flat, her first ever, she was glad to have him along. Without even having to be prompted to do so, he replaced the tire, cautioning her that the spare wasn't in much better condition. When the Mitsubishi pickup with the motorbike strapped to the top sailed past, she didn't see any point in mentioning it. Asked where she was going, she replied, Yucatán.

Not in this car, he said.

She looked at him in consternation. Why not?

Not with that knocking sound.

She laughed. It's been doing that for days.

To her relief, he didn't argue. Instead he asked if she was heading for the ruins or the beaches.

For the eclipse, she stated, not wishing to be typecast as the predictable tourist.

He pursed his lips. His silence—an act of criticism. You've got it wrong, he said finally. There's no eclipse in Yucatán.

There is too, she maintained, avoiding his gaze.

No way. He was adamant. You'll be able to see it from Hawaii, Baja California, Tecolutla . . .

Yucatán, she insisted, clenching her jaw.

Not this year. Now he was staring at her legs as if some message were to be extracted from them.

Where's Teco . . . whatever?

Tecolutla. On the gulf. In the state of Veracruz. Not far from El Tajín, which has some of the greatest ruins . . .

Discouraged, she slowed down. Are you certain?

Of course. The wide smile was contagious. I'm from these parts. Trust me.

She stopped the car along the side of the road and fished for a map in the glove compartment.

There it is, he said, pointing to Tuxpan on the map and nearby Megalen on the coast. See, it's not half as far as Yucatán. Right near the ruins of El Tajín. If you're lucky, you'll get to see the dance of the poles.

I want to—

It's a special dance, he said. The tourists love it.

I'm not a tourist, she said pointedly.

Five men scale a tall pole, and then, while one plays a flute on top, the four voladores, suspended by ropes, spin around it. . . .

Have you seen it?

He grinned. Many times, and admitted that he came from nearby Veracruz.

You just want me to drive you there?

He pantomimed affront at her charge. What do you take me for?

To her question if there was anyplace where she could stay in the vicinity of El Tajín, he rolled his eyes comically. Many . . . When she hesitated, he promptly offered to drive. I'll take you—

Her hands tightening on the wheel: No, no.

OK, OK, he said hastily. Take the next left. Here . . . In showing her on the map, his bare arm brushed her shoulder.

I'm not sure that I want to. . . . Her nervous reaction made him withdraw his arm. I just thought . . . His face lighting up the moment she yelled, Stop making sense.

He was startled. D'you like the Talking Heads?

"Psycho Killer," she screamed.

"Once in a Lifetime," he yelled joyfully.

"Slippery People."

Crestfallen, he shook his head. He didn't know that one.

OK, she said, trusting that someone familiar with the Talking Heads couldn't be up to anything reprehensible.

I have a friend in Zacatlán who is a mechanic. He'll fix that knocking sound, he assured her.

Where's Zacatlán?

On the way.

Exuberantly singing, *We're going boom, boom, boom, and that's the way we live,* she followed his directions. Reaching Zacatlán, she had to remind him of his friend the mechanic. We're almost there, he reassured her. However, when they arrived at the garage, she couldn't fail to notice that the mechanic—despite the hitchhiker's attempt to indicate the contrary—didn't seem to know the hitchhiker. The mechanic was cordial enough, explaining that he was about to close for the night but he'd look at her car first thing next morning.

Is he the friend you mentioned?

No, the hitchhiker admitted. My friend isn't on duty today.

Then I'll come back tomorrow. The mechanic, discerning her mistrust, assured the hitchhiker that if she'd leave the car, he'd be back within an hour. That's all right, she said. Tell him I'll return tomorrow.

He said to tell you not to drive the car. One more kilometer and the engine will go. They looked at her, trying to gauge the depth of her apprehension.

I'll be OK. She would have driven away then and there had not the mechanic motioned her to drive up to the hydraulic lift. She intended to wait, but the mechanic objected, waving his arm. Go, go. He doesn't like people hovering over him, explained the hitchhiker as she watched the car being elevated on the hydraulic lift. I can't leave the car. There's a cantina nearby, the hitchhiker said. We can get something to eat and be back in an hour. When the two men shook hands she felt they were sealing an agreement. You don't even know the guy, do you? she said.

When they returned, her foreboding was borne out, for the garage was shut—and her car nowhere in sight. My things! She pounded on the locked metal gate, only to have the hitchhiker

open the office door with a flourish, pointing to her possessions, all piled neatly on the bench.

Through a small window in the office she could see into the
darkened garage interior.

We'll wait for him to—

Furious, she demanded her car. She could see it raised high
on the hydraulic lift.

OK, OK, he said, raising his hands in a gesture of appeasement. I'll fetch him.

It was 7:15 on the garage clock when he left. From where she sat
she could see, framed in the window of the garage door, the front
wheels of her car on the hydraulic lift. When he returned, by
himself, it was pitch dark. The smell of liquor on his breath did
little to allay her fear. I want to leave. . . . Now! Trying to restrain
her tears of frustration. He'll come as soon as he finishes eating.
She stretched out on the couch, covering herself with a blanket he
found in the closet. Though it was warm she was shivering. He
busied himself with the portable radio on the desk, searching for
music amidst the static. She still couldn't decide whether or not
he had ever been in this garage. You're beautiful, he said, hand
extended. Don't touch me, she said when he put his arm around
her. Girls come here to have fun, he protested, clumsily fumbling
for her breasts. They like to— She picked up a wrench and raised
it threateningly. He laughed. It was the laugh of a juvenile,
taunting her: Go on . . . then, lunging forward, gripped her arm.
She fought him as he clawed at her clothes, squirming in his
embrace . . . then, suddenly, went limp, drained of all resistance—not obstructing, not struggling—as he shifted his position, wedging himself between her legs, now barely able to
contain his high state of excitement, in a frenzy of activity
unbuckling his belt, lowering his trousers . . . and in that split

second, as his exposed member, all rigid, was aimed at that singular part of her anatomy that was so often depicted crudely on walls in the most out-of-the-way places, he could no longer contain himself, and in a shudder of anticipation, feeling a needle of pleasure run up his spine, ejaculated, the first of several spurts reaching as far as her uncovered breasts, while he, head thrown back, grimaced his pleasure. She didn't react when he berated her, calling her a *puta*. . . . He even spit in her face. Later she heard him urinating outside. Was it his goodbye? Her hands were still trembling as she wiped the semen off her breasts. More than ever determined to retrieve her car, she went through the desk drawer, locating a bunch of keys, one of which fit the garage door. But once inside, she was no closer to getting her car than before. Frustrated, she tried several switches to no avail. One made the hydraulic lift hum loudly. But her car wouldn't budge from its position close to the ceiling. It was another mechanic, not the one from the night before, who opened the garage and found her asleep in the wicker chair. He had a few words of English. You are waiting? That's my car, she said in a voice that trembled.

Do you want me to check it?

No! She felt desperate. I need the car.

You leave it, my friend will look at it tomorrow.

She shook her head emphatically. No!

OK. No problem, he said, proceeding to lower the car.

When she drove away, the knocking sound had stopped.

Mexican Motel

Whom does she resemble? Her father or her mother? Bonny looked at herself in the streaked motel mirror. Some Mexican motels were just like American ones; one couldn't tell them apart. Perhaps that accounted for the presence of so many American guests. There was a pool and a small restaurant with a laminated menu that included freshly squeezed orange juice, 100 percent beef hamburgers, fries, and even milk shakes. The second garage to which she had taken the Olds was within walking distance. After listening to the motor, the mechanic wasn't hopeful. It's not worth it! he announced. What's the matter with it? It's the transmission. Can you fix it? Not worth it. Can I drive it for another hundred miles? I'll buy it from you for the parts. How much to fix it? Come back tomorrow. If you change your mind, I'll give you fifty dollars. I'll think about it, she said. I'll give you seventy-five. I want to see the eclipse. A hundred, he said. In the bar of the restaurant, the presence of several boisterous Americans, who were drinking Charo Negro and eating cactus called nopalito, cheered her up. Hello, little girl, one of the men said to her. Can I buy you a lemonade? She went to her room and lay down. There was no TV. She was low on batteries, and the music—*Me and you and you and me, no matter how they toss the dice, it had to be, the only one for me is you and you for me, so happy together, so happy together, so happy together . . . And how is the weather?*—on her Walkman kept fading. She wished she were back home. . . . Closing her eyes, she wasn't half trying to think of her father, but was it the presence of the Americans reveling in the motel restaurant that helped concentrate her memory, focused her attention? Helped her recall the dinner for Mercedes she and her father had planned.

Just before the guests, all old friends, were to arrive, she overheard her father say, Under the circumstances, Bonny's taking it very well. Very well, Mercedes agreed. Bonny's eyes widened as she watched them embrace. Mercedes, who was wearing high heels, arched her body backward like a flamenco dancer, closing her eyes as her father put his hand beneath the velvet bodice, exposing her bare midriff. They kissed hungrily, while shuffling in an awkward bearlike dance around the room. At the sound of the doorbell, Mercedes broke free. Later, she promised. Later! As soon as he had left, she ran to the mirror to repair her disheveled hairdo and the smeared lipstick.

Where Are They Now?

Despite the frequent power failures, the breakdown of services, the frequent strikes, and the ever growing possibility of yet another, even more severe quake, life continued with a renewed zest . . . You give the best parties, Terrence assured Rita, who needed no such assurance. Most of the tanned, open, agreeable tennis-court faces looked at home among the collection of pre-Columbian art—the Mayan reliefs, effigy jars, late-classical Mayan polychrome pottery, Aztec gold pendants, a skull inlaid with turquoise that Rita and Preston had capriciously juxtaposed to the works by such diverse artists as Bruce Nauman, Robert Morris, Robert Ryman, Agnes Martin, Dorothea Rockburne, in order to . . . was it tease or bewilder?

You'll want to meet Salas, Preston said as he scanned the room, while Alejandro, out of an innate Mexican politeness, refrained from apprising his forgetful host that it was he who had given him Salas's name in the first place. He was just here a minute ago, said Preston. I'll look for him, Alejandro promised. Do that, Preston urged, as he left his side, arms outspread, to welcome Juan, the banker, and his wife. Amigo . . . The men embraced. Amigo!

. . .

On the terrace, the soft breeze against his face carried an almost Proustian reminder of a once distant happiness . . . but where? with whom? For the first time in months, a few stars punctured the overcast sky.

From where he stood he had an unobstructed view of Terrence on a settee, facing a slender woman in a sleeveless metallic asymmetrical dress that exposed her legs, her hair alluringly piled on her head in an elaborate Spanish hairdo. The rapt expression on his face indicated that Terrence was paying close attention to her every word. As Alejandro stepped into the room he recognized her—it was Vali di Vanini. Their eyes briefly made contact, but she gave no sign of recognition. In the next room, at the sideboard, he found Raúl, plate in hand, somberly contemplating the Belgian endive and walnut salad, the poached salmon with white peppercorn vinaigrette, the fish mousse with lemon-butter sauce and flying-fish roe, the cold new asparagus with red pepper mayonnaise, the wild rice with green onion . . . Looking around, Alejandro was struck by the fact that virtually everything, from the chairs by the Italian Maurizio Peregalli to the carefully selected art to the well-trained attendants—the good-looking young Mexican barman at the makeshift bar, the three unruffled-looking Mexican waiters—indicated a disproportionate striving for perfection. Was it the perfection Mexicans expected to encounter in the home of Americans such as Preston and Rita Hollier? Aren't you going to dig in? Raúl asked, adding a stuffed artichoke to an already overloaded plate. Later, he said, walking into the next room, seeing like-minded intelligent faces—open, trusting, dependable—equably ready to converse, exchange ideas, discuss business, while women in seductively low-cut, bare-backed

clinging dresses glided about triumphantly, their eyes determinedly confrontational, seeking nothing less than unbridled
desire—though prepared to settle for a less unequivocal response. I walked out on him a week after we were married, he
overheard one American woman remark. He stopped to listen
to this irresistible exchange—not accustomed to uninhibited
female candor. So soon? Believe me, the elegant red-haired
woman admitted with a forced laugh, one week was an eye-
opener! He actually wanted me to . . . But he failed to catch the
rest of her comment. I don't believe it, said the other woman.
Are men crazy?

An editor for *fem*, the Mexican feminist magazine, in the
straightforward way some women have of striking up a conversation, inquired if he happened to be an associate of Pech.

I haven't even met him.

She regarded him skeptically. He's the Phoenix art dealer
who dredges up all those questionable pre-Columbian treasures
for Preston.

Is that him? Alejandro pointed to a tall man in a suede
jacket.

No. That's one of Rita's sycophants. Clinging to his arm,
like a blind person waiting to be escorted across a street, she
commented, After meeting Rita and Preston, it finally dawned
upon me that U.S. consumerism is not a passion but an
ideal. . . .

I'm not sure that I follow.

It is the means by which the historical imperative can best
be expressed.

How so?

What draws us to America is not the superabundance of
their malls but the underlying promise. . . . The Walt Disney
virtual reality of life dominates. . . . It's a kind of Edenic

promise of an extended childhood—a Nintendo existence: I'm a child, therefore I am!

In the study, hung with more than a dozen small works by Basquiat, Eric Fischl, and David Salle, a tall man in a dinner jacket, wearing Texas boots, had made himself comfortable in Preston's revolving armchair, as he talked business on the phone, while, indifferent to Alejandro's presence, he riffled casually through the contents of Preston's open desk drawer.

Alejandro turned his attention to the Salle drawings.

Take a good look, urged the woman, who had stayed at his side. The Salles and the Basquiats are the next to go.

Really?

Noticing him looking at a large David Salle, a friend of Rita's, an American woman in a tight black dress with a slit along one side that, every time she moved, exposed a leg up to the thigh, made an ironic quip about the painting's extravagant sexual content. In the ensuing lighthearted exchange, he disparaged the painting, only to stop short, suddenly conscious that what he was saying might reach Rita. When she mentioned that Rita had just purchased the painting from Pech, Alejandro asked if she could point out the dealer to him.

He's standing over there. On your left, examining the drawings. It was the man he had seen riffling through Preston's desk drawer.

Would you like me to introduce you?

No, no. Just curious.

As he was backing away, the woman slipped him her card. She did it dexterously. Mischievously. It was well timed. She did it after having deciphered the indeterminate expression of his face—or perhaps she did it as a dare.

.   .   .

A Mexican waiter who bore an uncanny resemblance to the once sprightly Jack Nicholson of *Five Easy Pieces* darted past like a wound-up toy, balancing a tray of hors d'oeuvres, turning on an imitation Jack Nicholson smile each time he stopped in front of a guest. Alejandro finally managed to come within reach of the tray and helped himself to a prawn wrapped in raw spinach. Munching it, he headed for the balcony, where Rita, speaking a droll mix of English and Spanish, was conversing with Salas.

There you are, Rita said, trying to mute her displeasure. Jacobus has been searching for you high and low.

Hope I'm not interrupting.

Not at all.

By now Alejandro felt entitled to kiss her cheek. Beautiful party! Thank you, she said, as Salas directed his gaze at the crowded room behind them, pointedly ignoring him.

You two must know each other.

Salas flashed a toothy insincere smile. Of course . . . we're old friends. Good to see you, said Alejandro. I was at Alejandro's wedding, Salas proclaimed, and then idly inquired if Mercedes was present.

Isn't she in the U.S.? Rita asked.

I just spoke to her an hour ago, Alejandro lied.

Rita said something, her voice too low for him to hear, that provoked Salas's snicker. Annoyed, Alejandro was set to leave, when Jacobus, coming from behind, blocked his retreat. I think you owe me an explanation.

See you later, Rita said.

Bye-bye, said Salas mockingly.

Why are you so intent on trashing Jurud in your article? Jacobus said, as he backed Alejandro into a corner.

That's absurd. The accusation doesn't even warrant a response.

Filled with indignation, Jacobus's ruddy face loomed larger than life. His lower lip trembled. I won't let you get away with it.

Defensively, clutching his empty glass, he tried to allay Jacobus's suspicions. I assure you, I have no intention of dumping on Jurud. . . . Why, I haven't even submitted it yet.

Jacobus, not accepting his response: By now it's common knowledge that you intend to trash Jurud. . . .

Alejandro, retreating to the bar, holding up his empty glass as reason for this withdrawal: I'm not . . . I don't arbitrarily attack . . .

Jacobus, growing more and more emotional: Alejandro, don't fool with me! His protruding eyes blinking rapidly.

I keep telling you, I have no intention of attacking Jurud.

I can vouch for that, said Francisco, who had overheard their exchange, cheerfully slapping Jacobus on the shoulder.

Why don't you fuck off, said Alejandro amiably.

Decency alone should have prevented you from accepting the article, said Jacobus, working himself into a rage.

I hadn't realized that this was for real, said Francisco, as he backed away.

Straightening his tie, Alejandro shrugged off Jacobus's restraining hand. Go soak your head.

Terrence and Vali di Vanini, still immersed in conversation, were now chattily discussing Latin American authors. To Alejandro, it sounded like an introductory course in contemporary literature. Yet it couldn't be for lack of anything else to talk about.

Machado de Assis?

Ah, Machado, yes. Divine. Really, the least likely candidate to become Brazil's most modern writer. Regrettably no longer considered fashionable. Reading Diderot altered his entire view of literature. . . . Borges, as one might expect, asserted his Argentinean supremacy by referring disdainfully to Machado as the mulatto writer. She wrinkled her nose. Borges could be so disagreeable.

Wasn't he a hunchback?

Borges? No, he became blind.

I mean Machado.

Absolutely. And in spite of or was it because of his disability, he became Brazil's foremost writer.

Paz? Terrence continued unchecked, as if rattling off the names on a list he had memorized.

He's the one who penetrated our psyche. There's no one to rival him. *Labyrinth of Solitude* remains the principal guide to our emotional repression. A magnificent mind. An indefatigable traveler, a literary explorer par excellence, he has one foot forever planted outside Mexico. We never know if he is coming or going. Terrence, without seeming to register her response, impatiently produced the next name. Borges?

A writer of multiple deceptions and concealment. One layer covers the next.

What's being concealed?

Personally, I've always considered his blindness as too pronounced. She blinked rapidly, as if something had lodged in her eyes. The absence of the erotic is more than made up for by his outlandish fondness for the exotic "other," those Talmudic scholars, and his strange partiality for extreme violence. I'm of the opinion that his short, mannered texts are meant to distract us.

From what?

From interpreting the emotional content. I wouldn't look too strenuously.

Is it true that Buñuel disparaged Borges?

Buñuel was known for his unmatched candor but not necessarily for his literary perception.

And Fuentes?

More productive than ever, he rightfully dismisses the critics who malign him, who spitefully accuse him of not being sufficiently Mexican . . . of being ideologically incorrect and textually too elegant, too seamless. He's even been accused of writing mainly for the benefit of Americans. It's grotesque, but today in Mexico a writer or filmmaker of genuine accomplishment must have the correct political credentials. . . . If only Fuentes could convert us.

To what?

Why, to the Mexico of his brilliant vision.

Is it accurate?

Does it matter?

He was astonished by the number of Latin American and Spanish authors Terrence was able to name and by her rapid if nonchalant rejoinders. This time Alejandro greeted her. Hello, Vali. She looked up, pretending surprise. Why, Alejandro. I never expected to see you here. Then, to Terrence: Alejandro's everywhere.

Terrence's question—Are you enjoying yourself?—struck him as fatuous.

Are you acquainted with the work of Juan Rulfo? Vali asked Terrence, for all purposes excluding him. Now, there's someone who deserves greater recognition.

. . .

The woman who had adroitly handed him her card was leaving by herself. Briefly their eyes made contact. His heart racing, he started in the direction of the door but then, inexplicably, as if allowing fate to intervene, accepted the glass of champagne from a beaming Preston. What could have prompted Preston to declare, in the presence of a dozen people, I'm free of rivalry. I bear no bitterness, no rancor. I feel no resentment. I am an open book. If you were to peer into my memory bank, all you'd find are the blueprints for the elevator shaft in the Pyramid of the Sun. To which Rita dryly commented, The emblems of perfection!

When are they going to finally begin the construction?

Concluding that Francisco's question was not intended as a challenge, Preston spoke fervently of the proposed project. Just think of it! Ascending to the glory of history by the push of a button.

To this day I rank second, Rita said, making a little curtsy to Preston.

Preston didn't appear to notice. It's a huge investment, he said somberly. I hope it'll serve as a model for other sites.

Do you have the money? asked Francisco.

What are banks for? joked Juan.

I suspect that in Mexico we are too quick to evaluate everything on the basis of cost, remarked Vali. From up close, under the bright light, Alejandro was suddenly struck by how much older she looked. Only her large eyes retained their luminousness.

You hear that? said Terrence, his admiration for Vali unchecked.

What about you? Preston challenged Francisco. Do you judge everything by its price tag?

All eyes turned to Francisco. Rita intervened. Francisco is

like every one of us! Isn't that why the need to bring Kmart value shopping to Mexico remains our priority?

Have you met Señora di Vanini? Juan asked Alejandro.

We've known each other for ages, said di Vanini. Then, capriciously, expressed her regret at Mercedes's absence.

Just before he left he watched Preston, who had had a few too many tequilas, bully Francisco into a game of tennis at their club the next morning. I'll come and watch, Rita threatened, with the simulated eagerness of someone who had no such intention. Men only, remarked Preston boisterously, gazing at Francisco with all the fondness one reserves for one's victims. . . .

The woman who had slipped Alejandro her card had left a message on his machine. Her voice was filled with promise: Call me. Then she gave her number, a number that did not appear on her card. He had drunk too much and staggered to bed with a pounding headache.

Once again awakened by the elevator door on his floor being slammed, he walked barefoot to the window, seeing a woman who must have been visiting his next-door neighbor briskly crossing the empty street, the sound of her high heels creating an echo that resounded in his brain. Was she the same one he had seen late at night weeks ago? This time a taxi, its engine running, was waiting at the corner. Alejandro couldn't contain himself. Leaning out the window, he yelled, Slut! Slut!

Bonny

Next morning, a small disaster. Her toilet overflowed, flooding the tiled floor. Feeling unwell, Bonny forced herself to swallow a slice of dry toast at breakfast, then sat under an umbrella next to the pool, concentrating on a letter to her father. After the eclipse I intend to visit the Pyramid of the Niches at El Tajín. She felt somewhat reassured by the presence of the two slender American women who had arrived only that morning—both, disregarding the Mexican sense of propriety, were sunning themselves next to the pool wearing only the skimpiest of bikinis. Paying no attention to Bonny, they idly chatted about their friends. One mentioned a well-known rock star she had met in San Diego. Bonny enviously staring at their fully developed breasts, could see their lives unfold. But as soon as the men, both lean and athletic, with close-cropped hair and aviator's glasses, joined them, their voices changed—everything they now said seemed to convey an additional meaning. They were teasing each other for the sake of the men, for the men's enjoyment. Don't they just love to chatter, declared the older man. Gary, that's not fair, the younger woman shrilly protested. The men burst out laughing. Even the women's laughter was directed at the men, as if to acknowledge their unqualified supremacy, their leadership. Bonny squinted in their direction, nothing escaped her. In her mind she could also see them make love. With a slight shift of her head, she was able to see her room. A Mexican was standing outside her door, watching impassively as one of the two men, after being splashed by the women, started to chase the younger of the two. Squealing, she ran around the pool, dodging the potted palms and deck chairs until he caught up with her and with one fluid motion seized her by the waist and effortlessly tossed her into the pool. Braying like a mule, he jumped in after her. Nothing else stirred. The huge Labrador stayed in the shade next to the office, large pink tongue protruding as he lazily kept an eye on the white and black cat, which, mesmerized by the darting motions of a lizard, was on high alert. When Bonny looked up from her notebook to watch the couple who had frolicked in the pool and now, after some good-natured back-and-forth banter, were going to their room, she saw the other man staring at her. He smiled, wagging a reproving finger—Naughty, naughty little girl—laughing aloud when she stood up and hurriedly walked to her room. In the late afternoon, again seated next to the pool, she watched the two couples set off for what she assumed would be a night on the town. What town? The women were wearing shiny, sequined, low-cut silver dresses. One of the women winked as she passed her table. Endeavoring to reach her father, Bonny tried the Holliers first, only to be told by an impatient-sounding Rita that her father hadn't arrived. Where are you? I'm having engine problems, Bonny explained, giving Rita the name of the motel where she was staying. Goodness, what do you intend to do? I'm heading for Megalen on the coast to watch the eclipse. Are you sure about that? said Rita. I was under the impression that it's to be seen from Baja California. An hour later she tried her dad again—this time leaving a message about her travel plans on his machine.

Flame-Stitching Female Friends

Whom did she most resemble? The young man at the wheel was sufficiently drunk for it to show whenever he laughed, which was frequently. The four of them, for her benefit, were boister-ously talking of their trip, recalling what had happened so far, day by day. Bonny wished that this trip would never end, as she listened to their hilarious recital . . . the description of dingy motels and terrible restaurants. Gary wore a Rolex watch. He was going fast. It felt as if they were not simply driving but somehow streaking through this foreign country at an intergalactic speed, their momentum emphasizing the immediacy as well as the urgency of their *mission* . . . and of their unity. Though they were on a narrow, bumpy road, he easily overtook one car after the other. What kind of a car is this? It's a fast one, Paul assured her, hugging Dotty. God, Bonny prayed, let this go on forever. It was Dotty she had first approached. That's a shame about your car, Dotty had commiserated. I know exactly how you must feel. When she mentioned the eclipse, her friend was sympathetic. Of course you want to see it. You only live once. And now that you're here . . . Hey, we'll be leaving tomorrow. It may be a little out of our way, but I'll see if I can persuade Gary to drop you in Megalen—if that's where you want to go. Now they were driving her to the solar eclipse . . . or rather, to the hotel from which she could view the eclipse. To her relief, no one inquired how old she was. No one asked her why she was traveling by herself. No one cared to know her surname . . . or what her father did . . . or if her parents were divorced. Or how she had come so far by herself. They treated her as an adult. When they set off, the first thing Dotty noticed were her boots.

Alligator?

No. Lizardskin.

Justins?

No, Tony Lama.

I just love the flame stitching.

My dad bought them for my birthday.

I wish I had brought mine along.

Hey, how old are you? asked Paul in a Pavlovian response to the word *birthday*. Dotty at once came to her rescue. Paul, that's not fair. One doesn't ask women . . . Excuse him, said Dotty's friend. He's been spending too much time away from women. . . . Stir-crazy, you know.

He duly apologized. Sorry. There were no more questions.

You'll love the place, Gary assured her, when they dropped her off at the hotel. If we didn't have to make it back to Acapulco, we'd stay here ourselves.

Have fun watching the eclipse, said Dotty.

Don't get lost in the ruins, Gary warned.

I won't. She kissed them—each one of them. She had never felt happier in her life. She waved goodbye, sorry she couldn't stay with them . . . Sorry that she wasn't twenty . . . Sorry that . . .

What Else?

Francisco's initial response to Rita's invitation was a courteous I don't think so, until she, with that conniving smile, mentioned that Preston would be too busy to accompany them. It'll just be the two of us. Doesn't Preston want another look at the place? He considers it strictly an investment. As a matter of fact, he's not paying for it; Eden Enterprises is. I see, Francisco said, not entirely convinced, for he considered Preston sufficiently devious to set a trap for him.

It'll be a wonderful day, she promised.

He tried to respond to her smile.

Isn't it glorious, Rita said when they finally reached the villa. The sun was shining. The garden was much improved since the gardener had started to clear away the overgrown bushes. Inside, in the rooms where the painters had begun to work, there were huge pieces of furniture, in every shape and form, under plastic sheeting. Uncovering several, she was mystified. These pieces of furniture weren't here on our prior visit. She uncovered another.

Take this rolltop desk . . . I'm positive it wasn't here. It's not too bad, said Francisco. I can't believe it. Did someone dump it? Becoming more and more irate as they walked through the house. I know that piece wasn't here. Francisco tried to reassure her, saying, The painters may have moved stuff about. Entering the upstairs bedroom, in utter disbelief she stared at the coats, jackets, dresses, including several antiquated ball gowns, that were hanging in the closet. I swear this was empty the last time we were here. . . . Mutely he listened as she called Señora Maggi's office to complain. What's going on? Where did all this junk come from? Señora Maggi professed ignorance. I assure you no one but the gardener and the painters have been anywhere near the house—unless it's the late Anadelle Partridge's ghost, she joked. That's not funny. The upstairs closet is packed with her musty ball gowns. But, Señora Hollier, I assure . . . I have no knowledge . . . Is this a practical joke? Rita demanded. I can come by. It won't be necessary. I'll have someone come by. . . . That's all right. I'll take care of it, said Rita angrily. While Rita was marking with her eye everything in the house she intended to discard, Francisco explored the upstairs. Looking over a moldy pile of books in the library, he unearthed a silver-framed photo of Anadelle Partridge at a Mayan excavation, the group of Mexican diggers, shovels in hand, standing at a respectful distance in the rear while in the foreground the tall woman in khaki trousers and shirt, face beaming, looking self-assured, had one lanky arm around Salas, who sullenly stared into the camera.

Look what I unearthed, she said, when Francisco joined her in the kitchen, and pointed to a china closet, which contained the remains of what had been a Villeroy & Boch Petite Fleur blue and white set for twenty-four and a decimated but elegant gold-rimmed Rosenthal porcelain group.

These must have cost an arm and a leg, he said.

I still can't get over it. She gestured with her hand. Dumping everything.

The more I think of it, the more I'm inclined to suggest that we should return to the city.

Why?

I have an ominous—

Oh, please. You're not going to spoil our stay, are you?

It was an effort for him to utter the word *foreboding*. I have a foreboding. . . .

Waking in the middle of the night, Rita sat up straight, staring at the Mexican night framed in the tall open window.

What is it? Francisco mumbled.

No. You tell me.

Do you know what time it is? He glanced at the luminous dial of his watch.

What's the matter?

With what?

You're changing. I sensed it the moment we arrived . . . in your foreboding . . . in your inexplicable desire to return. Then, grimly, asking, Is there another woman?

Of course not.

I saw the way you were eyeing di Vanini at the party.

I wasn't even close to her.

She tried another tack. You're not going to back out?

He was totally mystified. What are you saying?

You're not going to refuse Salas's commission, are you?

Now he was on safer ground. It depends on what it entails.

All that money? They're being *extremely* generous. . . .

I suspect you've had a hand in that.

Do you find the terms unreasonable? Her hand found his chest, caressing it.

Look, it's three-thirty. Let's . . .

You don't think you can write the book?

He was exasperated. Of course I can.

I can get you more commissions. Don't you see? We could be independent. . . . I have contacts.

It's not that.

Why do you think I wanted this house?

It's beautiful, he said, trying to sound sincere.

I had us in mind. You and me. Here! It's to be our get-away. . . . Her hand had sneaked across his warm belly and now was cuddling his prick. She felt it pulsate with a life of its own.

What about Preston? Is he no longer part of the equation?

I don't wish to discuss Preston, she said sharply, withdrawing her hand. I don't want you to bring him up, ever! Is that clear!

Calm

Her second day in Megalen. The sea was far more turbulent. In the morning the sky was overcast, but by noon the sun was shining. Lillian, who was from San Diego, complained that the nearby newspaper kiosk had sold all its copies of *Time*. Bonny walked over to the newsman to inquire if he carried *YMS*, *Sassy*, *Seventeen*, *Glamour*, or *Interview*, finally settling for a Mexican fashion magazine. After tomorrow the kiosk will only be open to five, the man said in English. At least can you get *Vanity Fair?* In the open-air café, a gray-haired man in a white terry-cloth bathrobe was trying to read a newspaper while battling the strong sea breeze.

No one questioned her when she first arrived—it was as if

the hotel staff had by now grown accustomed to American teenagers traveling by themselves. Even her statement, I'm expecting my father to join me soon, appeared quite redundant.

In the restaurant overlooking the beach there were fewer than six for lunch. . . . How are you, dear? asked Mme Sabaia when she took her seat at the adjacent table. Bonny tried to read the title of the book that so absorbed Lillian. Each time the waiter emerged from the kitchen, Bonny noticed that Lillian would glance up, and whenever the waiter's and her eyes met, as they frequently seemed to do, Lillian would say something in Spanish and reward him with a wide, inviting smile.

After lunch Bonny took the local bus to Megalen Antiguo, on the hill . . . The main thoroughfare, a narrow winding street, was packed with boutiques and restaurants. As she was walking back to the hotel, Mme Sabaia, passing in her car, slowed down to offer her a lift. She declined. I'd rather walk, if you don't mind. Mme Sabaia drove off, honking twice in response to Bonny's wave. At dinner, Bonny found herself seated at a table with a garrulous lawyer on her right and the rather massive figure of Mme Sabaia to her left. How did you ever find this place? Mme Sabaia inquired.

I came for the eclipse, Bonny explained.

That's not for days, declared the elderly lawyer, with a testy look. Besides, we'll only have a partial eclipse. It's Baja California . . . that's where the ecliptophiles are heading. Eyeing her keenly: You're in the wrong place.

Seeing Bonny's look of distress, Mme Sabaia advised her to check with the desk. They know everything.

In any event, you'd better not stare at the sun at the time of the eclipse, warned the lawyer, to whom she had taken an instant dislike.

Bonny pouted. I know that.

The Aztecs believed that during an eclipse their gods would come down to devour men.

By slightly turning in her chair, Bonny was able to exclude him from her vision.

I've been coming here for ages, Mme Sabaia explained, then, looking closely at her: You haven't been here before, with your parents, have you?

No.

I feel as if I've seen you somewhere.

You must be confusing me with someone else, said Bonny.

Did you say your name was Jurand?

It's Jurud. Bonny Jurud.

An unusual name, said the lawyer, who, refusing to be cut by Bonny, kept staring at her profile with limpid blue eyes. Are your parents of Dutch or German extraction? She pretended not to hear, only to have Mme Sabaia gently remind her, Dear, Mr. Wahr is asking you a question.

I don't think so, she said, resentfully, when he repeated his question.

Don't you know?

They're not of Dutch descent is what she's saying, interposed Mme Sabaia.

Are you traveling all by yourself? he persisted, with a disagreeable lopsided grin . . . which may have been the result of his loose-fitting dentures.

Yes.

When I was her age, Mme Sabaia said, I had to get permission to go to the local cinema.

Where did you grow up? Bonny inquired, without any desire to know.

In Beirut. I don't suppose you know where that is?

As a matter of fact, I do.

How old are you? he asked.

Bonny bristled at the question. Almost seventeen.

He laughed, not concealing his disbelief.

What are you reading? asked Mme Sabaia.

She held up her book.

Mme Sabaia was enthused. How marvelous! When I was your age, I read all her books. Have you read any of her other books?

No.

She was growing exceedingly tired of this conversation. If not for the dessert cart, heaped with all sorts of promising creamy pastries, she might have left there and then.

On Monday Bonny was awakened by voices: one a raspy, low, measured man's voice, the other higher-pitched, irate, a voice she took to be that of a young Mexican woman. Sitting upright, she could see the ocean. She stepped out on the balcony and located the source of the voices as being directly above her. The more she listened the more convinced she became that the voices were familiar. Yet, how could they be familiar? The older, more subdued voice definitely belonged to an American, who, in fluent Spanish, was trying to placate the younger, shriller voice. What do you want? he kept asking, the question eliciting an angry tirade that Bonny couldn't understand.

On the beach she looked in vain for Mme Sabaia. Evidently she had stayed indoors, not even going to the restaurant. When she left the beach at eleven, the hotel interior was pleasantly cool. Hello, Bonny, said the desk clerk as he handed her the key.

After lunch Bonny walked to the nearby harbor, crowded

with dozens of small craft. Passing a line of expensive stores, boutiques, and jewelers, a boating supplier, a real estate office, she stopped at a watchmaker's to buy a strap for her watch.

Later that afternoon, from her fourth-floor balcony, Bonny watched Lillian swimming back and forth in the pool while a young Mexican, sipping a soft drink, perched himself on the low stone wall and stared alternately at the sea and at Lillian. Soon he was joined by several compatriots . . . Bonny assumed they were locals. All intently watched Lillian, absorbed by her rhythmic pacing as she swam lap after lap.

An hour later Bonny found Lillian, in her revealing red bikini, stretched out on a mat between the long row of beach chairs and the rear of the restaurant. Immersed in her paperback, Lillian did not respond to Bonny's greeting. At first Bonny couldn't fathom why she would choose to lie down in such a confined and incommodious place, in proximity to the kitchen, until, seeing Lillian raise herself the instant Luis the cook's sonorous voice became audible and, with a sensual look, scissor her legs so as to catch his attention the moment he looked out, she understood—and instantly left the beach, for she felt that she was trespassing.

When Bonny entered the hotel lobby, the staff were watching football on TV. Mazatlán versus Tampico, 1–1.

Gilbert, Lillian's husband, arrived on Thursday, wearing a clubby-looking blazer with gold buttons, a white turtleneck, and tasseled moccasins. He had picked up a car at the airport. At dinner, with a lewd laugh, he remarked that in La Jolla one can telephone a service that allows one to listen to an erotic conversation between two women. Lillian laughed in a fine show of confusion and, with an almost Oriental gesture of embarrassment, hid her face in her hands.

There were now fewer than a dozen guests at the hotel. But as yet Bonny hadn't come face-to-face with the angry couple staying in the room above hers. She never saw them on the beach or in the restaurant. Where could they be spending all their time?

The following morning she was awakened by the same duet. Again the older, more subdued manly voice was squabbling with his girlfriend. The querulous young woman, who was doing most of the talking, accompanied her words with what seemed like angry slaps on an arm or a leg—as if to pace her sharp responses. Though the older man's remarks were almost inaudible, Bonny could sense his growing impatience. When Bonny rang room service and ordered breakfast, she was informed that the electricity would soon be cut off. Why? It's the entire area, the desk clerk explained, as if he were addressing a small child. As a result of the power failure, the rooms would not be cleaned and the small polished metal elevator, with the manufacturer's name, OTIS, prominently displayed inside, wouldn't be running. Bonny took a shower. By 9:30 there was no electricity. There was also no hot water, no radio or TV. When she tried the telephone, it was dead.

An hour later she set off to explore the town, following a path she had taken the day before, but, missing a turn, retraced her steps and found that she was lost. She walked past boarded-up villas and well-tended deserted gardens with guava and avocado trees. On the gates there were only the street names and numbers. Calle de la Violeta, Calle de la Represalia, Calle del Destino, Calle de la Verdad. Now and then, on a yellow tile on the house or garden wall, the snarling head of a dog was depicted. Instead of finding the street back to the hotel, she had reached a dead end.

It took her an hour to locate the main road and return to the hotel. At the desk, the clerk smiled at her when she asked if there were any messages. None, he said. There was still no electricity, but the phone had a dial tone. She dialed her father's number, only to be informed by an English-speaking Mexican operator that the lines were not in working order. She tried again and again with no success. As she stood on the balcony watching the darkening landscape, she saw a large motor launch on a trailer being hauled past the hotel, the boat incongruously towering over the small houses farther down the street as it serenely sailed inland.

Could anyone still be in the room above?

Before leaving the dining room that evening, Lillian and Gilbert briefly came over to her and Mme Sabaia's table. They were departing early the next morning, Gilbert explained. He was tipsy. Tonight we finished an entire bottle, he said proudly, then abruptly excused himself, saying, We must be off. When I arrived a month ago, Mme Sabaia noted in a lowered voice, Lillian had hardly any Spanish. However did she learn so fast? Mme Sabaia smiled knowingly. She spent all her free time with the locals. . . . I'm told it's the only way to pick up another language.

Toward ten that night Bonny spotted Lillian and Gilbert with Luis in the bar. They were laughing at Gilbert's droll attempts to make himself understood in Spanish. To Bonny's ears the laughter sounded forced. It was the first time Bonny had seen the cook in a jacket and necktie. He was trying his best to look cheerful as he nursed a bottle of Carta Blanca, pretending not to notice that the barman wasn't paying the slightest attention to him. If Lillian noticed, she didn't seem to care. Of the four, she was the only one who remained composed. Some time later, Bonny overheard her give Luis their home telephone and address. Be sure to phone ahead, and we'll meet you at the airport, she instructed him in Spanish. Even though he kept saying, Sí, sí, he seemed befuddled, as if not comprehending what was being said to him. . . . It was plain to see that he was just dying for this wearisomely protracted encounter to end. Lillian now insisted on speaking only Spanish—while her husband listened, appearing to be enthralled by her performance.

Choice

There were fewer guests in the hotel and, in the harbor, fewer sailboats. Nonetheless, as on the previous days, the attendant set up a row of reclining beach chairs and planted next to each a beach umbrella, as if, at any moment, a crowd would descend upon the beach from the empty hotel. From her balcony Bonny saw Lillian crossing the road to join Luis, who was waiting for her on the deserted promenade. Side by side, for what seemed an interminably long time, the two stood at the railing, gazing out to sea. Was she witnessing a lover's goodbye? Only after the idle beach attendant had joined the two did Gilbert elect to leave the hotel and head unhurriedly in their direction, as if he didn't have a care in the world. When Gilbert returned, with Lillian in tow, she was contentedly smiling to herself. Less than an hour later, they departed. Luis came to the car to see them off. Bonny, watching from the fourth floor, saw him shake Lillian's hand and then embrace her husband. Lillian, leaning out the car window, laughed self-consciously as the men hugged each other. There was no indication on any of the hotel staff's faces—all cheerily waving goodbye—that they found this farcical leave-taking the least bit unusual. When a relieved-looking Luis at last rejoined his friend the beach attendant, who had followed the departure from a safe distance, the latter clapped him on the shoulder, smiling broadly. Seeing the lewd expression on the beach attendant's face as he closely listened to what Luis had to say, Bonny could only conclude that the cook must be giving him a blow-by-blow account of his conquest.

At lunch, Mme Sabaia mentioned that in two days she intended to explore the ruins of El Tajín. El Tajín, she said, reading from her guidebook, is named for lightning and the Totonac rain god. It's said to be one of the most striking pre-Columbian sites. Little is known of its builders. . . . The Pyramid of the Niches was built on top of an older, similar structure, which dates back to 300 B.C. Each of the four sides contains row upon row of niches. . . . At the summit of its six-tiered construction are the remains of a sanctuary. Each tier has an overhanging cornice, under which there are niches that add up to the number 365. There are two ball courts, one of them next to the pyramid.

Do the niches stand for the number of days in a year? interrupted Bonny.

I don't know, said Mme Sabaia. It seems plausible. In fact, it seems more than likely. Then, as if the idea had just occurred to her, she asked Bonny, Would you like to join me?

That should be fun, said Bonny.

Villa

When Preston called late Saturday night to ask Alejandro if he'd care to accompany him to Megalen the following day, he agreed at once. Sure. Gladly. And he was . . . glad to have the opportunity to revisit the villa in which he and Francisco had spent so much time together. To his surprise, Preston arrived by himself. Rita is visiting a friend, he explained. Without Rita or Terrence, Preston seemed more relaxed. They had started late and soon found themselves in heavy traffic, since everyone who had access to a car that day was seeking to escape the suffocating city air for the nearby mountains. As they inched along, Preston spoke of the restorations at the villa under Rita's supervision, and then, almost by the way, mentioned that Pech would be joining them. He's found something for me. Pre-Columbian? Yes. He has these marvelous sources. Alejandro could not remember ever before feeling so unconstrained in Preston's presence. . . . Asked how he and Francisco had come to work for Anadelle Partridge, Alejandro explained that a professor had recommended him. Señora Partridge was looking for a librarian to catalogue the rare books she had acquired for the museum library. Given my limited experience, I didn't think I stood a chance. I went to see her in Mexico City, where she had a town house—to my surprise, she appeared satisfied with my credentials, and after a brief exchange offered me the job, saying, Oh, you can have it, or words to that effect, as if it wasn't anything of great concern to her. The salary, while not excessive, was reasonable. The only drawback to the job was that I'd have to spend at least four days a week in Megalen. Several months later, when I realized that I wasn't making a dent in the enormous number of books, I requested an assistant, and suggested Francisco. She hired him at once. Now there were two of us without any experience in cataloguing scholarly books. How did she come into all that money? She married a corporate lawyer, and when he died, a year later, she was the sole beneficiary. The family contested the will.

They fought her tooth and nail. They even had his body exhumed and examined for evidence of foul play. All to no avail. As you might expect, there are rumors . . .

When they reached Megalen, Alejandro at first didn't recognize it, so much had changed. Preston drove fast, appearing to know his way around, but on reaching the outskirts of the town he must have overshot the lane to the villa. It's a dirt road. I don't suppose you remember it, he joked. Driving past a neglected-looking field, Alejandro spotted a black car emerging from what he at first took to be a thicket. A Jaguar, Preston exclaimed, sticking his head out the window, craning his neck, as the driver, a woman, unnerved by the loud sound of Preston's horn, with a great burst of speed set off in the opposite direction. That must be Rita, said Preston. In his haste to turn the car on the rutted unpaved country road, Preston backed into a ditch. . . . By the time they had extricated the car, there was no hope of catching up with the Jaguar. The bitch, Preston swore, banging his fist on the steering wheel, while Alejandro, too discomfited to say anything, looked away. The bitch, Preston repeated under his breath . . . then, as if to retract his emotional outburst, remembered that Rita had said she intended to check up on the repairs. The mind likes to play tricks on one, Alejandro said. Only last week I was positive that I had spotted Mercedes in a restaurant. It wasn't her at all. What we need is a drink, Preston decided, beaming goodwill at Alejandro. There should be something at the villa. Following the narrow winding lane the other car had just left, they reached the villa in a matter of minutes. The grounds and the building were the way Alejandro remembered them, though he couldn't recall the stone statues in the wooded area. They must have been placed there after he left. Those idiots, said Preston when he discovered that the painters had begun to paint several rooms on the ground floor, leaving each unfinished. No wonder this country can't get its act together.

On the small round table on which the painters had left their brushes stuck in open cans of paint thinner, Preston spotted a package bearing his name. Rita tells me that the painters keep unearthing all kinds of stuff behind the shutters, he said, gingerly unwrapping the package and eyeing the contents, a thick pile of letters addressed to Anadelle Partridge, with distaste. What have we here? More material for Francisco's book? Then, with a puckish smile, Preston said, You haven't told me what Anadelle was really like.

Frankly, I tried to stay out of her way. . . .

Didn't you and Francisco accompany her on a trip to Yucatán?

Oh, that. Did Francisco mention it?

No, Rita did. Looking at Alejandro impassively: As you see, she's able to acquire the most surprising bits of information.

There's nothing much to recall. Initially we were delighted to get away, welcoming any diversion. I presume Señora Partridge had us along to provide additional security. . . . We hadn't expected her to take this outing quite so seriously. We certainly didn't anticipate the lectures. It's amusing when you think of it. She, the American, trying to clarify the complexities of ancient Mexico to two Mexicans. . . . On the other hand, she could be so obtuse. I remember when Francisco informed her that the Aztecs kept the heads of their sacrificial victims on display racks in a kind of storage space, she wanted to know what they did with the bodies. I can still see the expression on her face when Francisco said, They ate them.

Is that true? Preston asked with a foolish grin.

What?

The cannibalism?

Father Sahagún, who arrived in Mexico three years after Cortés, observed it at firsthand. For details, you can read the articles and books by scholars, such as Carrasco, Sanday, and Harner.

Admittedly, the Aztecs were brutal—

Don't exclude the Mayans or the Zapotecs and Totonacs. . . .

Preston, going through the pile of letters, extracted a faded photo. Have a look at this!—handing it to Alejandro. It showed Anadelle Partridge next to Salas in what appeared to be a fashionable restaurant at the seaside. Both were laughing, as Salas tossed a handful of bread crumbs into the air, thick with diving gulls. It was dated June '81. Bet they had something going, commented Preston. I guess so, Alejandro said guardedly. What about you and Francisco? Seeing his look of indignation, Preston apologized. Sorry . . . I didn't mean it that way . . .

She was an elderly lady, said Alejandro, trying to contain his anger.

That must be Pech, Preston concluded, when they heard the sound of a car on the gravel path. Alejandro followed him to the door in time to see. Pech, who had parked his car at some distance from the house, standing by as two Mexicans forcefully extricated an Indian from the back seat . . . What's going on? Preston demanded, at once recognizing Emilio. Don't worry, it's all right, Pech called out reassuringly, as the young man stumbled and fell. He's going to lead us to the codex. He swiped it while in the employ of Anadelle Partridge. I'm convinced he's concealed the missing sections in the villa. . . . You expect me to pay for something already on my property? If not for us, how would you even know of it? countered Pech, not the least put out by Preston's indignation. What do they intend to do with him? Alejandro asked, as without a by-your-leave the two Mexicans walked Emilio in quick step past an unprotesting Preston into the house. He's a petty crook, declared Pech, squinting at Alejandro, trying to place him. Was it to offset Preston's growing displeasure that Pech demanded to know the reason for Alejandro's presence? He's my guest, said Preston. Do you mind? When Pech failed to respond, Preston pointed to the house. Is this absolutely necessary?

If you want the codex it is. Then, leading Preston away from the villa, Pech explained, The Indian claims it's somewhere in the attic.

It's chock-full of stuff, Preston said, falling into step with Pech, while Alejandro, lingered behind, still gazing at the entrance through which the three men had passed. Let's go, let's go, Pech called out. We're taking a little walk. Anyone watching the three of them would have concluded that they were out for a stroll before lunch. However, the moment Alejandro wished to obtain a closer look at the pool in the sunken garden, where Anadelle's friends used to frolic while he and Francisco were inside the villa cataloguing books, Pech at once, in the voice of an irate custodian, called out, Stay!

I was only going to—

I said stay, warned Pech.

Exasperated, Alejandro sat down on the grass. I don't like this, said Preston. Pech offered him a cigarette. Preston declined. No one made a move to return to the villa, which was bathed in sunshine. After a quarter of an hour, Preston looked to Pech. Well?

Patience, said Pech, hands in his pocket. Patience. But even he tensed when the first shrill scream was heard. It was followed in quick succession by another and yet another. Alejandro scrambled to his feet and started in the direction of the house. This has to stop!

I wouldn't, warned Pech.

Stop them, urged Preston.

The next scream was more muted, ending in a high quavering note.

Alejandro turned to look beseechingly at Pech.

You must stop them—

I can't interfere, said Pech, then apologetically to Preston: These men live by different rules.

A robin redbreast descended from a tree, landing on the lawn between them and the house. After a few indecisive hops in their direction, it pecked at something in the grass and flew away, just as Alejandro rejoined them.

You've found yourself one beautiful house, said Pech, puckering his lips appreciatively. In ten years or less you'll triple your investment.

So I'm told, Preston said unenthusiastically.

Was it like this when you were here? Pech asked Alejandro.

That's so many years ago. . . . Francisco and I used to work in that room over there—pointing to an open window on the ground floor.

Did you ever see any of the codices?

We catalogued several.

Anadelle used to buy from me, Pech said. When I found something I thought she'd like, I'd send her a photo. She used to bargain . . . offer to buy three for the price of two.

Preston laughed. He was beginning to feel more relaxed.

Aren't these pistoleros dangerous? Alejandro asked.

I wouldn't go so far as to consider them pistoleros.

A triumphant shout reached them from the house. They could see one of the two men waving his hand to catch their attention from an upper window. Cupping his mouth, he yelled, We've got it.

That's over, said Preston, showing relief.

The garden has possibilities, Pech observed, not making a move in the direction of the house.

One wouldn't think this is Mexico, mused Preston.

You should have seen the books, said Alejandro. It was an unbelievable collection.

Ah, yes, said Pech wryly. Adding gratuitously: But you and your friend didn't seem to do such a thorough job of it. . . .

Alejandro was about to launch into a defense of his and Francisco's cataloguing, when Pablo, hands clasped over his head in a gleeful victor's gesture, emerged from the house. It was in bubble wrap, he shouted. When he reached the three of them, he repeated the words: Bubble wrap.

Preston looked ill at ease. How do we proceed?

Let's have a look at your codex, shall we? said Pech. But first we must reach an agreement on what took place.

We have Emilio breaking into the house from the far side, Pablo offered. . . . We've picked the window next to the toilet . . .

What's he talking about? Preston asked, nonplussed by Pablo's remarks.

They're establishing evidence, said Pech curtly.

Exactly right, said Pablo. Emilio cases the villa. Believing it empty, he breaks a window to enter. Pablo looked to Pech for his approval.

He's caught entering, Pech explained. It's quite straightforward. You and your guest—pointing to Alejandro—have come here to check on the repairs. You catch the Indian entering through a window—

I may be a little dense, but I still don't understand.

The Indian pulls a knife on you. You defend yourself—bang, bang, bang, said Pablo, laughing helplessly as he pretended to stagger after being shot.

Not on your life, said Preston firmly. I have no intention of being a witness to whatever you have in mind.

I'm out of this, said Alejandro.

Pablo, squatting on his heels, head at a slant, cocked an eye at Pech. He was amused by their reaction. The codex was under the floorboards, he explained. We had to pull up several . . .

It's not what I planned, said Pech, showing regret. We'll just have to make the best of it.

The best of what? Preston was outraged. If you think I'm going to lift a finger to . . .

Did you hear that? Pech said in jest to Pablo, who, rising to his feet, fastidiously began picking a few blades of grass off his tan trousers.

I suggest you pack up, said Preston.

You are on your own property, Pech replied evenly. Our Indian has a criminal record. There's no one to dispute your evidence.

Pedro's a very competent man, Pablo assured Preston, not understanding the latter's scruples, lauding his compadre as if he were extolling the skills of a carpenter or painter and not a killer.

Take the codex. I don't want the damn thing.

Eyebrows raised in mock exaggeration, Pech looked at Preston quizzically. You really expect me to tell them the deal's off?

Precisely. The deal's off. O-F-F. Off! Preston repeated, just as the first shot rang out. The birds took off from the trees, screeching. Alejandro hadn't been aware that there were so many. Pablo sprang into action, running toward the house, while Pech, in one quick motion, raised the flap of his jacket, pulled out a pistol, and, crouching low, headed to cut off Emilio's retreat, which left the two of them exposed in the vicinity of Pech's car.

This isn't what I had— Preston began to say, his face chalk white.

Alejandro heard Pablo yell to his colleague, as Emilio, blood streaming from a facial injury, ran from the back of the house, one hand clutching his leg where he must have been hit. Another shot rang out, but it missed its target.

They're out of their skulls. . . .

We have to get out of here! Alejandro said urgently, as another wave of birds swept past overhead.

Preston averted his face . . . Alejandro could hear retching. It sounded as if Preston were trying to dislodge his innards. Yet another shot. Horrified, Alejandro saw Emilio stumble, then recover himself and continue running. He was praying, Please, God, let them miss, seeing Pech, as if in slow motion, grip his pistol in both hands, legs apart, and carefully take aim, and in that second's interval catching a glimpse of a terrified Emilio glancing over his shoulder as another shot rang out. The sun was shining . . . but Emilio didn't fall. The birds were now wildly circling the house . . . Alejandro watched the three men, guns drawn, fan out and cautiously approach the thickly wooded section into which Emilio had disappeared—but for some reason they didn't pursue Emilio. He got away, Alejandro said quietly. Is that good? Preston asked, wiping his mouth with tissues he kept pulling from a small package. . . . You can't be serious, said Alejandro. He saw Pech say something to Pablo and Pedro, and motion in their direction. As the two men came running toward them, Alejandro panicked. They're heading for us!

However, to Alejandro's relief, the two barely glanced in their direction. They ran to Pech's car, jumped in, and took off with a burst of speed, narrowly missing the gatepost.

Mexican fuck-up, Pech said, when he rejoined them. Alejandro watched him slip his pistol back into its holster with the motion of someone long familiar with the use of the weapon. Somebody's been sick, Pech said, not concealing his contempt as he stepped back to distance himself from the odorous evidence of Preston's regurgitation, while looking from the offending patch of grass, already alive with flies, to them, as if to seek out the culprit.

What now? Preston asked helplessly.

Here's someone, said Pech, as a gray van with three Mexicans came bouncing their way.

It's the painters, said Preston, recognizing the burly driver.

Just remember, we're friends enjoying ourselves, Pech cautioned them.

Goddamn, I told them to stay away. They're not supposed to be here today.

The van came to a halt on the gravel path, not far from where Pech's car had been standing. The driver got out, hands partially extended as if to show he was unarmed. Señor, he called out, managing a look of concern. We heard shots and were worried. . . . Is everything OK?

Preston looked to Pech. It was a thief, said Pech calmly. He was inside the house when we arrived.

The man nodded. There are lots of thieves. . . . He stopped to mop his face with a colorful kerchief. Alejandro could see he was trying hard not to show any awareness that anything out of the ordinary might be taking place.

You weren't supposed to be here today, Preston said, his voice conveying anger, annoyance, and alarm.

Señor, I came for a few brushes and the tarpaulin, the painter explained. We have another job.

Come back tomorrow, said Preston.

Yes, señor. The painter kept his eyes averted so as not to see Pech. Saying, We are leaving . . . we are leaving. He retraced his steps, the kerchief dangling from one hand.

Tomorrow, shouted Preston a little too shrilly.

Tell him next week, said Pech.

Next week! shouted Preston.

The panic was now evident on the man's face as he got behind the wheel, Sí, sí, he yelled. Frantically he started the van, only to have the engine stall. Son of a bitch, exclaimed Pech, heading toward the van. Just as Alejandro was beginning to fear for the driver, the engine came to life. The painter made a wide U-turn that took him off the gravel path, uprooting patches of grass in his haste to get away.

That's just dandy, said Preston, upset at the damage done to his lawn.

Not your day, is it? said Pech.

It was Pech who led the way back to the house. The bubble-wrapped codex was on the table in the room in which Alejandro had catalogued Anadelle's library.

Shall we have a look at it? Pech asked Preston with a teasing smile, not prepared for the latter's curt: I don't give a hoot what you do with it. For all I care you can stick it—

After all the trouble we've gone to.

Preston followed Alejandro's gaze, only now seeing at the

jagged outlines of a head in the smashed windowpane. How did that occur?

I don't know, said Pech. He might have tripped. . . .

Tripped? Alejandro hooted.

Hearing a car outside, Pech left them with the codex.

It must be the pistoleros, said Alejandro, while Preston, palms pressed to his temples, as if to help him concentrate, walked to the table. God help me, I'm trying to think. To Alejandro's relief, he did not open the bubble-wrapped package.

Well, what's it to be? Pech asked when he returned.

The answer is *no!*

I'll bring it around to your house. Let you decide in peace.

You had no right to involve me in this frightful escapade, Preston stated somberly.

Suit yourself, said Pech, picking up the package. If you change your mind, you can reach me at the Hotel Paraíso in Megalen. I'll be there for another day or two.

That's that, said Preston as they watched Pech and his two pistoleros drive away.

They hardly exchanged a word on their drive back to Mexico City. They had run out of things to say. When they finally said goodbye, they sounded like two men who had no reason whatsoever to see each other again.

Blurred Vision

The next morning, still in bed, feeling unwell, Bonny heard the disputatious woman arguing again with the older man. This time there appeared to be another person present. But she was far too sick to pay attention. If anything, their raised voices were an irritant. By now she was running to the toilet what seemed like every few minutes. Finally, in near despair, she called the desk. Within minutes a solicitous chambermaid came up with chamomile tea and a giant pill. Since the hotel had a dish antenna on the roof, Bonny was able to watch the eclipse as seen from Baja California on CNN. With the curtains drawn, she lay in bed, staring hypnotically at the total solar eclipse on TV—according to one commentator, the longest eclipse until 2132. There was mention of the thousands of "Eclipsophiles" who had come from all over the world to see and document this event. Scientists referred to it as The Eclipse of the Millennium. In western Mexico it would last for nearly seven minutes, long enough for scientists to try to determine the fate of interplanetary dust as it spirals into the sun—the dust being the cause of the "zodiacal light" in even the darkest night sky. Also mentioned were the ludicrous measures to which the Mexicans on the Baja peninsula were going to protect themselves from the sun's lethal rays. Staying indoors, wearing red underwear. The CNN commentator had joked that many had even attached red ribbon to everything of value on their property: fruit trees, fences, farm animals. They're not taking chances, he said.

My dear child, I was looking everywhere for you, said Mme Sabaia when Bonny came down for dinner. Are you better?

Much.

Every time I see you I have to revise my estimate of your age, said Mme Sabaia, laughing nervously. You seem to be getting younger and younger . . .

It must be the way I do my hair.

Puzzled, Mme Sabaia looked at her, dubiously shaking her head. I can't understand it.

About your offer, Bonny began hesitantly. Does the invitation still stand?

Offer? said Mme Sabaia, looking a little startled.

I wonder if you're still going to El Tajín?

Of course . . . Willingly. I'll be leaving tomorrow immediately after breakfast. She then once again launched into a description of the ruins, repeating most of what she had said on the previous occasion. As you can see, they're in the thick of the jungle. It'll be ever so exciting.

What time?

How is nine for you?

I'll be ready.

View from the Roof

The floating circular stairway, with its gleaming marble steps and polished metal handrail, was a triumph of design. There were blue floor tiles on the fourth level, green on the floor beneath; below that the tiles were yellow. Sections of the blue tiles were chipped. When Bonny climbed the final flight of stairs, she discovered that the flat roof was paved with red bricks. Emerging from the small structure housing the staircase, dodging the laundry lines, she walked to the railing. There was no one about. From where she stood she had a view of the distant mountains enveloped in a reddish haze, of desolate stretches of beach, an empty harbor, the nearby villas, mostly shuttered, a deserted tennis court.

Drawn by the sound of music, she leaned over the railing and gazed straight down into one of the fifth-floor balconies, at first not comprehending what she was seeing—feeling that despite the familiarity of the ubiquitous objects, a round metal table and the folding chairs identical to the ones on her balcony, she was looking at an unidentifiable topography. Perplexed, she kept studying what she took to be a garishly colored giant doll or mannequin. Could it be some kind of Mexican fetish being prepared for a celebratory occasion? Finally it dawned on her that what she took to be a giant doll was the lifeless body of a man, lying faceup on the tiled floor, his eyes staring blankly at the sky, a rag stuffed in the distended mouth, hands and feet tied with brightly colored neckties, and with what she now realized was blood, not paint, seeping from the dozens of wounds in his body. Did she linger to commit the details to memory? The swimming trunks neatly draped over the back of a folding chair, while on the table, next to a pair of binoculars, rested a carafe of coffee and cups for four. On the tiled floor, in a pool of blood, she spotted a pair of rubber gloves and a knife. Instead of a handle the knife had tape wound around it. A transistor radio played a lively salsa tune. Her heart pounding, she raced down the stairs to her room on the fourth floor. As she shut her door she heard footsteps rapidly descending the stairs. . . . Peering through the peephole, she saw a man striding past . . . Her relief was short-lived, for a few minutes later there was a knocking on her door. Not the polite knocking she had come to associate with the hotel staff. When the knocking persisted, she crawled into bed and, drawing the covers over her head, tried without success to shut out the sound.

As soon as she was able to achieve a modicum of self-control, she picked up the bedside phone and, after dialing 95 for long distance, feverishly dialed her father's number. To her dismay, he didn't pick up. When the machine came on, she left a less than coherent message. Dad, I'm really scared . . . I can't explain, but I must leave the hotel where I am staying . . . A lady is giving me a lift as far as El Tajín. Please hop on the first available flight and

meet me at the El Tajín ruins tomorrow . . . You must
come . . . I'll be waiting for you . . . I don't know what to do
. . . Help me . . . Please!

When she stepped out on her balcony an hour later, she could
still hear faint salsa music from above . . . and then, to her
consternation, she noticed drops of blood on the railing and the
tiled floor.

Ruins

The two policemen at the reception desk turned to look at her
as she stepped out of the elevator. The desk clerk, in sharp
contrast to the two dour-faced men, smiled. Buenos días,
señorita. Buenos días, she replied, heading for the dining room.
What do you make of all the furor? Mme Sabaia asked as soon
as Bonny took her seat at the adjacent table.

Furor?

You mean to say you weren't woken by the police sirens
this morning?

No. She avoided Mme Sabaia's steady, unnerving gaze. I
was fast asleep.

Mme Sabaia eyed her skeptically. Something happened on
one of the upper floors . . . I asked the receptionist, but he
wasn't very forthcoming. As you can see, the police are here.
She tittered self-consciously as she admitted, It's unsettling.
Aren't you even the slightest bit curious?

I didn't hear a thing, Bonny maintained.

How could you have slept through that commotion?

Mme Sabaia could no longer hold back her misgivings. Are
you intending to stay on?

I thought we'd . . . She waited for Mme Sabaia to complete the sentence.

I've been thinking, Mme Sabaia began to say with a shade of embarrassment. It might not be wise, after all, for you to accompany me . . .

Prepared to burst into tears at the slightest rebuff, she looked apprehensively at Mme Sabaia. Why not?

My dear, after visiting the ruins, I'm heading straight for the coast to return the rental car. Then—

That's fine, Bonny assured her, quite undeterred by Mme Sabaia's reservations. You needn't worry. . . .

You are much younger than I thought . . . I don't think it would be responsible of me. . . . If you don't mind my saying so, you should be with your family or friends . . .

That's why I asked if you—

Surely you didn't come to Mexico by yourself?

I'm expecting my father to join me.

There you are.

He is coming . . . but I can't stay here.

Why not? They'll look after you until he arrives.

I can't . . . You don't understand.

I realize that I am going back on my word, but in your interest . . .

At least let me come with you as far as El Tajín . . .

The ruins are in the jungle. The only access to the ruins is by car. I couldn't possibly. . . . If you speak to the receptionist, he'll be glad to arrange some—

I desperately need to leave. What's more, I've told them I'm leaving. Please. Just as far as the ruins . . .

Mme Sabaia looked doubtful. A young girl like yourself . . . It's foolhardy. As I said, you should be together with—

How do you think I made it to here?

That's what I find so puzzling.

Please . . . , Bonny begged. Please.

As you can see, I'm not very social.

You asked me . . . You invited me . . .

Mme Sabaia sighed. She couldn't deny it. You make it so difficult.

I'm fine. Really . . . I just spoke to my father.

Then, he's definitely coming?

Yes. I told you.

That's settled, then. . . . Marvelous.

That's why I need a ride.

Surely he's not meeting you there?

You don't know my father. He has hired a helicopter.

I can't believe that. She looked reprovingly at Bonny. What's happened? You're shivering. It can't be that important . . .

I promise—

A helicopter? Really, you shouldn't exaggerate . . . If you want to come along that much . . . I just don't see how you'll manage after.

But he's meeting me there. I've left a message . . . this morning.

But, my dear . . . Then, leafing through her guidebook: Here, look for yourself. The ruins are in the middle of nowhere. . . .

I'll be fine. If you just . . .

According to the guidebook, the ruins stretch for miles of jungle. I couldn't possibly leave you there. . . .

When Bonny went to the reception desk to check out, the clerk pointed to a man nearby in the lobby, reading a newspaper, explaining that he was from the police and wanted a few words with her. About what? You mustn't be afraid, said the detective in English, rising from his seat, folding the newspaper as he approached the desk. To her relief, the questions were few and not in the least demanding. Did you ever see the couple staying in the room above yours? he asked.

I only heard them . . . each morning.

A man and a woman?

Yes. That's what it sounded like to me.

Are you sure?

Yes.

In what language were they speaking?

Spanish. I couldn't make out what they were saying.

What were they doing on the balcony?

I'm pretty certain they were having breakfast. I could hear the sound of dishes. One of them, the man, spoke with an American accent.

Did you hear anything yesterday?

I was ill. I was in bed with the TV on . . .

What were you watching?

The eclipse.

That was the day before.

I don't know what I was watching. I said, I was ill.

The receptionist told me you are waiting for your father.

Yes.

When do you expect him?

Any day now.

As Bonny and Mme Sabaia left an hour later, the staff lined up at the door to wave goodbye. Goodbye, Bonny . . . , they shouted.

Goodness, I've been here twice before, and I've never had

this kind of a send-off. You must have tipped very generously.

I haven't . . . I just handed them my Visa card. . . .

How extraordinary.

At first the road was well marked, and they had no difficulty finding the turnoff to El Tajín. It was hilly country. On the way they passed fields of maize and what Mme Sabaia maintained was cocoa. Just imagine, this is what everything looked like when Cortés landed in Veracruz.

I haven't had time to read up on Cortés, Bonny admitted. Was he the good or the bad guy?

Goodness, I suppose that depends entirely on your historical perspective.

My father maintains that history and fiction are interchangeable.

Mme Sabaia could not allow that statement to pass unchallenged. History, she said, is the untrammelled flow of energy that defines our essence.

OK, said Bonny, who had not understood a word. What about fiction? By this time they could see the pyramid. It overshadowed their conversation. It diminished any need Mme Sabaia may have felt to offer an opinion.

Majestic, isn't it? said Mme Sabaia, gazing at the stately pyramid with an expression of awe. Bonny was all set to go and explore the ruins the moment they arrived, but to her dismay, Mme Sabaia kept stopping to consult her guidebook: The center here was first occupied in the Early Classic, but the peak activity was toward the close of the Late Classic (A.D. 600–900). The inhabitants, she went on, were obsessed with the ball game, human sacrifice, and death, three concepts closely interwoven in the Mexican mind. It was midday, and there weren't many tourists about. What were the empty niches used for? Bonny asked as they began their ascent of the pyramid. I don't think they know, said Mme Sabaia. Unlike the Pyramid of the Sun outside of Mexico City, large sections of this far more decorative one were crumbling. Reaching the top of the first of the six tiers, Mme Sabaia decided to rest, perching herself on the narrow steps of the central staircase, fanning herself with the guide-book. I'll think I'll stay here for a while . . . Then, eyeing Bonny, she said, Don't let me stop you—you go right ahead.

Bonny was about to do so when she saw in the parking lot two giant tour buses disgorge dozens of excited kids. A make-shift sign on one bus read MITZWA EXCURSIONS. Just what I need, said Mme Sabaia. I think I'll go down to have a look at the new arrivals, if you don't mind, Bonny said, barely containing her excitement.

By all means, said Mme Sabaia, by now resigned to their impending arrival. Take all the time you want. I'll be back soon, Bonny promised. As she neared the parking lot, the youngsters were receiving last-minute instructions before heading for the pyramid. . . . Surmounting her shyness, she approached, overcome by a strong desire to mingle with the others—was it a desire to return to what at first sight the group represented, the family or the familiar? One of the counselors looked quizzically at her, undecided whether she was part of the group or not. How to explain—for the first time since she had left her father she felt at home. Where are you from? a young girl asked, looking at Bonny's boots as if the answer were to be found there. New York. The city? Yes. Now, looking more attentive, the girl wanted to know, What part? Central Park West. We're on Eighty-ninth and Broadway. They giggled. But when she asked Bonny what school she attended, Bonny could only recall the name of her grade school. As the group began to follow the counselors in the direction of the ruins, the girl, in what to Bonny sounded like an invitation, volunteered that there were a couple of empty seats on the bus. I love your hat, said Bonny impulsively. I'll trade you, replied the girl, and they did. In the distance she could see Mme Sabaia sitting on the steps, immersed in her guidebook. I'll catch you later, Bonny said. If you're on your own, come join us, said the girl. They won't even notice. Couple of girls failed to show . . . and at least three of the counselors are last-minute replacements. They don't even remember our names.

Second Thoughts

Isn't life full of coincidences, Mme Sabaia said, looking decidedly relieved when Bonny informed her that she had met up with some friends from New York. . . . See how things work out. She walked Bonny to the parking lot, where Bonny collected her bag and accepted a sandwich. Mme Sabaia checked the car doors to see if they were locked before setting off to visit the Building of the Columns, with its reliefs of human sacrifice, and the ball courts. In case you should need me, she said, I'll be around for at least another two hours. I intend to save the museum for last. However, in case we miss each other, I'll say goodbye now. Kissing Bonny on the cheek: Goodbye, my dear, goodbye. . . . It was a treat having your company. I hope your father won't keep you waiting much longer. Bonny, a little taken aback by the abruptness of Mme Sabaia's goodbyes, picked up her possessions and fled.

An hour later, while sharing a box lunch with her new friends, Aubrey, Nancy and Constance, Bonny saw Mme Sabaia walking to the low building that served as a makeshift museum. She waved, but Mme Sabaia was too lost in thought to notice her or hear her call.

We were about to fly to Israel, Constance explained, when the Iraqis began to shell Tel Aviv.

I'm not sorry to have seen Mexico instead, Nancy remarked.

For one thing, we wouldn't have met you, said Aubrey.

Is Bonny your real name? Nancy asked, wrinkling her nose.

Bonny hesitated. My dad calls me Buddy. . . . My mom calls me Bon. . . . Just thinking of them made her want to cry. My friends . . . She faltered. They call me Bo.

In the late afternoon, Bonny making herself as inconspicuous as possible watched from the side as the American kids, having formed the letter *F* on the steps of the pyramid, posed patiently while several counselors, using everything from Nikons to Instamatics, took an endless number of shots. Seeing her by herself, one of the younger counselors approached and asked where her parents were. She tried to oblige. Think hard, he said earnestly. I don't know, she finally admitted, looking around, as if expecting them to materialize at any moment. He looked concerned. When did you last see them? She was vague. It's been some time. . . . At noon? This morning? Not receiving a reassuring response, he walked to where the other counselors were standing. Bonny saw them in deep discussion, every now and then turning their heads to glance in her direction. The senior counselor finally walked over to her. He had his hands in his pockets.

He tried to look cheerful. Hi, there! What's your name? When she told him, he inquired, Did your mother tell you to wait? Not receiving a reply, he half knelt and asked in a near whisper, Do you consider yourself lost? Yes, she said, I think so. Do you know where you are? El Tajín. Do you know where you just came from? The Hotel Paraíso in Megalen. Can you see your parents' car in the parking lot? She wanted desperately to please him and say yes. Well, do you? he asked. She looked at the cars—there were fewer than a dozen—and reluctantly admitted, No. Who did you come with? A lady who was staying at the hotel. Well, we must reunite you, mustn't we? Yes. Is she here? I don't see her. Just wait; we'll help you find her. When he rejoined the group of counselors, their discussion seemed if anything to grow more heated. By now she felt too tired to even think. All she wanted was something cool to drink. She was about to walk to the Coke machine in the gift shop, when she spotted Pablo and Pedro standing next to her old bookmobile. Clutching her belongings, she fled . . . Nothing else mattered as she ran—as fast as she could—in the direction of the line of trees. Wait! yelled the counselor. Little girl . . . wait! She was in a state of terror. She had to find a place of concealment. Bonny, yelled her new friends. Bonny, stop . . .

She kept running toward the safety of the jungle.

Attendants?

The two men greeted Mme Sabaia as she walked to her car. Hello, señora, Pablo called out in a lilting, seductive voice. Did you enjoy the ruins? Anywhere else she might have considered the greeting as intrusively familiar, but here, in this magical setting, in these astonishing pre-Columbian surroundings, furthermore reassured by the fact that the two "simple" Mexicans maintained a "safe" distance between her and themselves, she was able to assimilate them into the historical if savage splendor she had just experienced. They're magnificent, she warmly agreed, more than ready to accept these two young Mexicans as presenting a link, tenuous as it might appear, to the ancestors of the Totomacs, the builders of these amazing edifices—now remnants of what was once a great imperial society.

Something to take back home, said Pablo.

She was happy to share her pleasure. Yes, exactly. Given the occasion, she was totally uncritical of what she took to be a well-intended if trite statement.

We could see from your face that you liked it.

Liked? No, she protested. That word doesn't approximate the feeling this spectacle arouses in me. It's awe-inspiring . . . But I expect that to you it conveys a more meaningful truth. She wasn't being patronizing. On the contrary. She felt supremely contented, having viewed in the small museum the startling relief panels that showed the sacrifice of the captain of the losing ball team in what must surely be the very same ball court she had visited earlier . . . She wanted to communicate not only her boundless admiration . . . but as well her abiding belief in man's ingenuity and inventiveness.

They stared at her—taking stock. Seen one, seen them all, Pablo said finally, with a laugh so coarse that it startled her out of her reverie. I must be going, she quickly said. Now her smile was forced.

Are you returning to Megalen?

Flustered by the question, she hastily said, Oh, no . . . I'm heading East.

Leaving Mexico?

She turned in the direction of her car, fumbling in her bag for her keys.

The men followed. They were the only people in the parking area.

Key in the lock, door half opened, she looked at the men, who now stood next to her.

Where's your little girl?

At the mention of little girl, an alarm was set off in her head. . . . Pretending not to understand, she looked at her watch, feigning surprise. I must be off.

We like Bonny, said Pedro, with a disarming grin.

She slid behind the wheel and rolled down the window. There was a young woman. I only gave her a lift. . . .

Isn't she returning with you to Megalen?

She slammed the door shut. Eyeing them mistrustfully, she said, She's expecting her father . . .

When Pedro stepped up to the car, placing his hand on the roof, not seeming to mind the intense heat of the metal, she panicked, turning the key in the ignition, shifting into first gear, wanting to put this disconcerting encounter behind her as quickly as possible.

Reading her mind, Pablo smiled. Drive safely.

She looked in the direction of the pyramid as she exited the parking lot, aware that she had been negligent . . . that she should return . . . and if necessary wait with Bonny until her father arrived.

No, she decided after having driven a short distance, she was reading too much into what they had said. Bonny could look after herself.

The Immutable Self

Bonny spent the early part of the night near the Pyramid of the Niches. She found a spare box lunch and two Cokes one of the counselors must have left for her. When she saw several Indian boys nearby, she quickly hid. They were stalking an animal, and she soon heard thrashing and wild inchoate animal screams. After thrusting her bag in the niche nearest her, she started to climb. Though it was not a very tall pyramid, as pyramids go, it took her the better part of an hour. She opened a can of warm Coke on reaching the midway point. She was near exhaustion . . .

Each time she shut her eyes, her brain assembled, piece by piece, the by now nauseatingly familiar picture of the dead man on the balcony, compelling her to see his eyes staring blindly at the sky while—was this a figment of her imagination?— either Pedro or Pablo, standing near the body, dropped a pair of soiled plastic gloves to the tiled floor. The salsa music from the portable radio on the balcony's metal folding table did not drown out the sound of the shower going full blast inside the man's room. Finally, to dispel this disconcerting representation, she forced herself to escape, to run down the hotel stairs . . . in passing, seeing a DO NOT DISTURB sign dangling from the handle of the dead man's door.

She woke with a start. It was pitch dark. Soon her father would be there, she kept telling herself. Soon it would be light. An owl hooted.

She watched the sun rise . . . The trees, some almost as tall as the pyramid, were alive with birds . . . She covered her ears to block out their cacophonous songs. Below, a mangy dog scurried past the base of the pyramid. By nine it was warming up. An hour later it was roasting. She had drunk her last Coke and finished the box lunch. There were several cars in the parking lot. One, a jeep, seemed to belong to the custodian. The people working in the gift shop and in the museum had arrived in the others. She feared everyone. Descending one level, she hid at the back in the coolest of the niches and tried to get some more sleep.

Boys

The three boys climbed the ruined pyramid to search for coins, sunglasses, cameras, trinkets, anything tourists might leave behind. They found the girl sprawled lifelessly in the tiny sanctuary, next to her Sony Walkman, a couple of empty Coke cans, and an empty lunch box. One prodded her gently with his foot. One shook her shoulder. When she failed to respond, they assumed she was dead and panicked—what if they were blamed? Given the conditions of life, it did not seem at all farfetched to them. How she died was of no importance. They'd be culpable because they were Indians. After a brief discussion, they decided that the best way to dispose of her was the old Mayan method: they slung her down the back of the pyramid, seeing her land on a ledge several levels below. Having tried the Walkman without success, the tallest one, the leader, pocketed it as his booty. They kicked the cans and the remnants of her meal over the side. Barefooted, they raced down the steps, with a dexterity perfected by generations of Indians climbing and descending the steep incline.

Search Party

It came flying low over the giant trees, creating a wind that bent and twisted the treetops. Making a sharp turn, it came straight at the pyramid, circling it once before landing in the central plaza. No one came forward to greet the pilot and the three passengers who, after alighting from the chopper, on the side of which was the word EDEN, huddled over a map to get their bearings. Are you sure that the guide is to meet us here? Terrence asked the pilot. Yes, señor. He is a linguist who'll be able to communicate with the local Indians. What could have brought her here? Jurud wondered aloud, as he looked at the sixty-foot-high, seven-tiered pyramid with its row upon row of niches.

Mishearing his remark, Terrence said, I'm told it was Thursday. As far as we could determine, a Mme Sabaia, whom Bonny got to know at the hotel in Megalen, brought her here. Incidentally, Mme Sabaia mentioned to the desk clerk that Bonny was expecting to meet her father at the ruins.

I don't know what to make of it, said Jurud despondently.

That'll be our guide, Alejandro said, catching sight of the tall man in a bush jacket who was striding toward them. You must be the linguist from the Partridge Museum? Terrence said, addressing the man in English. No, señor, I am the archivist. Terrence looked perplexed. I understood that a linguist familiar with the local dialect was coming to assist us. Peering closely at Terrence the archivist asked: Are you the gentleman whose daughter is missing? No. I am, said Jurud. Sir, let me assure you, we'll locate her, said the archivist. The local Indians, on whose help I'm counting, know every square inch of the terrain. But you're not the linguist, Alejandro protested. We need someone who speaks their language. Who cares if he is a linguist, as long as he can communicate with the Indians, said Terrence. I've never experienced any difficulty yet in *communicating* with my fellow humans, the archivist replied, clearly nettled by the latter's remark. Terrence, seeing Jurud's baffled look, responded with a shrug that implied, I'm no wiser than you. Still, there was something appealing about the archivist's tall, gaunt figure. His ungainliness counterbalanced by a sprightly youthfulness. His features accentuated an intense discord. Each element, each detail—eyes, eyebrows, mouth, lips, chin, forehead, even ears—was set on a course that was entirely independent of the others. As if reading Jurud's cogitations, the archivist proposed that they begin the search by climbing the pyramid. Leaving the uniformed pilot standing at the side of the helicopter, the four of them, with the archivist in the lead, headed for the pyramid. We must do this methodically, the archivist said as he bounded up the steps, displaying more energy than one might expect from a deskbound man. Shouldn't we first get in touch with the local Indians? Jurud asked, as he tried to keep up. First we need to look at the top, said the archivist, maintaining his lead. I'd take it easy, Terrence cautioned Jurud. You're not accustomed to this elevation. It looks easier than you— I'm fine, said Jurud, determined to keep up with the others. Eyes fixed on the archivist now nearing the uppermost level, Jurud continued to climb, the perspiration beading his face, all the while berating himself for delaying the search . . . for misinterpreting Bonny's letters . . . for failing to heed her earlier messages. He was on the verge of collapse when he reached the top just ahead of Alejandro. The archivist, on all fours, was already examining the rough, uneven stone surface for clues. Here's something, he said, holding up a white plastic spoon—then, triumphantly: Here's something else. It was a torn gold chain. I just don't know, said Jurud wearily as he examined it. She had a gold chain, but how am I to tell if it's this one?

What was she wearing?

I wouldn't know. She ran away . . . I don't know what she was wearing. He handed the archivist a photo. That's her. It was taken over a year ago.

A güera.

Jurud was confused by the archivist's pleased look. A güera? A blonde, said Terrence.

The archivist radiated optimism. We're ready to set off for the village, he said. If she's here, the Indians will find her. . . . Jurud was too exhausted to express any opinion. By now the news of the copter's arrival had spread, and dozens of scrawny Indian children and several adults stood gaping at it and its pilot from a respectful distance.

We should question those Indian kids if they saw Bonny, Terrence said as they made their descent.

But when they headed for the helicopter, to Jurud's dismay the children, seeming to sense what they had in mind, scattered in all directions, shrilly laughing as they ran toward the shelter of the trees. They're exceedingly shy, the archivist explained. They distrust strangers.

Can we fly to the village? Alejandro asked.

The custodian has agreed to drive us, since the copter would alarm the villagers, Terrence explained. However, we'll make good use of it in our search.

As they walked toward the copter, Alejandro seized the opportunity to commiserate with Jurud.

Bonny's an independent spirit, said Jurud.

The custodian, a short, muscular man, with a large pistol strapped to his belt, greeted them deferentially. When questioned by the archivist, who had taken charge, he explained in Spanish that he had seen the young girl they were looking for. She was dropped off by a middle-aged woman. . . . She met up with some girls—American children who had arrived in two buses. At first, he said, I concluded that she was part of the group. But then I saw her running away . . . she was frightened. . . . I also saw two Mexican men, who arrived in a small bus, looking for her. How do you know they were looking for her? That's the impression they gave. Hours later I caught sight of her climbing the pyramid. But I didn't give it any thought.

When the American teenagers left at sunset, I assumed she was on one of the buses.

When did you last see her?

He scratched his head. It must have been when she was climbing the pyramid. I thought she might have left something behind. Tourists frequently do.

The archivist inquired if any attempt was being made to trace the busload of children who had visited the ruins, to see if by chance Bonny had left with them.

It's being done, said Terrence. We have people in Mexico City trying to locate the bus.

Do you think it's possible that she'd be on that bus? Jurud mused.

Alejandro was astonished to see Jurud so controlled, so unemotional.

There's a good chance that she cadged a lift and then . . .

If not, then she must still be in the vicinity of the pyramid, said Alejandro. We'll have to look into all the niches. There are over three hundred, each one large enough to accommodate her and her luggage.

The custodian drove them over the deeply rutted dirt road to the village with an abandon that could only come from a firm belief in the hereafter. I kept receiving her letters . . . Jurud explained to Terrence, who was seated at his side in the antiquated jeep. I assumed she was all right.

How could you tell? Alejandro interjected. He was not yet prepared to acknowledge that his anger and his resentment of Jurud was being supplanted by an emotional warmth, a feeling akin to affection.

Reaching the village, really a collection of huts and ramshackle houses, the archivist, who seemed to know his way around, sought out the local cacique, a man of power in the community. The cacique, who seemed to have been expecting them, invited them into his hut. Though Alejandro could not understand a word of what passed between the cacique and the archivist, both smiling to signal their good intentions, he detected something at once sly, underhanded, and ingratiating in the cacique's response to the archivist's request that he organize a search party. I wouldn't turn my back on that man for fear he'll pull a knife on me, said Terrence, reading the look of disgust on Alejandro's face. However, their suspicion of the cacique was not shared by the archivist who, declaring himself satisfied with the meeting, went on to say that it was only a matter of time before Bonny would be located. I'm more convinced than ever that she's around here, somewhere. They were about to head back to the copter when an old woman came forward, hesitantly holding out, as if it were an offering, a battered-looking yellow Sony Walkman. That could be Bonny's! Jurud exclaimed. While answering the archivist's questions, the woman kept looking in all directions, as if fearing the wrath of some unseen spirit or person. She claims that some of the local boys found the Walkman. Where? She's being evasive, the archivist explained. Can we speak to the boys? said Alejandro. I suspect that she was asked to bring this to us. I wouldn't press her. We need their cooperation. Examining the Walkman closely, Jurud saw the initials *BJ* scratched into the back. Excited, he exclaimed, It's hers! Ask her, when was it found? Seeing his fiery look as he advanced on her, the old woman let out a muffled screech and fled. Please, control yourself, said the archivist. I suggest we stay on while they organize the search, said Terrence. They agreed. As they waited in an open hut, buzzed by large aggressive flies, watching men rush back and forth, Jurud had the impression that he was witnessing a parody, a burlesque show, an aimless exercise performed purely for their benefit. When the cacique served them pulque, Jurud, though thirsty, did not conceal his squeamish apprehension. What is this? Try it, urged the archivist, raising his cup in a toast. Salút. It's fermented juice from the maguey plant, said Alejandro. It's quite heady. Overcoming his initial reluctance, Jurud tasted it and not finding it as unpleasant as he had anticipated, he accepted a second cup. Before we leave we must pay a visit to the curandero, said the archivist. The medicine man, Alejandro explained. More than likely he's the real power here. The cacique laughed when Jurud, rising to his feet, wobbled slightly. I warned you, said Alejandro as they set off. The curandero, who was sitting by himself in a thatched roof structure supported by wood beams indistinguishable from all the other dwellings, responded in a guarded manner to the archivist's ebullient greeting and questions. I can see he's not going to be cooperative, said the archivist. Money? suggested Terrence. No. The archivist shook his head. On an impulse, Jurud pulled off his eighteen-karat-gold moon-phase watch and handed it to the curandero, who readily accepted it, albeit with a puzzled expression. The archivist looked upset. What do you think you're doing? The curandero held the watch by one end of the strap, not looking at it. For you, said Jurud, gesturing with his hand to indicate that the watch was intended as a gift. That's unnecessary, said Terrence. You now have put him under an obligation. Precisely my intent, replied Jurud. I wish you'd leave this business to me, grumbled the archivist. This is not the way to proceed. . . . But Jurud, indifferent to the latter's disapproval, extended his hand. The curandero who was still seated, took it. Bonny, Jurud said, pressing the curandero's hand. Bonny, the latter replied with a blissful smile, as if the name were a greeting.

. . .

Their jeep was stopped at an intersection by a police patrol, four men carrying submachine guns. After one look, they were waved on. Everything's upside down since the murder of Pech, the American art dealer, Terrence explained.

A macabre incident, Alejandro said to Jurud. He was found murdered in his hotel room, just about the time your daughter was staying there.

Had she met him?

I doubt it. The police claim it was a sexual crime. I don't believe them.

Did you meet Bonny in Mexico City? Jurud asked.

No.

She kept me informed, letting me know where she was staying.

What did Bonny say in her last message to you? Alejandro asked Jurud.

She sounded frightened out of her wits. She said, Meet me at the ruins . . . I am counting on you.

What did you do?

Well, before hopping on the first available flight, I called the embassy in Mexico City. I also informed the Mexican police— equally futile actions. I then called the Holliers. . . . I am most grateful to Preston for putting the company helicopter at my disposal . . . and to you and Terrence for coming along.

You know, I was to interview you on TV, said Alejandro, a slight edge to his voice.

So I was told.

You didn't show up.

Sorry about that, said Jurud lightly, as if he were apologizing for missing a luncheon and not an event planned in his honor.

We felt let down.

I had to cancel . . . Jurud's voice trailed off.

You should have let us know.

But I did. I had my agent get in touch with Jacobus. . . .

Incidentally, was the watch you gave the curandero hand-wound or quartz? the archivist wanted to know.

Quartz.

He'll never be able to find a replacement battery for it, said the archivist with ill-concealed glee.

It was just a gesture, murmured Jurud.

When they returned to the helicopter, the pilot, out of Jurud's earshot, informed Terrence that he had intercepted a message sent by the search party to the Megalen police, reporting that they had evidence the missing girl was in the Indian village, under the care of the curandero.

We'll just wait, said Terrence, and told the pilot to remain on the alert for further messages. The sun was setting when a policeman drove up to the helicopter and in Alejandro's presence informed the archivist that the young woman had been located. We're not one hundred percent certain that she's the missing girl, he admitted.

What's going on? Jurud demanded to know.

For one thing, she doesn't match the photo, the policeman stated.

What's he saying?

So what, shouted Alejandro in exasperation. A young woman is missing, and you find one, ergo, she's the missing—

Patience, patience, said the archivist.

The policeman explained that a doctor was on his way. She's suffering from exposure . . . dehydration.

All the more reason for her father to see her, argued Alejandro.

Will someone tell me what's going on? Jurud yelled.

On being told, he shouted, Take me to her . . . do you hear me! Then, yelling to the archivist, Translate, for God's sake. What's happened to her? They'll be here shortly with her, promised the policeman. Ten minutes.

But it took an hour for the ambulance to arrive. Bonny, wrapped in a blanket, was carried in a stretcher to the helicopter. She appears to have fallen down an incline, said the Mexican doctor who accompanied her. She's badly bruised. I can't rule out neurological damage . . .

Where was she found?

The doctor looked distracted. From what I understand, she was found somewhere on the pyramid. The curandero in the Indian village was treating her. . . . God only knows what he may have given her.

I suspect that whoever found her, the archivist said, perhaps some of the local boys, may have been afraid of being implicated . . .

At first the doctor had insisted that she be flown to the hospital in Megalen. After some bickering, during which time the pilot radioed Eden Enterprise, requesting that they get in touch with the American-British Cowdray Hospital in Mexico City, the doctor was persuaded by Terrence to accompany Jurud and Bonny. For lack of space on the copter, Terrence and Alejandro stayed behind with the archivist. They spent the night in the Hotel Paraíso in Megalen. At dinner, to Alejandro's dismay, the archivist having ascertained that he, Alejandro, had been one of the two librarians who had catalogued the Partridge Museum library, began to revile him for his ineptness. The next morning, when Terrence, who had rented a car for their return trip to Mexico City, offered the archivist a lift, the latter turned it down. Not with that man. Don't take it to heart, said Terrence as they set off. He did help locate Bonny.

Two days later, after extensive examination had ruled out any serious neurological damage, Jurud was permitted to return to the U.S. with Bonny, even though she had not uttered a single word. She's in a state of shock, the neurologist in charge of her case explained. Once back in familiar surroundings, she should recover quickly. She's young and resilient. A nurse who Alejandro had befriended confided to him. They're not convinced that she's the missing girl. Who else could she be? And why would the American accept a girl that wasn't his daughter? That's what's so puzzling. One hears so much about the skills of the curanderos. What are you implying? She shrugged. If they have any doubts, why don't they get more information? There must be a dozen ways of identifying an American teenager. Obviously, she's lost a lot of weight and is dehydrated, the nurse conceded. Furthermore, Señor Jurud seems so positive.

Alejandro insisted on accompanying Jurud to his plane. It was an Aeroméxico flight. I wish I could have been of more help, said Alejandro. You've been very helpful, Jurud assured him.

Bonny sat staring vacantly into space, as the ambulance sped them to the airport.

Why am I here? Alejandro asked himself. Was he waiting for Jurud to mention Mercedes . . . to reveal something?

The Critic Has No Past to Speak Of

In full view of passersby, two men, one from each side, grabbed hold of Alejandro, and half dragged him to where their car, its engine running, was parked. Expertly they bundled him into the back seat. If you can tell me what it's about, he pleaded, once he had recovered from the initial shock, I'm sure we can reach some accommodation. Receiving no response, he mentioned that he had a class at 2:00 p.m. This time the burly man next to him chortled, I guess you won't make it. Alejandro did not give up, using the term *to see reason* to suggest his willingness to pay. He should have known better. The traffic, as if divining their special mission, parted for them as, ignoring traffic lights, they drove at breakneck speed along the tree-lined Paseo de la Reforma and, after a sharp left on Amazonas, stopped in front of a large, tightly shuttered mansion that might once have been a foreign consulate, even a legation. It was well synchronized. The door opened, and they passed through with not a word spoken. One man took him up a flight of stairs at a run. Alejandro was out of breath when they reached the top, certain that he was being rushed to an interrogation, only to find himself left, a little bewildered, in what might once have served as a reception room. On the wall a framed map of Veracruz under siege showed the disposition of the invading French land and sea forces. The furniture, what there was of it, was covered with dust sheets. There was no carpet. The tall windows gave onto the street. To his surprise, when he tried the door, it was unlocked. Stepping out on the landing, he looked down into the white-marble interior courtyard. There was not a sound to be heard. On a chair near the stairs, someone had left a copy of *Alarma*. On one of the inside pages there was mention of Pech's death. He wondered if the paper had been left for him to see. It contained nothing new, aside from the information that Pech, the American art dealer, had been staying at the Hotel Paraíso in Megalen with a young Veracruz Indian. The only other detail that caught his eye was an unsigned editorial that condemned American homosexuals who came to Mexico to corrupt its youth. Are we lackeys who dare not speak out? Isn't it time that we convey to the U.S. that we will not tolerate their sexual excess? the editorial writer raged. Half an hour passed. An hour. He looked at the comic strip. He began the crossword. Getting up from the chair, he tried another door but found it locked. He was halfway down the stairs, when someone whistled. It was the burly man. Resting against the banister, he lazily beckoned Alejandro to return: Come back, come back, as if addressing a pussycat.

What have we here? their boss, the jefe, said by way of greeting when Alejandro entered the room. A critic, replied his sidekick, a short man with bloodshot eyes. What does the critic do? He examines what should be left unexamined, was the insouciant reply. To Alejandro's relief, there were no bright lights. No overt threats. Only a bottle of Tehuacán carbonated mineral water on the metal desk served as a warning. Would you like some? asked the jefe's sidekick with a suggestion of a smile, as if to remind him of its other, less orthodox utilization. A third man, the youngest, was studiously taking notes. There's no mention of Preston Hollier in his file, stated the sidekick. Alejandro nervously watched the jefe, who kept toying with a massive gold ring bearing the initials *DG* on his right hand. The eyes revealed nothing. Is he going to be cooperative? the jefe asked rhetorically. Given the context, an interrogation, and the setting, a former consulate or embassy in the heart of the city, their every move, their every motion, appeared rehearsed. They seemed to luxuriate in the commonplace, investing it with their unquestioned authority. In this environment, the banal was cherished. The jefe absentmindedly fingered his chin. They were in no hurry. The first blow landed on the bridge of his nose. If the backhanded chop was intended to get his attention, it more than served its purpose. In order to sock him, the jefe half rose from his chair and, with one hand on the table, leaned forward. The blow was delivered with the left, the ringless hand. He didn't even put any effort into it. Alejandro fell to the floor. It must have resembled a comic routine out of a Stan Laurel and Oliver Hardy movie. His glasses flew across the room. He lay on the floor, too stunned to move. No one came forward to assist him. He shook his head to get rid of the loud ringing noise in his ears. The chief interrogator motioned him to stand up. With an apologetic look, Alejandro said from the floor, I have to use the bathroom.

The jefe nodded to the somber-faced young man, who on his way to escort Alejandro to the bathroom bent down to pick up his glasses. The young man even held open the door and switched on the light for Alejandro. It was a huge bathroom, with an old-fashioned marble basin. The admonitory words DO NOT HOLD BACK . . . GIVE US WHATEVER YOU HAVE. WE'LL TAKE IT FROM YOU ANYHOW! on the inside partition of the institutional-green metal cubicle, beneath the roughly drawn giant-size prick and a dotted line to indicate a spurt of semen seemed to convey a special exhortation. By now Alejandro was far too nervous to retain any kind of critical balance. So that's how it's done, he thought, as he examined his throbbing, swollen features in the mirror while vainly trying to stem the trickle of blood from his left nostril. Though there was no one outside the bathroom when he finished, he didn't even contemplate an escape as he retraced his steps to the interrogation room.

The men had traded places. To his relief, the soft-spoken younger man had traded seats with the jefe. Before sitting down Alejandro took the precaution of edging his chair away from the green metal desk. No one appeared to notice. The fan rotated stale warm air and the smell of tobacco. Only the jefe preferred American cigarettes. The others, he noted, smoked Casinos and Record.

The younger man, on receiving a nod to proceed from the jefe, began by asking, How well do you know Preston Hollier?

He tried to inject sincerity into his reply: Not well. He looked at them with an expression of someone with nothing to conceal. We're just acquaintances. On one occasion I accompanied him to Teotihuacán. He suggested that I could be of use to him . . . that I might write favorably of his commission to build an elevator in the Pyramid of the Sun.

Were you of assistance to him in his acquisition of pre-Columbian artifacts?

Only to the extent of giving him the name of Señor Salas, a former colleague of mine who is the curator at the Partridge Museum. I believed that Preston Hollier might find Salas useful, inasmuch as Salas has all kinds of connections. . . .

The sidekick eyed the fly that brazenly had settled itself on a saucer containing a tea bag. Alejandro could see that he was tempted to swat it.

How long have you known Salas?

Since university. However, nowadays we hardly see each other.

Was Salas of any help to the Holliers?

I believe so. But I didn't ask in what way. . . .

Did you receive anything in return for this quasi service of yours . . . this introduction?

A trifle.

The fly settled on the table's surface, now challenging the man with the bloodshot eyes. He slowly furled a newspaper.

Such as?

A small pre-Columbian figurine from Preston and a small fee from Salas.

Just for a name? Are you in the habit of rendering this kind of service for your American friends?

Certainly not.

They were amused by the indignation in his voice.

It wasn't payment. I regarded it as a gift. I would have been embarrassed to return it.

Didn't you once work for the late Señora Partridge?

I and my friend Francisco catalogued the scholarly books Señora Anadelle Partridge had acquired for the Partridge Museum. We worked in the villa in Megalen.

Did you catalogue anything else of value?

All the art was crated by the time we arrived. We were there for one purpose, to catalogue the books and codices for the museum library.

Had you had any cataloguing experience prior to your stay with Anadelle Partridge?

I had assisted cataloguers at the university library. You might say that I was acquainted with the procedure.

Did you complete the job?

To start with, we made a complete list of all the books, and also arranged them by category. It's fair to say that when we left, the job was far from complete.

Were there any codices in the collection?

Several.

Did you mark the codices to indicate that they had been listed?

Yes, in pencil. I considered some too valuable to be stamped.

Did you ever steal any?

Codices? Certainly not. Seeing the men laugh, he added, I may have picked up a novel or two that had found their way into the collection.

Was there any reason why Preston would invite you to accompany him to the villa in Megalen? the younger man asked.

I imagine he didn't want to make the trip by himself.

Tell us again: What was Hollier's reason for the trip?

As far as I could tell, he wanted to inspect the house, see what progress the painters had made.

You went along for the ride?

Yes.

We think that Preston Hollier may have been trying to catch his wife together with your friend Francisco at the villa. That you were brought along as a "reliable" witness.

I wouldn't knowingly have gone along with such a scheme.

Salas pays you. Preston pays you. Why shouldn't you do Preston another little favor? asked the jefe.

When did you first discover that Francisco was involved with Preston Hollier's wife? asked the young interrogator before he could respond.

When I saw them together leaving an art gallery near San Angel. I could tell from the adoring way she looked at him. My suspicion was confirmed when Francisco on some pretext came to see me, bringing her along. He requested that if asked by Preston, I should say that they had spent the entire afternoon with me.

You agreed?

Of course.

Any payment in return for the favor?

I'm not in the habit of requesting payment for favors.

You just told us that you had received money from Salas and—

Francisco is my best friend. I accepted Salas's gift because he's not a friend. It enabled him to demonstrate his importance.

Did Francisco ever mention the gifts he's accepted from Rita Hollier?

I'm not aware that he's received any.

The official looked pained. The expensive suits . . . ? The jefe snorted. The exorbitant silk shirts . . . ?

Silk pajamas, the jefe corrected him.

No.

On the day of your drive to the villa, did Señor Hollier refer to his wife?

Only to say that she'd taken charge of redoing the house . . .

Looking at the calendar, Alejandro saw it was turned to the wrong month.

The local painters maintain that in addition to you and Preston there were others present at the villa. An American . . .

Yes, Pech. Preston had told me that he was expecting the art dealer.

Had you met Pech before?

I had seen him once at the Holliers'. But I didn't speak to him.

Had he come to the villa to sell Preston Hollier something, or was he there for another reason?

I understand that Preston Hollier was always buying something from Pech.

Think hard, said the beefy man.

Preston Hollier is a major collector.

Think hard.

I am . . . I'm trying to.

Was it a pre-Columbian artifact? Or a codex, perhaps?

I don't—

Think hard.

Alejandro jumped in his seat when the young interrogator brought his fist down on the green metal desk.

There was a codex, he admitted. I didn't see it.

Did Pech bring it with him?

No. It was concealed in the attic by the Indian, a former employee, who tried to sell it to Pech.

Did you ever catalogue that particular codex?

I didn't get a chance to look at it. Preston Hollier wanted no part of it, after what happened. But from the description—

Did you advise Preston Hollier to buy it?

He didn't consult me.

Did Pech offer to pay you a commission?

No.

Why aren't you telling us the truth?

I am trying to.

Was Pech by himself?

He arrived with two Mexicans and an Indian. Both Mexicans were armed. They dragged the Indian to the attic to look for the codex.

Was Pech armed?

Yes.

Did they kill the Indian?

No. They shot at him, but he managed to escape.

Who gave the orders?

Pech did.

And they were his accomplices?

Yes.

To do what?

Act as his guards, I suppose. Do his dirty work.
Why are you lying to us?
I assure you, he pleaded, I'm not.

When he least expected it, he was punched in the face by the young man behind the desk. He toppled backward, this time banging his head on the floor. His glasses flew in the same direction as before. Again, his nose began to bleed.

The Imaginary Father

There are so many ways of harming a person without leaving any traces, the heavyset policeman said to Emilio, who, with his hands tied behind his back, dangled upside down, suspended by a rope tied to his legs from a hook in the ceiling. Please . . . , he quavered, in a voice no longer his own. People resist and resist and resist, until at last they gratefully cave in, the policeman maintained, not appearing to hear Emilio, while his two visitors, Pedro and Pablo, hands folded across their chests, calmly watched. The policeman laughed when Pablo playfully gave Emilio a small push that sent him swaying back and forth, his words of entreaty, his *please*, becoming indistinct.

How the Actress Responds
to the Ladies' Man

Her smile had not changed. It was the same seductive smile Francisco remembered from the screen. There was a pianist playing jazzy tunes from the thirties in the front room where the ladies liked to meet for tea and pastries. The maître d', who wore a bright red rose in his buttonhole, was reluctant to leave Patricia's table: If there's anything else you need . . . Thank you. Again that bewitching smile.

What are you doing here? Francisco asked.

Waiting for *your* publisher . . .

Jacobus?

She invitingly stroked the plush velvet seat beside her on the banquette. Join me.

He hesitated. I'm meeting someone.

Pouting: If you don't wish to . . .

Sitting down next to her, he looked at her again. Did anyone tell you you look ravishing?

Boldly returning his stare, she said, You're not bad yourself.

His response was instantaneous. Are you very *busy* these days?

Is that an invitation?

Absolutely.

She studied the place setting on the table as if trying to extract a message from it. I heard you're leaving for the U.S.

I'm not leaving until tomorrow.

He tapped his fingers lightly on the table to the lively phrases of the music that drifted into the back room and, beyond it, into the garden, as she, pulling out her diary, pretended to examine it, playfully saying, That doesn't leave me much time.

Are you busy later?

And she, in no way discomfited by his straightforwardness: When?

This afternoon?

She laughed. Francisco, you're impossible. I don't set eyes on you for years, and now—

Not years, he protested.

Why don't you call me when you return?

I'll be gone for two weeks. To impress her with the serious-
ness of his intention, he jotted a reminder in his pocket diary.
Then, looking cheerfully at her: So?

What's this about Alejandro?

He's vanished. A neighbor saw him being picked up.

Cops?

The police deny arresting him.

When I ran into Alejandro not long ago, he mentioned that
Mercedes was in the U.S.

She's returning any day now.

Are those two still together?

I'd be the last to know.

Francisco, you know everything.

Well, at this stage, I'm seriously afraid for Alejandro. Jacobus is trying to galvanize PEN to intervene.

Could it have something to do with Preston?

Why do you say that?

Alejandro is close to him.

I don't believe that's true. In any event, as an American
financier, Preston is virtually untouchable.

All the more reason . . .

Nonsense, he said brusquely.

Could this have any bearing on the Partridge Museum?

How do you mean?

Preston is funding it.

I hope not. . . . I have a contract with them. I am to write
about the late Anadelle Partridge.

She laughed. Then, seeing a couple eyeing them from the
entrance to the dining room: Are those the people you're
meeting?

He glanced in the direction in which she was staring. No.
I'm meeting Vali di Vanini.

Are you ever without a woman?

He was amused. Señora di Vanini is strictly business. . . . Not every woman I meet jumps into bed with me.

I don't think I believe you.

Francisco pretended to be shocked. Patricia, what are you trying to suggest?

She, calmly watching him: Just seeing you, looking so masterful in your double-breasted suit, eyeing us women, selecting . . . selecting . . .

I wasn't, he protested.

Yes you were. You can't help it. I can see you measure them. Planning the seduction.

You are going out of your way to make me uncomfortable.

I am flattering you. I bet every woman in here is just dying to—

The lady-killer? That's absurd. I don't do anything that women don't encourage me to do.

What about the beauty Alejandro saw you with—you were coming out of a gallery?

Did Alejandro mention that?

He was discreet. Wouldn't give me her name.

My lips are sealed.

Admit it, you're banging Preston's wife.

If you must know . . . I appear to have fallen out of favor.

Is that why you're leaving for the U.S.?

I was planning to leave all along.

Wistfully she said, We could have had fun.

We could meet for a drink at five.

At five? She laughed. How much time do I get? A full hour? That's unfair.

We had what? Two months?

Why harp on the past?

I'll admit I don't have Rita's prospects.

Why are we focusing on Rita?

Did Alejandro introduce you?

If you must know it was Jacobus. It was at a dinner for Preston who had acquired a share of the publishing house. I was seated next to her.

And?

And nothing.

How could you tell she was available?

That wasn't too difficult to establish. One learns to read expressions. . . .

How do you read my expression?

He was about to answer when she saw Jacobus. She waved. Jacobus frowned when he saw Francisco. What's he doing here? he asked in mock indignation.

I'm stealing your woman, Francisco said, standing up.

Francisco is meeting someone for lunch, she explained, as Francisco stepped back from the chair.

Stay. Have a drink.

I must go. . . . Any news of Alejandro?

Alejandro is behind lock and key. No one knows exactly where. All I've been able to establish so far is that he's being held by the Department for the Prevention of Delinquency.

Nice bunch.

They have a reputation.

You mean torture?

They wouldn't dare . . . , said Patricia.

I see my luncheon date, said Francisco, waving to Vali, who was standing near the door.

Why, that's di Vanini, said Jacobus. Join us . . .

I think Francisco has business to attend to with the lady.

Another time, said Francisco.

Jacobus waved to Vali. She waved back. When Francisco had left, Jacobus said, At least they haven't arrested Salas.

Why would they?

Preston Hollier has underwritten the renovation costs of the museum. Anyone even vaguely connected to him might be at risk.

Where does that leave you?

Let's talk of something a little more cheerful, shall we?

Critical Exposure

The jefe and his sidekick watched as the film crew set up the lights and camera equipment, while a makeup man worked on Alejandro's face. Just a little touch-up, he joked.

Ready? said the jefe. The next moment Alejandro was blinded by two spotlights.

Could you shift those? I can't see.

While this was being done, Alejandro requested a glass of water.

Get him some water, said the jefe, and then signaled the cameraman to start.

Let's start at the beginning, when did you hear from Preston Hollier?

It was late on Saturday night.

What happened?

He rang to ask if I would care to accompany him to his newly acquired villa the next morning.

Did he usually call late in the evening? the jefe asked.

No. Never.

Did he give any reason for his call?

He said that he was acquiring a work of art and wanted my expertise.

Had you ever before accompanied him on a trip to purchase pre-Columbian artifacts?

No.

Describe what happened.

He picked me up at nine-thirty the next morning. I had expected his assistant, Terrence, and possibly Rita to accompany him, but he was by himself.

Does he usually drive?

He has a chauffeur who drives him to work. On other occasions he prefers to drive himself.

What did he say?

He mentioned that we would be joined by Pech. I concluded that Pech would be bringing the work of art.

What did you speak about?

He wanted to know what it was like working for the late Anadelle Partridge, whose villa he had purchased. He also more or less intimated that if not for Rita, he would not have purchased the villa, which he considered a liability. Then, on the subject of Rita, looking me straight in the eye, he asked if it wasn't true that she was seeing a lot of my friend Francisco.

What did you say?

I was embarrassed. I said that he must be mistaken. He smiled, as if what I had said confirmed his suspicion. I also noticed that throughout the drive he kept checking his watch, as if he was timing his drive, intending to reach the villa at a certain hour. We arrived shortly after twelve. It was my first visit to the villa since I worked there over ten years ago. The grounds and the building looked deserted. For some reason he chose to park the car at some distance from the house. As we

walked toward the back entrance, he kept looking around—
I had the feeling that he was expecting someone to be there.
The house was empty. On entering the main living room, I
noticed that one of the windows overlooking the garden was
smashed. There was glass all over the floor. Someone must
have broken in, he said. He seemed quite calm. Not in the least
surprised. When I suggested he call the police, he said that we
should first inspect the house to see if there was anything
missing.

Was there?

No.

Did you accompany him all the time?

He seemed to want me to.

The bedroom as well?

Yes.

Did you notice anything?

He picked up and pocketed a woman's comb that may have
belonged to his wife. When I again mentioned informing the
police, he said it would be a waste of time.

When did Pech arrive?

About forty minutes later. He arrived together with a Veracruz Indian.

Did Preston mention the break-in?

No. . . . Pech apologized, saying that he was sorry things
had gone awry. The Indian explained that they—it was clear
to me that he was referring to Rita and Francisco—had come
and left earlier than expected. . . . Preston was outraged. He
accused the Indian and Pech of shoddy planning.

Did you follow what he was saying?

No. At first I didn't get the drift of it.

Did Pech speak to you?

That was so odd. The three of them behaved as if I wasn't present. . . . We're not going to have such an opportunity again, Preston declared.

Did you know what he was referring to?

I was totally mystified.

Then what happened?

Well, Pech offered Preston the work of art—which turned out to be one of the codices that had belonged to Anadelle Partridge—only to have Preston say something to the effect that he'd buy it when the other job was completed. That the payment for one, namely the codex, included payment for the other job.

Did you know what he meant by that?

It was beginning to dawn on me that the Indian was to hurt or even kill Francisco and possibly Rita.

How did the Indian react?

He stood there mute, looking to Pech . . . Pech was his boss.

How did Pech react to Preston's refusal to buy the codex?

He was furious. He left, saying that he was staying at the Hotel Paraíso in Megalen, implying that the codex was still available. He also maintained that come hell or high water, the Indian had to be paid.

Did you know that Preston had donated a substantial sum to the Partridge Museum?

Yes. Jacobus had mentioned it to me.

Did he expect anything in return for his gift?

Preston and Rita were able to acquire from the museum a few pre-Columbian artifacts at bargain prices.

Are you saying that Salas, the director, enabled this American industrialist to make use of the museum as if it were a bargain basement?

Yes.

Did Preston kill Pech?

No. He couldn't have. As soon as Pech had left, we returned to Mexico City.

After the spotlights were turned off and the camera crew removed their gear, the young man who had sat apart from the other two interrogators came forward to shake hands with him, saying, You probably don't remember me, but I was once one of your students.

When was that?

About five years ago.

Alejandro stared blankly at him. Yes, of course, he said without remembering.

I enjoyed your course on Cervantes.

When will I be able to leave?

Soon, the man promised.

Very soon?

Certainly . . .

An Unfolding Sense of Unending

How did things evolve? How did one thing lead to another? Naturally. As one might anticipate between a man and a woman with so many similar enthusiasms. Now? Summer intensified the tender lightheartedness of their brief involvement. Even though he knew what her answer would be, he asked, Why are you returning to Mexico?

I must.

You don't intend to come back, do you?

What makes you say that? she protested.

You are running away.

On the contrary, she said. I'd be running away if I failed to return.

Does Alejandro care for you?

I'm sure he does. . . .

You say you're sure, but I detect an equivocation.

You sense wrong. Besides, it's not the issue. He's disappeared.

What can you do?

I don't think you fully comprehend what that means.

People don't disappear in Mexico, he maintained. It's not Brazil or Peru or Argentina. He may have gone off. Have you considered that? Found someone?

That just shows how little you understand. In Mexico, people like ourselves are politically privileged only as long as we don't rock the boat—as long as we confine our discontent to the critical left-wing journals no one reads.

Are you implying that Alejandro has suddenly rocked the boat?

Not intentionally, that's for sure.

You think you can extricate him from whatever mess he's in?

Not I . . . but people I know.

Why Alejandro?

Whoever is holding him may simply be trying to get at someone else. . . .

Who might that be?

I have a hunch it's Preston Hollier. He's everyone's target.

Will you come back to stay? I mean, permanently.

She laughed nervously. You're not serious, are you?

Of course he wasn't serious. He had looked baffled when she said chidingly, Mexico is my home. Perplexed, frowning:

Think of it, America is user-friendly. Within two months you'll consider yourself an American. . . .

That's not the issue. I am not trying to replace Mexico with—

I was under the impression that you liked it here.

I do . . . immensely. Now, I must—

I'd like to make it possible for you to come back to stay.

Arrange to find employment for me?

Didn't I—

Precisely.

You can stay here as long as you—

Under what circumstances?

Stay . . . We'll find something.

I can't.

The pre-Columbian ruins are holding you in their wayward grip, he joked.

What? No way.

You're enchanted by that dark, pestilent past.

No . . . She laughed at his suggestion.

Now they were flying above the clouds. Lowering the window shade, she settled back in her seat. The two young women in the seats next to hers were lazily leafing through a pile of fashion magazines. She felt a pleasant lassitude . . . detached, sipping her drink, eyes closed. . . . There were hours yet before any decision would have to be made. In fact, some decisions could be postponed . . . delayed . . . indefinitely.

I can take a taxi. It's easy. No need for you . . . But Jurud had persisted. I am driving you. She could detect, despite his words to the contrary, the relief her departure would bring . . . a relief he was not ready to acknowledge.

. . .

Are you Mexican? the woman in the next seat asked Mercedes.

Yes?

Would you know if the Hotel de Cortés—I believe it's located on Hidalgo—is near the center?

Center of what?

You know . . . the museums, the restaurants and stores.

Absolutely. It's walking distance to the Zócalo and to the Zona Rosa. . . . I'm sure you'll enjoy it.

Chicken or beef curry? Startled, she looked up at the flight attendant . . . Sorry, I didn't catch what you said.

Will you translate my next book? Jurud had asked in a bantering voice.

I'm not the only Spanish-language translator.

My friends were fond of you. They said . . .

Yes?

Don't let her get away.

They blame me . . .

For what?

For what happened to Bonny . . . Instead of our spur-of-the-moment vacation, you should have—

Nonsense. Bonny is much improved. She looks happy. She's beginning to speak. Today she said that I—

She's become a seven-year-old.

Not through any fault of yours.

The flight attendant collected the trays, then the lights were dimmed. Passengers were adjusting their seats and disentangling their earphones as a male flight attendant came on the public-address system to announce the movie.

Mercedes tried to follow the movie, but her mind kept wandering. She forced herself to concentrate, if only because the actor in the lead role was the spitting image of her father. Less stern perhaps, but the same immaculate suits, the same stance, the same lack of forbearance; the same fondness for young women . . . well-trimmed beard . . .

A damn silly film, commented the young woman at her side.

On landing, she called her father at the ministry, expecting a long wait. To her surprise, he came to the phone at once. Yes, my dear? He was reacting to her call as if they had been in touch only the day before instead of not having spoken to each other since prior to her wedding. Yes, my dear. He wasn't patronizing. He sounded warm, contrite, even solicitous. What can I do for you?

Alejandro has not been seen for a week. He has disappeared into thin air. I was in the U.S. when it happened. I flew back as soon as I received the news.

Ah, that is serious. Are you sure it's not just another woman?

Our neighbors, I've been told, saw him being forced into an unmarked car. Jacobus has information that Alejandro is being held by the Department for the Prevention of Delinquency.

I'll look into it.

She waited for more questions, but there were none.

Thank you.

I'll be in touch. She couldn't detect any animus in his voice.

I'm most grateful.

I'll see what I can do.

She felt it necessary to tell him that she would be staying in their apartment.

Which one? he asked teasingly.

There's only one. I still have a tiny studio in Zona Rosa. But I'll be at home.

As soon as I know anything. These things may take time.

I understand.

I have a certain amount of influence, but . . . There was no need for him to complete the sentence.

I understand.

As long as you do.

I'm in your debt.

And he, by saying Fine, agreed.

Goodbye.

Complicity

How did things evolve? How did one thing lead to another? Fear? Was it the fear of the untold degradation, disgrace, dishonor? The shame? The humiliation . . . the whispers and the knowing smiles of his predatory neighbors? Perhaps terror would be a better description. What could happen, what might happen . . .

Now?

When he was told that he was free to leave, Alejandro looked uncomprehendingly at the young man, his jailer. Now?

Yes.

He walked down the steps, holding on to the banister, afraid of losing his balance. The man who accompanied him to the front door held it wide open. Adiós, señor. Was that said deridingly? Once on the street, he felt so confused he didn't know whether to turn left or right. Free, at liberty to go wherever he wished, he felt far from free. He was discomposed by their matter-of-fact manner, by their allowing him to know where he had been held. The feeling of shame that in order to obtain his freedom he had betrayed Preston Hollier had not yet fully sunk in. It was four in the afternoon. He didn't know what to do next, where to go. He crossed the street, convinced that he was being followed. But why should they take the trouble to do so? Hadn't he provided them with what they needed? The means of pressuring Preston to do what? He stopped to buy an afternoon paper and a pack of cigarettes. Finding a small café, he entered and ordered coffee. He hadn't smoked in ages but suddenly was overcome by a craving for tobacco.

Now?

He scanned the newspaper. There was no mention of him or of Pech. In the interrogation, the jefe had offered him unconditional freedom if he gave evidence against Preston. At first he had balked—I don't see how . . . I mean . . . I couldn't. . . . Then he capitulated. OK.

I despise these intellectuals, the jefe said to his assistant, for their sly evasiveness, their continuous lies and deceptions, and the way they demonstrate their triumph. . . . What small victories!

Next to the café's toilet there was a public telephone. He knew the number by heart. Though the coffee shop was air-conditioned, he was sweating. . . . Finally gathering his courage, he dialed Preston's home. He waited patiently until Preston came to the phone. I have betrayed you, Alejandro said. I've lied about you.

I'm aware of that, but why are you calling? Preston said.

His hand gripping the receiver was coated with perspiration. He wasn't able to think of an adequate reply. The silence grew until it became intolerable.

I'm sure the alternative was not a pleasant one, Preston finally said before gently hanging up on him.

Hommage

Waiting for her father on what was neutral territory, she tried to compose herself. Any appreciative lover of beauty glancing in her direction could see that she had a perfect face. A face one could enjoy gazing at for hours. In profile, that long nose, the lips firm and compressed, the fine-boned face . . . A bit too rarefied? The eyes too pronounced? Where did it come from? That imperfect perfection, Alejandro would say. Soft dark silky hair . . . But all this exquisite beauty suddenly marred as she began savagely to bite her lower lip, then the inside of her cheek . . . so that the portrait of her lineage was suddenly destroyed for the admiring viewer. . . . What could it be? A sudden attack of apprehension? Fear? But fear of what?

He entered the restaurant, nodded to the unctuous waiter, and headed toward her. He hadn't changed. He leaned down to her and kissed her cheek. Well, I think I have good news.

Thank you.

I think we can celebrate, he said, settling into the seat across from her. It appears that Preston Hollier has enemies, but for the time being everything has been settled. Preston was made to see reason. He has agreed to accept Senator Galindez as a full partner. Alejandro was a cog . . . the means to put pressure on Hollier . . . They promised to leave him alone. Nothing more to worry about. Incidentally, this may be an opportunity for Alejandro. That is, if he wishes to be on the board of Eden Enterprise.

How can I thank you?

Well, for one thing, I would like to get to know your husband. . . . You must bring him to see us on the weekend.

Sunday?

No. Come Saturday and stay overnight. We have a lot to catch up on.

Coming Together

They were holding hands in the back of the limousine. Her father's chauffeur was driving them to the estate.

You're not afraid, are you?

A little nervous, he admitted.

He's eager to meet you.

If this ghastly situation has brought you back to me, then I'm glad it took place.

No, no. I would have come back. I intended to.

I met Jurud. I accompanied him when he flew to El Tajín.

All she said was, Bonny is improving.

Good.

One problem. She's regressed, she's like a seven-year-old.

She'll recover.

That's what the doctors say.

She hadn't been to see her family since before her wedding. The car pulled up in front of the entrance. Not a servant but her father came to welcome them. He embraced her and then, treating Alejandro as a son-in-law, hugged him. Her father, though so much older, towered above Alejandro. When Alejandro entered the large house, a sea of pale Spanish faces greeted him . . . They were smiling, going out of their way to make him feel at home. Later, as they were having tea, Mercedes's mother glanced at a newspaper and noted that a Veracruz Indian, a certain Emilio Jesús Monte, had confessed to the murder of the American Pech. These American raiders of pre-Columbian art, Mercedes's father said irritably, keep coming to rob us blind. Pech had it coming to him. Then turning to his daughter, his face softening as he gripped her hand in his. In the end, he said, I always knew that you'd come back to me.

Alejandro felt the intolerable itching sensation long before he detected the rash on his body. As he looked at himself in the bedroom mirror, he saw that a red rash covered his groin, his genitals and the lower area of his stomach. To his dismay, he could see that the rash was spreading to his armpits and chest. It must be nerves, he decided. Just a bad case of nerves. When he left the bedroom to return to his new family, he could hear their voices all the way from the dining room. They were already seated at the festive looking table when he entered the room, and looked to the left and to the right to determine where he was to sit.

ABOUT THE AUTHOR

WALTER ABISH is the author of two novels, three collections of stories, and a book of poems. He has been a Guggenheim fellow and a MacArthur fellow. He is the recipient of a Lila Wallace–Reader's Digest Writer's Award and the 1991 Award of Merit for the Novel from the American Academy and Institute of Arts and Letters. He lives in New York City.

A NOTE ON THE TYPE

The text of this book was set in a digitized version of Fournier, a typeface originated by Pierre Simon Fournier *fils* (1712–1768). Coming from a family of typefounders, Fournier was an extraordinarily prolific designer both of typefaces and of typographic ornaments. He was also the author of the celebrated *Manuel typographique* (1764–1766). In addition, he was the first to attempt to work out the point system standardizing type measurement that is still in use internationally.

The cut of the typeface named for this remarkable man captures many of the aspects of his personality and period. Though it is elegant, it is also very legible.